ADVANCE READER'S EDITION

HAPPY BAD

A Novel

Delaney Nolan

Astra House

New York

Copyright © 2025 by Delaney Nolan
All rights reserved. Copying or digitizing this book for storage, display, or distribution in any other medium is strictly prohibited.

Permissions Acknowledgments tk

For information about permission to reproduce selections from this book, please contact permissions@astrahouse.com.

This is an advance reader's edition from uncorrected proofs. If any material from the book is to be quoted in a review, please check it against the text in the final bound book. Dates, prices, and manufacturing details are subject to change or cancellation without notice.

This is a work of fiction. Names, characters, places, and incidents are products of the author's imagination or are used fictitiously. Any resemblance to actual events, locales, or persons, living or dead, is entirely coincidental.

Astra House
A Division of Astra Publishing House
astrahouse.com

ISBN: 9781662603280 (hc)
ISBN: 9781662603297 (eBook)

Design by TK
The text is set in TK.
The titles are set in TK.

HAPPY BAD

Chapter One

I lived in a box in the desert. I slept in stiff white sheets. All night my dreams swam with the things the girls drew, on class assignments and birthday cards: lilies and blades and lopsided skulls, impossible planets lit like lamps from within. They didn't know how things worked. I had to tell them: stop drawing. Pay attention. Listen.

Every two weeks, I received a paycheck, which I spent on bleach and wine and then, at home, delighted, I changed my sheets, I wiped the window, I touched the floor, thrilled to be someplace clean. The things that happened at work—the vomit, the mania, the tampons thrown at heads—all that I kept in a hazard-orange bucket in my heart which was sealed the moment I walked out the doors of Twin Bridge. Home was safe. Work was work. I had a system. I had a system in Askewn, in Texas, so that I could successfully oversee the girls, who started every morning sleepy in the cafeteria, learning to dance.

Usually, at Twin Bridge, I was on the morning shift. That morning the girls were lined up in the caf, shaking their feel-good hips, flipping their hair; Askewn and the hideously boring earth pinwheeled around them. Above: cold light. Drop tile ceiling. Below: white linoleum tile that had weathered very many feet and bodily fluids. The oldest girl, Teresa, stood in front of the line, her back to me, instructing the others. Her manner was military.

"Pay attention," she commanded.

She took a big step backwards, shifted her weight, and fell to the floor like she'd been shot, her limbs in a pile. Then she rose up slowly, turning to the side, and bent at the waist, gyrating.

"That's what," she said.

The other girls dancing in the cafeteria with her all leaned back on one leg and then fell, cautiously, to the floor. One, two, three, four, etc: down on the ground. *Fall harder!*, screamed Teresa. Sick dancehall beats seethed up underneath their voices.

Teresa was seventeen. At eighteen, presto, she'd be a grown-up, booted out the Twin Bridge door to the waiting maws of the wide wide world. From the doorway I watched her chew on a tassel of her own hair. Statistically, Teresa had a 50–50 chance of landing in one of two places:

1. Jail

2. Psych unit

But that's just math, I thought, as I leaned against the doorjamb; math hardly applied. What lecherous villain would compile such numbers? They've got no relevance to the daily trudge of Twin Bridge Residential Treatment Center, home for the traumatized/neglected/abused/criminal, oblivion addicts as a rule, where dominated (once) a regimen consisting mainly of school, therapy, chores, sleep, the occasional screaming and drug-addled fit.

"Step back on your *right* leg," Teresa scowled. She swung her own leg back to demonstrate, then twisted a plait of her dark hair about her hand as she watched the others. Step, fall, up, twist, then the bizarro waggle.

So there we were in the coop. Although technically I held the grand title of *coordinator*, all those wild chickens would not be coordinated, nor corralled; they belonged entirely to themselves. The truth is that they, the girls, wanted to fight all the time; I wanted to fold my leathery wings over them and hold tight until they stopped, until they calmed and the rage lifted out of them like a cartoon ghost, evaporating in the sun. But at Twin Bridge nobody got what they wanted.

Twenty-nine girls, aged thirteen to seventeen, four to a room, prowling the halls, refusing their meds, huffing glue, prying up tacks from the backs of couches to ram through their own thumbnails, malnourished and obese or skinny as a rail, all sent to Twin Bridge due to drugs, theft, truancy, neglect, etc., all under supervision, no boys, no telephones, no real fun. Watching them fling themselves on the floor made me cringe. It was six in the goddamn morning, but they were awake, hyper-alive, electrified through each flailing limb, practicing for the television camera that they had constructed in their hearts. Most of them planned to be famous.

When Teresa first arrived, about a year back, she'd tried to smuggle in cocaine stuffed inside a ball of knitting yarn. No success! Kicks, shrieks. Sobriety. Headaches. Ravenous hunger, aversion to food. These were our dear and constant companions.

The girls set their faces dead serious, twitched to the bass. I left them to rehearse while I did the rounds, put on my *merrily merrily* face to walk the Twin Bridge halls.

Long before the era of Twin Bridge, the place was a B&B called Alice's Cottage—way back, when people still visited the middle part of the country. When there was still grass outside. Alice, the owner, got got for selling off-brand amphetamines to new brides. Foreclosed, the bones of the buildings shifted but did not buckle. In the 90s, a Turkish wheat heiress named Fatima scooped the building for a pittance, renovated it, and reopened as a supportive residential center for teens. Thirty years later, when Fatima died and her son, Arda, took over, the center was in financial ruin. It would have collapsed totally were it not for the site's necessary reinvention, which Arda says he was strong-armed into: teetering on the verge of bankruptcy, the center fell into the clutches of private equity and was thereafter purchased by a private social services company, within whose subsidiary, named TENDER KARE, we snugly nested. The state had privatized these social services and outsourced them to TENDER KARE, who had in turn partnered with a multinational pharmaceutical company whose record of lawsuits I once Googled in despair. Our bosses were bureaucrats at the TENDER KARE headquarters. None of us had ever met them.

I know Twin Bridge was shiny and hygienic, once, with a welcome board and a long veranda. But years of wear and tear had scuffed the walls, torn down the veranda rails, shattered fanlights and splintered latticework. Welcome boards and murals now displayed crudely sketched anatomy alongside instructions. The anatomy bore hairs, sometimes teeth. We scrubbed and repainted; impossibly, despite infinite confiscations of markers, the graffiti multiplied, toothier, hairier. The welcome desk exhibited a fist-sized hole.

All the girls' rooms were upstairs, opening off a balcony that circled a large inner courtyard, so everyone could see everyone, a panopticon nobody wanted in ugly cream vinyl tile. I circled the balconies, poking my head into rooms: *get up, get up, go to school, time to learn about the Civil War, chlorophyll, long division*!

I stopped at Room Four, where Amy lived. Amy had been practicing—or attempting to practice—witchcraft. She had discovered a website. Twin Bridge didn't have a rule against it, exactly. We weren't the type. Missionaries had certainly shown up in the rapidly changing roster of Twin Bridge staff, but none of those folks were here now. No anti-witch rules, and no mandatory prayer, though god-talk sometimes slipped in all the same: it could be helpful, and we needed all the tools we could get.

The new medication from TENDER KARE, though, BeZen, had been so successful over the last six months that I suspected it could replace god-talk all together. Heaven wasn't necessary; BeZen required only water and a swallow, no further sacrifice, and all your troubles would be swept down to the bottom of an inner sea.

I knocked on the doorframe.

"Enter," Amy sang.

The other three girls who lived in the room were getting re[ady for] class; they crowded in the bathroom, sharing an old stick of black eyeli[ner.] Amy sat cross-legged on the floor in the center of a wobbly pentagram she'[d] made out of salt. The saltshaker sat next to her. Incense was burning. The whole room smelled like old furniture and melted ice-pops.

"Where," I asked, "Did you get incense?"

She looked at me and didn't answer. Open flames: strictly forbidden! Incense, though, was allowed.

I sat at the edge of the pentagram.

"What does this do?" I always tell the Twin Bridge staff: exhibit interest in the girls' hobbies.

"It gets rid of demons," she told me. Bad energy. Ghosts. Negative thoughts. Evil. The devil in his dark green coat cannot come in. She put her hands up on her cheeks and squeezed them. "We may be sitting in the only safe place on earth."

Amy had had to remove all the metalwork in her face when she checked in, and so her lips, chin, nose, and ears were dotted with piercing holes that held nothing. She was allowed to wear makeup, and she used black lipstick liberally across her sweet, pinched elf's face. Dandruff showed in the white part of her dark hair as she looked down at her ankles.

I kneeled inside the pentagram, my knees touching hers. On a plywood bookshelf above the twin bed sat a dozen teddy bears of varying age and quality, some patchy and furless. They sat in a line and their dead eyes tunneled past me. The bear on the end wore overalls with plastic daisies sewn on. The rest were naked.

"That's interesting," I said. "What else helps you feel safe?"

Sage, she told me. Telephones. Garlic. Cherry pits. Pudding cups. Wild thyme. Boars' tusks, hares' heads, chalk, music videos, blue glass, turquoise, pearls, reality TV shows about miserable chefs, eggs—especially an ostrich—a gland from the neck of a donkey, her bears, gold coins, ock's spur, new underwear, scented moisturizer, blankets, holding hands, salt, and the best thing was to spit in the face of a child. On her bed, atop the green acrylic blanket, lay three black and white printed pages; they seemed to be from a website explaining the difference between Wicca and Satanism. I could make out a section title: BE YOUR OWN BARBARIAN HORDE.

"We have eggs," I volunteered.

Amy made a face. "They're grown in a lab. Not from real chickens."

"Nobody can taste the difference. Would they work?"

"I'm going to find out," she said, and picked one up from where it had sat hidden behind her. How had she managed to smuggle an egg from the kitchen? She cradled it near her face and whispered to the shell, *if you don't protect me, I am gonna crush you.*

"All right, come on," I smiled. "Show me a spell."

Amy put her hands palms up on her thighs, eyes closed. She hummed, breathed in through her nose, and straightened her spine. She radiated calm. When I put my own hands down, palms up, they were shaking. I wasn't nervous. Don't think I'm a nervous person. My hands, they'd just taken to shaking. I'd worked at Twin Bridge for three years, and for the last nine months or so, I'd begun to have doubts. I couldn't articulate exactly what those doubts were. I think the trouble was that I sometimes understood the girls. And, that there was a goblin, squatting in my skull, rattling a metal pail full of bolts and hissing *failure, rot, spoil*. I wouldn't speak to the goblin. The goblin kept rattling. My hands, they weren't steady.

"I want to be strong enough to wrestle a person," Amy was saying. "A fat person." She considered for a moment. "A medium-fat person."

"Don't say fat," I reminded her. At Twin Bridge there were words whose utterance was forbidden, but no one could stop you from thinking them AS LOUD AS YOU CAN. Sometimes I sat, glass-eyed in the main office, holding a cold coffee and think-shouting SUICIDE, BLOWJOB, FAT, just to assert my autonomy, my status as a 31-year-old authority figure who could go home at night.

"This spell will make us powerful," Amy was saying. "We're going to have muscles the size of cinderblocks. No one will ever touch us again!" She smiled wide, her face all dreamy. Then she opened her eyes and took down the printed pages. She turned to the second page and began reading.

"Money, money, come to me, in abundance three times three . . ."

If anybody ever tells you money's not important, steal their wallet. My sister said that. I knew a little of Amy's story, but I'm not allowed to tell you. I can tell you this: when she was a child, there were welts. Uncontrollable fits of rage in the elementary school bathroom that cracked the glass. Her mom is in jail.

Amy touched her forehead, her breastbone, both shoulders. The other girls left the bathroom; on their way out, one noisily tore through a striped shoebox beneath her bed, pulled out a spiral notebook, and flounced from the room rolling her eyes.

"Bring me wealth and prosperity, oh Holy Lamia, goddess of snakes, eater of flesh."

Amy's wall was covered in pictures of white celebrities, lilac angora rabbits, stiletto heels. She will never be able to have children. Already I'm telling you things I'm not supposed to tell. She seemed to forget, for a moment, that I was there, because she clasped her hands together and started whispering, listing the things she wished to buy: a boat, a dog, an island, new teeth, flip-flops, lip gloss, a mint green Ferrari with a top that goes down.

While I watched her shuttered eyes the incense smoke caught in my dry throat, and I started to hack into my hand: two sharp coughs that I caught in a fist before I made it to the sink in the back of the room, where I drank from the faucet. Ferraris, islands, new teeth! What madness is this? Almost-normal desires: exactly what we aimed for. BeZen was a miracle. BeZen made it difficult, apparently, to think about the bad parts of life. And so they floated through class, giggled at the dick graffiti on the welcome board, fantasized about coconuts with frilly umbrellas, though I'd never heard of a Twin Bridge graduate making it to the echelons of upper-middle class, nor middle-middle. This was the thing that made me so sad, sometimes: that they were hopeful. When it was already almost definitely too late. I'd scuffed the salt of Amy's pentagram, breaking the line. I bit my own lips hard until the painful lump went away: where was the spell for that? Inexplicable sorrow, the lump in your throat. Snake Mom in the Sky, hand me a grimoire that will replace the urge to wail.

"Amy," I barked from my position, hunched over the sink, "You're going to be late for class."

Her face was a bank of hope, coins in her eyes, and when I scolded her that vault slammed shut.

"Thank you for showing me how all this works," I added, more gently.

She turned away. I turned away. I was scrubbing my sleeves together as I went back out to the hallway, as though I'd spilled something on them that threatened to stain.

"All right, Beatrice?" Arda, my boss, asked as he passed by.

"All right," I said. "Just cleaning up."

The girls were getting ready for the on-site school, filing into the classroom, as Arda and I and the rest of the staff urged timeliness. A few minutes later, Linda came in, sweating.

Linda was the teacher. She'd run the six miles to work, Monday through Friday, up the shoulder of the dusty highway around dawn before it got too hot. She mused out at us from beneath a blast of frizzy yellow hair, carried herself taut as a violin string and with as treacherous a vocal pitch, her high voice pinging off the walls. She'd been the teacher at Twin Bridge for about two years and this had taken its toll. At some point, she'd taken on an apocalyptic bent, insisted on teaching the genocides, Titus Andronicus, imaginary numbers. I was growing concerned, but also, interested in where all that would go. Revelations, Jonestown studies? Anything was possible. No one ever came to check on the syllabus. No one was listening at all. Hello, hello out there! Echo! We could maybe do anything we wanted. And Linda's quadriceps! So large and unyielding that she looked like a statue, the very interpretive kind, the bottom half shaped from a wedge of wet dark clay sliced in a slick clean line with a palette knife at the back. Her musculature compelled trust. In addition, nobody else would ever want that job, so we were generally very grateful for her.

"Any news?" she panted to Arda and me. She pressed her fingers to her wrist, taking her pulse as her chest heaved.

"Everything's normal," I assured her. She looked at me with suspicion. Fair.

Though Linda had been there longer, and was a bit older than me, I was technically her supervisor. Under the guiding hand of TENDER KARE, Twin Bridge had shifted from support center to support center + drug testing pilot program + mildly punitive arm of the state. And so Twin Bridge was now kept afloat thanks to the combined profit-reaping private investments of TENDER KARE pharmaceuticals, an insurance company, and (in name only) the state government. Each benefited in different ways from the drug trials conducted here. As coordinator, I'd been tasked with compiling the qualitative results of the on-site clinical research for BeZen.

In practice, this meant I monitored the girls' BeZen-modulated behavior, noting improvements (many!) and side effects (generalized dreaminess, swollen ankles). The drug was not yet approved by the FDA. These were Phase III clinical trials.

I compiled my notes in a report which was strictly confidential. This, Linda did not like. Linda had a great deal of ambition, but it took the form mostly of boundless physical energy. She thought I was the problem, blocking her dreams of climbing the ranks; in truth, there were two problems: firstly, despite her interest in formal education, she was not in possession of an organized mind. My mind, in contrast, is strictly organized. I could take you on a tour of the compartments. Secondly, there were simply no ranks to climb.

"And the report?"

"Normal. Good," I repeated.

Linda was referring to the BeZen report, which would in effect determine our futures. If BeZen were a success, our funding would increase, and Twin Bridge would relocate to Atlanta. We would bring some of the girls, though we were still waiting for TENDER KARE to send us the official list of names. If BeZen were not a success, the pharma company would end the trials, we'd stay in place, and our funding would dwindle. Maybe it sounds, here, like there were two possibilities, just two options, but really the paths into the future were countless and impossible to grasp, like a nest of eels. "The numbers are looking real good," I added.

"We'll begin packing the office tomorrow," Arda announced. "From what Beatrice has been saying, it sounds very sure, our move. Atlanta. Georgia. I don't know. I've never been to Atlanta, Georgia." He rubbed his wrist, blue with fuzzy ancient tattoos. Arda was in his seventies, sweet as pie, covered in ink. He told me once he'd spent his childhood in Izmir, before he and Fatima came here, and he bore the faintest trace of an accent. "It's strange, strange to think about moving."

Linda just frowned at me as she stretched, bending her leg up behind her like a swamp bird. "Strange, all right."

"We'll miss you," Arda said to her, "No new Georgia teacher could replace you. I wish you would join us, transfer to Atlanta with us."

She shook her head and her stiff hair bounced. "I couldn't leave my mother here alone."

"Well. We are going to miss you, very much. You and Carmen also." Carmen, the main day-time counselor on site, was perhaps making the right choice in remaining behind. She was the newest staff member, and herself a former Twin Bridge resident who had returned, a decade later, to be a counselor. This made her very good at her job, sometimes, but also created predictable types of problems.

Maria, 15 and with permanent circles under her eyes, popped up behind us.

"Excuse me," she said. "Teresa threw up. On my bed. She came into my room and threw up twice on my bed." While Teresa was throwing up she had, apparently, looked Maria directly in the eyes. Linda walked away, hugging herself to stretch her triceps.

"That's impossible," I assured Maria. She wore pink sweats from head to toe, her face a bowl of worry. "Nobody can vomit with their eyes open."

I told her to scamper off to class and slumped with an automatic movement of the body to fetch a mop, I mopped, this was it, my calling, the goblin was rattling the bolts—

Twin Bridge sat on the plains. What was the plains.

This was east and far enough north that you saw a lot of Oklahoma license plates. I've seen the photos, and I know that when I was born, this area was covered in grassland. Well, no more. A hundred miles from anything, brown and flat and endless; wrinkly hills with no allegiance: the type of country that could be anywhere, the depths of Romania, a Mongolian wasteland. Tricks of light, palisades. Pablum and static on the radio. Heartbreaking stuff. If you leave Askewn, for hours it's dead crater country, skinned tractor tires and the occasional grain elevator with its roof stoved in. No rain, no nutrients left in the soil, everyone on their way out. Everyone leaving for the coasts, cooler climes, or Minneapolis.

Once, it rained. None of that, now.

The building itself sat a few miles from downtown, on the shoulder of a highway. Nearby was mostly rocks and snake holes. And a gas station. At the gas station they sold lighters and knives. The knives had camouflage-colored handles or were etched with PROUD TO BE TEXAN. Around us was flat land, ex-pasture, ecological deserts where soybean and corn and soybean and corn and corn and soybean and soybean and soybean and soybean and soybean once grew, crop dusters dusted, enormous metal arms trawled around pissing chemicals and then all the insects died and the land flooded and then dried and baked hard and cracked and there's nothing much you'd want out there, now.

Every once in a while you get a nice day. The sun eases off. Some clouds scamper by and throw shapes on the dry brown grass. Once I saw a pigeon. It hopped and left. Jackrabbits swarm everywhere, by the thousand. They find whatever tufts of brown grass remain. But for the most part, none of that mattered; we'd stay inside, as the girls didn't have a lot of time allocated for outdoors and the outdoors wasn't very healthy, anyway. You wouldn't want to breathe too much of the air is what I'm saying. You wouldn't want to get caught in that sun.

Late afternoon, when the heat eased, there was an hour of free time when one of us would supervise the parking lot, bring a basketball maybe, and, if it were winter and the sun was gentle, they'd lie on rough towels on the tarmac with their shirts rolled up to stop just below their breasts and tan on their backs with their eyes closed. A row of bellies, lying supine on the asphalt, eyes closed, still as surgical patients; then past that a strip of brown land and then the flat white sky so bright it strained your eyes.

Indoor living, though: that was the Twin Bridge mode. And indoor living plus a meager budget meant smells, stains, conditions that bred lice and cough. I lived in horror of tracked fluids. We tried, anyhow, to be clean.

I mopped the vomit off the floor in Maria's room (Room Two), and then dragged the mattress, sheets and all, down the hall, trailing the smell behind me like a length of ribbon.

In the supply closet was where we kept the spare bedding and tacky motel art, the posters that read BE KIND. WASH YOUR HANDS. If you just stayed in that closet, if you kept yourself walled in with the linens, you could believe that Twin Bridge was a paragon of healthy behavior. ALWAYS SAY PLEASE.

Once I'd cleaned up, I took out another cheap cot mattress, then a set of fresh sheets, starched and stiff. I brought them to Room Two and carefully made up the empty bed. Then I lay down on it and put my face in the pillow. I breathed in deep. It smelled like piss. Piss and spoiled milk. I got up and took the sheets off the bed. I threw them in the dumpster out back of the building. Affectations of wealth, luxury, a move like that—to simply throw a set of sheets away! An indulgence! Normally we would never, but we were about to move, so it was time to toss things. I took out a set of fresh sheets from the storage closet, stiff, starched. I covered the bed completely with the sheets. I placed my face on the pillow and inhaled. Spoiled milk. Piss. I snapped the blanket tight over the tucked-in sheets. Then I walked out the room, shut the door behind me. There was no making it better.

WELCOME TO YOUR BRIGHT FUTURE. This poster was tacked above the front desk where I sat. The words hovered over the image of a nondescript, sun-drenched highway. Recently a girl had tried to bolt. I was stationed by the front door to ensure no one else gave it a try. Sometimes, the girls would get inspired, and we'd get a streak of attempts.

"I'm hungry," Amy announced, strolling over. Her dyed black hair stuck in sharp dry points around her shoulders. She picked at her lips, leaving her fingertips smeared with the cheap black lipstick; anxiety made her hands crawl all over.

"You just came from lunch," I said.

"I was too bored to eat." She leaned both her elbows on the edge of the desk and huffed a sigh.

I opened one of the desk drawers and fished out a bag of sweet corn puffs. "Here," I offered.

Amy swung a hand limply at the bag, knocking it onto the scuffed tile floor. "Gross."

"Pick that up, please," I said evenly, "And go to school. Lunch break is over. Class time."

Hanan, who lived in the same suite as Amy, wandered up. "This place fucking sucks," she sang. "Ooh! Corn bites." She picked the snack bag up and stuffed it into her pocket—not to eat, but to trade, later, with one of the other girls.

"Did you take your BeZen today?" I frowned.

Hanan made a gesture suggesting fellatio. She was 16 and weighed about 80 pounds. Shortly after she'd first arrived at Twin Bridge, we'd caught her in the toilet after her brother snuck her in an Oxy; she sat in the stall wearing a bath towel as a cape, high as hell and rapping slowly in Pashto until we made her throw it all up and tucked her in.

"Girls," I said.

"I took it," Amy smiled sweetly.

"Me, too," sang Hanan. I could tell it was true. You could always tell. Their pupils were big and their faces relaxed, even as they gleefully defied me.

"School," I repeated. "Class."

As I spoke, the lights flickered, dimmed, and then went out.

The emergency exit sign cast red raw light onto the cheeks of the girls. Hanan's were all hollowed out. They both whooped and grabbed one another by the arm, ready for lawlessness, but in another moment the lights surged back on. It wasn't so unusual—the electricity glitches in Askewn had been happening more and more often. "You're both late. You'll give Linda a heart attack."

Arda appeared, rounding the corner; he had that nervous look. He zeroed in on me.

"The new girl, what's her name, Alina," he frowned. "She keeps covering all her arms in hand soap. Up to the shoulder. Keeps saying 'I'm a fetus, I'm a fresh fetus.'"

Arda was made deeply nervous by the girls. As a rule, he didn't want to upset anybody. He was obviously in the wrong place for that. He was often found out back by the dumpsters with a cigarillo clamped between his teeth, muttering about responsibility.

"Tell her to wash it off," I shrugged.

Arda grimaced, reluctant to be The Bad Guy in the face of trouble, though this hardly qualified as trouble. A few months ago, soapy arms would not have even been on our radar. But with BeZen: no more fights. Significantly less vomiting. Everyone asleep by nine. It was (so I said in my report!) a miracle drug, nothing short of wonder. Of course, it wasn't all linear improvement: some days were better than others, and still, often, Twin Bridge wrought its awful spell.

As Arda opened his mouth to speak, footsteps dopplered up the hallway towards us and I saw, in a flash, Teresa, sprinting for the doors. She was heaving and crying, breathing raggedly: "I'm done, I'm done!"

She slammed out the fire exit, making a mad dash for the road. I chased her into the parking lot, the heat hitting us in a wave; I was taller, faster; I caught up shouting, *Teresa! Stop! Teresa, stop now*! She was thirty yards from the highway, twenty, ten. And then I tackled her to the ground.

She screamed a banshee scream.

The dust settled. We had both skinned our hands and knees on the gravel, the tarmac so hot from the ruthless sun that it felt white, then sharp, then cold. The restraint technique is essentially a hug of death, a limb-gripping squeeze. Teresa had dark hair, eyes black. I'd forgotten the new restraint technique; her arms were meant to be crossed in front of her, but she'd gotten them free, screaming, *fuck you, shit, let me up, fuck-lips*, and squirming, and tried to elbow me in the face so I hugged her tighter.

The rule is five minutes. After five minutes, no matter what, I'd have to let her get up. As I held her there, trying to get her to calm, repeating her name in a false strained assurance, waiting for Arda to show up and help, Teresa bit into the meaty swell of flesh at the base of my palm which I'd left exposed because of my poor technique and I actually screamed, out loud.

"God dammit!" I shrieked, snatching my hand back. Teresa had found her satisfaction, teeth-first. She quit trying to crack my skull with her skull. Arda arrived, panting, and I scrambled up clutching my hand. We asked if she would come inside, and she sat up, brushed the dirt off her clothes.

"Okay," she said, calm as anything. "Sure."

"Wait," I said, and took a minute to cough my grossly incompetent lungs out; the dry dry air made gasping hurt. "Teresa, puke? I mean, you threw up on the bed? Yeah? What's that about? You okay? You feeling sick?"

She considered for a moment. "No," she decided, before Arda led her gently back inside. "No, now I think I'm feeling better."

While Arda took custody of Teresa, I washed my hands off, wrapped the hurt bit in toilet paper, then walked Hanan and Amy, who'd been loitering, watching the drama unfold, down the halls to the dingy room where they learned. Linda was teaching while she did her bicep curls.

Hanan and Amy settled in and I took a seat in the back to help with classroom control. Biology time. Animals. Oceans. Jamie, the youngest, 13, kept opening her jaw and cracking it and opening her jaw and cracking it again. She rubbed the stubble of her shaved head. She had arrived only a week before and was still on Level One privileges: no television, no makeup. I wasn't in charge of making the rules.

The class was studying the jellyfish bloom that had taken over vast swaths of the Pacific Ocean. She clicked through slides with one finger. I pinched the skin around my chin and neck.

"Jellyfish," Linda coughed in her high, musical voice, "Which you've seen if you've ever been to the coast, are remarkable animals. Most of their natural predators," she went on, a tremor of delight in her voice, "Have gone extinct. Salmon, for example, haven't been spotted in years, since this particular bloom of billions of mauve stingers wiped out the last known school off the coast of Alaska." Click: a photo of a slime field, roiling with plastic bags and ribbons of flesh, which I slowly understood was a mass of jellyfish in the Alaskan Gulf. Next to me a student wrote in her notebook: SAMMON??

"Around 2028, nomura jellyfish were killing four hundred Japanese fishermen per year by overturning trawlers and clogging engines. They would fill nets, burst them, and drag men—"

"And women?" interrupted Hanan.

"—and women—into the sea."

"I saw the ocean, once" Amy offered. "Full of gooses."

"That's a lake, dumbass." Hanan flicked an eraser at her.

"Girls," I said.

Linda went on: jellyfish had clogged the intakes of coastal nuclear power plants; disabled the cooling pipes of American aircraft carriers, taken down floating oil rigs. They were streamlined, perfect; their mouth and anus was the same (cue more giggles); she clicked through pictures of jellyfish the size of foldout couches, yellow and purple and pink, some ripping along canals at a dog's jogging pace.

"The fishing industry tried chopping them up," Linda went on, undeterred, "but nomura release sperm and eggs when divided, so it made the problem worse!" She cackled, and half a dozen girls also giggled at the mention of sperm. I walked to the front to make my presence known. "Furthermore, some jellyfish are immortal," Linda wrapped up, and did not elaborate. I sat back down.

"Nitrogen runoff," she continued, clicking to the next slide: a photo of fertilizer plants and, on the other side, a satellite picture of the Gulf of Mexico, chewing away at the ragged coast, striped by a neon blue band that glowed most brilliantly around the widening mouth of the Mississippi River, "It causes plankton blooms. The plankton suck up all the oxygen in the water, creating deadzones where nothing can survive except—you guessed it—jellyfish!"

Someone put down her pencil and began to clap.

"Sh!" I hushed.

"In fact," Linda went on, "In Precambrian times, jellyfish biodiversity dominated the seas. So we have restored balance. In a sense."

"What's Precambrian?" asked Amy.

"Four point six billion years ago," Linda enunciated. She began to write it on the board, all the zeroes intact.

She was interrupted by a knock on the door. Carmen was there, motioning for me to come into the hallway. I left Linda behind with her doomed seas.

Carmen, all daisy overalls and melanoma-scarred cheeks, was hugging her arms tight.

"We need you outside," she said quietly.

"What for?"

She answered, in a voice so careful it betrayed a dizzy tick of joy: "A kid is up on the goddamn *roof*."

The roof! A kid on the roof! Miracle of miracles, in fact, that it hadn't happened before, given that the windows stayed unlocked due to fire safety regulations; in truth incredible that teens didn't blitz themselves on the daily via gutter plunges, but yes, at last, Carmen repeated, a kid was up on the goddamn roof.

I ran outside. A few others were already standing around, gawking.

There was Arda, his brow knitted, and some people I didn't recognize; a few visiting family members about to trudge for the bus. Somebody's dad discretely pulled a Fanta from his bag and opened it with a fizz. When he saw me staring, he lifted the bottle and silently offered some. I turned around.

"Jesus Christ," somebody said, and then I realized it was me—I said it.

Teresa was standing on the edge of the roof, the very edge, in front of the AC units. She had that look. Ratty pale jeans, band t-shirt. Clenched jaw. Dirty hair in strings around her face. Jaundiced-looking skin, dime-sized bruises on the arms; a whole defiance in her posture that spoke of boys with pellet guns, hours in mom's car idling outside the Quick Check, Virginia Slims with the filters clipped by pocket knives. Here is a girl, I thought, that will never see the ocean or be on a plane. I was so wrong, but I didn't know that then; I only realized, to my dismay, that she had found a place in my heart. Quickly, I built a wall around it.

"I thought she was on basement restriction after she tried to run?" I muttered to Arda.

"Carmen went to use the toilet and then, you see, she escaped." His eyes were fixed on the roof's ledge, and he kept taking a step towards me, then towards the building, then towards me again; he was near epileptic with worry. "What have we come to? What is this, with kids on roofs?"

I clucked my tongue. So she'd escaped from basement duty. So she wanted to get closer to the sky. Or really, it seemed, move rapidly away from it. Who could blame her? Sometimes the things we did for the girls' well-being constituted such awful acts of mental violence that I basically had to stop thinking and move around using only my most basic physical senses, like some nocturnal, subterranean animal. A mole, maybe.

People thought I was good at my job because I possessed some deep reserve of empathy, but actually the opposite was true. I was good at my job because I lacked imagination. Only occasionally, in raw accidental bursts, did I think about the unhappiness of the girls. Mostly I forgot about it completely. Or if not completely, at least sometimes. Or if not sometimes, at least I could go to the laundromat. I could wash my clothes. I could pour out the blue, flowery soap. Count quarters to the tune of the anti-musical music they played inside. Anyway I'd been good at my job, historically, because I was able to largely ignore the mental/emotional anguish around me but lately it seemed that the years at Twin Bridge were eroding this superpower, thus the goblin, thus also the overwhelming gratitude for BeZen, which made all of our lives medium-easier.

The girls at Twin Bridge generally fell into two camps: half had been "removed from unsafe homes," while the other half had been siphoned out of overcrowded juvenile detention facilities thanks to good behavior and luck and generally a heaping dose of racist bias, hence a population whiter than your typical child jail. So the state got to claim it was offering humane rehabilitation for kiddies, while the drug company had a place to test newer medications. We'd sampled sedatives and sleep aids, meds for non-insulin diabetes and asthma, pills for ADHD and high cholesterol and weight management; a whole cornucopia of antis: antidepressants, anti-psychotics, anti-anxiety drugs and anti-hypertensives. But nothing—nothing!—had ever worked so well as the beautiful blue miracle of BeZen, which, according to the ad copy I'd browsed once in the nurse's station, promised "a smoother life." If the girls were late taking a pill they got blinding headaches, and sometimes they seemed to forget whole glacial chunks of their past, okay, but generally they seemed much better, almost like whatever bad stuff had happened before had gotten carved right out of them. Generally.

Teresa shifted forward a bit, so her toes peeked over the edge of the roof. This was, of course, upsetting. The tile could crumble at any time, and then: presto, splat, disaster and news cameras. Teresa rocked back and forth, slowly, running her eyes over the crowd.

"Call an ambulance!" wailed a woman behind me.

"Let's not get ahead of ourselves," Arda scowled. We had to ration our ambulance calls or the operators got tetchy. He turned to me. "Would you please go up there, please, and speak with Teresa?" Arda was very polite.

The building was three stories tall. Would that kill you? Probably you would break both legs. Would you die? If you were trying, I decided, you could die. You could throw yourself on your head, and die.

"Can we drag out a mattress or something?" I hissed.

"I don't think that would help so much," frowned Arda.

"How did she even get up there?"

"Honey?" called the same woman from before. "We're going to get you down, okay?"

Teresa breathed in a deep breath, raised her arms. "Stop talking about me!" Her voice was half carried off by the dry wind. It was too hot to breathe; in the sun the heat was a boot on your neck.

On the off-limits third floor, around the corner from where Teresa stood, I could see a window that'd been swung open. I told Arda I'd be back, then dipped inside and ran up the stairs two by two. The window turned out to be the window of the men's bathroom. Rarely used, it smelled faintly of piss and fake lemon; dead flies lay thick in the rubber lining of the window. I set myself in the frame and swung a leg out. Down below: the parking lot, mute and heartless.

Between the window and the roof's cornice was the top landing of the fire escape. The stairs had long since fallen off, and the landing was a disintegrating platform of dust-blasted rust. I could see how she'd gotten up there, but I could also visualize myself trying to copy her, tentatively shifting onto the platform before it suddenly gave way, crushing me under its weight, my eyes bugged out, skull cracked, and then, later, standing in heaven's mudroom, asking for permission: what good deeds have you done, they'd say, and I'd say, if you could actually just let me wait right here I'd be fine. I feared this vision, and additionally I wasn't confident enough about Teresa's jump being imminent to take that sort of risk. No one had ever—

ever!—successfully suicided at Twin Bridge before, and so it would have been quite the achievement for Teresa to upset that record.

"Teresa," I called. "Teresa!"

Her face appeared suddenly over the edge of the roof, preceded by a shower of tiny black pebbles.

Teresa, snag among my paperwork nightmares. She had not learned the habit girls are taught of blinking often, of looking down away from eye contact. She stared at what she wanted to stare at. She carried some extra weight, but most of it was there in muscle. She had dark, nearly black eyes, set deep back in the sockets, a thin mouth she kept tightly shut; she wore one of three loose t-shirts every day. I'd offered to wash them, once, and the eyeroll I'd received about singed my brows off. Tired-looking, faint yellow undertones from a life spent too much indoors. But what really made her trouble was not the roof-climbing itself, nor the attempted escape, nor the bite still stinging my palm: it was the fact that she was doing all these things despite radical levels of BeZen, almost three times the dosage of the next girl, the sort of dosage that should make even the most frantic hooligan slow to a steady, boneless drone. Yet she was running. Climbing. Biting. Fucking up my compiled rates of success, the report I'd been preparing for TENDER KARE. Her behavior alone had brought the numbers for successful treatment down so much that we would fail, we would not be receiving funding—Twin Bridge would have had to close, had I not done some soft doctoring of said numbers. No one else knew how close we were to shutting down.

Up on the edge of the roof, Teresa pressed her chapped lips together.

If she could have spit far, she would've spit in my face. I waited. She was a champion of not blinking. Finally I couldn't stand it.

"Will you come inside?" I asked. "We can talk just us two, if you want." The glare from the white sky made it hard to look at her. "You're making a lot of people nervous as hell."

I glanced down and saw Arda, in the shade now, on the phone, sweating with anxiety. I looked back up and her face had disappeared. Then a shape soared off the edge of the roof.

I shuddered and grasped the ledge tight, turned to look—her shoes; both her shoes were lying in the lot below. Beyond the lot, the dead brown land. I could see jackrabbits scurrying around out there, nibbling the last of the grass.

"Those are your shoes!" I yelled idiotically. Down below I heard the same woman holler: *her shoes*!

"I'm not a convict," Teresa cried from above, "You've got no right to keep me here, I'm not in prison, this is America!"

Only partly true. Okay, it wasn't a prison-prison, but we did have custody of them. An anecdote: one time a girl, Lucy, left a tampon in for two weeks straight to give herself TSS because she was so determined to leave. What's the lesson you take away from a thing like that? Me, I think: angry young women are the most goddamned resourceful people on the planet.

After the shoes came the rocks. Why the rocks? From where the rocks on the roof? There are some mysteries we'll only get answered after death. Chunk, chunk: bits of asphalt went flying, like confetti from a dark god of construction. Teresa grunted as she hurled a fist-sized piece out into the void, tracing a black parabola. I waited for the crack of a skull, but there was just shrieking as the crowd shied away, ducking behind cars. One landed on the hood of an SUV, leaving a dented bowl that flashed sun in our direction. The car alarm blared once, twice, three times, then quit.

"Jesus Christ," sang a high voice.

"I am the sun god! The only machine!" yelled Teresa.

"Didn't somebody call an ambulance?"

"You all look like shit!" she added.

"Look, Teresa," I called, "Standing up there is only going to make things worse. It won't make them better."

Her feet appeared over the edge, kicking near my face, and then she dropped down and kneeled on the metal grate of the fire escape, a foot from me, glaring.

"Tell the truth," she said, still crouched. "Are you going to strip-search me when I get inside?"

For a minute I was too surprised to answer. Because for one, no, we wouldn't strip-search her: everybody got searched when they arrived, to check for drugs and weapons and signs of injury, but only that one first time. And secondly, it was strange to hear her name the action out loud; something in me recoiled. And third, crouched there by the corner of the roof, her eyes dark in her yellow-gray face, her body still, the sky empty behind her, her jaw set as though she had bones that unhinged, Teresa appeared not like a girl but like some small, furious angel, cast down out of the gates and cursed to live among us. I blinked.

"Okay, Teresa," I said. "I'm going to tell you the truth." I kept talking while I stretched my arm out, offering my hand. "We aren't going to search you, but you are going to go back on basement duty. And if you do this again, we're going to send you to the hospital." My hand remained empty. "We do this because the number one—the most important thing—to us is keeping you safe. As long as you're here with us, you're safe. Okay?" My hand hung in the air.

"I don't want to be kept safe," she growled. "I want to throw rocks."

I dropped my hand.

The crowd of spectators had shifted around the corner of the building to stand under the window and fire escape.

"If you hate people staring, why not come inside?" I tried.

She looked at the window, down at the crowd, back to the window. She waved me away, and then before anyone could protest she was climbing across the wall, fingers gripping the frame and brick, one bare foot edging in the window while the other swung wide through the thin air like Spiderman. She was already inside by the time somebody screamed. I was so keenly relieved that she was back safe, indoors, that before I realized what I was doing, and though spontaneous hugs are strictly forbidden at Twin Bridge, I'd clapped her to me with both arms and Teresa proceeded to pull her fist back, aim, and punch me in the stomach as hard as she could.

I released her, coughing, as Carmen and Linda rushed in to help. I let it all play out while I watched the sky, from the ground where I had chosen to lay, catching my breath. I considered Linda's jellyfish. Teresa was dragged away, howling. They are so successful. They are so successful, the jellyfish, Linda had said, because they need basically nothing. Everything that goes wrong—the hypoxic seas, the pollution, the decreased visibility, the rising temperatures and acidity and overfishing—only helps the jellyfish to thrive. That was the lesson under the lesson. I could see it there, from the floor. In order to thrive, you must thrive on nothing; you must love nothing. This time next week, I thought, we'll be out of here forever. We'll live like royalty. With steady money, in the Kingdom of Atlanta.

Chapter Two

Fair, I can see how maybe the screeching, the flailing, the climbing of roofs and punching of guts could make it seem like I was bad at my job, even dangerously so. Not true! Through sheer force of will and the memorization of terminology I'd discovered online (e.g. locus of control, protection issues, diminished capacity, failure to thrive), I'd shaped myself into an apparent pro, a real treasure of an employee. Despite everything (everything (everything!)), I was good at my job.

My family taught me the lessons which would make me good at Twin Bridge. I grew up in Edenton, a small town on the North Carolina coast, where things were okay until we lost almost everything we owned due to the environmental problems and I thereafter, thanks to lucky stars, secured safe passage to Texas. I've never gone back.

My father was a Code Enforcement Officer. He went around town ensuring buildings were up to code. He stood in the Regal Cinemas lobby, among the violet carpeting and tubs of neon ice-drinks, testing the darkened doors of fire exits. He visited the Post Office and took long breaks bumming menthols off clerks. He walked the harbor past the hauls of sick mackerel, checking for proper drainage; he infuriated contractors by frowning over roofs and wall insulation, ensuring the presence of hurricane straps and properly screwed-down stormproof shingles. I thought it was heroic then that he was keeping the people safe from Severe Weather, the Severe Weather I heard murmurs of all the time. There's Lesson One: enforcing rules would keep us safe.

After all this time peering and poking about at construction sites, in the sun, in the wind, it is maybe no surprise that he developed a problem with his eyes. Pterygium—a thin pink growth over the jelly of his eye— which required surgery. This was expensive, and him with no health insurance; discount surgery led to shoddy work, corners cut. A scene, watched through kid eyes from the doorway of the bathroom:

"It stings," said my dad, standing at the sink with his back to me, face upturned, swaddled in gauze.

"Hold still." My mother gripped his face with one powerful hand while trying to guide the dropper with the other, the one from the veterinarian, where liquid antibiotics were cheaper.

"Ow, ow, ow, ow, ow, ow, *ow*—"

"Hold still!"

"I am."

"Don't blink so much."

"Don't claw at my face so much, Daisy."

"Oh, oh no. Okay. It's bad." My mother daintily lifted up a pinkish corner of gauze with two fingers. She looked into whatever loose mess he had there about his eyeball and sucked her teeth. "To be honest, hun, it's gross."

"Ow!"

"And it don't look happy either."

He pulled his head back so the bandage dropped back into place. "Gross and unhappy?"

"I'm saying it looks infected."

"Don't tell me that, don't say that to me, just put the drops is, don't touch the bandage, don't touch—"

"It's all red and wet, honey."

"Why would you tell me that? Why do you think it helps to tell me that?"

And so on. I gnawed on one finger, watching my parents flail in the mirror, all limbs and hiss and bandage.

The bandage contacts got infected and a hard callus formed. Within a few months my father couldn't see out of his right eye at all, nothing, nada; the left one wasn't too hot either. What I'm saying is I had a blind-ish dad. What he got was handicapped parking tags; what he lost was his ability to drive safely, and he couldn't write well, though he was not entirely blind, not quite. He could read large-print magazines and dodge a slowly moving object. But sometimes, for example, he would walk into the kitchen and bark, "where's the pears?" when the pears were just there, in reach of his right hand.

"Catch!" my sister would shout, pelting one at his solar plexus.

Our dad swung his arm in front of himself and missed; the unripe fruit bounced off his belly and landed on the floor, where it split open, and my sister sprinted out the porch door cackling, but our dad said nothing, admitted no fault or difficulty, just bent over to catch his breath and touch the floor, like somebody poisoned or dying of laughter.

Lesson Two: never show the kids your weakness.

With Dad out of work, collecting his paltry disability, Mom started ringing up groceries at the Harris Teeter. Times were tight. From her I learned the grim pleasures of self-deprivation, in that sometimes I think she enjoyed sublimating her small, accumulated rages into a strangled self-righteousness, which, sure, appeals. If, for example, my father, in one of his odd, high, increasingly frequent moods which set the household vibrating announced that he was ordering four Nepalese harps online and we were to start a band, she would sigh, grip a dishrag, run a delicate hand down her face, and say nothing. She deprived herself from even the pleasures of out-loud outrage. Instead, our meals were precisely budgeted, our kitchen spotless. And it was on us—my sister Jemma and me—to modulate our father's bursts of enthusiasm, and, being children, we had no interest in modulation, and so we did get the Nepalese harps. They were opulence itself, gorgeous, carved from a rose-colored wood, and I plucked at mine continuously for four days until Jemma lost interest and I snapped a string, upon which my father burst into tears. The harps must have cost as much as our electric bill. Jemma whisked me into the yard to play.

Lesson Three: mistrust enthusiasm.

Jemma was four years older than me and several registers better-looking. You might describe her as handsome. In the yard, her attentions at play were laser-focused and adhered to an unshakeable structure. We did not simply dig for rocks: we gathered rocks no larger than my hand and no smaller than a penny, because we were building an impenetrable wall in the muddy backyard, behind which we would secure our kingdom. She had a streak of rage within her, but it was never turned against the family. Her violence was a mode of protection only. For example: the last time I was stung by a bee, when I was six, Jemma found it seizing, stinger-less, on the ground. A few minutes later, while I nursed my ankle with ice, wailing, Jemma approached me solemnly, hands cupping a napkin. She opened them close to my face.

"I chopped it up for you," she said, revealing a bee that had been sliced into many careful pieces. I sniffed and blinked, looking between her and the bee. This was a lesson, too, though I didn't take it to heart. Cutting enemies into pieces can be an act of love. Stabs as care. She would grow up in an altogether different direction from me.

Unlike the rest of us, with the mousey coloring and potato noses of Bolshevik peasants, Jemma turned out blonde and light in her features. She kept her hair trimmed in a neat square style. Our mother criticized this style under the pretense of concern, saying she looked like the lesbian captain of a spaceship.

"Leave her alone," my father would say, squinting at the pictures in a magazine.

"What's wrong with being a lesbian?" my sister would snap, at our father. She wasn't gay, but she did want to needle him. He would make no response, turn the page in careful silence. The messy family web was too fragile for him to hazard a reply. Due to his habit of rocketing moods, my sister nursed a sustained grudge. Most things were his fault.

Lesson Four: a tolerant silence, a willful deafness, is a powerful tool in the arsenal.

But the main skill I learned, which I brought to bear constantly, constantly, at Twin Bridge, was an uncanny ability to disconnect myself from the events at hand. That same summer was a 101 on that skill, as it was also the summer of my mother's 40th birthday, the day when we tried to kidnap the Mayor, for her, as a gift.

That bee stung summer was the last time I saw a bee. It was August, vacation, maybe my favorite summer ever. I had, that year, been deemed old enough to swim on my own. I had taken full advantage and spent long, luxurious days lying on my towel on the grass at the edge of Albemarle Sound with Jemma. My father had been in one of his good moods for months, which put the rest of us in good moods too. Jemma had "taken up gymnastics," which really meant that we snuck into our neighbor's yard after dark and tried to do catapults on the trampoline. I scraped my knees and our mother sent Jemma for ice pops, and I'd hold a frozen one against my knee while eating it and getting sticky red food coloring all over my face and hands and leg and suck the plastic till I got sick.

But around us, around the country and the world, things had begun to change very slowly, and then very fast. I mostly got glimpses through television. There were floods. The floods widened and stayed. Towns, and then whole counties, in Indiana and Iowa and Nebraska had two feet of water sitting on them for months. On TV, there were wars, and then wars that came closer. Encampments with blue tarps. There were people crying against a fence. After fires upon fires in the West, whole swaths of California jumped ship, headed East; a dozen families wound up in the Walmart parking lot in nearby Elizabeth City until the city council agreed they would have to leave. They left. Some things got hard to get; Jemma and I whined on the occasional days we sat in long gas lines, then stopped whining when we heard the hushed arguments it caused between our parents. Southern Louisiana more or less disintegrated, Oklahoma ran out of water, heat waves left Southerners dead in nursing homes and hospitals, Chicago and someplace called Vermont got blasts of air so cold that birds dropped dead out of the sky: *hello birds*, said the newscaster on TV.

People started moving, a lot of people. After dinner, in the living room dark, the TV glowed with awful visions. Mobs with hand-painted signs and camo jackets rallied at state borders, standing in the road to block cars with out-of-state plates, screaming at the passengers until cords stood out on their necks. Soon after that, a new term trickled down into the elementary school lexicon: Pink Cards, newly created by Congress, required to move from one state to another. Katie Sullivan got one and she flashed it around the playground looking smug. It looked like a driver's licenses, with a picture of a bald eagle flying over Mount Rushmore, in pink monochrome. I wanted one, because I was a kid, and I wanted to see my name stamped in print. But they were very hard to get. They're expensive, my mom would explain, and anyhow we don't need them, why would we leave our home? And meanwhile, in the parking lot of the strip mall, taking her Harris Teeter nametag off, she would shade her eyes and nod at her coworker Lorena and say, "Miami, now. All those buildings. Neighborhoods. You hear?"

Storms were what we got. Being on the coast, we knew *hurricane*, though the word for this danger only slowly seeped into my peripheral awareness. At the Cape Fear Public School, just before summer break, our teacher had taken it upon herself to teach us all about it.

"Hurricanes happen when warm air from the ocean is sucked up into the sky," said Ms. Trinidad. "These become big, big storms, with very fast wind, and lots of rain." She was standing at the front of the class, with her big eyes and lime-green earrings. We listened obediently, because a sense of arts and crafts was in the air. Piled on her desk were plastic bottles, dark construction paper, and tubes of glitter. These made hurricanes seem easy, even sweet.

"Hurricanes can be very scary," Ms. Trinidad continued, "But if you listen to your parents, they'll keep you safe." Ms. Trinidad was from Chicago. When she married her husband, they'd gotten a Pink Card to come to Carolina, but she'd only come South the year before and had never actually seen a hurricane.

Ms. Trinidad handed out the plastic bottles, and we began to fill them with glitter and dye. We attached them at the mouth and created water funnels of our own: look at the perfect symmetry. The water spinning down looked harmless and lovely. Safe, we thought; yes, safe.

Towards the end of summer, inexplicably, they ripped out the lights on our road and never replaced them. This was the new economy. They had no money to invest in the creation of new, innovative green projects, but they would dole out contracts of destruction. Jemma and I went out to watch. We liked the machinery. Enormous trucks; the beeping, rattles and noise; the clawed yellow bucket which came down and tore up the earth. That whole August we watched the poles come down. Waves of heat shimmered over the asphalt roads. Salt and gasoline came in on breezes from the shore. At night, when the construction workers left their equipment behind, we would creep to the machinery and climb the huge treads of the tires, the rubber still warm from the day's sun.

"Jump," commanded Jemma, and I jumped.

"Now you," I said.

The crabgrass in our yard and everyone else's turned brown and crisp. We weren't allowed to water our lawns; that summer there were all sorts of new rules in our house: no lights on during the day, no baths, careful monitoring of the garbage cans to ensure they held no plastic. I didn't realize until much later that these were not well-intentioned bits of activism on the part of my parents: all these things had been tagged with fines and fees. We had not been provided with alternatives, but our usual modes of consumption were growing ever more expensive, and that was, so far, the solution presented for the environmental problems.

Jemma and I relished these changes. As water prices skyrocketed (*temporarily*, muttered our parents and neighbors), we went days without washing, just had our necks and armpits roughly scrubbed by our mom with a damp cloth; we made believe we were sailors, pirates too tough for hygiene, that the scratches on our arms were from fish scales, our sun-cracked lips from the sea. My skin turned deep brown from UV rays and mud. Jemma's was constantly pink and scorched. I watched new moles appear on her arms and back.

Afternoons, when it was too hot to be in the sun, we crept about the half-lit house, the warm murk of summer filtering through the shades meant to keep the house cool. Every window was thrown open. No air conditioning. On the truly scorching days, we set up a box fan in the window, and then we'd spritz water onto our bellies and lie upside down on the couch, in the path of the fan's air, luxuriating in the coolness, listening to the cicadas drone, and later, as it darkened and we prepared to climb our tires, the croaking of peeper frogs and crickets. She slapped my stomach and I threatened to cry. We relaxed. One evening our father stopped us as we prepared to rush out.

"Do you know what tomorrow is?" he asked us. He was tall, but his school athlete muscles had melted largely to fat. He kneeled down to see us better with his bad eyes.

We shook our heads.

"Tomorrow is your mom's birthday," he said. "Should we get her a present?"

"Yes, yes, yes," we chanted, our dirty hair swinging while we hopped. He put his finger over his lips, and told us to get in the car.

My father was absolutely not allowed to drive. He most especially wasn't allowed to drive in the evenings, when the light was fading. We knew this, but who were we to stop him? He bubbled and sang, a sort of dazed smile on his face as he talked in one continuous stream, buckling us into our seats. There were gnats in the air, ones so small and fine that they stuck to your sweat-damp skin and disintegrated into tiny black parts when you tried to wipe them off.

"Because she loves boats so *much*, you know, the *concept* of boats at least; your mother's never sailed in her life, of course, a land-locked landlubber, but it should be easy to learn, we'll take classes, all of us, because practicing is the best way to learn. Learn by doing, isn't that what we always say, girls? And there could be nothing better than learning while doing while in a boat—what is it they say in your book? Those books you like, what are they, the ones with the frog and the other frog?"

"*Frog and Toad*," I corrected him.

"That's it, that's it exactly," he cried, slapping the wheel, turning around to smile at me as I pulled the seatbelt strap away from my chest and tucked it behind me. Jemma and I were both sitting in the backseat, bouncing: a car trip with our dad alone was the rarest treat. Our mother was at work and we had him all to ourselves. These were early days, when Jemma's hair was long and she still adored our father. "Frog and Toad say there's nothing better than fucking around in boats, don't they? Sorry, girls, cover your ears! But they make a point; all the best points come from children's books. It's the perfect situation, the perfect kind of balance of freedom and control, isn't it, girls? Ideal cooperation with nature; not the capture of wind, but a symbiosis—" He stopped, suddenly, mid-stream, and turned around. We were still in the driveway, his hand holding the key in the ignition. He looked at us both. His okay eye and the cloudy one, from behind large square glasses; the high rectangular forehead and its deeply carved lines. The sun was low, and sweat stood out on his face, which had a kind of trembling energy, like a sensitive instrument for measuring sounds undetectable to the human ear. So attuned it was nearly painful to look at. I didn't like it. "Do you love me?" He turned to both of us in turn. His voice was taut. "Girls—you love your father?"

"Yes," we said, in chorus, my volume dampened somewhat by a fear whose source I couldn't articulate.

We were rewarded. His face transformed instantly, to a hungry delight, itself so sharp that I was glad when he turned back around and twisted the key to start the engine. "Love makes the car's wheels go!" he crowed, and we shot backwards out of the driveway.

We made our way, under the happy rants of our father, toward the harbor. We lived on Moseley Street, on the Western edge of town, in a cul-de-sac from which you could clearly hear the highway. He came to abrupt stops at lights which set our bodies rocking forward in a fun way. He snapped furiously at cars which erupted, honking, because he'd changed lanes without seeing them.

"Jemma, Beatrice," he said, looking left and right out the windows, "help me with your eagle eyes. Do you see Fountain Street?"

We eagerly scanned the outside world. Our father wheeled in circles from block to block, muttering and jabbing at the radio. We were driving through a neighborhood much nicer than ours, with large white houses and lawns that still grew green and lush. They must have paid their fines without a second thought. They must be taking long, cool baths; they turned on pink lamps in clean pink bedrooms, and unwrapped packages of ice cream and apples, and stuffed their plastic in the trash. I was imagining this, not with envy but an idle curiosity, when I saw the sign.

"There!" I cried, victorious.

Fountain Street was lined with drooping yellow oaks.

"Excellent work, kiddo!" sang my father, and he whipped the car around, and I beamed, while Jemma looked on jealously.

He parked haphazardly in front of a big yellow house, the passenger-side tires up on the lawn. We walked up the brick footpath, Jemma and I shyly trailing our father. A smell of dead crab from the harbor came up and left with the wind. Our father rang the bell.

An older man opened, one with a hunched, owly posture. He looked surprised, gaping at our father and then at us.

"Can I help you?" He had a soft drawl, and seemed to barely open his mouth to speak.

"I'm here about the four stroke Sun Tracker pontoon," our father rapped out. He grew suddenly serious, but a strained kind of seriousness, one he'd put on sometimes like an ill-fitting suit in the company of other men. Though I was a kid, and so my attention slid naturally away from adults engaged in these plain exchanges, I noticed his odd rigidity, his hands folded neatly at his belt, as though he expected to be harangued. There is something sad, something suddenly aging about seeing your parents when they are trying hard to be liked. Instead I inspected the bottom of the sidelights. The bottom had little thumb-shaped smudges: they had a dog.

"Oh, oh, oh," the stranger was saying, rubbing his forehead. Smells of money came from inside the house, roasted meat and candles. "You should've called, we're just setting down to dinner."

"Shit, I'm so sorry!" my father erupted, waving his arms around in the air, "Oh, I'm so, so sorry, of course I should've called. Fuck. God damn it. I interrupted your dinner." He bugged his eyes down at us cheerfully, like: look what your pop did now.

The man said it was fine. He stepped out and led us to the garage, saying, "You've owned one of these before?"

"It's a gift for my wife," our dad said, taking deep breaths of lawn smell, "A birthday gift."

"Look," Jemma whispered to me, lifting her hand. I hoped it was the dog, but she was pointing across the street, where we could see into the neighbor's backyard.

There, atop a tool shed, was a strange kind of gargoyle, the size of a toddler. It was a funny shape, finely carved, with a thin neck and no head. But then the gargoyle moved. In the dimming light, it expanded, stretched out its strange reticulated stone wings, and adjusted the gray body on the gray clawed feet. I gasped as my understanding of the world shifted within me.

"That's the big big biggest bird I've ever seen," Jemma went on close to my ear, her breath reeking of ice-pop. I blinked: yes, it was an enormous bird, the biggest one ever, standing hunched on top of the shed roof.

"Here we are," said the soft-voiced man. We tore our eyes from the gargoyle bird as he led us in the garage side door. Here was a long fiberglass boat, with a blue tarp tied over it.

"A beaut," said our dad.

"We just never use it anymore, since they say you aren't supposed to swim in the Sound recently. It's got E. Coli."

"There's no sail," said our father, in the voice of a man who's spotted an opponent's weakness.

"Well. Yes," said the seller, shifting uncomfortably from one foot to the other. "It's a pontoon boat."

Our dad had already moved on. "A photoshoot," he was busy saying, "You think, girls? With your mom, in the sun, on the water, cocktails in our hand . . . what kind of engine this thing got?"

"Um," the seller twisted his mouth, "Well, it's a four-stroke. Seven-fifty horsepower . . . you said you ever driven one of these before?"

"I'll learn! We'll all learn; a family activity, see—we've been wanting to learn about boats, boats and engines."

The men talked about specs and money, our dad doing most of the talking, launching into story after story. The man listened with his arms crossed, nodding rapidly; then began to shift his weight from foot to foot as it dawned on him what he was dealing with.

We shuffled around while we waited, looking at the sawzall and chainsaw and organized glass jars of screws, not touching.

It didn't take long.

"You don't understand, I have the money. I just need to transfer it out of my IRA—"

"No—" the stranger was shaking his head. "No, no, I'm sorry, I can't take installations. It's up front or escrow."

"Man," our father huffed in anger. He turned away and, for a second, examined the sawzall hung on the wall, orange and perfectly clean. "People are like this now, huh? Neighbors don't trust each other. Where you from, man?"

"Houston," the man said quickly, his nervousness making him polite. "We moved here after the storm."

"I knew it."

"Knew Houston?"

"You have that smell around you, the newcomer smell. What you don't get, man—what you don't understand about this town," he was squinting, having trouble seeing in the weak garage light, "is that this is a community, and we support one another."

"I think you should go," said the man, stiffening.

"I think you should—"

"Leave. Now, please."

"Okay, okay, okay, okay, okay, okay, okay," our father scowled, and smacked a case of drill bits off a shelf, so they scattered across the floor. "C'mon, girls," he said, yanking the door wide. We hurried out behind him as he stalked to the car. He stopped once to yell, "I'll find someone else to give my money to, then! Shit head."

We piled onto the backseat, and he rocketed us out of the driveway before we had our seatbelts fastened. Jemma and I gripped each other's hands. Knocked against the door by his driving, I caught a last glimpse of the gargoyle, almost invisible now in the dark, though I had a chill feeling it watched us back. It stretched one wing out with a slow, liquid movement; I shot down in my seat.

"Shall we sing a SONG?" our father bellowed. He began punching radio dials at random.

"That man was mean," Jemma offered meekly.

"Mean," I agreed.

"And ugly."

"When I'm the mayor," our father mused, not looking back, "Selfish, rich assholes like that—excuse my language, girls—will be first against the wall." He stopped at a radio station that was playing mariachi music.

"We saw the mayor!" Jemma cried.

"That's very good. I see him all the time, way up there in the sky, kind of lonesome-looking, but who can say? Who can say, a carrion-eater like that, a scavenger—that's what the boat asshole was, wasn't he, hm? A scavenger."

"No, not in the sky," I piped up. "In the yard. Back there. The big bird was in the yard."

Our father braked hard at a stop sign, and Jemma and I let go of each other's hands to brace ourselves. The mariachi music played on, trumpeting cheerily. Our father turned around in his seat. In the feeble light we could see only the shape of his face, not what was written there under shadow.

"Girls," he said. "You're sure you saw the mayor?"

We nodded. Slowly a smile dawned on him.

"How do you spell 'boat'?"

"B-O-A-T," we answered quickly.

"And how do you spell bird?"

We informed him.

"Well, then," he said, putting the car in reverse, "That's close enough. Isn't it?" From the sound of his voice, we knew he was smiling. So we began to smile too. "Let's go pick up the mayor."

What happened is that back then Edenton was a little southern town nursing a dread of sea change and mega-hurricanes, and so the townspeople elected a turkey vulture as their mayor. This began as a joke, and continued to be a joke through the middle part of the election, and then stopped being a joke near the end.

The vulture's electoral victory stemmed, really, from the zoological shortages. Raccoons, for example, had not been seen in months. Deer were reported witnessed by children, but who could believe them? Owls were strictly out of the question. This wasn't a problem unique to Carolina; in class, Ms. Trindad sometimes taught us about America's most charismatic rare animals. Wolves, obviously. The brown bear and tuna and bison, again. And birds, wild ones, all kinds.

But then, overhead, the vulture appeared.

Children discovered the vulture at the edge of town, sticking its pink, fleshy head into the bloated torso of a rat. This was a good portent. We had a vulture. *Other* towns didn't have a vulture. Other towns speculated that we had, perhaps, lured the vulture; that even, perhaps, the vulture had once belonged to their town; that we had procured the vulture by deception. The people of Edenton pointed out that the vulture had likely flown south from the Virginia swamps, which had gone half-rotted from saltwater intrusion. Our Mayor, Roscoe Bond, sneered, smiled, accused the neighboring towns of being wild with jealousy, and immediately died. His death was due to natural causes—Mayor Bond was 83—but tensions were high.

Relationships between Edenton and its neighbors soured. People booted from storm-damaged homes in Edenton were no longer welcome in Bethel and vice versa. In Mackeys, we heard, they were stitching nets. This seemed ridiculous; this was a bird, and a scavenger, and not even a pretty one. But if they wanted the vulture so badly, well, then we wanted the vulture badly too.

So we had to lay further claim to the vulture. A name? Name the bird? Yes, but a name was not enough. A name was only a handle that anyone—even the sneaky neighbors—could grasp. A name, in fact, could make our vulture vulnerable. We considered capture, we considered cages.

Those plans were thrown over by more reasonable voices. But what would help us possess it?

The proposal, then, the joke, went around the electorate. And the next month, when the special election ballots were counted, it was official: the vulture. Our new mayor cast his shadow from the thermals. Someone made a small blue sash, stitched from satin and fringed, but there was no possibility of hanging it, so it was folded away. And besides: it was only a joke.

But that joke was why my father stopped the car and reversed, then popped the battered trunk and fetched a pellet gun, and told Jemma to shoot it.

"But Dad—" she protested.

"Well, then, Beatrice will. She'll bring Mom her birthday present. Won't you, Beat?"

"Yes," I bluffed.

That was all it took; Jemma set her jaw and took the pellet gun. It was long, the kind that was supposed to look like a Remington, and she was graceful enough as she raised the barrel and settled the stock on her shoulder, then pressed her cheek against the gun that was too big for her. I watched with my mouth open. Jemma was a decent shot; we practiced sometimes behind the house and in the woods on the husks of computers and old tires. But she had never shot something that was alive.

The vulture sat on the garden shed's roof with its head tucked under its wing. It had a tip of white at the end of its beak, but I couldn't see much more than that in the dark. As we all stared, the bird lifted one claw and clenched its yellowy talons, like an old man stretching. Watching Jemma's face, I saw that her lip was trembling—she was ready to cry—and that meant I was ready to cry, too; then I burst into tears.

"Don't kill it," I choked quietly, afraid the people in the house would hear. The vulture was big and ugly and I knew it had something to do with death, though I'd only ever seen it way up in the sky, circling, when someone on the playground pointed up and said, *look!* I still didn't want Jemma to kill something.

"She's not gonna kill it," our father assured me, putting a big warm hand on my shoulder and pulling me towards him. I leaned into his hip; he was warm; he smelled like our couch. "She's just gonna wing it. So it can't fly. Then it'll be stuck down here on the ground and we can bundle it up and put it in the car with us for the drive home. This is good, good for you; you girls need to be able to face the real world, the coming world, you understand?"

This information was weirdly comforting for a second, but then I realized with horror that I might be expected to touch the vulture, and I started to cry harder. Jemma, panicked by the sound, raised the pellet gun, clenched her whole body, and fired. The shot made me jump and shut up. Nothing else happened.

"I missed," she said, and looked back at Dad to see if she had permission to give up. He nodded, signaling she should try again: she should never, ever, ever give up, not on her dreams nor his.

She lifted the gun again, aimed, squeezed the trigger, and again there was a crack and a whizzing noise as the pellet flew and hit nothing but leaves.

"Keep trying," our father said. She obediently lifted it once more. I was standing behind her, but I saw her shoulder move and relax as she breathed out, this time, in the moment when she squeezed the trigger. And then it hit.

Vulture Mayor made an awful high squawk, and we watched as the bird spread four feet of black and terrible wing, extended the head on the swooped neck, and then lifted off from the low roof. But of course, something was wrong: it flapped, squawked again, and then fell awkwardly back to earth. It got up onto its feet, testing its spooky wings.

My father—not one to back down—was thereby called upon to fight the vulture. He was our leader. He snatched the pellet gun from Jemma and ran towards the bird. The Mayor of Edenton was doing a funny little shuffle and ticking its head from side to side. It stopped moving as my father approached.

My father looked at the mayor. The mayor looked at him. My father paused, then dropped the gun—I think he might have been panicking—and moved forward with his arms spread wide, like he intended to grapple it into submission. The mayor, unfazed, reared its head and coughed. The cough grew longer, and longer, and the mayor deployed a skill endemic only to turkey vultures known as defensive vomiting.

"Wait—" said our father, ineffectively, but his checkered shirt was splattered. Even for vomit, it looked particularly rough. Yet our dad was so brave, undeterred: he scrabbled in the grass briefly before coming back up with the Remington, then stepped forward, the gun cocked behind him, ready to swing and clock the bird on its little skull, knocking it unconscious (at the least) so he could toss it into the trunk of the car like a kidnapped princess from a fairy tale.

But the mayor screamed a true scream. My father, disturbed by the shriek, stinking of coughed-up rat organ and bile, hesitated a second, and that was all the turkey vulture needed to take an odd, loping trot and lift off again, somewhat unsteady but whole enough, disappearing swiftly into the dark.

"God. Damnit," our father said, and ripped off his shirt. He turned to us, his big square glasses flashing streetlamp light. There was a moment there when I think it could have all tipped either way—his mood, the night, our hunt.

But he grinned.

What can I tell you? That we were afraid we'd failed? That we had to narrate the whole drive home from over his shoulder, hollering *left! Right! Slow down! Watch out,* along the dark roads, and him with his bad eye, still stinking of carrion? That our mother was home weeping? That for months the mayor wasn't seen; that fights occurred at cross-town bars; that long, long after the scandal had settled I had nightmares of the mayor's brutal revenge? Black wings at my window, the awful curved beak, scrabbling at my door and searching for the soft flesh of bellies? How I developed a panicked cough when I saw movement in the sky?

No. I choose not to remember any of that. I remember, instead, how we turned on the garden hose. The faucet was on the side of the nearest house, and they weren't worried about water quotas. Dad unlooped the hose with a finger to his lips, then washed off his shirt, and then turned the hose over his own head, and then us too, jumping up and down and squealing, because the night was warm, warm. Grass from the green lawn stuck to our feet. My hair was plastered onto my neck, and when a light came on in the window, we all cried *Run!* And took off together, hooting like a band of thieves, loyal forever and ever till death to one another only. Beaming under the streetlamp at our dad, who was ready to shoot the last living thing on earth just to tell our mother *Happy Birthday, I got this for you.* And then: then we went to the Hot Bag, and we got an entire rotisserie chicken, a food I had not had in months on months, and we ate it in the car with our fingers because it was our special treat, he said, for his brave girls, his hunters of wild fowl. We peeled loose the meat and sucked the bones. "I'm proud of you," he said again. He was still way up, still muttering about our culinary revenge on the craven bird kingdom while outside, past the edges of town, waves pulled beach sand back to the bottom of the sea, disappearing the coast. But he gave Jemma and me the wishbone. Chickens, too, have wishbones, though most people misbelieve they are too small for wishes, so small and delicate, small as the walking bones in your feet. My sister and I both got to hold an end. I closed my eyes. I thought of what I wanted. I pulled.

"And?" asked Arda. "Did you get it?"

I had been telling Arda about the night we shot a vulture for no reason. We were in the back office of Twin Bridge, packing up.

"Did I get what?"

"That thing you wanted."

"Oh," I said, ripping some tape with my teeth. "I don't remember."

He had been flipping through a stack of papers, slowly, licking a finger to flip through one at a time. He gave me a skeptical glance. Then he straightened the pile of documents by knocking them once on the desk, and slid the whole stack neatly into a trash bin. "We keep these records," he said, "And nobody cares. Ah, Beatrice, we may as well write *replaced child with sack of rocks* for all they care. Nobody asks!"

"Mm-hmm. When did we get these?" I lifted a sealed plastic bag of bracelets, the kind that light up when you crack them. They had flowers on them and the flowers were smiling.

Arda frowned. "One of those delegations from the pharmaceutical company, maybe." He put it in the USE NOW box. "Always bringing useless shit for the kids. Stuffed animals. Candy. Nobody needs candy! We need money! Give us money!" He rubbed his fingers together in the air.

We'd been packing, slowly, for weeks. Not just Twin Bridge, but Askewn at large had, for years, been emptying out: the summers, the dust and blackouts; who wants to live like that? I don't know where other people went. Arda and I planned to move with Twin Bridge to Atlanta.

That relocation was going to require a van, or a bus. I had to arrange that too. To do that I'd called a man named Frank, a handyman type with whom I'd gone on 1 (one) date, a single forgettable date, years ago. He didn't remember me, obviously, but I remembered his funny light eyes and his nervous, tumbling manner of speech. We'd be handing all these boxes over to him soon.

"I'm glad the vulture survived," Arda was saying.

"Me too. We would've caused a riot."

"It's bad luck to kill them."

"Really?" I dumped a whole drawer full of old papers into the trash.

"I don't know. Probably." Arda fanned himself with a folder, frowned around at the mess. He turned and opened a window behind him, then leaned out to survey the dry world.

"I'm just glad Jemma didn't end up a political assassin."

"Hm." Arda nodded thoughtfully. "But you watched? Watched her shoot?"

"Of course."

"You would watch your sister become a killer?"

I shrugged. "If the worst thing ever is gonna happen in front of me, I'm gonna watch it."

This route was typical of conversation between myself and Arda: we didn't talk about work, or the girls, but we did talk around them.

"Do you know," Arda said slowly, "My mother—Fatima—she first named this place *The Lower Plains Home for Girls*? That was—oh, fifty years ago."

I had my leg knee-deep in a garbage bag, smashing down trash so I could fit more in. "How come she didn't name it, like, 'Fatima's Corner for Lost Children' or something?"

He scrunched up his face like he'd tasted something sour. "You're very American." Then he laughed. It was a rare pleasure to see Arda looking relaxed. He had a neat, square smile, and always offered his happiness for sharing, it didn't count if he wasn't making eye contact with someone.

"It must be hard to leave," I said. A blast of hot wind came through the window, scattering files, and Arda slid it shut, then took the tape from me and began to seal the cracks to keep the dust out. I picked up a loose paper: a printed list of the dwindling grants we applied for yearly, me and Arda, work spread over the course of weeks that invariably culminated in a long gaunt 3 A.M. night poring over reporting requirements while we pried ourselves awake with energy drinks and corn puffs. Mostly the applications got denied because we already had corporate funding, though TENDER KARE, too, met all our asks—real-deal therapists, more teachers, ED nutritionists—with *sorry, but no*, and I'd begun to suspect that all that time was a net loss, that those wasted hours could have been better spent playing Parcheesi. Arda had been doing this for 20 years.

"I will tell you a secret," said Arda. He turned to me and cupped his hand around his mouth, then said in a stage whisper: "I think the others are crazy not to leave."

I laughed and leaned against the desk with my bad hand. "Ouch," I said, shaking it.

Arda frowned at the bite mark on my palm. "You should get that checked." He looked around. "There's nothing else in here worth saving, I think."

He was right. I went to the office of Nurse Bell, a drooping 60-year-old hunchback from Kansas City who looked always so very sad, as though she were staring into the face of oblivion. She had some mysterious difficult personal life about which I did not ever ask, and which prompted from her long, long sighs, and many personal unpaid days off. She gave me antibiotics in a little orange canister with a seal for safety and said to take with food.

I swallowed my first dose at home that evening. Then I popped two aspirin and cupped my hands under the faucet in the bathroom sink to wash them down, trying to keep the bandage dry. I swallowed and looked around my face, then tried to imagine feeling wanted. What if someone were happy to see me naked? Seems morbid. In the mirror, my hair was thin and dirty, my lips white, covered in pores, there it is, my face, whatever. That's just something I carry around. I opened my mouth to see the fat pink worm inside. I considered calling Frank.

Our date had been maybe three years back, after we met outside the psychic parlor that a former staffer, Jasmine, had been running out of her front living room. I hadn't gone for a reading—I don't believe in that stuff, planets—but Jasmine had left her beaded purse at work, and I'd come to deliver it.

Frank had been up on an aluminum ladder, rattling away and struggling to install a light, a big neon hand that flashed pink and beckoned: fingers out, folded, fingers out again. He'd just finished when I arrived, and as I knocked on Jasmine's door, the hand sparked on, turning the sidewalk rosy and knocking me back a step.

"Jesus," I'd said.

"Georges Claude," he'd said from above.

"Oh." I looked him over quick. Long, bony, but hard to say really how he looked at all, under the pink flashing light. I still had Twin-Bridge-brain; it seemed an enormous effort to make regular adult conversation, like pulling myself up from out of a snowbank. He was holding a socket wrench away from his body. "Hi, Georges. I'm Beatrice."

"Sorry," he said, looking down with surprise. "I meant Georges Claude invented neon signs. I was just messing."

"Oh." I hated him briefly. "Funny."

He came down off the ladder and handed me his card. His card was just a torn bit of blank paper with his phone number and the words ODD JOBS, MOVING, HANDYMAN!

Jasmine had unlocked the door then, dressed in tie-dyed fabrics, smiling and holding a bottle of sake. "Beatrice," she'd cooed, "you're an angel." Flustered by the gaze of the backlit stranger, I'd pushed my way past her to get inside, then hid among the flouncy fabrics and patchouli scents gulping acrid sake while Jasmine burbled about the mystic cross on my palm.

"You might predict the future accurately," she said, while I hissed from the rice wine's burn in my stomach. "Or, you might have an interest in the occult."

All evening the neon man flitted in and out of my awareness. By the time Jasmine emptied the last of the sake into my glass, I was squishing her sweet plump cheeks in my hands and jabbering, *you absolute vixen, are you trying to get me loaded?*, and then we took turns trying to do headstands until Jasmine looked green and hiccupped and I rolled myself to the bus stop and fell asleep on the bus, waking at 5 A.M. surrounded by nurses going to work. Later, at the center, we were embarrassed around one another, and the faint threat of friendship hung in the air, but I spoke to her of nothing but Twin Bridge plumbing problems until the specter of camaraderie dissolved. No point befriending coworkers. Not a good practice. Because Jasmine, for instance, only lasted another week. Then was replaced by Angela, then Casper, then Sarah or Kendra or Claire—hard to remember. Carmen was on **month four**. Our average was about three weeks. Sometimes, Arda and me, we took bets.

I opened my phone and mulled this over, looking out the window where our nearly obliterated town lay itself open before me. Blank buildings, solitary men who walked occasionally down the road's shoulder in heavy steps against the heat. Dry earth ticking at the window. I closed the phone and opened a bottle of wine instead.

It was obvious I spent too much time alone. And thus enjoyed too much the crush of strangers on the bus. I was always telling the girls: find the locus of control. If there's a problem in your life, who is making it? Could it be you? Could you un-make the problem? I was my own problem-maker, and the problem I'd made was spending my days off in bed, trying not to get up or move, unhungry, listening to a playlist I'd found online called "Ambient Home" which contained tracks with titles like "Clothes Dryer Sounds" and "Smooth Brown Noise." This was fine, except for the occasional moment like this one, when I had nothing to do and so was struck by ravenous want—wanted raw red meat, pins in my skin, a mouthful.

You're an adult, seek vengeance, said the goblins, and so as I drank I marked on a paper map the houses of our six city council members, drawing six black stars. Sometimes I suspected that the rage of the girls was so powerful it got into my hair like the smell of gasoline. It's hard not to respect an anger like that. And moreover they were right to be mad; policymakers and power nodes at every conceivable level had filled their futures with a series of impossible hurdles, flaming hoops. What the girls already knew— what I'd first learned with Jemma as she wept with fury in the glass-spangled Social Security office—what anyone who's spent 90+ minutes on hold with a federal disaster management agency already absolutely knows, is that in order to remain operational, your internal engine does require the occasional burst of limitless rage. The alternative, of course, is despair.

I filled six white envelopes with baking soda and then, on the inside of the envelope flaps, I wrote ENJOY YOUR ANTHRAX, VIRGINS, in loopy handwriting, giggling. The last time, it'd been dead worms and roaches swept from the supply closet floor. The time before that I had coughed, weeping, into the envelopes, and mailed them out to the three richest men in Texas. My father used to rant about poisoning the politicians. A rant so loud, so enthusiastic, it earned us a ban from not one, but two breakfast-based national chain restaurants.

    I addressed the envelopes, writing ASKEWN, TX, at the end of each with a flourish. I sealed them up, laughing unsteadily. I had no stamps. Sure, it wouldn't help, but I was off the clock, and so to hell with helpfulness. I put the envelopes on the kitchen counter and flopped down onto the floor tile, leaned against the fridge and ate black beans out of the can with a spoon, too tired to cook. I considered my furniture. Soon I'd be gone! I tucked the envelopes under my arm, finished the bottle, and went to bed, putting a six pack on the pillow next to me, for night time, in case of emergencies, night emergencies. I lay there and thought about masturbating but instead I fanned out the threats in my hand.

    "The mail," I slurred in the dark of the room. "The American mail, what an invention." I opened a corn beer and craned my neck to drink, trying to think of more American inventions. "Cowboys. Hot sauce. Double vent turbo engines, taser guns, anti-lock brakes, the lunar module, Nicotine patches, predator drones . . . corn syrup . . . what else, what else?"

    I fell asleep with the beers by my head and the fake poisons resting on my belly, and my thoughts about justice, and above that the ceiling, and above that a vacuum. Teresa's shoes flew through my dreams, then her teeth. Somewhere way up there in the dark, the contrails of airplanes were being scrawled. Sulfur and ice crystals, 30,000 feet above our heads, a straight line showing us exactly where some other, better people were heading, over this land that nobody comes to.

Chapter Three

"I know exactly what you're up to," Teresa was saying. "I see you talking down to me, you pig-faced, nasty old box of horse guts. Sitting there, smiling, like I'm not gonna put your skull in a big old pot of boiling baby oil and watch your skin bubble up." She yawned. "Like barbecue."

Frankly, there was something weirdly pleasurable in sitting face-to-face with Teresa's barrage of creative threats. Something about her extreme vitriol, the way it slid right off because being hated had become a regular part of the job—it was like standing at Chernobyl in a radiation-proof suit.

"I'll kill you," she was mumbling now, half-hearted. "Boom, splat, pow."

We had her in the nurse's station. Nurse Bell had taken the day off again. Teresa was sitting in a hard-backed chair where the symptomatic typically went, across the desk from the two of us. Linda had her arms crossed and was listening attentively. I noodled around with a plastic gidget on Nurse Bell's desk, but was listening; I was curious about Teresa, who had a blunt edge to her anger, a sleepy implied violence that reminded me of Jemma in her later years.

"I'm gonna put a knife through your fingernails, one by one, and pin you to the desk, and while you're stuck I'm going to pour wasps in your ear holes. Then I'll pull out the knife and peel the skin off your leg and feed it to you, like that nasty fruit leather candy." She was speaking with the diction of a furious psychopath who's been apprehended at last, but actually, she wasn't being restrained, and she didn't even seem that excited. She relayed her plans with a plain expression on her face, concentrating, like she was pulling the words up from someplace she only partly remembered and was a little bored.

Finally Linda sighed, uncrossed her arms, and said, "You can't talk to people that way." She leaned forward across Nurse Bell's desk, which was strewn with papers, candy wrappers, and crumpled receipts. "Making threats is not allowed at Twin Bridge. You can be expelled for that. You know that, Teresa; you've been here for what—a year?"

Ten months. I'd fished her chart out of Nurse Bell's chaotic files and flipped through. The chart was patchy: referred to Twin Bridge as part of the diversions program. Diagnoses written and crossed out: dyslexia, oppositional defiant disorder, ADHD, PTSD, depression. Medications prescribed, canceled, switched; one note that just said "generally agitated brain." When she first arrived, she seemed to be adjusting—then a setback, six broken windows on the residential hall. Shortly after, BeZen was introduced, so we put her on it. Wonderful improvement. Star patient. Total leveling of mood swings—until another sudden incident, unexplained, unprompted, in the cafeteria, moments away from pouring near-boiling water over the head of another girl. They hadn't even been fighting. Some talks. More BeZen. Fine, fine, fine, then suddenly every surface of every car in the parking lot is keyed, and, incidentally, possibly not connected, a jackrabbit flayed open along the belly and left on the hood of one car. Added to the therapy waiting list, more BeZen, and steady sailing, until this week, with the run and the bite and the roof.

"I am not afraid of you," said Teresa.

Linda sighed.

"You're not supposed to be," I offered, clicking one of Bell's pens.

Linda checked her watch. "I've got to go get ready for class. You okay here?"

I waved her off. Then it was just me and Teresa. I leaned back, peeked at her from underneath the horrible invisible leather mask I wore when other staff were around.

"Teresa," I tried, "Do you like it here?" I needed her to be responding to BeZen. As it was, she was snarling up our report, trampling our chances.

Teresa flipped me the double deuce. "Eat shit."

"Well, okay, maybe we can be polite."

"Please," Teresa smiled, "consume feces."

"I think there's room here for us to respect one another," I tried, spreading my hands.

"Look," Teresa stood, "*You* don't respect *me*. And I have a right to privacy. That's in the constitution."

"It isn't," I said. Is it? "We don't want you to get kicked out of here," I went on. Out in the hall, Hanan and Amy sprinted past, cackling. "It's your choice. If you choose to get on the roof again, or do, you know, shenanigans—"

"What the fuck did you just say to me?"

". . . Then policy says you get transferred to a residential psychiatric facility."

"Boohoo."

"You won't like it," I said, sounding sad, because it was actually sad, because that was the truth. The facility was horrible, horrible; permanent spider brain inflicted anyone who entered. "But that is your choice. It's up to you."

"Who makes the policy?" she asked.

"Um," I said. She smirked; she knew she had me. "It's just policy. It's the conditions of the Diversions program you're in," I added, "So I guess it's the District Attorney?" Not for diamonds could I have named the DA. The smell of Nurse Bell's office was getting to me, a smell of latex glove powder and something else, sour and human, wafting from behind the mint-colored curtain behind which girls got sick or searched. "Three write-ups," I concluded, "And then you get booted."

"Can't you guys just, like, choose *not* to write me up, then? I mean if you really, actually don't want me to get kicked out and put in a facility?" asked Teresa, curling her lip, sliding back and forth against her chair now like a bear scratching her back. "Or maybe you were lying?"

It was impossible not to admire a question like that.

Yes, I thought. But you can't admit that kind of thing to a kid in crisis, that some consequences are overly punitive and arbitrary, that my boot was poised over her neck because a boot was on mine; that it's boots on necks all the way down. Rather than lie to her face, I got up and fished around in the nurse's cabinet. We weren't really supposed to distribute meds ourselves, but sometimes we forgot we weren't allowed, so I handed Teresa a little paper cup of BeZen and another one for water. Teresa made a face, eyed them for a second, then took them all.

Somewhere a dingy white binder, already packed up in a box, contained a blurry photocopy of the 'post-crisis debriefing questionnaire,' a series of spooky questions we were meant to administer after a thing like this. I hadn't actually pulled it out in about a year, but I'd gone over it so many times I had questions memorized: *Are you having any thoughts of harming,* etcetera, etcetera. But lately mostly I improvised.

"Teresa, did something happen yesterday? To upset you?"

Teresa shrugged. "I guess I was thinking."

"About?"

"About home."

"About your friends? Your family?"

"Yes," Teresa said. Her voice already had a tinge of mellowness. "My family."

"I see," I said carefully. This part was always a little nerve-wracking. The unpeeling. Sometimes they would tell you things and you just had to know those things forever. "Have you heard from them, lately, maybe?"

"No." Teresa smiled bashfully, as though recalling a secret. "I saw a movie trailer. It made me think of my dad."

"Okay. And what was the movie trailer?"

She lifted her eyes, made them wide and round, and lifted her cupped hands towards the sky, reading the neon title in the air before her: *"Rocket Dude."*

"I know that one," I said. "It's about a guy who makes a rocket."

Teresa nodded vigorously. "My dad's an engineer," she explained.

"So. Thinking about your dad made you upset," I prompted.

She nodded, once, slow, letting her chin drop heavily onto her chest. Quiet sat in the room for a minute. I held my breath and waited. Behind her, in the white griddle of sky through tempered glass, I could see a single hint of cloud. "Because he was always busy building shit in the barn."

And then, still hostile but softening, Teresa explained. Her father, once an aerospace engineer and rarely home, got laid off and spent the last several years seized by uppers (intravenous) and schemes (half-baked), had become obsessed with propulsion engines, with rockets, mechanisms of escape in their ratty barn instead of, say, ensuring his daughter was not huffing aerosols at the strip mall. She spoke of long highway walks she was sent on to search up scrap metal, socket wrench retrieval when he did his work high. By the way she began to recite the startling technical detail, it was clear this project had been explained to her many, many times.

Her father's vision was an orbital carrier eight feet across and 95 feet high, converted to use kerosene, housing three separate liquid-burning engines and welded together carefully over the course of years, based loosely on the old Soviet Vostok. Her father, Semaj, created the fins from the panels of busted combines, from troughs he'd split and spliced. He sent Teresa to fish nuts and bolts from the slow unwinding of defunct machinery that once belonged to their neighbors who'd left (a trailer hitch pulling down the road, an escape to the smothering southern sea). She found a seed drill for the tip of the nose cone. A well-washed pesticide tub reemployed as the housing for the oxidizer. An automatic gyro control fashioned from magnets and weather vanes.

As she spoke I could see it: on winter mornings, in the blue dawn, Semaj would go out to the would-be rocket. He'd put on his clothes in the cold, muttering, and hack red dust up for minutes into the kitchen sink. Then walk to the silo. The earth held no heat. Locusts skittered in the sparse grass. Above him wheeled the satellites. In the grease and hay smell of the silo he walked in silence around the rocket with one hand on the cool metal, anticipating the rivets before his fingertips crossed over them, having memorized the shape of his own escape route. Velocity thrummed in his hands, his legs. He had set a goal and by steps he would achieve it. And each morning, in crystal-clear language he would explain to Teresa, as she rose from the fold-out and set about her chores, that there would only be room for one person, the pilot, him.

"Sorry, daughter," he'd tell her, "But we each of us pay for our own way."

He had no love but for the vacuum of space. His heroes were not among the living nor the dead. He admired only the rings of Saturn: the neat slice of their ice and dust, the perfect geometric disk embedded with moons. He was ready for the soundless black, to see earth remote. Because all Semaj knew for sure was that this world wasn't right. For long years, he'd been biding his time, maintaining the vast corpuscular machines that work the desiccated and failing land, watching the government subsidies thin and disappear, his neighbor's abandoned houses erode. Not even the blackbirds came anymore to pick at his seeds. The rabbit blight chewed up roots and moved on. It was time to go.

"And then?" I was leaning forward, breathless, caught in her story. Teresa shrugged. "Then it blew up."

"Oh," I said, "Wow."

I think I was supposed to say something reassuring, about human fallibility maybe, but all I could hear in my head was the pop song clip from the *Rocket Dude* trailer. In the trailer, a wealthy actor wipes fake mud from his brow and looks up at the sky, his macho index off the charts. I tried to swap this image for one of the ridiculous exploded barn, Teresa trudging up from the schoolbus stop to discover a lunar seabed of charred and smoking tractor bits. In another lifetime maybe I would've said, *buddy, don't talk to me about abandonment, my dad went crazy, too,* but usually when you try to relate to teens like that they recoil, see you as a warty bruja trying to sponge up their youth. What was clear was that she'd only shared the cinematic parts of the story, the easy bits to explain. Her file said something slightly different, but I suppose *my dad slammed speed and neglected me* is less compelling than *my father, the genius, was called to outer space.* I cleared my throat and asked, "Listen, while we're on the subject of hobbies, did you really slit that rabbit open?"

BeZen was working its magic; Teresa, melting, shrugged. I made the shape of a rabbit with my hands while repeating, "The rabbit, dead, cut open? Cut open here—" I drew a line up my belly.

"No, no," Teresa said lightly, slowly straightening one leg out in front of her in the manner of a ballerina. "That wasn't me."

"But keying the cars, the boiling water thing, the smashed windows, punching staff—"

"Just you," Teresa interrupted helpfully.

"—trying to pierce Martha's tongue while she was asleep, smuggling in porn, drinking White-Out, snorting eraser dust, pissing out the window, spitting on staff, scratching staff, unscrewing the steel door handle from inside your room and chucking it at staff, putting used tampons in the water dispenser . . . that was all you, Teresa. Right?"

She was on her feet now, spinning in a slow circle with her arms out in a hoop. She completed the pirouette and huffed her hair out of her eyes. A slow, dopey smile broke across Teresa's face; the ambling and absence-based happiness of BeZen spreading throughout her body and affect like an oil slick over a harbor. The debrief, now, was hardly possible.

At that moment, the lights—the building's electricity—flickered off. For a few minutes, we just enjoyed one another's silent company. There stood some mutual, wordless agreement to put it on pause. How sweet! How normal! Then the lights flicked back on, as Teresa was drifting into a pleasant BeZen nap. I gathered my useless notes and Teresa's useless chart. I was anticipating a visit from Frank, so we could coordinate all the packing up and putting-of-things into moving trucks. It was me who'd hired him—fished the ODD JOBS, MOVING, HANDYMAN! card out of a drawer, where it'd sat, languishing, for almost three years, since our silly date.

In just five days, we were meant to skip town.

As I left, Linda, who was stalking up the hallway, called me over in a whisper.

"This—" she gestured to Teresa, who was closely examining a nearby crack in the wall—"This won't be a problem, will it? With the report? The funding?"

"No," I said. "No problem." Because I would lie, lie, lie. "It'll be fine. The report will be fine. We'll get the funding secured. The move is on." I smiled a tight smile. "Get your farewells to the girls in order. There's still time to change your mind—if you'd like to come with us."

But Linda shook her head. No, she would stay in Askewn. Like a goober, a fool (in my opinion), wasting a rare shot at a Pink Card. Oh well.

I glanced back at Teresa. She and I, we were the lucky ones. She looked up, blinking her eyes, slowly, one at a time. All her talk, her threats of knives, had drained out of her. She smiled and showed her wet teeth. I left.

In the hallway, I sank into the quasi-pleasant rawness of my hangover, tenderized by daytime colors and noise, my nerves thrillingly exposed. I blinked down into the cup of BeZen I was still holding. Plucked out one pill and held it up to the overhead fluorescents: a blue and red gelatin capsule with teeny balls of neuro medicine inside. Already it grew warm and tacky in my hand. If I held it long enough, would it dissolve into my skin? What a pleasant gift, the dreamy ease Teresa had floated into; people search their whole lives for a feeling like that. I dropped the pill back into the cup and rattled it around. Her knives tucked away. Who would BeZen make me—no mailing of fake chemical weapons, but docile and soft, floppy as an anesthetized puppy, and perhaps I would cook a vegetable, read a book—learn to knit!

"What are you smiling about," scowled Hanan. I started and saw her, sliding along the corridor with her full weight leaning against the wall like a gunshot victim.

"I'm not smiling," I protested pointlessly. "Are you okay?"

Hanan paused, turned, and sang her next word into the wall. "I have a seeecret."

I stiffened. Horror of horrors. She continued sliding, right on past me, and I turned and followed her.

"Would you like to tell me?" Hanan was capable in a way I found both admirable and alarming. She'd gotten put in the Diversions program for jacking cars, more than a few over a summer. She and two friends wouldn't do anything with them, she told me once; it wasn't for money, they'd just drive, around and around, rolling through stop signs and nodding out the window at little old ladies "like we just got our dicks sucked" while the radio bass thrummed at bone-rattling volume, as she explained it once, until the sun came up and they dumped the cars in East Askewn where people burn tires.

Hanan spun around to face me so abruptly that I nearly crashed into her. "Green," she whispered. "And I had to clean their cages."

"Yes?" I braced myself. You never knew when the girls might relay some shocking information, and you had to not act shocked. When it rained that one day two years ago, we'd all gone outside, giddy, even Arda, electric with the feeling of rain, real rain, drenching our clothes and tamping down dust, until Katya, a girl now long gone, had taken my hand in the doorway and explained she did not like rain on account of the time her sister had tried to drown her.

"The parrots," Hanan continued. "The parrots we had." She closed her eyes. "That's the *last* time I had a pet."

"What?"

"And they made a sound like this," she said softly, and then, into my ear, she shrieked, *AAAAAAHHHHH!* A glass-cracking shriek, a blade to the brain.

"Jesus!" I cried, wheeling back. I clapped my free hand to my ear and scrunched my eyes up, then my whole face, tightened all the muscles in my face as tight as they would go, which is the exercise I do sometimes to keep myself from snapping.

"HA!" Hanan finished, then spun and sprinted down the hall, cackling, "Suck my dick, zookeepers!"

"Hanan!" I yelled. "School is the other way!"

She was gone, had disappeared around the corner, but I heard her yell: "Your man is here!"

I began to walk in her direction, baffled. I gave up.

And thus began my day in full.

I ducked into a bathroom, gargled water and checked my teeth while I combed fingers through my somewhat-dirty hair. I jumped when somebody bellowed from behind a stall door: "No negative self-talk!" I'd been muttering *idiot, idiot* at the mirror. Embarrassed, I fled into the hallway.

Around the corner, I found Frank standing just inside the front door, listening with his brows knit to the atmospheric grumblings of Twin Bridge: somewhere upstairs the heavy chunking about of furniture, the smack of a hand against a wall, a high and sustained moan.

"Thanks for coming," I said, keeping several feet away from him.

"Sure. Consultations usually take about 30 minutes. That okay?"

On the phone, when I'd called, neither of us had acknowledged remembering each other. Now it seemed that he either did not remember me, or else we had both agreed to continually pretend not to recognize each other; we'd committed now and were in too deep to change course.

Unfortunately, I was attracted to him. Though you wouldn't call him a classically handsome man. The first time I'd met Frank, I'd thought something like, *this is only practice for the real thing, he's too unusual-looking.* Maybe then I'd thought that over so much I had tricked myself, because now I saw the appeal: he had a lean, capable energy. His nose was interesting, a kind of odd bulbous shape that I could never recreate in my memory. If you'd pointed a gun at me and told me to draw Frank's nose, I would've pissed myself from fear. None of this explains how he attracted me. I struggle to tell. He had a chipped tooth. I guess it had nothing to do with an accumulation of perfect features. A tattoo emerged out of his left sleeve and onto the back of his wrist and hand. What was it? A fruit? A clown?

"That's fine. Let me show you what the story is." I avoided eye contact and led him towards the office.

"Samuel came, too," Frank said as he followed. "He'll be handling the van rental. He said he had some questions."

I stopped and peered behind Frank at a man who seemed like Frank's photo negative. If Frank were a picture of surprise desire, Samuel was the picture of conventional disappointment. Squat, muscular, in a tight polo the same color as the rest of him: pale yellow, the shade of bile that comes off milk when it spoils. His mouth was a dollop, small and pink. His eyes had long lady lashes. He had his chin tucked down a bit, and his fists balled. He stuck out his hand to me, making me cross the distance to shake it.

"Samuel Paratory," he said. "I'll be arranging transport."

"Great," I said, as he squeezed my hand and pumped it twice. His hand was sweaty, his shoulders were tensed; sometimes people got acutely, aggressively uncomfortable in Twin Bridge, the way you might in a hospital or morgue or strip club. "I didn't realize you'd need to come in person to rent us a van."

"Actually, I came to talk about payment."

"Ah," I said, "The vouchers. Yes—"

"That's the issue," he interrupted. "We don't accept them."

I stopped short. This was a quandary. Twin Bridge's finances were labyrinthine and cash-strapped, and we had only government-issued vouchers, like the kind you might get for Section 8 housing, except that these were for transport across state lines. Usually they went to people fleeing an area destroyed by the environmental problems. Linda was hovering behind Samuel, pretending to adjust the thermostat, eavesdropping.

"Let's figure this out in the office," I said, hustling him further up the hall, not looking back.

"The vouchers are state-issued," I explained. We were sitting in the almost-bare office. In the corner were boxes we'd taped up and bags of trash. The desk was clear, except for an ancient computer and a phone that no one ever called. "The money comes directly from the Department of Health and Human Services. It's guaranteed. Totally common," I went on, bluffing; I knew basically zilch about the vouchers and had never had to use any before. "People love them!"

"Sorry," Samuel shrugged. I could see Frank's shadow through the door as he paced around in the hallway, waiting. "We aren't required to accept them. And we don't. That's our policy. Cash or credit only." Samuel's unblinking eyes stared at a spot in the middle of my neck. His scalp, underneath the mustard-colored hair, was spotted with blisters, as though he'd been very badly sunburned at the top of his head. "Cash, credit," he repeated. "That's it."

It was hard to argue with that, but I was shaking my head and waving my hands in front of my face, saying, "Look, look, this is guaranteed—all you do is say yes, and the state, the state mails you a check—or maybe they transfer it, whatever you want, okay? This is source of income discrimination, this is a waste—"

"No exceptions," he said, shaking his head. He wet his lips and smiled thinly. "Look, we're the only moving company in the metropolitan area that's allowed to go across state borders. But margins are tight. We don't take risks." In the hallway Frank was whistling a jaunty tune.

"It's guaranteed," I repeated, trying to suppress the pleading note in my voice. Nothing. "Can you hold tight while I get someone from the central office on the phone? They can explain it better than me."

He shook his head and stood to go. "We're happy to work with you," he wrapped up, "But we need real money. Up front."

And with that he was gone, passing a concerned-looking Frank, who quit whistling to watch him go.

I cursed, quietly.

"What happened?" Frank boldly ducked his head into the office.

"Nothing," I sputtered, surprised, then, "Looks like we've got no wheels."

He opened his mouth but before he could speak I pushed past him, declaring, "I'll show you around."

I stalked down the hall with Frank in tow, pointing out rooms that would need to be emptied.

"This is the classroom," I said, opening a dented metallic door on our right. He peered over my shoulder. I flicked on the lights and rows of desks appeared. "We'll take the teacher's desk, but you can leave the students'." From behind us floated the sounds of the Spanish-language romcoms Carmen watched on break. I poked a desk with my toe. On its surface, in pink highlighter, one of our beloved gremlins had scrawled YO AMO EL SEMEN. From Carmen's office, a burst of *jajaja!* "Linda will show you which teaching materials go with us. I don't know. Probably the globe and stuff." I drifted around the room for a minute, idly touching things. What good was a voucher, then. There were some clumsy displays up on a bulletin board. Linda had cut the words OUR ROLE MODELS out of construction paper (the optimism, still coming off her in waves!) and then, below that, cut from magazines, the girls had stuck up different figures: Oprah, Godzilla, the Grim Reaper, three photos of cats, a diagram of an alligator burrating deep under mud, all labeled in the spidery scrawl of the girls. Up front, no more Precambrian zeros stacked on the whiteboard: now a large triangle covered in question marks. "These desks are bolted down, anyway, so you can't move 'em." I added. "The chairs, too."

"That's a hassle," Frank said, from where he lingered in the doorway.

"It's so they don't throw the furniture," I explained. I uncapped a whiteboard marker and took a whiff. "God. I hate packing."

"Me too," he said.

"But you're a mover. You can't hate packing."

He shrugged. "Everybody hates their jobs."

"Haven't you ever had a job you liked?"

He thought for a minute. I squeezed past him, out the room, and he shut the door behind us as we moved slowly on.

"This is the recreation room," I said. "Most of this is just garbage."

"I liked installing that neon sign," Frank finally said. "The job I was doing when we met. When you asked for my business card. Even though you don't have any neon lights at this particular child prison."

"This isn't a prison," I protested. But facing away from him, I flushed with confused pleasure—so we remembered one another after all. And yes, bullseye to the horrific truth, that we here are the inept prison guards of kids. I smiled and continued to point around the room, indicating various objects slated for the landfill. "That's garbage. That's garbage." I indicated the broken foosball table, the broken tub where we kept the mashed-up crayons and colored pencils. "Garbage. Garbage," I continued, pointing at a broken chair which was ripe for use as a weapon.

"Lucky for you all that I'm a jack-of-all-trades, hm?"

"Lucky," I agreed. "Georges was a Nazi, though."

"What?"

"That name you said. Georges Claude. The guy who invented neon. He collaborated with the Nazis in France. After the war he was supposed to spend life in prison for it. But the French let him go because he invented a way to create energy from cold deep sea water."

"Shit," Frank cursed.

"Lots of people were Nazis," I assured him.

"What a downer. Fuck."

"No cursing," I said reflexively. We were standing in the middle of the rec room, looking around at the dinginess and marks that seemed so stark in the daylight. We'd both grown suddenly embarrassed.

"Have you worked here a long time?"

I started to say, *so very very long*, but at that moment a knot of girls burst in, laughing, having just been released from 'group therapy,' an awful process led by a graduate student in Missouri over a video platform, something I'd sat in on once or twice and then sworn never to witness again.

They saw me and froze (a bad sign), then looked at one another and burst into quasi-stifled laughter (a worse sign). In the complicated semiotic system of delinquent teen, this froze my blood; this meant plots, plans. Amy caught at my hand.

"Have you met the new girl?" she asked.

"What?" I frowned. The others elbowed Amy, shushing her. They cut eyes at Frank, some blushing.

"She's really short," smiled Maria, sweetly, Maria of the vomitous worry, scrubbing at her face with the dingy sleeve of her pink sweats.

"Where?" I asked, a faint panic fluttering up in my chest. "The new girl, where is she now?" Unexpected arrivals might mean a girl got gooned, 'gooned' being when parents report their own home as unsafe (warranted or no) due to a girl's drug use and/or violent behavior and/or reluctance to follow Biblical law, etc., etc., and then hire some guys in a van, guys who surprise the teen in the night, with zipties, flashlights, *easy way or the hard way* talk, and the girls get bundled off through brute strength towards a surprise drop-off at a treatment center—dark stuff, nightmare pulp, very messy. We do not recommend. They come out of that van all teeth, all claw. It can take them years to recover from the damage. "Take me to her," I urged them, forgetting all about Frank for a moment.

"She's right here," Hanan piped up from the middle of the crowd, and brought her hands towards my face. Some spooky guttural noise humped out of my throat as Hanan opened her hands to show, wrapped up in an old dish cloth, a living, sniffling rat.

"Fuck!" I shrieked, then, "Hanan! Drop that now! The—diseases—" I sputtered; the girls burst into uproarious laughter; the rat twitched its nose. "Right now!" I cried again, recovering, and clutched Hanan's shoulder with one hand while I tried to bash the bundle to the ground with the other. The rat squealed and lashed its naked tail.

"What's happening—" Frank began, but in quick succession Hanan dropped the rat and slammed her foot down on my instep.

"No!" I hissed, the room gone white with pain.

"Docky, docky!" cried several of the girls.

"Docky?" Frank repeated helplessly, as Maria whispered to me, *that's the rat's name.*

"It's short for Doctor Bubonic," wailed Hanan.

"Everybody leave please right now," I groaned, standing on one foot. The rat was nowhere in sight, the dishcloth empty on the ground like a bad magic trick.

"Come back to us, come home, come back to your mommas . . ." Amy squatted down to scan the classroom floor.

"Now," I barked, "Let's go!" I pushed the classroom door open too hard and it slammed the far wall. Reluctantly, the girls began to float away, still calling the rat's name in a mournful, minor key.

"Don't worry," Maria added wobbily before she drifted off. "She'll come back. We've been making friends with her for months. Leaving out crumbs."

Frank frowned at me helplessly. "Crumbs?"

Maria pointed at Frank. "Is he a, you know—" she lowered her voice to a whisper—"a retard?"

"For God's sake," I said, clenching and unclenching my hands. She sulked away.

I spent a few more seconds bent over, resetting. Bolts, pail. Breathing deep box breaths through my nose. Once. Twice. I don't snap at them hardly ever, really.

"All right," I said, straightening up and clapping my hands. I turned around and faced Frank, whose face was knotted with pure, uncut horror. "Next room."

I waved Frank along with me and we continued the tour—offices, lunchroom, resident rooms, and so on. We did not talk about Hanan's pet rat. As we wrapped up, we fixed a date for him to arrive with a moving van to transport all our things, and awkwardly shook on it as Linda approached to hand over custody of Teresa, still zonked, standing still as a statue as she examined her own palms.

On our one date, those years ago, Frank had taken me downtown: through the dry suburbs; past the long-closed golf course now overrun by saltcedar and noxious cogongrass, the ponds brimming with whiskery Asian carp; past blue-tarped businesses, their roofs torn off again and again by dust storms until the owners gave up; easing his busted-up car around potholes the size of hogs. The sun was high. We stopped at the old frontier museum. The museum was not technically abandoned. An elderly man worked the front desk, napping in a black vest that said POW/MIA, and he sold us two feather-soft tickets. Inside we walked, chatting, past where many high schoolers had gone before, past cracked windows and settler mannequins which teens had posed, both kneeling and prone, in intimidating sex positions.

"That isn't real," Frank kept saying, pointing to different poorly taxidermized animals. Some of them, I was pretty certain, could still be found alive at places on Earth: a prairie dog. A horse. "That's not a real animal." He was joking, I'm nearly sure.

He sat on the tailgate of a model covered wagon that bore cigarette burns on the canvas, drinking a tall beer we'd smuggled in in my purse, nervously fiddling with some old timey buckles while he asked me about myself. I'd already finished my beer. The museum had been his idea—I'd never been to a museum in Askewn; am anti-memory, as a rule. Around us were dioramas with white, Germanic-looking colonists and Indigenous people in various states of fictionalized harmony.

"I don't remember learning about this stuff at school," Frank was saying. "Do you?"

"Which stuff?" I went up to one diorama, where pioneers crowded around a huge fiberglass ox that was stuck on its side in the mud. The colonists were scratching their heads. Faceless and bent double, they looked less like distressed pioneers and more like medical actors in the throes of IBS. Visitors had scrawled mustaches on their faces, carved avowals of love into the ox's haunch. Someone had glued a feather boa around the neck of an elderly pioneer man.

"Pioneers. Oxen. Covered wheelbarrows. The big slog West."

"Sure. Of course. It's the other stuff we didn't learn about. Land theft. Ethnic cleansing in Mississippi." I tugged at a fake plastic pistol, holstered at the hip of a worried pioneer.

I heard the sound of Frank thinking. Then, "We learned about the Devil."

He'd surprised me. I straightened and looked over, extra wary, in case he was a cuckoo, dragging me here to proselytize.

"Very Christian school. Nebraska City." He drew the shape of something enormous with his hands in the air. "Cherubs have ox feet, says Ezekiel."

"Interesting."

"I'm not religious. To be clear. Not at all, at all. Are you—wait, sorry, not supposed to talk about religion on a first date. Sorry." I managed to pry the pistol out of the holster, almost falling backwards as it came loose. "Were you a troublemaker?" He asked, watching me potter around. "Is that why you do this now—helping the *youths*?"

"No," I answered, as he joined me before the diorama. I handed him the pistol and he took it graciously. "No, not at all. No trouble. Just late to school." I crouched down and poked at the ox's fiberglass leg: here was the tragedy. Two big red holes indicated snake bite. "And I wouldn't call it 'helping youths,' honestly."

"Right. Corralling the madhouse?"

"It's more like . . . have you ever had one of those dreams where you're trying to put a bunch of puppies in a basket, but every time you turn around they're gone, running towards the cliff, and your legs aren't working?"

"Let's even the odds," Frank said, and stepped over to the next diorama, ripping a plastic pistol out of the hand of another pioneer, this one raising it against a Caddo man. He tried to twirl the two fake guns, like an outlaw, laughing, but he dropped both on the floor. "C'mon," he said, waving me into the next room.

A fake frontier kitchen, a lady in a bonnet, a black iron stove—everything vandalized and cracked. In pyrex display cases, rusting chaps, spurs, dented murder bits.

"Please don't think I'm a gun nut," he said, running one finger along the beveled edge of a display case. I watched his hands.

"No," I assured him, "Not religious, not a gun nut. Just a nut for the Great American Myth."

"Not that either," he said quickly, darting a look at me. His hands ran along into a neglected, cobwebbed corner, and he brushed them off on his jeans. "It's just that it's always quiet in here. And the air conditioning works."

"You come for the myth and the air conditioning."

"The myth, the air conditioning, and the spiders."

"The myth, the air conditioning, the spiders, and the ox feet."

"The myth, AC, spiders, ox feet, and to impress pretty women with my knowledge of the cherubim."

"Aha," I said, spinning a gold spur. "How's that usually go?"

"Not great. But I keep trying."

"Try someplace with more spiders, next."

"More spiders," he repeated gravely, closing his eyes. "Next time I'll remember."

Afterwards, we'd gone to a bar with neon CORN BEER signs and a red felt pool table. Advertisements pasted over the windows, painted shut to keep out dust, made the place dim, like we were at the bottom of a boat. People stood around in happy islands; on the wall were mounted the heads of a half dozen jackrabbits. Frank sat down across from me and pushed a fresh pint glass into my hands, his fingers brushing mine. We leaned forward and got loopy.

"I swear," he was saying, "I have seen some dark stuff happen on that pool table."

"Oh," I took a big gulp and brushed foam from my lip, "Let's not compare what dark stuff we've witnessed." I cringed; I hadn't meant to perform a competitive cynicism.

But he was deep in recollection, looking off at the back wall. Look at that face! Like a, like a—what was he like? "This lady, during one of the blackouts, she had a battery-powered fan . . ."

"The blackouts, I've gotta say, I'm sick of them."

"Sick!"

"And they're only getting worse, right? That's not just in my head?"

Usually the blackouts happened at night. I'd be in a good loopy way, drinking maybe, about to drop into sleep, and then, like the world was in accord, the light from my bathroom would go dark, the green glow of the microwave's clock, the thin red dot of the router, and outside my tempered window, the orange haze of Askewn too would snap into darkness. And then night was real. Hard to explain how dark that is, with no lights anywhere. From my pillow I could see Venus, hot and distant, rolling around the sky and blathering on about love. The air would grow stale; I'd sweat in my sleep. By morning, the machines would be humming again while midnight blinked on the clock.

Frank was shaking his head, then nodding, saying, "A fan," and here he made the puckered face of a fish, "and everyone was so hot, here, they started paying her 10 bucks a pop for a turn in front of it—"

"How many minutes?"

He furrowed his brow and guessed, "Five."

"Five minutes is a long time."

"Then somebody didn't want to give the fan up, so he got in an argument, and smashed it on the ground. We lost the breeze. Isn't that sad?"

He looked sad. "We all sang "Danny Boy" and tried to cover the bar mirror with trash bags."

I drained the rest of my glass.

There were other moments. I guess more serious ones. He asked:

"Really, really, it must be hard, right? Working with a lot of traumatized teenagers?" It had gotten quiet, briefly; the bartender was flipping through stations looking for better music.

I grimaced. "It's a mixed experience. 'Helping' is generous."

"Why do you do it?"

"Oh, it's just a job, just a job; I just like getting paid to play Parcheesi."

"Really?"

I frowned. "Sorry, buddy, I've got no One Big Wound to serve you on a silver platter. No big terrible thing that made me—"

"No, no, no—I just meant—Parcheesi?"

I leaned across the table and seized him by the collar. "We can't just sit around being sad, Frank. We've got to play Parcheesi or we'll die, we'll die!"

And still later, I asked him:

"You ever have a nickname?"

He drummed on the table. "Not one I'd like to share."

"Something bad? I'll guess. Toilet boy?"

"Toilet Boy was my father."

"Lil Toilet Boy? No. Gorilla Mitts? Dust Bunny? Hot Dog?"

He was laughing. It was good. A good, really good laugh. He reached across and touched my elbow.

Anyway, it went on like that—laughing and talking over each other about nonsense—but here's where I may have miscalculated. Easy talking led to easy drinking, on my part, and having skipped dinner I wound up sloppy, unkissable, had to pour myself into the rare indulgence of a taxi at some late bar-closing hour, and I recall Frank's face, soft with concern, the flat wide lips over the chipped tooth, as he closed the door of the taxi and asked me to call him and let him know I made it home, which I did not do. Instead: throttled my thoughts. Had taxi driver drop me ten blocks from home. Would not be rube suckered into the romance racket. Would not go for Frank, whose attentive eyes were brimming with fondness, blackberries and movement, whose presence was both warm and roomy, reflecting a better version of yourself, like a mirror full of breath. No. No, no. I staggered homebound through nighttime to clear my head. I keyed three e-commerce delivery trucks on the walk home. And did not call Frank, not then nor ever, out of embarrassment, and the need to keep a tight, tight, tight control over my time. Until I fished his business card out of the drawer.

"She's already better, Beatrice!" Linda was saying. She'd come up to me as I stood in the hallway, blankly regarding a wall while I sorted out my thoughts about the move.

"Who? What?"

"Teresa. She's been an angel this morning, since the interview." Linda briskly cracked her knuckles on each hand, one at a time. "Sat in the front of the class. Listening. Raising her hand. Really participating—not mocking me. We were doing physics, biology. Kept it light. What's a proton? What's a neutron? I say, autocannibalism is a normal part of the animal kingdom; even the short-tailed cricket is known to eat its own wings—and I see her taking notes. Notes!" As she spoke, I watched Teresa slowly, slowly reach back to touch her shoulder, where her own edible wings might be.

"Wonderful," I said.

"I thought that, instead of taking her down for basement duty, she deserved some time up here. So. You two have fun," she said, pushing Teresa towards me for my turn at custody, and for a moment I felt a powerful hatred for Linda, but then it melted away and I was left with the core, which was just nausea and fatigue. The girls were on their post-class break. Soon I would have lunch with them. There would be noise and smells. I wanted to do something nice, something to reinforce good behavior, and that's how I spent my last normal afternoon at Twin Bridge painting Teresa's nails.

Of course, it wasn't a real manicure—just cheap pink polish from the self-care kit, which we kept hidden away so they wouldn't try to huff the acetone. I chaperoned her to the rec room and we found two non-broken chairs to sit in. We pulled them up to one of the plastic tables. Scattered about the floor were crumbled bits of colored pencil and stray board game pieces catapulted from the boxes they belonged in. The table was speckled gray and barely holding itself together, trembling when we touched it. Someone had drawn a series of smiling faces on construction paper, the faces grinning with a blind rictus, bald and noseless, and superglued them directly to the wall. Whatever. We'd be out soon.

"Give me your hand," I said gently. She was subdued and sleepy. She gave me her left.

She looked at her choices: just the pink and an old bottle of black, nearly empty due to high demand. She pointed at the pink. Someone had named it Aruba Sunset. "It's nice," she said softly.

"Really nice," I agreed. I shook the bottle and twisted off the cap, shedding dried bits of polish. First, I carefully pushed back her cuticles with my thumbnail. I'd always hated that sensation, but she didn't flinch. I began the first coat, remembering the one time my mother had painted my own nails. It was shortly after the shooting of the mayor, which our father had proceeded to brag about (*"my girl, Annie Oakley, a crack shot!)* This in turn had not endeared my father to the community.

Around that time, also, our dinners changed. I believed we had grown rich. I was ten. The people in the cities wanted steak and pork chops, which they could afford despite the ever-higher meat taxes, so the livestock industry bought out all the corn and soy that survived the droughts and floods and then there was none left for us: what was left was hoof and offal. Freeze-dried, vacuum-sealed, canned giblet. Only once I'd accompanied our mother to the Save-a-Lot and watched her walk primly past the deli counter, not looking, did I understand it was a step down.

I accepted this, though I understood, the way children readily absorb shame, that I shouldn't talk about it amongst my friends and teachers. We were ninety to a class then: kids from the tri-county area bussed in and assembled to sleep through lessons in the defunct auditoriums of The College of Albemarle-Edenton-Chowan, and in the noise and tumult I worked on the expansion of my imagined constructs as on a master project. Hourly I was possessed by childish visions: our teachers staggering with the symptoms of vampirism, superheroes bursting through the painted cinder block walls, teenaged detectives recruiting me mid-class. They wore pink trench coats and spoke urgently. Hourly, they failed to appear. Desperately, I waited for radical change. It dawned on me that it was possible the drudgery was inescapable. The boiled meat, the greasy auditorium chairs, the increasingly sterile earth, the punishing summers. Could it all become normal, permanent? No; I knew further wonder awaited me, stretching endlessly away like hot dunes. I only needed to grow bigger and freer. I would learn a new language, and the names of carnivorous plants. Someday I'd stand on an iceberg.

I'd had to ask my mother for the manicure. She'd been standing out under the carport, carefully painting a crack in the windshield with clear polish. A sweet smell of damp grass and motor oil soaked everything. I stood behind her, watching.

"It won't fix It," she told me, unprompted. "But it'll keep the crack from spreading."

I kept on watching for a minute, standing at her shoulder in the humid garage. I was jealous that this was what my mother had chosen as the outlet for her exhaustion and stress. She had the polish, she had the time—why not me?

"Will you paint my nails? I asked.

She looked up, entirely surprised, as though this had never occurred to her. She was generous, my mom, and she tried hard, she did. Despite often being silently cross with our father, she loved and respected him, and she tried her best with us although the enemy of her care, really, seemed to be a distraction driven by directionless faith. Every five years or so, she found God. She believed also in elimination diets, cold water, and the lessons of mythology. I don't know much about her childhood, but I know that it took place at Fort Bragg and was very difficult, and thus she wanted peace, as an adult, above all else, at any cost, and seemed to feel the cost was self-deprivation. Being raised this way meant she was not cold; it simply didn't occur to her to be warm. She never argued. She had her hair cut in a short brown tousle, and whatever she wore it seemed not enough, because every part of her—shoulders, forearm, ankles, neck—revealed sinew, tendon, parts pulled taut and somehow profane, living as she did on her staples of diet soda and smoke, cigarettes she rolled herself in secret, thinking we smelled nothing, papers packed with cheap tobacco from the Piedmont. It's typical perhaps of children to have no real idea of what their parent's personality is, but I believe my mother didn't know, either, because she'd tried hard for too long to cover up everything with a show of right-acting. She did have secrets, though. Once I saw her, through the blinds, pouring salt around the base of my father's prize peonies. Once or twice, too, I saw him calling for her, blinking about with his ruined eyes, as she stood nearby, unseen, not answering. This, although when he got home she kissed him on the cheek. I'd heard her cussing in her sleep.

Now, in a purple work shirt with the sleeves pushed back, her jaw working in anxious concentration, she blinked at the glass bottle in her hand.

"Sure, honey," she said. "But all I got is clear."

"That's okay," I said. I kept my voice deliberately casual in order not to betray my joy.

She sat us both on a bench and put down an old dish rag to protect the wood. She smacked a mosquito from her arm. I splayed my hands eagerly across the rag. My mom took one in her right hand and, though I'd imagined this to be a delicate process, she simply held my pointer finger and started painting with a pragmatic gesture indistinguishable from what she'd used on the windshield: one, two, the first nail done. Then the next: one, two.

"You have good nail beds," she said, without looking up.

"Oh," I smiled shyly. "How?"

"They're long. Feminine." She briefly took my chin in her hand and smiled at me, softening. When else have I allowed someone to look into my face like that, so completely, without flinching? In another ten years, she would be near-mute with guilt and fear and a twisted inspiration, so changed I barely recognized her. But in the garage, she said, "You're going to grow up to be such an interesting person." Then she began to look very sad. Gingerly, afraid to waste the polish, I clutched her left knee. And though I'd heard that nails got two coats, she screwed on the cap and put the bottle away.

She looked out the garage door at the overcast sky—it was what we'd jokingly begun to refer to as 'the wet season,' as in the afternoons it poured with savage intensity for hours.

"Oh," she said, "There are these things, all these things I wish you coulda done. Swim in the harbor, even. Fish." I made a face; I would never do those things: the harbor bore E. Coli warnings, and daytime summer play was suffocatingly muggy, could lead to heatstroke. "I just don't remember it being like this," she sighed.

"I like how it is," I said immediately, urgently, because all I wanted on earth was for her to be happy and perhaps also to be the cause. I know she was saying that she feared her generation, and those before, had undone the world with jet fuel. And yes, maybe living has gotten more difficult. But wasn't I just recently laughing? And listen, I've seen an egg with two yolks. I've fallen asleep on a bus and woken up in a brand new town, with just-washed streets. I've seen a dog rescued from a storm drain. And look at me, now, painting pink the nails of a girl who just recently bit my hand to bleeding—doesn't that mean my joys also include forgiveness? Couldn't a smaller kind of ordinary still be okay?

"I saw a dog once," offered Teresa, "but it was stuffed." I'd been rambling a bit. Her zonked-out catatonia was the perfect sounding board, and I'd painted her nails with four somewhat sloppy coats. "My neighbor had it up on top of her TV. The eyes were marbles, but they fell out. So she stitched them shut."

"Some people still have dogs in their homes," I said, screwing the cap on. "Living ones, I mean. I'm sure you'll meet one someday."

I cleaned up and ushered her off to the basement. Then I sent off the rest of the girls who lingered. Amy complained she wasn't tired, so we played a round of Parcheesi. I hadn't spoken to my mother in years. I turned off the lights. I shooed Amy to bed. Hushed bickering and snores from the various rooms, the occasional muffled sob. What can you do? Each sleeps with risk of nightmare, except Teresa, being blotto, pie-eyed, soused: she will sleep all night with no dreams at all. The fortunate duck. I had the overnight shift and would sleep on the office cot. If a nightmare drove a girl into the hallway, I'd rush to meet her with the melodious, whisper-soft voice that I was only able to produce at night, at Twin Bridge, and a paper cup of bad imitation tea. I sat on the thin mattress and kept the door open. Behind me was window. Outside was night everywhere. Tall buildings glowed over the horizon. Up in the sky, the city lights turned the blurry clouds of dust orange and red, like there was some sign there, advertising a product past the rim of heaven, where the oxen cherubs walked, where Semaj's rings still spin, or higher, someplace I could not see.

Chapter Four

The day had arrived! Our moment of truth! Report in hand, I pep-talked myself for the drive to High Rock, the small city an hour east of Askewn where lay our headquarters, where I had never been. This was a special occasion, worthy of special feelings. I would see fresh landscape. I would drive the company car (battered as it was, with a bumper held on by zip-ties). I would thrust my face into the greasy driving air of roadside America.

I had hot car to myself. I had files, the thoroughly/falsely documented improvement of the Twin Bridge girls, only medium exaggerated. I would be in an actual city. I would purchase, perhaps, an iced drink, and smell the smell of grilled meat. Would I stand in a crowd? I might. Possibilities were rich.

Askewn was a dump. Ask God, clean roads, buy ads; nothing worked. Nothing made people want to live in Askewn, remote, with the utilities getting less reliable all the time. Every winter when the winds came up, wires snarled, blackouts descended, dark for days. Every summer when the AC cranked, rolling brownouts, targeted blackouts to ease the grid. Hospitals, elderly, etcetera, in deep trouble. Deaths in elevators. Traffic accidents.

The Texas grid was overloaded and our town was shuddering down into emptiness, shrinking to fit again the word *frontier*. Where grows no green, no lights at night, yes jackrabbits by the million. Fauna reduced to hog and cow. Flora blighted. After I said *So long, wish me luck* to Arda, I rubbed Vaseline in my nostrils to keep the fine outdoor silt from getting inside; as I stepped outside, I had to kick away the wet sheets we jammed under the outside door to keep the dust out. On real bad days, you tied on respirator masks from the walk-in clinic. Cases of dust pneumonia: you heard about them.

Squinting, I got in the burning car and said a little sing-song prayer as I turned the key: sometimes the static electricity in the dry air made the engine lock. On the worst days, you got a black wall, a snapping light, and then the siren yelped and we all ran to the basement. That's a dust storm, that's a bad one. I wore sunglasses, but ten miles into the drive my eyes were still sore from squinting in the glare.

Soon enough I found myself in the black parking lot of a strip mall. It turned out that our headquarters—TENDER KARE INC.—was sandwiched between a discount haircutters and a long-shuttered barbecue joint, from which no longer blinked a ghostly neon pig. This was all disorienting. I'd been expecting a high rise. I'd seen the tall buildings, shimmering glass towers, from a distance as I'd approached the city. But the high rises, it turned out, were not made for us. They contained financials, and financial people. This seemed suddenly obvious. No floor-to-ceiling windows for TENDER KARE's regional headquarters. And no shade, here, in which to park the car.

Inside, I introduced myself as Beatrice Campbell, operations coordinator from Twin Bridge. The secretary was bored and polite. I sat in a gray cloth chair. On the walls, along the top, advertisements were plastered. Sunscreen. Water filters. My hair was a vicious knot from the wind coming through the car window. I folded my hands in my lap and thoughts about an enormous gray factory in China that pumped out chairs like these. The secretary said my name.

In the office of the TENDER KARE regional manager, a plastic plaque on the desk read Bing Hooper. Unmistakably this was the name of a rodeo clown. Yet Bing Hooper stood and shook my hand.

"Welcome," he said crisply. "Great to meet you." He seemed less jolly than the name first suggested, but affable enough. Older than me, but with a round, youthful face and a neat haircut, more well-preserved boy than man. His eyelashes were long and dark and hard not to notice. "How's the move shaping up? We're all very much looking forward to reading your report."

"Me too," I smiled nervously. "I mean, I look forward to hearing what you think."

I had spent hours upon hours reviewing the report, tightening the loose bits, adding false details to behavioral descriptions: after second dosage of BeZen, Client 297F exhibited stabilized mood and began consuming meals regularly (for details on improved physical health and weight gain, view Table 5).

"Well," Bing Hooper smiled, "From what I've heard, it certainly sounds like BeZen has been a resounding success. Our pharmaceutical partner is enormously pleased, and looks forward to pushing BeZen ahead into the final stages to pursue FDA approval." The name of the pharmaceutical company that provided half our funding was kept secret from us, for legal reasons I couldn't quite parse. "The state agencies are also pleased, as you may imagine. We're looking at Twin Bridge as one of our pilot programs. Given your success, they want to expand the program to centers in a dozen more locations. And in Atlanta—have you seen the new facilities?"

I shook my head.

"What!" He lit up with delight in a startling way. "You are in for a treat. The building's brand new. I've got photos—would you like to see some photos?"

I nodded. This was not the grilling I'd expected.

Bing Hooper pulled some pictures up on his computer screen. We scrolled through them together: white walls, big windows, a kitchen with a zinc island. Three stories. Double the rooms. I kept nodding as he elaborated on the facility's advantages, thinking all the while how much work it was going to be to get everyone adjusted to a new routine in a new place. There was a lot of glass to keep clean. Glass smears and shatters.

"You'll have additional staff, of course," Bing was saying. "We've already got people on the ground out there, so you'll be able to settle right in. Cleaning people, kitchen staff—you know."

I brightened; I hadn't known; this was news to me! But no matter what he'd said, even if he'd explained I'd be sanitizing the floors myself by tongue and by bleach, I'd have nodded and cooed assent, because the office of TENDER KARE deepened the feeling I carried always: a sense of myself as scuttering, sneaking under the barrier into the vaunted halls wherein people employed and employable mingled, talking in sotto voce, muttering into wine glasses upon whose rims they left no print of plum matte lipstick, twirling the stems with manicured nails whilst I stood among them, tying not to make eye contact lest I reveal that I was in fact not a young female professional but rather one hundred cockroaches stacked in a trench coat.

"It all looks great," I said, "So great." I pulled out a bound copy of the report and placed it on the desk, resting my hands on the cover. "I submitted this already, of course. But I brought a copy so we could page through and discuss it. If you have any questions." Around me the wine glasses clinked; I smoothed back my antennae.

But Bing Hooper waved his hands. "No need, no need, Beatrice! I already forwarded it to the people at the CRO. All we really needed was that number—90% success rate! And now," he rapped the report with a knuckle, "we've got it. Outstanding." He stood up. "This late in Phase III of a clinical trial, the CRO has invested a great deal of money, time, and resources into the drug. Investors are excited. It would have been an enormous loss if we didn't meet the efficiency threshold." He opened a drawer and took something out. "You can imagine what a relief it was, then, to get your numbers which confirmed our best hopes." He handed the thing over: it was a packet titled WELCOME TO ATLANTA!! in pink bubble letters. "Great work. We're very pleased." I took the pamphlet. My mouth was open and I snapped it shut. "There's some coupons in there," he confided. "Half off a ticket to the zoo." He crossed the office and held the door open. He stuck out his hand for a shake. "I hear they have a hyena."

I was about to be ushered out the door. As it turned out, I hadn't needed to polish my professional mask much at all.

I drew towards him in a trance, but stopped. "Wait," I said. "There's a problem with the vouchers."

"What?"

"The vouchers we got. To hire movers and the transport van." I shook off the hypnosis. "There's only one moving company in Askewn, and they won't accept them." Bing Hooper, frowning now for the first time in our rodeo, reluctantly closed the door. I swallowed and added, "We also need a stipend for lodging—we're going to have to spend the night someplace on the way there."

He sat back down behind the desk, steepling his fingers; I was in pain, hating to ask for things. Though moments of boldness came through for me, they mostly happened at night, after drinks, whereas here in the fluorescent daytime buzz of TENDER KARE all my boldness was drained.

"You're asking for money," Bing Hooper observed, clicking at his screen, which I could not see, "But I don't see anything here from you that includes a Medium Purchase Transportation Stipend Request."

"What?"

Hooper pursed his lips. "Did you ever submit a 1085A?"

I shook my head.

"Well," he sighed sadly, "That ties our hands. Form 1085A? The MPTSR form." He was saying it more slowly now, and with increasing frustration.

"I don't—I don't know what that is," I said, vaguely ashamed.

"There's nothing we can do," he said flatly, showing his palms in a gesture of helpless regret, "if your staff haven't submitted the request form 45–60 days before the move." He was speaking slowly and enunciating, but it didn't make his words make sense. "An upfront stipend for cross-border transportation—Ms. Campbell, TENDER KARE can't just give those out."

"No?"

"Why wouldn't you make an official request?"

"I thought that I did," I repeated, and I could feel, to my horror, some locked-tight part of me squeezing, bending inwards, threatening to push tears out of my eyes. "I thought I filled it out online?"

He clicked around a bit more, the sedimentary layers of concern deepening. "No, Ms. Campbell, it appears you requested the *form*."

"I what?"

"You requested Form 1085A. That request takes three to five weeks to process. Then when you receive the form itself, you mail it to the financial processing unit, along with an invoice and notarized statement of need." He clicked around more. "It's all here on the accounting guidance form in the administrator's portal. Do you need the website?" I blinked at him. "I'll email you the website." He began furiously clacking away.

"But we don't have time for all that. Can't you, like, expedite things?"

"I wish we could help. It isn't up to me."

"But—" Hot guilt was sloshing around the front of my face; I brushed the Atlanta welcome packet with my fingertips. "Who makes that policy? I mean, there is funding, right? I mean, can I exchange the zoo ticket for cash, or—"

Bing was shaking his head, looking vaguely embarrassed for me. "Listen, Ms. Campbell, we can't just *give* you *cash*."

He paused, but his eyes were telegramming something. He seemed to be implying we couldn't be trusted with money? That we, irresponsible wardens of the poor, would blow it all on malt liquor and scratch tickets, rather than housing our precious charges?

"What about a check?"

He started to laugh, but saw I was serious. "Look," he frowned, clicking around more, "We have redundant accounting practices to ensure financial security, and we're dedicated to reducing costs for consumers and maximizing shareholder delights by taking full advantage of federal grants. Our policy is vouchers only. You're going to have to talk to the transportation company and work it out." He looked up brightly. "Or try a fundraiser? One of those online things."

"Okay," I said; my spirit was broken so easily, I'd never have made it as an outlaw or martyr. I was trying to do quick math in my head: the (remaining balance on the company credit card)—((cost of 1 motel room) x ((number of girls + staff) / 2))—(cost of mover)—(cost of van rental). It didn't work out.

Bing was typing rapidly at his keyboard. He rapped a final key and swung back to me, smiling again. "All set. Anything else?" Even as he asked he was standing back up.

"That's all," I said, wanting badly for this whole interaction to be over, and then suddenly I was back in the waiting room, staring at the secretary, disoriented from how quickly it had all happened.

TOTAL UV PROTECTION, read a billboard overlooking the strip mall parking lot. I put my hand over my face. The light was a bully. It got into everything. I steered numbly towards downtown, thinking only about achieving some minutes of relief by landing myself into the company of emotionally stable adult strangers. As I motored up the highway, Bing

Hooper's frown and Form 1085A condensed, hardened, and settled to the pit of my stomach, a painful and infuriating knot I would simply have to ignore forever.

High Rock is a town for marketing executives, young gun enthusiasts and low-profile sex criminals; people I'd spent my whole life avoiding. The residents are spared water quotas, spared too from the rolling blackouts. Meanwhile, in Askewn: hundreds of heat deaths per year; overcrowding at the emergency cooling centers; outbreaks of hantavirus and Valley Fever. Not so in High Rock! In High Rock: gumball machines and ice water! White linen, outdoor weddings with fans! And along the roads, working street lamps, alive all night, casting a streak of sodium lights that wind towards the city center like a vein of ore.

I drove through downtown, past hotels with intact glass windows. Busy intersections. I stopped at the big mall, at the edge of the smell cloud composed of parking lot oil and food court and chemical soap, staring at the bustling crowd through the windshield in the manner of a dumbfounded cosmonaut at the base of an alien structure on some black moon. Then past the parked cars, through the gleaming double doors and into the sanitized and anti-romantic glow of the department store. A pop song bobbed. Smooth mannequin faces beamed their smiles around. Cleanliness! Calm! Security guards in tactical gear stood with shields and ammo at the exits; it gave me the jitters. But I had only come to bask: the ding of the elevators, the neatly pressed cloth, the flawless planes of the model cadavers, all suggested there was no squalor, anywhere on earth; that squalor and Form 1085A and Twin Bridge itself were bad rumors.

To the food court. I would spend ten minutes sitting at a plastic table, slobbering my way through synthesized red meat, spewing crumbs and germs that some other person and/or mechanized trash vacuum would clean—but not me! Not me!

"A hamburger," I enunciated at the greasy counter, practically high. I looked around: no children projectile vomiting from the second floor balcony, no dead pigeons in the toilet, no weeping sores on palms burned by smuggled BIC lighters, not an abscess scar in sight. Families with teeny babies wandering in and out of shops. Several of the shops were shuttered, because times were tough all over, but there were still goods: sun protection, cooling jackets, portable fans, nutritional supplements, wrinkle-defying cream, double-productive stimulants and convincing meat substitutes. Housewives wandered around with heavy black-lensed sunglasses tucked on their collars, their dust masks looped about their wrists.

"Having a normal time," I muttered to myself, and failed to suppress the weird giggle that clambered up out of my throat.

The man behind the counter called my name. The paper was transparent with grease. I pushed past showered strangers who were all capable of taking care of themselves.

"Hello," I said to the strangers as I headed for my own plastic table. "How do you do." No answer, but I flashed my tight smile around: socialization, socialization, now was my chance to lap it up! No one replied. They passed me in their ironed trousers. I sat.

I hung my head low towards the rich meat smell. I chewed with my mouth open and glared around; fine, then, they thought me degenerate? I could be degenerate. I bared my teeth in the general direction of Everyone Else and let the meat show. The relief I'd expected to feel on this tiny vacation did not materialize. Instead, I thought: who are these people, to be walking around, snapping photographs, scratching their ankles carelessly? Who are these people, who buy new running shoes, and have blood in their cheeks, and clean fingernails? While 100 measly miles away—the rats? Of course, I knew that was not fair. But I couldn't help myself; I was suffused with bitterness. The air conditioning was so powerful it brought up goosebumps on my arms.

As I finished my heavy-smelling bag of food, the lights in the mall—the mall in High Rock!—suddenly flickered once and went out. My mouth full, I moaned my disappointment. Here? Even here? The soft pop playing from the overhead PA system dipped, stretched, and stuttered. The people at the tables around me paused their chewing and looked up. The ceiling said nothing. The AC drone was silent. The security guard who patrolled the food court stopped, stiffened, off-kilter at the whiff of change.

Throughout the mall, hoots and cries. In the dim light I jammed the rest of the burger in my mouth, balled up the trash, and threw it at a passing lady's head. I ignored her cry and left the table, hustled towards the red emergency exit light sign as my phone dinged: there was no escape mechanism, no exit hatch that would let me slide far enough from Twin Bridge. It was a text from Arda reading, *Scabies alert!!: (Do u have rash?*

It didn't matter. Who knew what ailments could be cured by Atlanta? Atlanta! They had a zoo! A live hyena! Perhaps a curtain of vermicide at the town line, through which you step into a pest-free place. I burst out the door into a blast of hot air. Cleanliness was possible. We'd lead a good life, if only to spite the likes of Bing Hooper.

Within the mall, the music came on again for a moment, and then stopped. And didn't come back. Because hundreds of miles away, in one of those depth charge moments that happen while you obliviously examine a scab on your arm, an overburdened transmission line shorted, and a cascade of failures began.

As I sped away from the darkened mall, my phone buzzed again.

EMERGENCY ALERT, it read. POWER FAILURE AFFECTING LARGE AREA OF TEXAS. RESTORATION TIMEFRAME

UNKNOWN. UPDATES WILL BE SENT DIRECTLY TO OUR SUBSCRIBERS WHEN AVAILABLE. THANK YOU FOR YOUR PATIENCE:) [POWERGY CSTMR SRVC]

    I drove back to Askewn with the radio off. Silence was a rare commodity and I had to treasure it where possible.

At the edge of town, traffic congealed. Traffic lights weren't working. At every intersection, people stopped and politely took turns. Odd, I thought. This blackout is long. And far-reaching. I wasn't watching too closely. I was practicing conversations in my head: how I'd convince Samuel. How I'd explain the cashflow problem to Arda. What I wished I'd said to Hooper.

    Someone darted into the road and I slammed on the brakes. A man in a suit, his arms carrying a stuffed duffel bag like a baby. His hair was messed. His eyes wild. We stared at each other for a second, and he ran on.

    I plugged my phone in to charge as I crawled toward the dead stoplight. Just in case.

    When I arrived back in Twin Bridge, the generator was thrumming along cheerily. Inside, heat and dust smell was creeping in. Arda snagged my arm as I turned a corner.

    "Gasoline," he hissed. My face was damp with sweat, just from the brief time outside as I brought in my things from the car.

    "Low?" I cringed. I dropped my bag on the floor.

    "Gone," he said, "Empty!"

    "No."

    "Emptied the last canister into the generator twenty minutes ago."

    "Who was supposed to get more?"

    "Andrej, the maintenance man, the one with the arms like—" He swing his arms in the manner of a built gorilla.

    "He died. Months ago!"

"I know, I know he died," Arda agreed, nodding vigorously, "But that's why the gas was not restocked."

Andrej had seemed like a nice enough guy, kept his distance, made the big repairs, once caught Lucy trying to freebase tobacco soaked with Windex (a move theoretically possible!), and when he alerted us, asked earnestly that she not get in trouble. I'd heard he'd died of a sudden, strangling asthma attack, but who can say? Rumors ran rampant out there, all dirty half-cocked cowboy truths.

"Let's send Linda," I suggested.

"Never."

"Please, Arda, you're killing me here, I've been driving for hours—"

"Fine, fine, fine, fine, fine, fine," he scowled. "But if she comes back with some damned cat or other thing, it is your fault," and he blew past me. Arda was funny in this way. He sometimes characterized others by a single action they'd made, once, assigned it to them for good. Linda liked cats and had once let one inside the building.

Linda went on her mission. Nurse Bell didn't show up. We were short-handed, and the girls complained about the noise of the generator, which could be heard from every corner of the building even though it was outside. Jamie rubbed at her forehead, wrung out from a migraine. We found her a quieter room and brought lukewarm bottled water.

We opened the day's pre-made lunch, which we generally received in massive vacuum-packed boxes: re-hydrated potato flakes, white beans, dried strips of some kind of meat product.

"Mm-mm!" sang Maria. "I love pig, I love pig meat, I love pork chops, I love ham—"

"Shut the fuck up," snapped Hanan, "I'm going to be sick."

"Do you guys remember tangerines?" asked Amy, wistfully, pointing her question mostly down the table. "I'd chew off my hands for a real tangerine." She got blank stares.

One blessing: even were we to briefly run out of gas, the food would be okay without refrigeration. All the meals we received, as a rule, contained enough preservatives to embalm Hannibal's elephants, along with a mysterious ingredient dubbed *decorative orange flavoring*. It was clear this had nothing to do with fruit. The fruit was not involved. The decorative flavor covered everything; not pleasantly, but effectively. It tasted like nothing so much as the non-toxic cleaning solution they used to wipe down the walls. These kids weren't allowed near bleach. The meals made me think of mop buckets. The news, which Arda played on his phone at top volume, gave no useful information, but between the mudslide crises in California and the commercials for hospice it did manage to leave me with the aftertaste of some human crime, like a castration or a scalping.

By the end of lunch, Linda had not returned.

Next was group therapy, led by Carmen. To qualify as a group therapy leader she'd had to watch a 40-minute video about positive thinking and the pharmaceutical company's liability and privacy policies. I sat in the plastic chair, mentally miles off, jaw clenched and mulling money problems, like the discontented prince of some Austrian empire on a throne of skulls.

"Who are you going to be when you grow up?" asked Carmen, her legs crossed, her pen poised to take notes. Her weeks on Twin Bridge staff were going swimmingly. She'd told us that she'd been a resident there when she was 14, over two decades ago. She believed in sun signs and chakras, lived in Oklahoma for years before coming back to Askewn, didn't chat much. She came to work in a dented blue sedan, blasting the saddest bolero music you've heard in your life. I liked Carmen. "What will you embody?"

"Sex!"

"Aretha Franklin."

"The President of the Goddamn United States."

"All right, everybody, now is silent goal-setting time. Think of someone you admire, and then think about yourself."

I joined in the activity, scribbling some thoughts on a ripped piece of notebook paper cribbed from Maria. Had I had specific role models as a teenager? After a minute I looked down to discover I'd written "*Boooooooo*," in loopy handwriting across the page.

"Hanan," Carmen chirped, "Would you like to get us started?"

Hanan stood up. "When I get out of here and begin my *career*," she gave us a little curtsy, "I am going to be the king of hell."

"Hanan," said Carmen.

"Here is what I will do as king of hell. I will give all the Twin Bridge girls a million dollars," [*Cheers, applause*], "I will make it so cats can talk—"

"In hell?" Amy interrupted, frowning. "There are cats in hell?"

". . . I will think up some new and creative punishments for the following categories: snitches, billionaires, landlords . . ."

"Hanan," said Carmen again, rubbing her temples with both hands, "What will you *be*. What *skills* do you want to *learn*."

Hanan seemed baffled at the question. Mostly what the girls were offered was discipline, was retribution, and in moments like this you got a horrifying glimpse of how that had already begun to mold their thinking. She mulled it all over and said, "I think that I could be a very famous rapper."

Polite clapping. Maria began trying to drop beats, messy enough to get her booed; then an outbreak of poorly syncopated competitive beatboxing, over the rising protests of Carmen. Group dissolved into dissatisfaction, as usual. The sun was coming through the windows at an angle, now, but we didn't turn on any lights.

FINALIZED REPORT, APPENDIX A

Table 1: Collected data related to residents (various; unordered)

She snores. She isn't sleeping. She has a black black tooth. She eats toothpaste and says *yum*. She had an abscess on her forearm and it got infect-ed. She's got track marks. She was adopted. She was abandoned. She was dragged out still swinging. She reads at a fourth grade level. She loves the books about the sexy British detective Sherlock Holmes. She smokes. She runs. She ran away, six times. She crushed them up, she snorted them, she slammed it, she shot it, she didn't heal up right. She sold them. She drank. A cop did it to her, and the other cops let him. She needed a colostomy bag for four months. She is allergic to penicillin! She lied. She lost all her clothes because her cousin got booked for murder and her clothes, well, they were at her cousin's house and so the police, they took the clothes away for evidence. She broke in. She walked here. She chewed up the inside of her mouth during, and after. She slept. She slept outside. She slept in a tent near the overpass. She slept wherever the floor was clear. She slept, and slept, and slept, and still she was so tired all the time, waking up after dark. The cops lost her Pink Card. The cops wrestled her to the ground. She hid. She whispered. She giggled like a maniac (a maniac!). She hid food under the bed and that's why it smells so crazy bad in here all the time, Ms. B. She was pregnant. She can't get pregnant again. She had a cat. She had a CT scan. She knows all the words to the Disney film *Aladdin*. She sipped. She was pregnant twice. She ate Vicodin and Fioricet. She slept with a knife under her mattress. She wasn't allowed to leave. She hit him, she punched him, she stabbed him, she ate the whole thing, tail and all, and she liked the way it shivered on the way down. She loves Jesus. She would like to go to outer space. She used to get high and do her own makeup for hours while eating slices of nectarine, slowly, with her fingers. She ODed. She got Narcaned. She stole cars. She snuck in. She used to have a family. She rode on top of a train car of wood mulch across the Smokies in the pink dawn fog of the foothills alone. She taught herself how to do it. She waved goodbye in a trance, in a trance, in a state like dreaming, waving goodbye through the ambulance window, *goodbye, goodbye, goodbye!*

Linda showed back up after Group. She called from the car.

I met her out by the generator, where it hummed and churned out a black diesel smell and carbon monoxide that (so the yellow sticker on its side warned) was DEADLY IN A GARAGE. She swam up out of the dark, making me jump. Her wild hair had gone limp with the heat, and her face shone with sweat.

"You were out there forever," I said. "You okay?"

"Everyone had the same idea," she said, panting a little and hoisting her prize.

"That's all you could get?" I frowned. Linda carried just two 5-gallon jerry cans.

"All they'd let me buy," she said, fussing with the nozzle with her thin fingers. She got it set up and began emptying the gas into the generator's tank. "The station had a buy limit. The line stretched blocks and blocks. I had to wait for two hours." She shook the last drops from one can and screwed open the other.

"What gas station did you go to?"

She looked at me over the glug of the can. "I checked, like, four." She shook the now-empty can and set it back down in the dust. "Shipping problems, they said."

"Shipping," I agreed. Ten gallons would get us about eight hours. If we raised the temperature of the central air, we'd sweat all night, but we could make it well into morning.

We headed back inside to wrangle the outlaws.

Once more, Nurse Bell didn't show. When we called her number it went straight to voicemail. So when the girls held out their hands for their bedtime meds, Arda had Linda scan the medical forms filched from the nurse's file cabinet, one hand covering his eyes, muttering wretchedly about HIPAA violations and the Hippocratic oath.

"You never took any oath," I reminded him, as we sorted various medications into paper cups. Tick, tock: time slipped around corners and disappeared like a giggling shadow as we dropped BeZen into each of the girls' outstretched palms.

Outside it hovered in the 90s, and with the thermostat turned up to 78, the hair stuck to our necks, but the girls drew cheerful things during our hour of pre-sleep wind-down, whereas pre-BeZen it'd been oak trees with black knots, rows of X's, open mouths with no lips and crenelated teeth like the top of a battlement at war. Now hearts, now circles, now traced roses. I loved BeZen with a true love. Maybe if they were boys, we would've had to figure out what to do with their anger; it would have emerged via fistfights, bitter screaming matches and firearms. But we didn't have the scaffolding upon which to arrange girls' rage. Instead, we got meds.

Each of us on site—Carmen, Arda, Linda, myself—agreed it was better to sleep there. Just for one night. Why fight traffic to go to homes without power, when the generator here still chugged? And besides, we knew—from experience—that it wasn't good to go out after dark in a blackout. People got strange. People got ideas.

I settled down on one of the staff room cots. In the hall, Carmen's galumphing footsteps, punctuated by the skitter of girls dashing by, then a detonation of laughter. Things were happening on the other side of the door and they had nothing to do with me. Only now that I was lying down did I realize my heart was hammering—I'd forgotten how nighttime heat did that, how the heart pumped blood to the surface of your skin to cool you down and, in the process, tricked you into thinking you were afraid. But actually it was fun sleeping someplace strange! Horizontal and disoriented. Even though being excited to spend the night at Twin Bridge seemed wrong, was maybe a little insensitive, was maybe a little like a mortician eating a popsicle. Still: had I comrades there on the cot, we'd've giggled. My comrades in Texas were exceedingly few. My first year in Askewn I went practically blind with loneliness, got bored even of drinking, finally drove four hours to visit a man, death take me. After sex he talked about car accessories. Another fifteen minutes and he'd run out of steam. We lay there in humiliating silence for a minute, two minutes, until I asked what he was thinking of and he responded immediately *gladiators*, and I realized then that only I had found the silence humiliating, implicating, because it wasn't really silent in there to him at all. Because he was surrounded by his room, his things, every object muttering meaning in his peripheral perceived as a low and constant thrum, a background frequency repeating *you, you, you,* whereas I heard nothing. Was a tourist, grinning stupidly at a lecture in Czech. Wearing the wrong clothes. Wearing the wrong shoes. Of course I hear it too, in my room too, the thrum of *you, you, you.* But at Twin Bridge? A sweet, baffled emptiness. At some point in the night Linda came in and put herself to bed, and when I woke up in the morning the whole room smelled like her gum.

On the second day, it was Carmen's turn to wait in the gasoline line.

    While she was out, I skipped breakfast to text Bing Hooper, turning my phone on just long enough to message him and let him know we were going to postpone the move by a day or two, until electricity returned.

    Any chance you can wrangle that transpo stipend? I added.

    Totally understand delay, he wrote back, *This is y we r relocating! Wut a mess :P* he replied, adding nothing about the money.

I called Samuel. I asked him—maybe, I confess, I begged him—to take the vouchers. I told him about the postponed date.

"Absolutely not," he said. "You know what business is like right now?"

I didn't. The line went empty.

No nurse, no therapist, and so no therapy. Carmen turned up three hours later with the two permitted cans, just as the generator must have been running on fumes, looking sunburned and harried.

"Lots of rumors," she said in answer to our questions. "And no bottled water anywhere." She took great, painful gulps from the faucet while I went out back with the gas.

We invented a new routine. Free write, 9–10. Dance time, 10–11. Art, 11–12. Jog in place from 12 to 12:30, then lunch. Naps? Sure. Linda taught a kind of free-wheeling, improvised curriculum in the afternoon. What did it mean that they didn't fight, didn't try to hurt themselves, once we were distracted by other concerns?

We'd begun to wilt, all of us. The heat drained energy from our bodies like an emptying bath. I went into the parking lot to try and catch a breeze in the shade. Traffic crawled at a painfully slow pace up the highway that ran past Twin Bridge. Some cars stood on the shoulder, their radiators having busted or their tanks empty. Their hoods were propped up, shimmering in the sun.

When I went back in, I found Arda in the kitchen, opening cupboards and pawing through them with blind urgency, letting the cheap doors bang shut. The kitchen was a big industrial joint, saucepans deep enough to boil a toddler in, though in fact we almost never cooked. The smell of fried potatoes and decorative orange flavoring hung heavy.

"What are you up to?" I asked.

Arda reached into the back of a pantry and emerged with a hand-crank radio. It must have been ancient, red plastic with an LED flashlight on one end. "Ta-da," he sang.

He put it on the zinc counter and cranked the handle. Pop blasted, tinsel and young lovers throttled to a hysterical pitch; he fiddled around, switched to AM. A voice resolved through the static.

. . . encompassing homes and services throughout Texas, affecting millions, said a calm white woman. *An overheated transformer in East Texas triggered a cascading failure that has knocked out service of the entire regional power grid. Powergy does not have a timetable for return of service.*

Arda slowly lowered himself onto a stool next to me, thoughtfully scratching his fingers through white stubble.

Powergy CEO Fenton Chain added that the expense of maintaining an outdated grid in a region with a declining population is unsustainable without serious subsidies.

Then a man's voice: *It's very simple: it is the federal government's responsibility to regulate these services. Whereas our responsibility is to shareholders.*

Back to her: *Hospitals report a growing need for evacuation assistance, while communications throughout the region are impeded. The National Weather Service has issued an excessive heat warning. More on this story as it develops.*

Then: proclamations of weather. Heat. Dust. Wind.

Arda slapped his knees. "I do not think we should wait any longer. Should you arrange the movers?"

Form 1085A hooted at me from the distance. It would be better to take care of things myself, rather than try to explain my administrative failure to Arda. I nodded slowly. "I can try." I would certainly try.

CURRICULUM FOR JANUARY TWENTY-THIRD:
> ELECTRONS AND PROTONS
>
> ELECTRICITY GRID
>
> - largest US blackout ever:
>
> - Michigan, 2028, ~2000 dead
>
> > - Extreme weather (BURNING, FREEZING) damages grid, repairs are EXPENSIVE

PROMPT QUESTIONS:
> - do you have a RIGHT to electricity?
>
> - if yes, who HAS to provide it? the government???
>
> - where is the government? who is "in charge"?
>
> - is anyone listening?
>
> - where is the National Guard? // do we want them here? where is FEMA? do we want THEM here??? would they come armed? would you? what will they be armed with? knives? tasers? guns? guns? guns? guns? guns?

"I'm bored," shouted Amy from the back of the classroom. I jolted awake and nearly tumbled from my chair.

"We're all bored," snapped Linda.

"Everybody," I hissed, "Tighten up."

I wasn't sleeping well. I mean at night.

The heat made it hard to think. All I wanted to do was lie facedown on the floor. I turned on my phone to try Samuel once again. I'd been preserving the battery life and only turning it on for 30 minutes a day. I glanced nervously at my email inbox, which I treated lately with the extreme fear and reverence of some Armenian monk before an eclipse. I had a message from TENDER KARE.

> The subject line read **Good News!**

Ms. Campbell,

How are you all holding up out there? I'm writing with some great developments: thanks to our outreach efforts with some colleagues at Askewn County's CPS Department, as well as collaboration with fellow juvenile justice reform advocates at the Askewn County Juvenile Criminal Attorney's Office, we've secured the release of the below Twin Bridge residents.

Please see attached documents, with discharge papers and designated custodian of each girl who has been deemed eligible for immediate release.

We hope this will make your transition to the new, brilliant facility in Atlanta more smooth. Recent information we've received indicates that travel with a large group will soon be relatively difficult. Therefore, we also STRONGLY encourage YOU TO HURRY:)

With all the faith in the world,

Bing Hooper

Regional Director for Lower Plains, TENDER KARE

Surprised, I sat for a second staring at the list. "Juvenile justice reform advocate"? This was akin to a professional assassin who preached nonviolence, while up to his elbows in blood. I jotted down the names on a loose piece of paper. Next to those who were getting early release from criminal detention, I drew a star, to indicate victory: no hesitation there, only good news. Fly forth and prosper, chickadee, under the long and tenacious shadow of the carceral state! I was happy for them. Excited. But with the others, sometimes it looked complicated.

"This is most of the girls," Arda said, when I showed him the list. His finger paused at Amy's name. He tapped it twice and didn't say anything, but I knew: no way Amy ought to be going back to who she came from. Ditto Jamie. Ditto Sabine. And others, some who'd come from badly abusive caretakers. And even if Amy were going with someone new—discharges shouldn't ever be this sudden; there were weeks of prep, setting them up so they could keep up their therapy and/or prescriptions etcetera; also there was the mental/emotional girding, the girls taking time to prepare themselves to face the world again as free agents with the anxious anticipation of Olympic athletes. Meantime, the schools were all shuttered thanks to the blackout, and the governor was on the radio begging us to quit panic-buying bottled water. This was no good territory for any of them.

"I don't like this," I said carefully.

"No," Arda agreed. "Some of these girls, they're going from a frying pan into fire." He rubbed his stubbly chin, thinking. He ran his finger down the list again. "But it is not up to us. Out of our hands. I'll start calling the contacts. You can delay the move a few days, until we get in touch."

I nodded. The gift of time, then. For all of us.

As Arda began the calls, Carmen and I did rock-paper-scissors for a gas run or basement duty. She got the gas run. I went down for a shift on basement duty with Teresa. We all hated basement duty. Basement duty was required by TENDER KARE's liability policy.

She was in the basement space, comprised of one big room with a bed and desk and chair, and one bathroom. The walls were pink. That wasn't my decision. It was her last day on basement duty, and then she could return to the Upstairs World.

When one is on basement duty, one is also on 'arm's length.' That meant I was supposed to keep Teresa no more than an arm's length away from me at all times.

When Teresa in the basement lay facedown on the bed, I stood near the bed.

When Teresa sat at the desk, I sat in a chair near the desk.

When she got into the shower, I sat on the floor outside the bathroom while she counted out loud. This was for safety: you'd be surprised how hard it is to hurt yourself when you're counting to fifty.

"One. Two. Three. Four. Five. Six . . ."

I kept staring at the wall. Carmen would be on hour two of the gas line. Teresa stayed in the shower for a long time, counting in a warbly voice, then got out without washing her hair. She looked at me with her eyes big, like I was about to pry her shell off.

"I heard you," she said quietly. "You're out here laughing at me."

"No," I promised. "Nobody's laughing." We could hear the chugging of the generator's labors through the walls.

I picked up a pen and asked if she wanted to play a few rounds of tic tac toe. After losing a few rounds to Teresa I suggested an exquisite corpse game, both of us taking turns writing lines of a story; that turned out something like: "Once upon a time there was a terrible queen, who / ate a bag of dicks and got sick. / She grew so ill, that the kingdom was forced to / [crude drawing of a corpse being defiled]," which almost made me laugh, and was the point, these little secure wormholes of subversion set up for her to slip through.

I was bored, she was bored, and up next she was in for a lifetime of waiting; hours and hours stuck in courtrooms and unemployment offices and rental assistance lines, at laundromats and bus stops. Just the sort of punitive time-sucks that used to drive Jemma crazy when she was taking care of me. She'd suck down beers on the phone with the EBT people, snarling.

"Do you want me to braid your hair?" I offered.

Teresa was scribbling an illustration of our story. She paused, and then said, without looking up, "Okay."

I sat behind her on the bed and gathered her dark hair, warm and dripping from the shower, gently into my hand. I separated the tresses and brought them together. Teresa sighed with something like contentment. I couldn't remember which category this fell into: protection, prevention, punishment. She scribbled all over the sympathy card, until it was one big mess.

Arda had reached most of the caretakers by day three, and as they showed, we began to give the girls the startling news: your [insert caretaker] is on their way. Surprise! No Atlanta for you, sugar plum. Invariably the effect was as though we'd hooked them on an IV of high-octane corn syrup: wide eyes, choppy movements, sometimes white lips and clammy hands *a la* hypoglycemia.

"My mom?" repeated Kristal, frozen in the midst of packing.

"Your mom," I confirmed. "She's on her way now."

Kristal sat back on her heels, swallowing, making some kind of mental calculation as she drilled her eyes into the wall and twisted an old t-shirt tighter and tighter in her hands. I wanted to stay, talk it out, but there was no time; Twin Bridge was sliding back-asswards into some collective delirium triggered by the blackout. Even as I began to ask *how are you feeling, Kristal?*, the sounds of hedonism bled through the walls: ghoulish cackles, the dull lumpen thud of bodies wrestling, and then the crash of a window breaking.

"I'll come check in on you later," I said instead, not so much smiling as contracting assorted muscles around my face.

"Daaaang, Kristal—" I heard from behind me as I left, from one of Kristal's roommates. They had one another for now, I remembered with relief. Each room a tiny nation. Each girl an ambassador, building alliances, making peace with others, even as civil unrest burned within.

On the fourth day, Linda came back with just one jerry can. Gas was running out everywhere. The can would last us eight hours.

We discussed worst-case scenarios and decided to open the faucets.

We washed and filled the mop buckets. We filled the toddler-sized saucepans. We filled the vase from the office. Whatever we could find.

While the water ran, Linda called FEMA. She put it on speakerphone, on hold, for the next hour. The hold music was fifteen seconds long and it looped, unbearably.

Once the containers were filled, I walked down the hallway crying, "Chores!"

Everyone groaned out of their sweltering rooms and trudged to get the weird non-toxic cleaning juices from the closets. A thick syrupy smell hung over the caf as they bustled around. At last someone picked up at FEMA and Linda ran out for a quieter room. A hand tugged on my shirt; it was Lucia, a girl who mostly stayed in her room listening to death metal, telling me the toilets were blocked up again.

"You have got to stop putting things in there that aren't supposed to go there," I groaned.

Lucia rolled her eyes. Amy flung herself into a chair behind us.

"She isn't helping," Jamie cried, storming over and pointing at Amy.

"I have a stomachache," Amy said. But her eyes were watering. A stomachache of the mind, I thought weakly, taking a step back from the girls; the mind, the brain? A stomachache of the adrenal glands. Wherever feelings go.

Carmen came up, swinging her arms. "Well, it smells like a Florida bus stop in here."

Arda tagged after her, looking cheerful. "Look at you all," he said, "What are we down about? It's a mild day before noon in the country, no dog-sized spiders in sight, the sun is a cheery yellow, and just now I found five dollars on the ground."

"Those are my dollars," Carmen said, reaching.

Amy groaned. "No more sun, please."

"Amy has a stomachache," I said, gesturing towards her.

"How about pizza," said Arda, and gently almost touched her shoulder (but there is no touching without asking permission at Twin Bridge). "Would pizza help?"

Amy uncrossed her arms and nodded.

We had some buried deep in the industrial freezer. We distributed slices on Styrofoam plates while Hanan taught the girls how to say "pussy" and "cannibal" in Pashto and I pretended not to hear. When they ate they were briefly quiet. The pizza was all sugary soft bread made from drought-resistant millet, sweet sauce, plasticky cheese and potato; nutrient-poor foods that needed little to grow and would last forever. I'm old enough to remember a different interpretation of the dish; I remember the tomato. Other treats I've not smelled in a literal decade: maple syrup, skipjack tuna, chardonnay, stone fruits, but the girls don't care; the girls grew up on soybean oil and powdered yam and this here is as good as it gets, their palettes have been bred in the new world and for that reason I guess they'll be happier. Well, good for them.

I sat down among the chatter. Linda returned and announced that FEMA had told her to wait 7–10 days for mail regarding possible assistance. To distract herself from her irritation she delivered an impromptu lecture on marine biology focused mostly on whale extinction.

Carmen sat across from me, cutting her imitation-pizza with a knife and fork.

"Have you been home yet?" I asked her.

She look up, startled, and shook her head.

"Don't you have pets to take care of? Don't you want to empty your fridge? You don't have people to check on?"

She shook her head. "No. You?"

"No."

She was wearing her eyeglasses on a blue chain around her neck, which made her look strangely old. "To be honest," she said, lowering her voice to a whisper, "I'm hoping to catch a ride out of here with you all." She pointed her fork at Linda. "I think she is too."

I smiled stiffly. "Perfect." Linda was now picking up where she'd left off at her last lecture, talking on deep sea vents, the merciless weight of ocean depths, the primordial chemical soup that sloshed around and sparked the first miraculous life under conditions bleak, impossible. A canister of glitter circled the room. Amy dropped a fistful into Maria's hair and cackled; not with happiness, but with a kind of keen relief asymptomatic to joy, the sort of laugh we heard a lot at Twin Bridge.

Jamie's grandmother showed up to claim her: a brittle-looking woman with a wicker cane who gave Jamie a walloping hug. Seeing her go home felt good. She was one of the ones getting released from juvenile detention early. Though most of the girls who'd been picked for early release were white, Jamie included. Next, a woman with an American flag tattoo on her bicep arrived, chewing her lips at the front door.

"I'm here to pick up Kristal Cormier," she said.

Kristal appeared behind me, dragging two bursting black contractor bags of stuff. "Okay, Mama," she said, pushing past me.

"Oh, my God," said Kristal's mom, and her face changed, squeezed tight around the mouth and eyes, while she opened her arms and Kristal walked right into them. "It's been a nightmare. A nightmare," the woman said, shaking her head as her voice grew thick with feeling.

"Okay," Kristal said again, and began using a handkerchief to roughly smudge a bit of snot away from her mother's nose—not very well, but with great intention, and silently as her mother talked on, about their plans, about how they'd evacuate now and head north, her and Kristal, Kristal and her, north towards lakes and winters and ice skating, the great frozen lakes of Canada, Manitoba, Ontario, as Kristal made low noises of agreement and her eyes roamed her mother's face, not with love exclusively but with the kind of specific attention and mental arithmetic native to a parent wrestling an infant into snow pants—the face of anyone figuring out how to keep the distracted body of the one they love smooth and clean and fed and well.

I had her mom sign the papers, gave her the discharge info, the numbers for therapists and social workers and community behavioral health specialists, Medicaid referrals and login info for WIC accounts and disparate assistance programs we'd enrolled Kristal in—a glut of technical-bureaucratic info that only the most dedicated social service nerd could hope to navigate with success. They got a bottle of BeZen to go, and instructions on how to ween them off over the course of a few weeks.

Kristal was swarmed with girls, hugging her and wishing her luck, pressing small gifts into her hands—an interesting rock, a pen drawing of a horse. She looked at me and Arda. With permission, I gave her a quick hug, swallowed all my questions. Good luck, I thought, and

"Goodbye!" I called at the door, as Kristal was led away.

"Goodbye!" said Arda beside me.

"Goodbye!" said Kristal's mom.

"Goodbye!" said the girls from overhead, leaning half their bodies out the windows, sending a flurry of panic up from my gut.

"Goodbye!"

"Goodbye!"

"Goodbye!"

As they reached their car, the distant chugging of the generator sputtered and stopped. The minimal breeze from the AC stilled.

The gasoline was gone.

At night, strange noises. Unmoored from time and routine, the girls awoke at random, at all hours, driven by inscrutable needs. Spooky moaning poked its fingers into my dreams and emerged in visions of Jurassic mammoths staggering in black tar pits. I dreamt the rat brushed my nose and I awoke with a start, sweating, kicking off the thin blanket and banging my head on the underside of the desk beneath which I'd been laid out. I gasped. I ran my hands all over my body, checking for fresh bites.

"You were choking," said a voice. The silhouette of a two-headed girl in my office doorway, watching me. "We thought you were choking."

The shape split into Amy and Hanan, their arms linked in the dark, the glow of emergency lighting over their shoulders.

"It was a death rattle," said Hanan.

I wiped drool from my chin and shut the door.

On the fifth day, conditions began to deteriorate.

It was too hot to do anything. Those who remained, *Lord of the Flies* style, were beginning to separate into tribes, and they roamed the halls in groups which we were more and more letting alone. Nobody wanted to take a shower in the warm, off-smelling water that now came through the pipes, and they were so united on this front that they'd conducted a hygiene mutiny and lived happily frolicking in their sweat and grime. And we let them.

Carmen and I found Sabine, a redhead who usually said about one word a day, locked in a closet by one of her roommates, clawing the door with fury. Linda pulled Maria off another girl after she accused her of stealing her shoes, but not before Maria knocked one of Amy's teeth loose with a kick. Somebody, somebody, god forgive them, shit in a trashcan in the unused boy's bathroom, a mystery for which there will never be satisfying answers, and Arda's brave-faced response to the situation, quietly cleaning up with gloves and a trip to the hot reeking dumpster, earned him (in my book) a nomination for sainthood, something like Our Father of Unthinkable Bodily Functions.

"You know what this is like?" said a voice from down the hallway, making me jump. In this stretch of hall, with no windows and no lights, it was too dark to see more than a foot in front of your face. Amy's face swam up out of the dark. "This is like a crazy clown hospital." She floated past.

I smelled the smell of used cigarettes, floating around the place like a stepped-on ghost, but whenever I tried to track it down, I found nothing. Just as I walked into the caf, Sabine burst in. Her face was puffy. She stood next to me and declared: "I swallowed a battery."

"For fuck's sake," I couldn't stop myself from saying, and Sabine burst into tears. I led her away while babbling nonsense, basically, about how we needed to find the peace inside us, the locus of control, etcetera, something like that, I couldn't really tell you, that mumbo-jumbo would get all mixed up in my head and then I'd vomit it out as a soothing drone or background noise at times when I thought it could help, a sort of verbal soft jazz. I guided her into the toilet and helped her to throw up.

We drew down the shades and made sure any cracks were plugged, trying to keep the cool air in. I could feel the thermometer ticking up, degree by degree, the air getting thicker and stiller by the minute. Carmen and I took the girls into the caf and encouraged those who knew how to play piano on the half-broken keyboard.

Tink, tink, tonk. A minor. E minor.

Teresa, allowed up now from basement restriction, bobbled her head, eyes closed, caught up in the dream of herself. She leaned over towards me.

"I don't trust these hoes," she said in a stage whisper. "I only pretend to."

"Good," I said distractedly.

"How's your bite?" Carmen asked, cocking her head towards my bandaged hand.

"Fine," I said.

"Have you been taking your antibiotics?" Linda asked, appearing behind me. "Human bites are notorious," she added gravely. "Over 700 strains of bacteria can be found the human mouth."

"The inside of a man's tooth is poisonous," Hanan contributed helpfully.

"I am almost 100% certain that isn't true," I said.

Hanan put her hand over her heart. "I read it."

"Where do you guys learn this stuff?" Linda mumbled. "You don't learn it from me."

Arda came in, wrestling with Amy, his eyes terrified and begging one of us to intervene. I ran up but she quit as I got close, her limbs going loose, her eyes vacant.

"She'd scraped the coating from her incense," he explained, "and had pushed it into lines to snort."

"Amy—" I began, but she pushed past me and sullenly joined the ring around the piano, and I was too exhausted to pursue. Anything to get high. The month before, a girl drank a bottle of hand sanitizer; the month before that, Maria huffing polish remover she'd swiped from the manicure kit. It was all so stupid, a tacky kind of discontent, but they demanded to be taken seriously, chose seizures, numbness, psychotic breaks, temporary blindness. They snapped a razorblade out of a pencil sharpener and took it to their own heel. Nobody likes to admit it but unhappiness shows up that way, inarticulate and cliched, expressions of pain full-hearted and maudlin that hold our attentions hostage. The off-key piano vibrated through the room while Linda muttered to Maria about brain weight and outside, the sun bored holes into every surface.

I fled outside to call Samuel once more.

It rang. No answer. A helicopter chopped back and forth in the sky, which was full of haze. A feeling like panic was starting to kindle, breaking the delicate twigs in my chest. I tried Frank. He picked up.

"Are you ready to move tomorrow?" I asked him. "Have you talked to Samuel lately?"

"I haven't," he said.

"I'm going to go down there tomorrow and try to get the van."

"Try?" He repeated. When I didn't clarify, he asked, "How you all holding up out there?"

"Okay. Not great. Unstructured time is the devil's playground and all that."

"Sure."

"Are you downtown? How's it look out there?" The feeling that we were facing the same trouble added a low-frequency hum to our conversation.

"Strange. Really hot. But . . . cheerful? Everyone's been grilling out, using the food in their fridge before it goes bad. Barbecues on every block. But now . . . I don't know. National guard trucks are showing up, but they don't distribute water. They say they're here for looters. I haven't seen looting. Just people hanging out, I guess. Still. A couple arrests. Things are maybe getting a little tense."

Traffic on the nearby road crawled on.

"Are you worried?" he asked in a softer voice.

"Yes," I admitted. "Are you?"

"I don't know. I think so."

We were both meant to pick up vehicles from Samuel's the next day: me a passenger van; Frank, the moving van to transport all our things.

"But I haven't been able to reach Samuel, either," he said. We made a plan: I'd go first, scope the scene, let him know how things looked. We hung up. Carmen joined me as I faced the sun with my eyes closed to see how long I could stand it.

"I don't think the power's coming back," she said, as we watched the sun slip down over the far hazy distance.

"We'll see what happens tomorrow," I said, and added, "I've got to go home and pack," because the next day I was going to go wrangle a van from Samuel, one way or another. With no lights it got dark, dark, as Carmen rolled the ash from her cigarette, crushed the ember completely, and put the butt in her pocket. We went back in and handed out the glow-in-the-dark wristbands Arda and I had found in the office, so they were a bunch of zooming pink and purple and green blurs. And then at last we urged the girls to sleep, told them it was their last night at Twin Bridge, their last night!, though they wouldn't sleep, and we eventually surrendered, canvassing the halls just to make sure everyone was breathing as they dropped one by one into unconsciousness, strewn in beds and on floors and couches, like the fairy tale of a town where plague has come.

Thump. Thump.

From somewhere in the building, an uneven, repetitive noise stirred me from my sleep.

"Kristal?" I called, addled. Then remembered. "Hello? Everyone okay?"

I'd fallen asleep in the office as I went over the checklist for the next day's move. I looked at the battery-powered clock on the wall: 8 P.M. The hair on my neck was damp with sweat, and the room was very dark. The thumping came from upstairs.

I followed the sound up the stairwell. The emergency exit lights, whose batteries would run out soon, glowed and turned the floor wet-looking, made the walls look somehow skinned. Sleep had poured my head full of soft, warm wax. A sour smell was strengthening in the building; whatever could spoil, was now spoiling. I paused again to listen.

Thump. Thump.

Up the stairwell—softly, softly; at night is the whispering rule. Somewhere under the scrim of sleep was my dream, the thin one unstitched by this mysterious noise, and in it, a great lizard rose from the sea, its skull-shaped head surrounded by roses, and the soldiers met it with their tanks on the shore, and burned in their tanks therefore, until a giant flying benevolent multi-articulated dream bug came, and pushed the lizard into the sea, and the bug, it died, it also died too. That's only a dream. As I climbed, the trapped heat got thicker, stiller. With no electrics buzzing I could hear everything too much.

Thump, went the sound, *thump, thump.*

On the second floor I entered a smell. Dark thoughts lived in corners here. The smell thick, nearly bitter, like the smell of dirt or beets. Do you believe, Carmen asked me once, that powerful feelings can stain a place? I pushed open the door on the left: empty. In the classroom, pencils and books strewn around, detritus that would be abandoned with the building, soon to be furry with dust. Like what kind of places, I'd asked Carmen. She'd said, like an insane asylum, or a lighthouse where an exile lives, or a basement full of orphans; do you believe, she asked, that surplus feelings can soak into the floorboards, smudge the wall, like soot after a fire? I froze; I was awake now. A new sound: something high, strangled, suspended; then it broke, changed, dove down as though from a great height into a long, deep wail punctuated by gasps. The hairs on my neck stood up. The sound came from downstairs: just a girl waking up from sleep, waking up screaming, as some of them sometimes did. I heard the normal after sounds: groaning and cursing, the rustling and whispers of Carmen offering the girl a glass of water. *Thump,* came from further down the hall. *Thump.*

I opened the door on the right. "Hello?" I called.

Dark inside. Kids make bad decisions sometimes, that's all there is to it. The noise was coming from the last door. The earthy smell was familiar, but I couldn't place it yet. *Thump. Thump, th-thump.* Out the greasy window the dirt stretched out under a pure night sky free from light pollution; sweat dripped down my neck. I flipped the light switch but of course, nothing happened. I peered into the dark.

"Teresa," I gasped, because her pale face resolved, and then what I saw was blood running out of her ears, down the side of her face and to her chin. Then the rest of the scene: this tribe of Teresa, Hanan, Maria, and Sabine, all shirtless, sitting in a corner of the room with some halved potatoes and bloody body parts. As I stood there, Hanan looked over, blinked impassively, and finished her project: jamming a sewing needle through Teresa's ear cartilage and into a halved raw potato, as Teresa grit her teeth down on the t-shirt she'd twisted up and jammed into her own mouth, slamming the wall with her fist to keep from crying out. "Hanan!"

Sabine's eyebrow, Maria's lip, and to my acute horror, Hanan's left nipple: each had new, bleeding jewelry.

"Ta-da," Maria whisper-sang nervously.

I walked to their corner and crouched to see the damage more closely. Bloody tissues, drawn and shining faces. They were proud. A wave of fear and anxiety rose in me, crashed through, and then left. Let them be;

what was the point? It was over now, and in the Atlanta center they probably didn't have loose sewing needles around. Gently, I put my hand under Sabine's sharp chin and tilted her face so I could see the eyebrow piercing better. She pushed her hair back to let me see. For a moment, we searched one another's faces. A rivulet of blood traced the outside corner of one dark brown eye. Even when she took it out, the mark would be there forever.

"Come with me," I said quietly. "And pick up those potatoes and throw them in the downstairs trash."

I brought them downstairs and unlocked the nurse's office. It was too hot, I didn't have the energy to scold them, and anyway it was done already, I reasoned; the point now was health. One by one, in whispers so we wouldn't wake anybody, I cleaned the piercings with saline. "Don't twist the jewelry," I told them. "Your body knows how to heal." They'd done the job nicely. The piercings were neat and clean. "Let it scab. Don't pick the scabs off. Soap and water and saline, nothing else. If it gets swollen, hot, painful, red—you tell me, okay?"

Yes, they agreed, each of them glowing, quiet. I patted each piercing dry with a clean cloth, letting Hanan handle her own, working by the dim exit lights. I looked them over. They were so happy. It made me happy. Things were nice for a minute. *Yes, yes, we will.*

The pierced girls settled down to sleep among the others, sprawled out on thin blankets and mattresses that they'd dragged down, as it was cooler here than up in their rooms. Their glowing bracelets dotted the floor like neon sprouts in a black field. It was impossible to sleep in late, because the sun sent heat charging in with first light. Without the buzz of any electronics, no refrigerator, no compressor, it was totally quiet but for breathing. I stepped among the bodies softly, little field of institutional poppies. Among the snoring girls, I heard Amy, talking to another girl:

". . . and so he curses her with a sleeping curse," she was whispering, "And she can only sleep when she removes her eyeballs."

I walked over. She was speaking to Zakiyyah, the quietest girl. Zakiyyah, or Zak, had her fist in front of her and was staring at it intently. I almost passed by, but then I stopped, crouched, and tapped lightly on Zak's fist.

She jerked back, startled.

"What you got?" I whispered.

She looked at Amy nervously. Amy shrugged. Zak opened her fist. Inside was a human tooth.

I took a deep breath. "Where," I asked, "did you get that?"

Amy grinned at me. Then she pointed at the left side of her smile, where there was a black gap. "I wiggled it all the way out," she said, through her grimace, "after Maria kicked it loose." She dropped her hand and looked up at me. "I gave it to Zaki because it's good luck."

"We'll find you a dentist when we get to Atlanta," I pledged Amy, who looked unimpressed.

I heard a snore turn into a cough. I looked around: the girls were all awake, blinking at me from the dark like lemurs in the jungle. Their silent attentions made me unaccountably nervous.

"Everybody deserves to keep their own teeth," I blurted, loudly, to absolutely no reaction. "Okey dokey! Sleep well!" Nothing. They eviscerated me with their silence. I backed towards the door, my heart still hammering, probably from the lack of AC.

As I left the caf, Arda waved me over, both of us radiating heat.

"No more gas," he whispered. "It is time to go. The postal system, the deliveries, all disrupted. We are running out of BeZen. No more until Georgia." He gave me a once over. "And you, are you taking care of yourself?"

I reached one arm into the air and mimed putting an oxygen mask over my face.

"Yes," he nodded, "Exactly."

Report for TenderKare to Be Forwarded to Parent Contract Research Organization: Topline results (91% efficacy) from TWIN BRIDGE Phase III Clinical Trial Confirm BEZEN® Efficacy Including Better Efficacy with Extended Treatment

Published: January 20

Statistically significant behavioral modification and improvement from baseline

Favorable safety profile

Following rigorous guidelines of pivotal clinical trials, data from TWIN BRIDGE confirms that BEZEN improves and corrects deviant, aggressive, antisocial, and violent behavior often associated with post-traumatic stress disorder, acute stress disorder, adjustment disorders and other stressor- and trauma-related disorders.

Primary contra-indication is as follows: BEZEN reduces patient's ability to perceive and imagine pain, including emotional pain, within themselves and possibly others.

Designed under a Special Protocol Assessment with the FDA, the BEZEN trial is a randomized Phase III trial involving 29 teenaged subjects.

I hadn't been to my apartment in nearly a week. Dust had accumulated on surfaces. The air was stale and warm, but I didn't keep much food at home, so there was no stink.

On the battery-powered radio we'd heard that the federal government was suing Powergy, and Powergy was counter-suing the feds. The transformer that had shorted out and exploded during the extreme heat wave stretching from Houston to Monterrey had led to a cascading failure of the already over-taxed electrical grid. Wires had melted for miles at a stretch. Trucks had headed out with generators, but replacing all the transmission lines destroyed in the fire could take weeks or months. Anyway, anyway, none of this was my problem anymore! Fortunately, I didn't have much to pack. My walls remained shiny and bare. I tossed my clothing and some odds and ends into four cardboard boxes and a hiker's backpack. And by 11 I was done, that was it. The place had come furnished. I didn't have mementos. No time nor energy for friends outside Twin Bridge. And I didn't read books anymore, couldn't concentrate. All the thoughts I enjoyed not-thinking at Twin Bridge scrabbled and pulled at me once I left the center, because the wonderful thing about working with the girls was that it tumbled you into the realm of the immediate; it undid time. You got to live in the land of crisis where there was no Earlier or Later, only what was directly in front of you. If a kid has ever waved a DIY aluminum knife under your nose, you may understand how it hurls you into the Now. But here I had space to think. Oh no! On the magazine cover before me a woman held up sunscreen. Oh no! Her flawless white veneers. No! No! No! I had to get out; I left.

   At the bar where Frank and I had once gone to, where a sign in the window now read GENERATOR ON!!!, I ordered gin and sat in the booth with an ancient, soon-to-be-trashed chemistry textbook I'd rescued from the classroom on my way out. Tomorrow I would simply have to go to the rental place and pay for whatever I could afford using the Twin Bridge coffers and my own measly checking account. Would they take a deposit? I paged through the names and structures of poisons and looked around at the other patrons, people drawn to the generator-powered bar and its relative cool in the dark like moths to a boozy bulb. They had a charging station from which a bundle of wires and phones emerged; I found a free spot and plugged mine in, thanking the bartender, sucking down a second well gin with ice. Ceiling fans moved warm air around and everybody shone with sweat. As a teenager, in Edenton, before Everything Happened and I left town forever, Jemma used to get some drinks in her and put her arm around me and say, *I would kill everybody in this room for you, every single person; I'd kill everybody in this building for you, you sweet dumb-dumb.* I don't know anyone who would kill everybody for me, now.

"Mind if I join?" asked a man with a black beard, polite but visibly drunk. He had a hawkish nose and ears that stuck out so they looked pink and translucent from the sodium lights over the pool table. He seemed like he was about to cry. He held a ziploc bag with a goldfish in it, more twitching than swimming.

"Sure."

"Jesus. What a night. What a night."

"I'm just studying," I announced, holding up the battered textbook. "Finishing organic engineering school next month. I'm an engineer!"

"Wow. Amazing."

"Who's the fish?"

His face crumpled up like an unloved gift. "Roger. With the electricity out, the filter in his tank isn't working. It's the end of the line . . ."

"You named your fish Roger?"

"He came that way," he said defensively, and then I waited it out while he covered his face with one hand. While he recovered I ordered us a round.

"There, there," I mumbled awkwardly, patting the hand that didn't hold the fish bag.

"He's my only pet," he said, sniffling. "Sorry. Sorry. Only, goddamn this blackout."

"Oh, yeah. It's a big mess." I tapped the bag gently. "Isn't it, Roger?"

"You're an engineer?"

"I was. I will be. I'm leaving town, it's my last night in town. Do you know anything about hotwiring cars?"

"Me? No. Do you?"

"No," I admitted.

"Why do you ask?"

"Just making conversation."

"I wish I had a useful skill like that," he went on, "But I'm a teacher. Special ed."

We jabbered on for a while, getting drunk, each in our separate pool.

"My boyfriend and I love animals," I was saying. "Oh, jeez, we rescue them all the time. We've got, we've got, we've got a goat and a hawk and a pig and a llama . . ."

"It's like I can't take care of anything, man, it's like the only pet I might be able to handle is, like, the canned meat at the dang grocery store."

"I tell him, 'Don't let the pig sleep in the bed with us!' But do you think he listens?"

"The truth is, I wanted a shrimp for a pet. Is that crazy? I wanted a shrimp for a pet. The way they dart around . . ."

"I get it. I get it. Listen, he's a jerk, he's a monster, he's a real piece of shit—but I love him. What can I do? I just love him so much." I slugged back the rest of my drink and grabbed the guy's fist and squeezed. "Let's flush Roger. It's merciful."

Soon, standing over the men's toilet, where the smell was powerful and ripe, we swayed a little as he opened the ziploc bag. He froze. "I can't do it."

"I'll do it," I volunteered.

"No, no, I'll do it."

"I can definitely, definitely do it."

"No!"

"Fine. Let's say a few words." In the stall next to us, somebody flushed. "Oh, Roger, who art in heaven . . ."

"That's the Lord's Prayer."

"Take my hand," I said, grabbing his. "You were a good fish, you never pissed the carpet, you kept your owner—what's your name?"

"Eddie."

"—you kept Eddie safe."

"You were a good guardfish," he sniffed. It was stuffy and too hot and humid in the bathroom. When I wiped the sweat off my forehead my hand came away brown with mudded-up old dust.

"What the fuck?" somebody stuck their bald, very drunk head under the stall. "No fucking in here. No weird stuff."

"Git," I hissed, and feinted kicking the man's head, then kicked him very very lightly. He huffed and disappeared and I heard the scuffling sound of him falling on his ass, then patting around on his hands and knees on the tile floor, trying to get up.

"Oh, well," said Eddie, suddenly seeming to surrender his grief all at once. He upended the bag into the toilet bowl, and we watched the fish twitch, shake out its fins, circle once, twice—then Eddie gave a swift three-fingered salute and pressed the flush lever. We watched in solemn silence. "Do you want some cocaine?" he asked.

Later, a little bit high, out behind the dark bar with my back against the brick, we made out for a minute and then did some hand stuff while I told him about my imaginary engineering career, all the things I'd invented, electrical spines, driftwood that recounted its journey, blue lightbulbs that revealed your feelings. Finally, he reared back and said, "Look, it's been nice getting to know you, but could you stop talking for a minute? I'm trying to concentrate."

"Sure," I said, and tried to focus on how his fingers felt, but couldn't get away from the thought of us as wet meat, and the powerful B.O. coming off the both of us after hour upon hour in the sweltering heat. In the end I pushed his hand away and concentrated on taking care of him.

When it was over, he sighed and said, "That was fun."

"My name's Lilith," I told him. I wiped my hand on his shirt. "I'm moving tomorrow."

I left him blinking next to the dumpsters and passed back through the bar to get my bag. Back at the table I dug around through his wallet that I'd pulled out of his pocket, pocketed the cash—$82, barely a dent in the van rental expenses—and dropped the empty billfold on the table. Then I left, jogged most of the way home, gasping at the stitch in my side while the goblin giggled in my head. A happy birthday: that's what I'd wished for on the mayor's wishbone. All the lights were out, the roads spooky, the streetlights swinging black and empty, and I lunged through the crosswalks without looking. My last walk through Askewn, my last night in Texas. Happy birthday, everybody, things were about to get better. Happy birthday, happy birthday, things would be better this year. Or anyway things would be different.

Chapter Five

Since we were understaffed—only myself, Arda, Linda, and Carmen to watch the remaining girls, and none of us getting a break or a decent night's sleep—we agreed that it made sense for me to bring the one truly difficult case, Teresa, along to get the moving van. As we hit the road I saw Arda's silhouette behind us, lifting one arm to wave.

Teresa swayed pleasantly, buckled into the car, as I nosed us at a crawl through slam-packed traffic towards downtown and Samuel. As we drew closer to the city, I could smell the burned smell. The aftermath of a house fire, it seemed, was still hanging in the sky, casting the horizon gray. Teresa stared straight ahead through the windshield. I turned the radio on low and listened to the bland voice of the emergency broadcast lady repeating, *This is not a test.*

"It stinks," Teresa observed helpfully. She watched the world slide by as a press conference started on the radio; they talked about curfews.

Samuel's rental place was, luckily, on our side of town, not far. Blue police lights spun in the opposite lane, two cop cars shooting up the shoulder with their sirens spooky silent. We took our exit, and on the street people hustled past with their shirts over their mouths and disappeared into the haze.

"Is there any water in the back seat?" I asked Teresa. She dug around and came back with a half-empty bottle. I splashed some into my hand and flushed my stinging eyes. She watched me, then did the same.

"How are you doing?" I asked her cautiously. We'd piled on an extra-high dose for the trip.

Her voice floated over to me, giggly and thin, like a flake of confetti. "I'm having a lovely time," she sighed.

At last, the sign that read CASK MOVING LINES in big red and white font swam up out of the bleary roadside. I pulled into a parking lot swarming with people. This was the largest crowd I'd seen in town in ages: dozens of people bustling, stumbling from cars, blocking the doorway. A line had formed by the front door, full of people coughing away smoke. I cursed under my breath.

"Right," I said. "Stay here."

I got out and walked very slowly towards the mess. It had abruptly gotten much colder, and there was a bruised color to the light. A definite fear vibration ran through the parking lot. A father got out of a car, slamming it behind him and locking it—"Stay here," he commanded, loudly, gripping the car key and pointing at his kids in the back. Two young women holding hands rushed past him, half-running, long hair tangling together in the gathering wind. The asphalt was coated with a thin layer of orange dust that lifted and snaked and eddied; the cars around us were strapped with suitcases. No one was in charge, here. At any moment, panic could catch like gasoline. A baby wailed. For no reason I could name I bent at the knees and filled my pocket with several rocks.

I simply needed the key to a van. This was, on its surface, very simple. This was the straight line I would follow between myself and success! I put my head down and started for the lobby entrance.

A sudden sound made me jump. The storm siren.

Blasting out of the various PAs around town: sweeping high, dipping low, nasally and unsettling. I stopped. We all stopped. We took the sound into our bodies, the awful deafening whoop. We'd all, out of instinct, hunched over, as though attacked. We straightened and looked around. And then, like a net thrown down from heaven, a terrible stillness came over the crowd.

Way out to the west, resolving out of the background of brown sky, we saw it: a strange wall a hundred stories high. It drifted like an enormous ghost ship, silently towards us from the horizon. The siren meant dust storm.

I took one step, two steps back. We got them from time to time, but I personally had not seen one this size.

When a thing so large moves as one, it follows a different concept of time. And so though the head of the storm was hurtling towards us at 60 mph, the dust storm's movements appeared, from the parking lot, luxurious and slow. There was a moment, I think, when it all could have gone either way—if even two people began to scream, the gasoline panic would have lit—but instead, after a tense pause, everyone resolved into a sort of tight calm. Those who were still in the parking lot began an orderly push towards the rental place, prepared to pack the lobby.

I backed towards the car. Look at those thunderous knuckles of god. They've not thought of us at all, racing towards us at highway speeds, secreting within wind gusts and hail. Though it was only 4 in the afternoon, the winter sun was already close to earth, and so it reflected light off the amber-colored dust, sending the sky above it purple and pink, and it looked soft, the front blooming continuously from inside itself, just like a thunderhead or a drop of blood in a glass of water, bursting slowly. The storm was coming from the far side of Askewn. I watched it swallow one tall building, then another. But it wasn't real until the smell of it reached me, on a stray gust of wind: something musty, not the sweet loamy petrichor of an oncoming storm but old, brittle, a storm come up from under floorboards. And then the sound. A muffled, still distant roar.

I snapped back to myself. Behind me, Teresa was leaning on the horn. When I turned around to look, she waved with both arms, ecstatic.

"Come on," I said, yanking the car door open.

"Are we going someplace fun?" Teresa asked.

"There's a dust storm coming," I said, as I pulled her up to a standing position and slammed the car door behind her. "We've got to wait it out inside."

"Ooh," she said, with a sweet note of delight, "Are we in danger?"

"No," I lied. We crossed the parking lot, past the angry dad, who was banging on the car doors, telling his frightened kids to get out. We mushed in with the crowding line of people around the building's front door, everyone pushing with polite restraint so far, muttering and coughing. I looked back over my shoulder. The storm, calcified soil boiling one thousand feet high, rolling like a mountain moving. When it reached us it would coat everything: hair, nose, throat, eyelashes. After bad ones you'd find the bodies of the jackrabbits, stiff and dead, their stomachs stuffed with fine sand. I saw tiny specks—the last of our birds—dashing madly for the far horizon. A dust storm that big could push cars into ditches, bury a road. Places like this, a century ago they had rain merchants, charlatans who rolled through town and promised to dynamite the sky to turn the weather. But we know better, now.

The siren was still wailing. Teresa stuck both her fingers in her ears and shouted, "Are we in danger now?"

What was the point? "You bet!" I shouted back.

We shuffled closer to the door, enclosed by the crowd, slow as the undead. A constant stream of shouting leaked from within the building. The angry dad pushed through, yanking both daughters behind him, elbowing others out of the way. I tightened my grip on Teresa's wrist until she hissed *Ow!* and snatched her hand away, so I stood behind her, hands on her shoulders, alert—it had gotten colder still—somebody yelped; a dozen jackrabbits were making a frantic dash across the parking lot, away from the storm's black edge—behind me it had rolled closer, swallowing the last of downtown's large buildings. The crowd pressed tight and I caught one worried woman's bloodshot eyes as the crowd pressed tighter still, and for a moment I was lifted off my feet, crushed and weightless, the breath out of me, still gripping Teresa's shoulders as the light dimmed a bit, and the first specks of dust, the pioneers, began to tick against my cheek, and you could hear it then, as my eyes met the wide, frightened eyes of my neighbor in the gathering haze, the sound under the siren sound, the note of panic in the crowd like a finger going around the wet rim of a glass, shivering, about to shatter, when at last and all at once we fell inside.

In the lobby the air was thick with the heat of anxious people. There were maybe forty of us surging around the cramped lobby, all unsure what was going on. A group of young men were arguing behind the desk, each shouting in a different key, but I couldn't tell if they were employees. I didn't see Samuel. Papers were scattered all over the ground; I plucked one from the air as a hot gritty wind from the open door blew it past, and two more people blasted inside:

VOLUNTARY EVACUATION, it read. *No time frame for power restoration. Leave if possible.* Then the useless FEMA hotline number.

It was dim in there. I pulled Teresa backwards and wedged us between the edge of the crowd and the doors. We looked outside in silence as the dust storm approached. The lobby grew quiet. The storm looked about twenty blocks away. We held still. People's eyes were glued on the doors. The lobby grew darker, the sirens somewhat muffled. Ten blocks away. Silent. Five blocks. One. And then it swept over us, and with a great inward gasp the lobby grew dark, very dark.

But the truth, the surprising truth about being within the cataract of dirt? It was nice. We were inside a cool bubble of time. Nothing but dust could reach us, not even sunlight, not even telephones. The doors rattled in the wind as the men who'd been arguing stripped off their shirts. A businesswoman emptied a bottle of water over the shirts, and they—we; I helped—stuffed the shirts into the cracks, between and around the doors, to keep out the fine brown silt, much of which had already found its way in, setting off fits of coughs. The wind and the hiss of sand covered everything. It could have been night time, dark and faintly orange. The world existed only two feet past the walls of the rental building, beyond that it stopped.

"It'll die down," said a girl in athletic clothes after a minute, her voice breaking through the soft timpani of dirt on glass.

"This is bullshit," groaned a young man who'd been poking around the counter.

"I've seen these before," said the athlete's boyfriend. "They pass. Don't worry, everyone!"

"Sure, we know," muttered his partner, now squatting on the floor, facing away from him.

"Does anyone work here?" I whispered to her, kneeling. "Is anyone getting keys?"

She shrugged and looked back at the black dust outside. I texted Frank, *chances of van rental not looking good.*

The crowd was hypnotized. We'd seen dust storms before, but this was a bad one. Some sat down to wait. Outside, we watched a loose car muffler throw sparks through the dimness as the wind dragged it along the sidewalk. Teresa drummed out a tune on the fire hose cabinet. Once, twice, three times, a pedestrian burst through the doors: visibility was almost zero, but each time someone resolved out of the darkness we'd haul open the doors just as they arrived, and they'd stumble in hacking and gasping, and we'd push the door closed ASAP on its pneumatic hinge while someone patted the arrival's back, congenially beating the dust off their clothes. I guess I was witnessing goodwill. The irritated man who'd been behind the desk now made runs to bring water in wax paper cups. Something about being trapped together was, somehow, lifting our spirits; a sense of camaraderie spilled around. We were part of something! People sat on their heels against the wall, trading *where were you when the power went out?* stories. *I was sweeping the floor. I was calling my mother.* I thought of the Askewn mall, Bing Hooper's simpering face. I did not want to be stuck here. I realized abruptly that Teresa was no longer at my elbow.

I wheeled backwards out of the crowd and looked around for her, white-knuckling my own calm. I had no bad intentions at this point. I walked the lobby. From the desk I plucked up a dusty and discarded surgical mask. I looked behind the desk, checked the toilets, considered the ceiling tiles with a pounding heart. And then I spotted her, sitting calmly in a plastic chair against the far wall, underneath a dead TV. She sat there, patient. Trusting me to figure it out. All the people back at Twin Bridge: trusting me to figure it out. I would have to be bold! I would have to take action!! The truth is, I saw people, children, do reckless things all the time, and they always always always survived in some sense, and what did they say about beauty and intelligence? You get to pick just one? I choose neither. I held out the surgical mask to Teresa, and for a terrible moment, we must have understood one another, because she lifted her hands from her lap, untwisted them like a trumpet flower or the cracked bottom of a vase, and revealed that secreted within she held a set of keys.

"You wanted these," she smiled gently.

I plucked the keys from her outstretched hand.

On a scrap of white paper scotch taped to the fob, the words VAN FOUR.

"Where did you get these from?" I whispered.

She pointed towards the back, behind the desk. "In there. A key locker."

It simply wasn't permitted for me to tell her, *good job.* I told her telepathically instead and then pulled her to standing. Without speaking, she followed me behind the desk. There was the key locker, standing open. Soon enough someone else would get the same idea.

I continued down a hallway which opened behind the desk, towards a glowing emergency exit sign that no one had surrounded because its sidelite faced a dumpster. I waited until she looped the mask's elastic around her ears. Gently, I pinched the metal band around her nose to keep it tight. Outside, in the darkness, were the vans. And now was the time to take one. I gripped Teresa's hand, and under the dim green light of the sign, pushed forward, into the punishing world.

When I was small, in Edenton, Jemma would take me on drives.
 She would sneak out and drive with just her permit—no license—so while she was driving at 15, I was 11 and still wearing overalls with daisy-shaped buttons, regarding her with awe. We'd take winding long ways, down Route 17 to Bear Grass and Grabtown and Merry Hill, or all the way down to Swanquarter, towns that must now hardly exist at all.
 "You know Mom loves you, right?" she'd say. I'd never doubted until she asked. "You know Dad loves you?"
 There were bugs back then. Here is something I've never told anyone: out of everything we've lost; the whales, the hummingbirds, okay; swimming pools, real coffee, The Maldives; salt marshes and glaciers and the Aral Sea; freedom of movement, commercial air travel, the Winter Olympics, fine: what I miss most, honest to God, is bugs.
 Because there were a few years, before I lost Jemma, when she drove me around all the time in the evenings. Or we'd go up to Merchants Millpond and wait for the sun to set and then sit there still, with the engine off, in the dark, in June's murmuring heat. Around us the bald cypress and the splash of night animals, possums, even alligators. I had by then, of course, become anxious that our parents didn't love me, not fully—anxious the way a child is anxious, secretly—perhaps, I considered, that was why they spent so many nights out with their friends, or glued to the television's

bad news, or going to meetings about Double Truthism. Absent love was, of course, an idea Jemma had planted in me by her very reassurance, an idea which I used the drives to drown out; my big sister's presence was sickness and antidote both. And as we drove, mindlessly, at night along the Chowan River, with the windows down, I heard them. Cicadas, I think. Maybe crickets. Sing, saw. They might have been frogs, the kind called crucifer. But that sound was warmth itself. A low atmosphere, something knit in the air, coating the night world black and bronze, softly. The sound said I was in a tent, sleeping, or in the deep felt of a carseat, cared for. It wasn't until the end, until just before the house burned down, that I realized I didn't hear that anymore. They were gone, those sounds of creeping love, and they weren't coming back.

The smoke had gotten mixed up with the dust. You can't tell apart smoke-haze from dust-haze, and neither can your lungs. Sandpaper air abrades every inch of uncovered skin: your face, your arms, your ankles; parts of your body you're in the habit of forgetting. Like a goldfish if you poured vinegar in the bowl, suddenly aware of the burning atmosphere. Pulling Teresa behind me as we leaned into the wind, walking in the direction of the garage, I tried to breathe as slowly as possible so I wouldn't get overwhelmed, but after ten steps my lungs were screaming, like I was about to drown in the middle of the day, spluttering and choking; I knew the door was behind us, and the sun above, and up ahead the garage. But I couldn't see anything at all in the dark of the dust, could barely open my burning eyes, kept them mostly closed and tried squinting out of one and then the other, Teresa stumbling behind me, my left hand out ahead groping for any surface. Bits of debris crashed into me; something heavier—a metal bowl?—clipped me in the side of the head, hard, and I cursed and clapped my hand to where it smarted. I squeezed her hand tighter, both of us trying not to go down. The sound was less like sound and more like pressure, sand in my ears, and keeping my back to it meant I had to shuffle sideways; I watched the ground in front of my feet, Teresa yanking my hand as she stumbled and I hauled her up again, then sticking my free left hand out—nothing—where was the door? I knew it was out here, in this direction. I tried to cover my head with my free arm, reached out with my foot, tapping along the ground in the direction where I hoped the door was; then I lurched forward again, groping the air. Creeping up on me came the paralysis of nightmares. I took another few steps—had I passed it entirely, missed the garage?—and started to cough, which only made me inhale dust until I coughed harder, and with my ears full of sand I could hear it in the echochamber of my body, rattling deep inside, had I made a mistake? Bent over double, coughing, something landed on my back. I straightened in a panic, my chest burning, nearly cracking Teresa's jaw with my skull, as it had only been her resting her head on my back a moment, and I saw her, not panicked, not coughing, half invisible under dust, and I took her hand again, yanking her forward; I could not find the door; if I had to call for help I realized I could not call for help, nobody was coming and then suddenly we were there, a metal wall, and I patted along it, following the wall to the right, banging against it until we found the garage entrance. I fumbled with the handle, huddled in the meager protection of the inset door. Just as I began to fear the knob was locked, it turned. We tumbled inside.

First I took big, heaving breaths, coughing up the shit I'd inhaled.

"Are you okay?" I gasped at Teresa. I spit on the cement floor. It came out yellow and brown. I started coughing again, hard, wracking coughs that made my guts hurt.

"Are we going to the beach?" she asked. She kind of spit dust out of her mouth, but she did it as a child would, slobbery and dribbling over her own chin. "I really love the beach."

I caught sight of my reflection for a moment in the darkened door window: I was gravy-colored, my hair all pointing in one direction. There was blood over my right ear from where the bowl or whatever had hit me, and my eyes were bloodshot and burning. Teresa was in the same state, but with the dreamy look on her face still. I began to beat some of the dust from her clothes.

"Y'all found me," said a voice from the dark of the garage. I started.

Samuel was there behind us. He was standing near the entrance to a glassed-in office. He faced us, but it was hard to see in the dim light that barely filtered through. He'd been the one to open the door and let us in. He'd retreated, and now was sitting on a bench, his hands on his knees, while behind him yawned the dark and cavernous garage. Several buses and vans. I gripped the key.

"Hey there," he added, squinting as the door rattled in the wind. I reached back and locked it without looking. A fly buzzed past, knocking into the glass. "You're the young ladies of Crazy Town."

"We aren't crazy," I said softly.

"The girl prison."

"It isn't a prison." I gently nudged Teresa behind me.

"No?" He scratched his head. I couldn't see his small eyes in the dim light, but he stayed where he was, ten feet away by the office door. The blisters on his scalp appeared to have popped and then scabbed over again—there were red, uneven welts there that looked painful.

"Do you have any water?" I rasped.

He leaned towards the office door and then slowly moved towards it, motioning for me to follow. I made a palm-down gesture at Teresa, asking her to stay where she was, and followed Samuel into the very small office, a narrow room four yards long with a Pyrex window looking into the garage.

He clicked on a hanging battery-powered light and I blinked rapidly, trying to adjust. I couldn't see Teresa with the light on, just our own washed-out reflections. A faint buzzing came from overhead. The air was warm and stuffy. Samuel poured me water from a plastic jug into a used, coffee-stained paper cup. I brought it out and handed it to Teresa.

"Wait right here," I said quietly. "Don't move." She smiled up at me in the dim garage, her face so coated in dust it was hard to make the shapes out. She took a dainty sip.

Back in the office, Samuel filled another dirty cup. The office was wrecked-looking: computer screens blank, of course, and papers and folders strewn over every surface, the ground, piles of trash under the desk. Someone had swept a bunch of tools off the shelf and they were jumbled in a heap. The place reeked of oil. On the floor, in patches, broken glass crackled in sticky halos, empty energy drink cans, rabbit jerky wrappers, something I definitely hoped was not a piss jug in the corner.

I was gearing up my pitch about vouchers and cash—take the vouchers now and I'll buy them back myself when we get to Atlanta; that was my newest angle—but Samuel was pacing a little, shifting his weight from one foot to the other. He seemed off. He kept checking over his shoulder and peering around, though no one else could have possibly been in the small office. We were very close to one another. It was very stuffy. "We're stuck," he said. "Stuck as a nail."

"Have you been in here all alone?" I asked.

Samuel shrugged. "Wish I could say no."

"You've got a few dozen people holed up in your lobby right now—"

"You know what I saw?" he interrupted, pulling at the collar of his tucked-in shirt. "Middle of last night? About a dozen Humvees loaded down, headed into the city."

"Oh."

"They're not coming to help evacuate! Right? They've come for riot control." He licked his lips. He was very pale, and sweat hung off the tip of his nose. He peered through the window again. Teresa was stretching, plunging both fists toward the ceiling, her shirt lifting to expose her belly. He pointed. "And who's going to defend her?"

"Listen, Samuel," I said slowly, "We're going to take that van. Van four. We'll pay for it in vouchers. Credit. We'll figure it out. But we're in an emergency situation. Okay?"

"Nobody," Samuel said, his eyes scanning the garage, fixing at last on the jumble of tools on the ground, "Nobody comes in a JLTV convoy with a chopper scout because they want to *help* people," he went on, ignoring me. "They come because they're afraid."

"Okay. You're right." Agreeing with ramped-up men was a tried and true protection mechanism and it came to me naturally, but moreover, he was right. I tried to imagine Samuel, sleeping in the garage, spending days alone, hopped-up on amphetamines and energy drinks, listening to the sirens and helicopters outside, the growing mass of people coming to bang on the lobby door and demand keys. "How long have you been in this garage?" I asked.

"First," Samuel went on, cracking the knuckles of his thumbs, "They're going to start arresting anyone who isn't evacuated. Put them in those big pop-up cage jails. Then, they're going to start getting paranoid about the ones that are left. So they'll start shooting people." He mimed hefting a gun and aiming the barrel just past me, at the door. *Rat-a-tat-tat.* My head was hot. In the corner, behind a shelf, something dripped. "I was there, I saw it, in Seattle, after all the fires. And people will shoot back."

"Samuel, how do we open the garage door?"

He looked at me. There was a weird smile turning his lips up at one corner. He seemed to be watching something invisible rapidly unfold, his eyes darting quickly back and forth. Then he turned and disappeared through a door I hadn't been able to see, hidden behind those dripping shelves. I heard him speaking in a low, urgent voice.

He reappeared, holding four one-liter bottles of water.

"I thought you said you were alone, here," I said.

"Nobody else is here." He put the bottle on the desk. "Anybody they catch goes in a cage. I'd say we've got about twelve hours before we're all considered looters. You got a gun?"

I shook my head. Then I gingerly picked up two of the bottles and tucked them under my arm. It had become clear that the best course of action was to disentangle myself as quick as possible and get away. The rocks were in my pocket. I took a step back towards the door. "Samuel, please open the garage door."

"Here's what we're going to do," he went on, his eyes roaming the space above my head. "We're going to wait here, in the garage. The lobby has a security camera—okay, it isn't working now, but it's a deterrent, and I got a couple .22s, we got food and water for another week. We'll sleep in shifts. Out there, the traffic's going to die down. We'll get raided, nothing we can do about that, but we can hold 'em off if they try to take our water, because—"

"Wait, wait," I said, stepping back until I hit the door. "Look, we're going to evacuate—"

"Evacuate?" Samuel spit on the cement floor. He was very close to me. A nervous, sour heat radiated off him.

"You spit on the floor," I said dumbly.

"I'm not going anywhere. This is my home."

I groped for the doorknob behind me. "This is a garage."

"Let me show you two something," he said. Samuel stepped toward me and took hold of my right arm, just above the elbow. I pressed harder into the closed door, scrabbling for the handle with my left hand.

"Stop," I sputtered, and turned to the left to shake off his hand. Samuel just adjusted his grip, reaching out now with both meaty hands to wrap his fingers round my right bicep.

"Just come here for a second," he spat.

I tried to jerk free but only clumsily threw myself sideways into the wall, dropping the water bottles I'd had tucked under my armpit and sending them bouncing across the floor. Samuel tightened his hands around my arm and yanked at me as my head was turned, sending me stumbling forward; I pulled my arm free and stood there a moment, frozen between him and the door. I shifted my weight onto my back foot and held both hands up, clawed like a wrestler.

"Don't touch me," I tried to say, but my throat was so dry it came out as a strangled noise. Samuel pressed his mouth into a white line of disapproval and took a deep steadying breath. I wanted to run but I couldn't, because if I did run then that would mean I was frightened; that would mean I was in danger, and if this man was only trying to help, I should not overreact, should remain polite but firm, though there was a hot fluttering now in my ears and sweat poured down the back of my neck. A cool draft hit me and I turned, shaky and ready to lunge—there was Teresa, prying open the office door, still blissed out with her sweat-damp shirt sticking to her ribs.

"Go," I hissed quickly, and moved to usher her out. But as I did I felt the thick hand on my arm again, then another, pulling my other wrist, as Samuel pulled both my arms sharply behind my back in a painful way, wrenching my shoulder as he pulled my left arm so that I was forced to turn my back on him. *Using force*: the phrase appeared in my mind as I went stiff all over, as Teresa stepped back and politely held wide the door.

Here the moment narrowed. My peripheral vision went dark.

"I'm just trying to protect you—" his right hand released my elbow and crawled around until he was touching my breast. I froze. I was facing Teresa. His fingers pressed, then released; he shifted his hand down to my stomach; it was that touch, his hand on my stomach, that sent my skin crawling, because the belly is mine, mine. I jabbed one leg back, catching his knee, then spun left to untwist my arm and as I turned I grabbed something from the closest shelf—a piece of metal from a broken jack—and brought it down across his head as hard as I could.

I saw his face clear as day for one moment. It was open wide, his mouth an O of perfect surprise. And saw it, still, like the afterimage that hangs burned into your retinas after a camera flash, even as he went stumbling backwards, enough for me to push fully away from the wall and cry, "Teresa!"

I think I thought that would send her to the van. But maybe my face was, instead, urging something else. Because she did a strange thing.

Teresa didn't move toward the van. Instead, she stepped inside, past me. I reached to stop her, but got only a handful of shirt, and then I saw her face had changed—it was not blissed, but something entirely new: her teeth clenched hard and bared in a kind of terrible/ecstatic grimace, her eyes gone unnaturally wide, her head tilted back so that her chin jutted forward, her face in an electric rigor. Without taking her eyes from Samuel, who still wobbled upright with one hand clapped to the top of his skull, she took a bottle from the counter that ran under the window. She held it by the neck while she smashed it against the counter in a violent, fluid movement. I watched, hypnotized. There was a momentum carrying us all by then. Nobody made this decision; the decision had been made already, before

Teresa swung the broken bottle in a wide arc at arm's length, before the glass, its jagged neck, connected at the place where his throat met his shoulder, before she dug it in. Immediately, a dark jet of blood shot from the place where the glass met body. I saw a pulse of muscle as Teresa, in a distinct movement, pushed the glass in further. Then she let go. A thick coppery smell slid up to meet us. The glass stayed in place, jutting from the curve at the base of Samuel's neck.

First, his right hand rose to the bottle, slow and tentative. A choked note of surprise jumped from my own throat, which I had unconsciously clutched with both hands. I stepped back, and then stepped back farther, pulling Teresa by the elbow until we were out of the office; I don't remember opening the door, closing the door behind me, stepping around the corner, but then there we were; I watched Samuel through the Pyrex window where he turned to look back at us, standing unsteadily still lit in the fluorescence while we two remained, mute, in the dark garage as though what happened next were playing out on a screen which we could at any time pause, reverse, turn off. On the other side, Samuel put his right arm out, waving it around like he wanted to put his weight on an invisible cane. His left arm, where blood was running, blood darker than I would've expected, stayed limp. His gaze roamed away, his face shining, feverish. And then gone, down. When I turned my head the movement of my neck was halted and jerky. This will hurt later, I thought distantly. I was squeezing Teresa's hand so hard it must have caused both of us pain.

"Don't look," I breathed, unable to quit looking. I let go and pushed her lightly towards the parked vehicles. My warm body, my moving arms. My wet and touchable iris. Watching Teresa, watching me, calm, curious, her face blank as a wall as I told her to get in van four.

Chapter Six

I was 11, 12, 13, and then, after months where my father's head was an empty swimming pool, dry and full of dead leaves, he popped back up with a vengeance. He'd been low—not working, barely getting out of bed, dragging his way through dinner table conversations, drinking alone in front of the cable news in the dark, saying things like "What's the point" and "There's no point" and "Oh no, no, oh no, oh my God, no"—frightening, but not novel. Our mom made sure he ate, showered, had friends check on him when she wasn't home. And then, after a couple months, something clicked and he was up, throwing sparks, forming plans. I came home one afternoon after school to find the north wall of the living room covered in news clippings, held up by blue and red tacks.

  I dropped my backpack on the floor. Below the clippings was tacked an old-fashioned map of the world, with pins stuck in and clustered at several places: the Michigan upper peninsula, the east coast of Argentina, some land that was probably brutal windswept steppes in central Asia. Clothes were strewn around the floor, and brimming also from a cardboard box that was pushed up against the television, which was blaring, tuned to the news. Next to it roared the vacuum, upright and unmoving. On either side were several stacks of newspapers, reaching as high as my waist, making the room smell faintly of ink and dust. I couldn't imagine where they'd come from; they never read newspapers. I went over to the wall and touched them: they followed a theme, the enthusiastic headlines of disasters, irrevocable glacier collapses, stories of lovers who drowned in the same hurricane storm surge, bodies stacked in an abandoned Connecticut airport after the Rockaways flooded. I saw he'd circled certain phrases: HOUSING EMERGENCY was one. Other places, he'd circled just words: BOTH or IMPOSSIBLE or TWO or UNCERTAIN.

From the kitchen came a hubbub of pots and pans, and then the sound of our dad singing and muttering to himself. The smell of peppery onions drifted in, along with the tang of burning. The door slammed: Jemma had arrived home too.

She threw her bag on the ground and looked around, 16 and scowling.

"Dad," she barked, "What the fuck is going on in this house?"

We looked at each other and then went into the kitchen. Our dad turned around, startled. Steam rose around him and fogged the windows over the sink. Here, too, weirdness: the cabinets had been emptied and the dishes were stacked on the counter and floor. The cabinet doors had been removed. Over the sink, the paisley kitchen window curtain flapped slowly, bearing scorch marks. Our father blinked at us, trying to make us out with his bad eyes. "Girls?"

"What the shit is going on in here?" Jemma hissed. She was furious, almost shaking. I slunk behind her. "This place looks insane. I can't live here."

"Jemma, honey, slow down."

"Where's Mom?"

Our mother emerged then from the living room, holding a sweater in each hand. "Oh, good," she said. "I'm glad you're here. You can help me sort things."

Jemma paused, off balance. Maybe they were cleaning, after all.

"What you making, Dad?" I asked, aiming for normalcy.

"Shakshuka and toast," he called over the sound of the fan and TV and vacuum, smiling. He wore an apron and oven mitts and held a spatula in one hand. "You girls hungry?"

"Yes," I said quickly before Jemma could protest. I pushed past and cleared the kitchen table. After a minute, she helped, plunking down four mismatched plates. Our mom carried away the sweaters in her arms. Through the doorway, I saw her stuff them in a box. Our dad put down a basket of toast. We sat. Our dad, his face shiny from the oven's heat, stood over the table holding a large cast iron pan in both mittened hands, beaming down at each of us in turn.

"My girls," he said. "All three, under one roof!"

We glanced around at each other, embarrassed by his sincerity. He started scooping sauce and eggs onto our plates.

For a while, there was a tense silence. It was the silence of a long-awaited confrontation that takes place at last, in the wrong place, in the daytime, sober. Jemma contented herself by savagely ripping off hunks of toast. Our mother kept thinking of other things we might want: pepper, water, napkins. She stood up and sat and stood and sat.

"Sit down, Daisy, you're making me dizzy," he said. We tensed. But she sat and they smiled at one another. He patted her knee gently. "Dizzy Daisy," he repeated softly. Then he took a deep breath and looked at us, grinning again. "I've got something to tell you girls."

"Are we moving?" Jemma asked.

"No," he said, "Not exactly."

"Because I'm not changing schools."

"We aren't moving," our mother repeated.

"We're moving because of the insurance thing, right?"

Jemma was referring to something I didn't entirely understand, then—rates had spiked due to the environmental problems, and continued to rise. More and more of our neighbors were defaulting on home loans. At some point that year, we learned that Ms. Trinidad was living in her car.

"Kids," our dad said, leaning forward over the table, "I've discovered something wonderful."

"Is this going to be a sex thing?" Jemma was sulkily poking at a warm lump of tomato.

"My literate little chatterbox," our father said, smiling into his food as he spoke. "This articulate visitor from a foreign planet. No."

Jemma laughed.

Our dad pushed his plate away and knit his fingers. He reflected for a moment. "I went to a very interesting meeting recently," he said at last. "It set some wheels spinning. Your mother understands its importance, too." He squeezed her bony knee. "And I'd like you—both of you—to read some material with me. You're smart young women. And Jemma, you've always seemed—" he raised his bad eyes to the ceiling as he grasped for words. "Dissatisfied; you've seemed dissatisfied with yourself. You know," he cleared his throat, "You've always been a bit of a complainer."

I watched her grit her teeth.

But he broke his wide grin out. "And that's great, I think, isn't it? The squeaky wheel gets the grease! You can't get anything in this life if you don't ask. And our family has been wrongly beaten down, haven't they? We never really get the things we want, do we? I got this problem with my eyes; your mother is always tired; you two, you girls, you could have it so much better, you're smart, you're capable, and I've never understood why you didn't make better lives for yourselves."

"I am thirteen," I pointed out.

"And just think about what you could have done with those thirteen years!" he crowed, striking his fist against the table with excitement. Our mother hushed him nervously but kept listening.

"I don't want your opinion on my life," Jemma said coolly.

"That's not what this is about," he said quickly. He had that look in his eyes by then, like he was listening to distant music, or seeing blueprints in the air. "This is about leaving our problems behind. This is about everybody finally getting what they deserve, and it's possible, in this lifetime, right now!"

"I get it," Jemma said, dabbing her mouth with a napkin. "This is about group suicide. Yeah? Okay. I'm ready." She tossed her napkin on her plate and stood.

"No, no, listen, sweetheart, when's the last time you thought, 'Oh, if only I'd . . .'" he stumbled, seeming to have difficulty in imagining Jemma's most likely regrets. "If only I'd asked that boy out before she did?" Jemma snorted derisively, still standing. He turned to me. "Or, 'If only I'd studied that part of the textbook, I'd pass this test?"

Something like that had happened to me, and nervously, despite Jemma staring daggers, I nodded, falling under the spell.

He lit up, and reached towards me with his right hand, as though physically pulling me in would get me spiritually hooked, too. "Well, that's what I'm saying. In another world, you *did* study! In another world, you did—"

"Suicide?" Jemma finished his sentence. Then suggested again, one eyebrow raised and hand out, as though offering chocolates to each of us: "Suicide? Suicide? Suicide?"

"Don't say suicide at the dinner table," our mother scolded.

"Look," our dad went on, hardly hearing, "There are infinite alternate universes, right? So every near miss, everything you almost did, in another universe you *did* do it."

Jemma sat down, sighed elaborately, and covered her face with her hands.

"I went to these meetings," our dad went on, "Two of them this week. The meeting is about Double Truthism. Not a lot of people know about it yet. But it's spreading. And the people—about a dozen people, including Ms. Schafer, remember her?—they've got some tremendous ideas, just—"

he slapped himself on the forehead like someone realizing something obvious—"ideas that make it all make sense. Everything. Let me show you something."

He got up and went to the living room. We followed. Our mom switched off the vacuum finally.

"Does this seem right to you?" He was pointing at some of the headlines: PERMAFROST THAWS; CORAL COLLAPSE; SOUTH LOUISIANA EVACUATES. Others, most printed out from the library computer: MUDSLIDES ACROSS CALIFORNIA KILL DOZENS. HEAT WAVE DEATH TOLL HITS 300. "Does *this* seem right to you?"

". . . No?" I answered.

"Correct!" he cried. "But that's the thing, that's the idea, in Double Truthism, we know it, we *know* this world isn't right. Something's been done to us. This can't be the way things are supposed to go for the whole wide world. But it turns out: we don't have to be stuck here! We can go to—we can access these other, parallel realities. You can train yourself how. It's about concentration and will, it's about having a very very powerful focus, and then you can see through it, you can see through the veil. That's how they know about it. That's how they know things are supposed to be better." He was talking fast, rocking back on his heels and shifting his weight while he tried to make significant eye contact with both of us.

"You're crazy," Jemma was saying, very softly, in a voice of actual wonder that broke my heart a little. "You're really just crazy, you're crazy."

"Doesn't it make some sense, sweetie?" Our mother was speaking now. She reached out and touched Jemma's shoulder. "Doesn't it seem strange, the way things happen, bad things, here, to people? Don't you ever think there are too many coincidences?"

Jemma was surprised by this, by our mother defending this in a voice of reason. "I don't know," she said, off-balance.

"Look," our father said, straightening up. He seemed to be preparing to launch into a speech. We sensed it and, quietly, Jemma let me hold her hand. "Let me show you." He left and came back quickly, with a chart he'd made on poster board like a high school science project. There were boxes drawn on it, labeled with each of our names: DAISY, JEMMA, BEATRICE, HAL. He tacked it up on the wall over the newspapers. From each box extended a web of red sharpie lines.

"Here, I've charted all the different versions of the world that I've glimpsed—in meditation, in dreams, you know," he began, and rocketed off, our father, on his own, doing what Jemma would later refer to as his 'manic mambo,' a frenetic electrification about him as he explained, the pressured pacing of his thoughts making him interrupt himself, tumbling from one fantastic shape of thinking to the next. Parallel worlds, he was saying. Imagine if you could go back to those certain forks in the road that each of us has pinned in our mind (at 13, I had few major regrets, so this was mostly lost on me). But, he argued, every other path *had* been taken. These other versions of the world rested snug up against our own, so close we could even step directly into them if we just learned how.

Who wouldn't be tempted? To hear that all you have to do to be a different, better person is to concentrate hard for a few measly minutes and then step through some door to Narnia in which all the labor of self-improvement has been done already, and there you are, presto, happier and sleeping well at night, eating your vegetables, surrounded by loved ones whose white teeth glisten in lamplight. All the lit windows you pass at night, fists deep in damp pockets as you go over your money fears again and again, dividing you bank balance by days left in the month, limping in bad shoes—imagine you looked to the left through that window, at the well-appointed rooms with the cut-glass coffee table and oil paintings on the walls, sconces and fresh flowers, and suddenly you learned that all you had to do to occupy this other, better life was to climb through the window. Of course I wanted this. I still want this. I want this so, so badly, all the time. To be the one who gets what they want. And deserves it.

But back then, I looked to Jemma for clues. I saw her eyes widen, her jaw clench, though she kept completely still except for her hands, which squeezed my own tighter and tighter.

"So what you're saying," she said, slowly, during a pause in his diatribe, "Is that there are parallel lives? And we can live them?"

"*Exactly*," our father said, nodding vigorously.

"Infinite parallel universes," she repeated dryly. She looked at our mom, who typically humored our father on crusades like these until he went too far. But she didn't seem to think this was too far.

"Not infinite," she said gently. "Just many, many, many others."

"And we get there how," Jemma scowled, "Do you have to say a magic spell? Climb through a hole in the ground? Is there sex tourism to the other universe?"

"Jemma!" our mother scolded.

But she went on: "How is it you guys think you're the only ones who've cracked this code? What, you're smarter than, like, astrophysicists? This is obviously some stupid-ass conspiracy theory." Her eyes shone darkly as her rage sharpened. "Honestly, y'all are embarrassing."

"Even Stephen Hawking—"

There was a crash and I flinched; Jemma had let go of me to viciously kick the vacuum, which clattered onto the ground. "Stephen Hawking, my dick."

"We have an opportunity—" our father started again, but Jemma was backing up.

"You sound crazy! Bonkers," she enunciated slowly, and spun exaggerated loops around her temple with her finger. "Loco. Out of your mind."

"We didn't raise you like this," said our mother, primly folding her hands in her lap and sitting back.

Jemma stormed into the kitchen, moaning, we all followed her. She spun around and grabbed the salt and pepper shakers. "Look at me, look at me, I'm switching the universe," she cried, and began to juggle them back and forth in her hands.

"Those are your grandmother's—" our mother reached for the shakers.

"I tell you I want to move out and you join a *sex cult*?"

Our mother was on her feet, raising her left hand to her breast in shock. "Jemma! Watch your mouth!"

"You're gonna move out?" I cried in dismay.

"About 13.7 billion years ago," our father was saying calmly, trying to start over, "everything we know of in the cosmos was an infinitesimal singularity." He pressed the flat of one finger to the tabletop and then showed it to us, his daughters, pleading. "Smaller than this speck of pepper." He shoved his finger towards my face and I recoiled. "Smaller!" he insisted.

"I'm getting out of here," Jemma snarled, then looked at me expectantly, standing tight as a vise.

What was here? The kitchen, my sister, my parents who'd grown to distrust the future. What could I say to make them all stay put and stop arguing?

"I have cancer," I blurted.

There was stillness like I'd spit up a kitten. Then:

"No, you don't," frowned Jemma.

"No," I admitted, "I don't."

"Jesus," our father gasped, putting his hand over his heart, "Don't do that."

"I was just trying to change the subject," I said meekly.

"You definitely don't have cancer?" Our mother said, putting the back of her hand against my forehead.

"I don't have cancer," I repeated, "Don't you feel relieved? Isn't this nice?"

"I'm leaving," Jemma declared.

"Honey, wait," said our mother, but she was already storming off.

I hurried behind her and made it to the front door where I stopped, watching her throw on her jacket as I hung onto the doorknob.

"We won't give up on you," I heard our father say, his voice down in his chest now, gruff with feeling. He reached towards her for a moment, then dropped his hand. Out over her shoulder, a neighbor was standing by their mailbox, smoking a cigarette and watching us. "Where are you going?"

"Dora's," she said, naming a friend. "For a while." She stopped and looked back at us. At me. But I couldn't do it, couldn't propel myself out of the house after her. I couldn't swing my allegiance fully over to my sister, give up on our parents and house, despite the tin cans stacked in the kitchen, the blackened curtain swinging in the wind. Jemma shook her head.

"I thought you'd get better," she said quietly. I wasn't sure who it was directed to—she could have meant any of us. But then she was down the driveway. And then she was gone.

Our father closed the door. I watched it sink into him: his lips twitched, his weak brown eyes focused in violent concentration on the opposite wall, and then all at once a smile broke through like a beam of day. He put out his hands and we took them.

"We're a family," he said. The relief across my mother's face was tidal. He squeezed my knuckles, and I felt comforted, too. I still had the same routine, the same address; this was a phase, they'd be over it next week, and Jemma would come back. So they had quirks: who didn't? These were my parents, who had invented holidays for us, had argued with my teachers, had carried me half asleep from the dark backseat of the car. "No matter where we are."

My mother kissed him on the cheek. All mistakes could be retrieved.

Chapter Seven

And then I was in the van. Sitting in the driver's seat. My fingers around the key.

Teresa, behind me, politely raised her hand.

"Let's go," she suggested crisply.

I took the key out of the ignition. I felt that I could see and understand things very clearly only my hand was moving by itself and trembling badly.

"Teresa," my voice said, "I'm so sorry you had to see that." As though she'd been a spectator. I stood from the driver's seat, stretched my hand out towards her and nearly stumbled. My balance made no sense? I couldn't figure out where my body was or where to move it? I sort of crouched down and patted the dirty floor.

Teresa raised an eyebrow. Then she leaned down and took one of my hands, like I was a dopey kid who'd dropped her ice cream, and she said, "Did you get any water?"

I looked around. Water? Water? One of the liter bottles of water that I'd tucked under my arm before was somehow sitting between my nose and the brake pedal. I pointed and mouthed *water*.

"Oh," she said, "Great!" She snatched it up and unscrewed the cap. I watched her throat as she chugged and then smacked her lips with satisfaction.

"I'm not thinking straight," I said to myself, out loud, very quietly. Samuel was 100 feet away, pale, dead, his lips parted, the tangy smell of blood coming off him.

A noise. I froze. Somebody was on the other side of the outer garage door, the one we'd come in through, trying the knob. The silver handle twitched and jerked, but the metal door, with its flaky blue paint, stayed shut. Then shook as someone on the other side of it banged with their fist.

"Hello?" came a muffled voice from outside. He banged again. "Hello, hello?" The knob rattled. "Let us in! We can see prints on the door."

Sweat prickled up painfully under my arms. The man rattled the knob again. Then it twisted, slow: first left, then right. I crept back into the driver's seat.

"Come on," a woman's voice said, then broke into coughs. "There's still too much dust out here."

The man muttered curses and banged on the door again. Then the knob was released. I heard the crunch of gravel. Then silence.

I realized I was staring at Teresa's face. She looked back with her sleepy BeZen gaze.

"I'm getting some real weird-o vibes from you, Ms. B."

I turned around and twisted the key. The engine rattled to life at once.

"Bravo!" cried Teresa, "Bravissima!" I smashed my finger against my lips, miming she should shush. She put her mouth against the window glass and blew her cheeks out, then made a face and wiped her lips on her sleeve. A wave of nausea rolled through me.

This side of the garage would be facing the road. Or the rental lobby? Which direction was north? Could two dozen people be out there right now, watching curiously, stepping towards us and the dead—over my shoulder I looked Teresa up and down: no marks, only her right arm was wet with a smear of blood, which she seemed to be ignoring. I found a rag in the glovebox and scrubbed at her arm furiously, leaving her smeared with motor oil.

"You're really sweaty," she murmured. When I was done I threw the rag out the window. She took a deep, slow breath and nodded once. "Okey dokey, artichokey."

I pressed a button on a clicker attached to the sun visor. Slowly, slowly, a crack of light appeared behind us. The garage door lifted and a rectangle of yellowy dry light yawned wide. I sweated, gripping the wheel, and took off the parking brake. I threw it in reverse and backed us outside, the engine's rattle quieter in the wide dry brown outdoors. I hit the brake too hard and accidentally slammed my head against the steering wheel.

"Ta-da!" Teresa sang.

I threw it into drive and sped for the road.

I drove through the remnants of the dust storm, absorbed by a vision: Samuel, revived, sitting in a hospital bed with a bandage around his neck; calm, merciful, declining to press charges. There were holes in this theory too large to mention, namely his arterial blood sprayed on the auto magazines, but I had heard that to make something happen you're supposed to picture it.

Teresa was humming sweetly behind me. I should technically call the police, of course. Of course. The van rattled slowly forward in the dusty traffic. I turned on my phone and dialed 9-1-1. It rang. I pulled over and parked on the side of the road. The phone kept ringing, and my face and lips were cold, while I began to pant like a dog to calm my stomach. I wanted to vomit and I wanted the feeling of wanting to vomit over with so I walked to the back of the bus and threw up carefully into the shadow of a tire. My face was cold and the sun was high. The phone was still ringing, still. No one was answering. I hung up and got back on the van. I looked at Teresa and started talking to see if the right words would come out.

"I know you probably feel confused," I began, "And that's okay."

Teresa squinted. "Did you just barf?"

"Just—let me finish—confusion is normal. Confusion is good? What I mean—"

"Look!" she chirped, interrupting me to point out the window.

Jaws snatched at my heart; cops, cops?? I scanned the view outside, just road and dusty landscape. Then I realized she was pointing at the window glass itself.

"It's a koala." Teresa had drawn a fat, smiling bear in the dust on the window. "It's burping." To demonstrate, she belched loudly.

"Oh."

"I drew it."

"Teresa—"

"With my fingers." She held them up in a claw position and waggled them, smiling with her chin tucked in.

"Teresa, listen, we've got to keep this all between us for now, okay? The—how you—once we get to Atlanta, then we can tell people, just—it'll be better for everyone if we wait. We don't want to go through all that here. Okay?"

Teresa gently took my face between her hands, forcing me to stoop. She brought her face closer to mine, close enough that I could see the faint rings in her eyes and smell her puppy breath as she whispered: "Burping."

As I drove the van back toward Twin Bridge, I tried to focus on individual objects. Things on the side of the road. Trash can. Traffic cone. Bicycle. Focus: Atlanta. I put everything about the garage, the tire iron, the bottle, away. Soon we'd be miles off. I blasted the AC until we shivered.

Years ago I was in a Dollar General, sitting in the shopping cart's basket, while my mother cried in distress that I had No Moral Compass. I didn't know what that was, the Nomoral Compass, but it was clearly important. I got it into my head that it was a bone, like the tailbone, that I had been born with. She was holding a packet of crackers that I had pulled from the shelf and opened, because I was bored and wanted a cracker. She was weeping. I got the idea—that I was sneaky, and the choices I made were bad, because I had Nomoral Compass, was boneless in the tail.

My mother believed that bad things happened to bad people. This was a tent of Double Truthism. She needed to believe this, because bad things continued to happen to her and around her, and she was frightened, and if she could control what happened to her by not being bad, or even if bad things happened to her and she deserved them, this would be a relief. But of course, it doesn't work that way. Nobody gets what they deserve.

And then we were pulling into the Twin Bridge parking lot, while Arda and Carmen and Linda came out the front door to meet us, waving, cheering, hailing us like heroes.

"You got it," said Arda, a true smile across his face.

"We got it," I echoed, my own voice cracking, climbing out of the van after Teresa. "Go wash off," I said to her quietly.

"Oh, shit," said Linda, appearing behind him. "You actually got it."

"Yes," I said.

"I didn't think you were going to pull it off, not with that juggernaut of a dust storm blowing through."

"O, ye of little faith," Arda sang. He was doing a weird little jig of happiness. "How many days have we got it for?"

"Um," I said.

"What kind of engine are we talking here," Linda muttered, circling the van. "Five liter? Ten liter?" She looked at me expectantly. "Twelve? No way—twenty?"

"Yes. No. Big?"

Linda pointed at the window. "What's that?"

"Nothing," I choked. Blood? Blood on the window?

"Is that a bear?"

"Oh."

"Yes!" cried Teresa, delighted.

"Go *wash*," I hissed.

"Bro, you are crazy pale," came the voice of Hanan, who had snuck up behind me. I flinched so hard I nearly hit her in the nose. "White, white, white. And twitchy!" She poked me in the hip.

"No touching," I said, brushing her hand away.

"How you gonna be this white with all this sun?"

"Are we ready?" asked Carmen, who had come to usher Hanan back inside. "Should we get the girls to come line up with their bags?"

Arda nodded and started to give out jobs. No one was looking at me; everyone was in a hurry.

"Linda," he said, "Tell the girls to come down with their luggage. Carmen, please empty the last of the refrigerator into those black contractor bags."

"Arda," I said, faintly.

He glanced my way and did a double take. "Beatrice," he shook his head. "You're very pale. Don't get heatstroke, please. Go inside, now, drink some water. Sit down." He waved me toward the door, out of the blinding sun.

"It's fine," I said. It was hard to concentrate on what he was talking about. I was tracking Teresa, who had slowly drifted back into the building.

Linda passed by, smiling. "Everyone's getting out. Even the nursing home evacuate my mom. So we're coming with—look who's here," she said, interrupting herself to point towards the van with her chin.

I turned around. Frank had pulled into the parking lot, in a limping sedan. He stopped in the middle of the lot, climbed out, and stood in front of the car without approaching. Heat rose into my face. I sat down abruptly on the ground.

"Beatrice?" Carmen frowned, tilting her head down at me. She looked at Linda. "Is that a swoon?"

I tried to read Frank's expression from a distance. Was there an accusation there? Was he holding so still because he wanted to give nothing away; feared tipping me off to the howling approach of a police car?

But he lifted a hand and waved. Looked off into the distance. Cracked his neck and slowly ambled over.

"Rental place was crazy," he yawned as he came up. "Like you warned me—no chance I could get a moving van. I'll load up everything that can fit into the passenger van and come back for the rest when things get a little more normal." Normal. Normal! "Hi. I'm Frank." He stuck his hand out to Carmen. "You all right?" He looked down at me with real concern— normal concern; no secret telegraphed there.

I got up onto my knees and then onto all fours. By climbing Carmen's leg, I lifted myself to standing.

"Hot," I croaked, and turned to rush inside.

I hustled to the bathroom to splash cold water on my face, and right away the sweet miracle of Twin Bridge urgency smacked me into the now. Hanan was in there, throwing up her lunch. When I entered I smelled the sour tang of bile.

"Hanan," I called, "Are you in here?"

I could see the bottoms of her sneakers under a stall door, treads worn smooth. Ah, sad fairies of food rejection! We weren't supposed to really scold them if they were purging—it could push them away. All we could do was express our disappointment and try to talk it out.

"No," Hanan said at last. I heard her spit, twice, into the toilet bowl.

"Well, I just worry. It's hard to become King of Hell when you're distracted by purging."

I waited. Nothing. I heard Camen and some girls pass in the hallway, Carmen chattering, saying ". . . if you're already packed, great, we can all meditate for two minutes . . ."

"Hanan," I tried again, "Do you want a coffee?"

"Yeah," she said, immediately.

I walked blankly towards the office, where we were leaving behind an electric kettle and packets of instant imitation coffee. Then I stood there. I'd forgotten I couldn't boil water this way. It was too hot for coffee. I split half a packet between two cups and mixed in the rest of an open bottle of water. When I met Hanan in the bathroom, she opened the stall door and leaned her hip against the wall, looking gracefully unimpressed, like I'd come to the door of her luxe Manhattan walk-up. I handed the cup of room-temperature sour water over and she held it with both hands the whole time, like it was really warm. We sipped the disgusting drink for a couple minutes and didn't say anything. It was the most relaxing thing that had happened to me in days.

Once I'd drained the cup without tasting it, I fished my voice up from out of my belly somewhere. "Are you excited?" I asked her, "To go to Atlanta?"

She looked down, consulted the cup, dug at it with one fingernail.

"I guess."

"What would you like to do before we go?"

Hanan shook her head, shrugged.

"Do you want to go say goodbye to all the rooms? Maybe cuss at them?"

She considered for a moment, toeing the tile. Then she nodded assent. We left to prowl the halls.

Getting the girls packed up and ready to go was itself an Olympic trial, keyed-up as they all were, talking in hyped and giggling knots. Frank moved past and among us, wheeling out boxes on a yellow dolly and packing them into the back of the van while we wrangled the human element. Among the boxes: our dwindling, now alarmingly small remaining supply of BeZen.

And so what was there to do but stalk the halls, barking, *leave the pillows, take the toothbrush* into the dorm-style rooms, turning a blind eye to those who were taking the opportunity of impending departure to carve their names liberally on door jambs and walls, helping Amy gently pack her teddy bears one by one into the black trash bag she was using in lieu of a suitcase. There were seven girls left: Teresa, Maria, Hanan, Amy, Sabine, Zak, and Lucia.

Back outside, the staff plus Frank waited in the shade.

"I can't believe it," Linda breathed. She looked around the parking lot, jaw slack, and then into each of our faces, a smile blooming on her. "We're leaving Askewn. Together!"

"I really thought this was going to be the year I retired," mused Arda.

"I thought I'd be quitting. I thought I'd be unemployed," added Linda. She beamed as sweat ran down the side of her nose. "Would've been bored out of my mind. I've got about two dozen lesson plans I haven't used yet." She widened her eyes at us, incredulous: "I was going to *volunteer*."

Hanan, whose spirits had lifted, was scampering around Maria, who was howling with a bizarre cave joy, and then began to frolic, actually frolic, gamboling in circles around the others. Jamie grabbed Amy's hand and spun her around, then did a series of karate kicks across the tarmac.

"They've gone mad!" Arda cackled. He had electricity in his face too. "They're too happy! They have to be stopped!" It was contagious; I started laughing, too, a weird high keening that traveled up through my body as I took his frail old shoulders and shook them gently.

"They're too happy!" I choked through a scrambled hysterical giggle.

Frank sidled up to us and Arda grabbed his shoulder.

"You, young man," he cried, "Tell us some bad news!"

"Um," he said. He closed his eyes and shook his head a little so his dark hair brushed over his eyebrows. "Sorry, I can't think of any."

Arda and I cried out in alarm.

"Disaster!" I moaned.

"Doom!" Linda crowed, her eyes burning. "Doom!"

"I don't understand how you run this place," Frank muttered, watching me. "I don't think I understand what your jobs are."

I grabbed him by the collar. "Sing a dirge," I commanded, "Something slow."

"Sing! Sing!" The girls had sniffed our joy like blood in the water.

"Sing some of that caucasian music, Nebraska boy," Maria cried.

"Sing, farmer!" Hanan echoed, merciless.

Frank wriggled out of my grasp, laughing but blushing—blushing!—as all eyes were on him. "I don't know any songs," he lied desperately, sticking his hands in his pockets and shaking his head at the ground, half-smiling, shy. The girls didn't care; they began singing themselves: some pop song from the radio about driving, driving with the windows down at night, too fast. Hanan began to ululate and the others tried, badly, to imitate her. They leapt, they wrestled; they jumped up and down, wriggling, fizzing, soda bubbles of the mind; Arda did a funny little soft-shoe, huffing. Linda was still crowing, *Doom! Doom!*

"Jesus," Carmen breathed, having come out of the building with the final bags. "What'd I miss?"

"On the van," Arda yelled. The girls had stopped singing and were trying out some new dance, shaking around while their arms stayed limp. "All aboard, let's go, let's go!"

They cheered and rushed aboard, hauling pink ratty backpacks, duffel bags with the straps missing. They clung to one another's arms, claiming seat buddies. Linda counted heads while Carmen gave directions to Maria in Spanish about where and how to store her suitcase, which was particularly delicate, made almost entirely from duct tape.

"Road trip," Linda was mumbling, rubbing her hands together. "Road trip time. Never been on one!"

Arda boarded last. "It's all locked up," he confirmed, and gingerly lowered himself into the seat behind me as I took the wheel. Before we pulled onto the road, I noticed the sign he and Carmen had made while I was gone, stuck in the road-facing window, intended for the would-be rescuers that probably never showed: *EVERYBODY HERE IS GONE.*

A couple weeks after the disastrous dinner with Jemma, I sat down at my laptop and typed *"double truthism what"* into the search bar. I was brought to a webpage. A banner across the top repeated my question back to me: WHAT IS DOUBLE TRUTHISM? The words were superimposed across a photo, over-exposed and gold-tinted, of several people smiling widely at one another. The selection of people was, I guess, meant to convey diversity, but by the way they'd been posed—an elderly Filipina woman beamed while clutching the arm of a young Black businessman, himself holding the hand of a middle-aged Hispanic woman decked out in what appeared to be a bridesmaid dress—instead suggested radical polyamory. Jemma would've found it funny, I thought, but I was too confused and annoyed to call her.

A video began to auto-play, startling me. First: a vast gold wheat field, somber piano chords in a major key. *Do you ever feel confused?* Asked the warm, textured voice of an old man. I was impressed. *Do you ever worry your life is a mistake? Do you feel a single choice in the past could have changed everything? Is the world around you unrecognizable? Have you ever noticed that there are more disasters than there once were?* As he spoke, certain words flashed onto the screen in heavy, bold type, glittering as they faded away: CONFUSED, MISTAKE, PAST, DISASTERS. Some of the feelings the voice articulated were familiar to me; some of the feelings I could imagine; and some of them seemed to appear, like an optical illusion, within me as the voice spoke them aloud.

Then a bar graph charged onto the screen, replacing the last glittery sparks of DISASTERS. I chewed on a knuckle while I watched. *Scientists have discovered that there are more disasters on earth than science can explain*, the man's warm voice informed me, the viewer. Something about that sentence didn't seem quite right to me. But the bar graph evidence disappeared too quickly for me to read anything on its axes, and was replaced by a live woman.

"We're actually sitting in one of the lower-quality universes right now," the woman explained into the camera, her face a rictus of delight. She had gelled waves of blonde hair and she lifted her translucent eyebrows to the ceiling as she spoke, widening her eyes, which were perfectly lined with black. Overall the effect was that she appeared aggressively awake. She wore a lilac-colored blazer and sat on a stool which seemed to float in space. Below her, text appeared: "MILA HORVAT / Advanced Cosmology Navigator," it said. These words carried no meaning, were the unflavored gelatin of words. "Everybody knows there are multiple parallel universes," she continued smoothly. "What people often *don't* know is that some of those universes are what you might call "high-achieving" universes. And with the right tools, *you too can get there.*" She began encouraging us to imagine the stuff we wanted, very vividly. Maybe we'd already imagined that stuff, or dreamt a world where it was true. The screen dissolved into a still photo of half a dozen people sitting cross legged in a sunlit room, the words *HEADQUARTERS, Raleigh,* at the bottom. I scrolled up and down as the blonde woman talked with great spirit. "You deserve to be successful, and you *are* successful, you *are* wealthy, in some of these higher-tier parallel universes." The rest of the webpage had section headings like "Success is Next To You" and made references to inter-verse contact. "With our donation-tiered system of self-abnegation and transcendental meditation," blah blah blah, I clicked another tab and she was cut off mid-sentence.

Does THIS seem right TO YOU??? asked the new page headline. Terrible photos collaged below: mountain-high flaming pile of black chicken corpses, burned for avian flu. A poorly lit and abandoned Toys-R-Us filled with body bags, drowning victims from the Rockaways. The smoking ruins of Seattle. Parking lots and warehouses in Louisiana overflowing with thousands of Black and Indigenous evacuees after Hurricane Svetla. I read the captions, trying to figure out what it all meant. That didn't help. I clicked another tab: here was a calendar of Double Truthism meetings, all over the Southeast, some even in Columbus and Clearwater. The photographs showed fireworks and dense, shoulder-to-shoulder crowds in large venues lit like nightclubs, with spotlights. The people in attendance had their arms thrown up towards the ceiling and faces twisted in ecstasy. The speakers wore expensive-looking, thickly-quilted suits. Their heads were enormous and tan, their hair ruthlessly tamed. American flags comprised of LED lights lined the stage's back wall. The whole setup gave off a sense of easy money and another feeling I vaguely recognized as sexual; this, I thought, much later, was the offer of a sugar daddy. He will solve it all. He will rescue you. Next I tried the FAQ page. None of the frequently asked questions were questions I'd have ever thought to ask. IS GOD ALIVE? was the first one. I skimmed the answer, which amounted to "probably." CAN WE ALL BE GENIUSES, was another question (the answer to this was yes). AM I ENTITLED TO GREATNESS? At the bottom, finally, I found a paragraph that clarified things:

"Double Truthism is the belief that, in keeping with superstring theory, trillions of parallel universes exist. Statistically, in many of those realities, we are happier. The increasing rate of extreme disasters around the world tells us that our current universe is not a good universe. Double Truthism shows us how, by meditation and non-attachment to this reality, we can access other, better universes, where we lead other, better lives. Why try to fix what's broken when you can leave it all behind?"

I turned the computer off. Tempting, but heady. They'd lose interest. I did my homework, but I couldn't concentrate, so I did a bad job.

Heading out of town, we got a clearer view of the conditions, and the kind of weird-o ecstatic hyperactivity everyone was gunned up on. People were embracing this soft apocalypse, the blackout, the evacuation; people were casually wheeling carts of tinned groceries out the smashed doors of convenience stores, sitting in the buckets of abandoned construction diggers with their shoes kicked off to get a breeze, walking around in their underwear; people were setting bad examples for our charges; people were flashing the van. Linda clapped her hand over the closest pair of eyes (Maria's), but she hadn't got enough hands for the rest, who whooped.

"Yes!" shrieked Sabine.

"Look! Ow. LOOK! OW!" cried Hanan, mashing her face to the glass and lifting her shirt to press her fresh piercing against it. Carmen half-tackled her away from the window and I caught a glimpse of Frank, covering both his eyes with his full palms like a child in a haunted house.

"Keep your shirt down," Carmen was scolding Hanan. "You've got to respect your body more than that."

"I respect the ever-loving shit out of my body," Hanan began protesting, but then went quiet as Carmen began to tell a story from her own teenager-hood. "My roots," I'd heard her call Twin Bridge. Despite those roots she was steady, even-keeled, had perfectly shaped thick black eyebrows under her bad haircut that made her face extra expressive. If Linda wanted to straighten the girl into right angles, Carmen was permissive to the point of alarm. Let me put it this way: during her first week she taught the girls palm-reading, and we spent the next few days putting out emotional three-alarm fires as each girl, in the manner of the Salem Witch Trials, worked out petty vengeances vis-a-vis accusations of devil-fucking and predicted one another's painful deaths with glee. Spiders in their eyes. Fistfights in the hall. Carmen stopped them, gently. And she held grand, heart-stopping ambitions for the girls; the only time she chattered was when relaying these fantasies as we cleaned up common areas—visions of Amy as a circus lion tamer, Hanan a war-zone journalist—all based on a level of faith and hope that struck me as mildly bonkers. Maybe she was steady because her mind was often elsewhere. But I liked it, and I liked hearing her hokey juju stuff, too—crystals and tarot—like telegrams from another world oiled by magic; they imbued her with confidence that she could flex seamlessly through problems with the assistance of sage smoke, snake oil and gems; faith placed in rocks kinder than the ones she'd left up north.

"Thanks for the ride," said Frank quietly, who'd moved to sit directly behind me. "And sorry the move got all messed up."

"That's okay," I said. "Couldn't just leave you behind." I glanced into the rearview and caught him suppressing a smile, which felt good.

"Guess I would've had to wait for a bus, otherwise. Going who knows where. But I'll come back for the rest of the stuff when things stabilize. Get it out there to Atlanta. I promise."

"I believe you," I said. "Or else you'll have to walk the plank."

"Aye-aye, Captain."

Meanwhile, all along the road, impromptu food stands had cropped up, bearing handwritten signs for FREE COFFEE or SANDWICHES 4 U or LOOTERS' BAR. Some were giving away meals. Stuff from dead industrial freezers that must now be well-thawed and almost spoiled. A man with an apron that read BESA AL CHEF was tending charred jackrabbit legs over a grill built in a half oil drum. Others stacked pallets of water bottles they must have dragged out of a store, cars pulling over to snag what they needed.

"Look," Arda leaned over my shoulder to get a better view out the windshield. "This is like a party."

We passed a man with a sign that said HONK IF YOU LOVE ASKEWN. Linda leaned over my other shoulder and put her full weight on the horn, causing me to cry out and swerve.

"For fuck's sake," I muttered, while people on the sides of the road, and every kid on the van, cheered and shook their fists. Out of the corner of my eye I saw Frank flash a thumbs up to the guy who was joyfully, drunkenly shaking the sign.

After another mile or so, approaching the turn to leave town, the cafes dwindled and disappeared. The traffic thinned out—most other people were headed north, towards Oklahoma, a much shorter distance to the blackout-border than heading East. Dust still lay thick on the shoulder. Something in the air shifted. The girls grew quieter. On a piece of plywood propped against a light pole, someone had written in grease marker: TURN BACK HERE.

"Spooky," Carmen said.

We turned a corner and found ourselves headed towards a line of armored vehicles that blocked the road. Tires as high as my shoulder, big open beds hung with brown camo netting, as-yet unmanned turrets at the top. Cars were rolling slowly through the checkpoint, single file, the occasional vehicle waved to the side for searching. And off behind them, on one side of the road: the cages.

I hadn't thought too hard about what it meant when the radio talked about "looters." People grabbing TVs, maybe. But here was the real meaning. Behind the checkpoint was a rectangle of hurricane fencing, 100 yards per side and 15 feet high, with a fencing roof, too. As we joined the stop-and-go checkpoint line, I could see figures inside: a few dozen, some leaning against the chainlink, others sitting on the ground. It was too far to make out much more.

"What's going on?" Lucia asked from the back of the van.

"We might get searched," I said evenly. Quickly, I took a mental trip through the steps necessary to ruin my life forever: 1. Someone found Samuel's body; 2. Someone deduced the license plate number of the missing van; 3. Police put out an APB to all the state agencies working the evac zone—not that many steps, really. The van had no emergency exit hatch. The metal fence of the living dead glinted in the sun ahead. I tried to catch Teresa's eye in the rearview mirror, but she was just looking glibly ahead, maybe even smiling.

Groups of police in riot gear emerged from one of the trucks and began to fan out along the road, in our direction. I gripped the steering wheel until the plastic squeaked. Nervous rustling behind me. For reasons that seem obvious, the girls didn't like police. Not just because they were hellions, or because they nursed sympathy with the general tenets of anarchy: their reasons were myriad and specific. Lucia, as a single example, had once called 9-1-1 because her mother's boyfriend had come back, screaming, hitting; the police arrested the boyfriend, and then wrestled the mother to the ground, too, Lucia crying, her mom crying, everyone yelling, the mom arrested for resisting arrest, and who couldn't afford bail, so after a week lost her job cleaning hotel rooms, so got evicted, so had to stay with the violent boyfriend, and after a few more steps Lucia wound up at Twin Bridge. Every one of the girls, so, already knew police as a force arbitrary in general and cruel in the particular; moreover, any adult in the van who'd lived through a disaster knew that the response of police/sheriffs/national guard in the 2–7 days following an acute crisis was akin to an occupying army—confused, and violent because it was confused. Nobody was handing out bottled water, I'm saying.

One of the clumps of police clomped past as we rolled forward. I looked out of the corner of my eye: they were Texas national guard, all camo and lace-up combat boots, with velcro flag patches on their arms, their eyes hidden by short-billed caps. Tense quiet on the van. I heard myself swallow. Another clump passed on the other side, peering through passenger windows. I rolled another foot towards the brake lights ahead. Two cops paused beside us. They peered up, conferred briefly with the others, looked back up at us, then detached from the group and headed our way, holding their weapons at an angle: absurdly large automatic rifles so clean and black and oiled they looked edible. I kept both hands on the wheel.

"Be calm," Arda said softly behind me. A ridiculous request. I was basically vibrating.

I glanced in the rearview and saw Arda, holding himself very, very still, except for his hands, which twisted brutally in his lap. The muscles in Frank's jaw were flexing as he gritted his teeth. It occurred to me that I didn't know that much about him, really.

I engaged the parking brake as the cops rapped hard on the door. I pulled the lever to let them in and the cool air fled out the door, replaced by gas stink and distant yelling and idling engine sounds. They stepped inside and immediately became the tallest things in the van, looking around down at the tops of our heads, keeping their hands on the guns. Their armor was layered, like scales.

"This city is under evacuation orders," the first one said.

"Excuse me. The orders are voluntary, yes?" Arda said, still seated, wilting even as he spoke. "I thought."

"Where are you headed?"

"Exit the van," the second cop said abruptly, in my direction. They were still standing at the top of the stairs, exuding a smell of hot metal and sweat.

"What?" I said.

"Get *out* of the *van*," the cop repeated, speaking to me, "And stand against the vehicle." He had tense, meat-thick shoulders. Jowls. His grip tightened around the rifle, which hung from a strap across his chest, though the muzzle stayed pointed down.

I stood up with a belly full of bees and stepped down the stairs, where the heat hit me again. I moved so that my back was against the van and concentrated on breathing evenly while I listened to the man follow me outside.

"ID," he said sharply. Well, this is it, I thought. My choices blinked out in front of me. Maybe they'd interrogate me in a room with air conditioning. The guard plucked the ID from my hand.

"Where are you going?" he asked, looking at the card.

"Atlanta," I said.

"Know anybody in Fort Worth?" he asked. "Arlington? Dallas?"

"No." Was this the correct answer? I hoped.

"What are y'all? School group?"

It was unbelievably hard not to lie. "We're a residential treatment center for teenage girls who've been removed from their homes."

He said, "What?"

I started to repeat myself but he waved his hand and stopped me, probably scowling, though it was hard to tell through his sunglasses. He walked a distance away, still frowning at my ID, speaking into a radio clipped to his shoulder. I watched him and breathed. Then took a couple steps forward and craned my head to see through the windows of the van—the other man was walking down the aisle, looking over everybody. His head disappeared as he ducked to look under the seats. He lingered at the back, where Maria, Hanan, and Zakiyyah were. My guard came back, repeating, "This area's under evacuation."

I waited another moment, but he wasn't arresting me. He didn't even say my name.

"I work here," I managed. "We're like a boarding school." Kind of. "For girls. And we are evacuating." On his vest, the man had three pairs of plastic handcuffs, and in his belt the taser, in his holster the gun. We stood there waiting. I tried to stay calm by thinking about exactly how expensive all the guard's belt accessories were but that did not calm me down. In the van, I saw the cop make Zaki stand up and spread her arms. He patted her down, tracing the backs of his hands over her locs, and a flash of hot and immediate rage surged up into my throat with such force that I was briefly dizzy. I clenched my jaw while the guard in the van motioned for Zak to sit back down and then he wandered casually back up the aisle. I couldn't see Zak's face.

Little gasps of warm wind were coming from under the van and licking my ankles. I made eye contact with Frank through the window but there was nothing to communicate but worry.

The second cop came back. Most of what I could see on his face were his thin lips, color bleeding at the edges. "Have you engaged in any looting or destruction of property?"

"What?"

"Have, you, engaged, in, looting?" Frustration made his lips whiter.

"No," I said. The word 'looting' was making less and less sense to me; I was getting the impression that 'looting' was like the trick story we sometimes told the girls about desert snipe—an imaginary animal, one that everyone feels they're just on the verge of catching, but which is never witnessed directly. "No. No."

"If we see you here again, Ms. Campbell," he said, handing my ID back, "We'll have to arrest you." He pointed at the van. "That goes for all of you. Everyone needs to get out. Hear me? Everyone. This area is out of control. Out of control." I watched a bead of sweat run from his mustache and into his mouth. His radio chirped the spooky four-toned song of threat. He pressed the button on its side and turned to talk into it, waving us off. I sat down in the stale baking oven the driver's seat had become as the fist in my heart started to unclench. We rolled on, not speaking, all the adults holding their collective breath. Before we picked up speed again we passed along the side of the fenced detention center: the people inside, mostly men, mostly Hispanic, sat and stood and slumped in the sun. There were no cots that I could see. Four latrines with their doors removed stood along the back. What Samuel had said, just a couple hours ago: *they're afraid*, he'd said, and, *they'll start putting people in those big pop-up jails*. Nobody spoke until we'd turned off the road and onto the highway, when Carmen went to the back of the van and sat in the seat next to Zaki, speaking in soft susurrations that went up at the end and then faded into quiet.

RESPONDER ANALYSES

Subject 1:

    Subject 1 had clinically significant behavior problems which caused her to be removed from her home to the care of TWIN BRIDGE. Subject 1 exhibited severe symptoms when untreated, i.e., violence against peers, violence against authority figures, truancy, theft, drug use and alcohol abuse, burglary, vandalism, etc.

    After six months administration of 20 mg BEZEN twice daily, symptoms abated. Patient currently exhibits clinically significant improvement and signs of well-adjustment. Testimony from staff:

    "[Subject 1] was a nightmare when she first arrived. She climbed out the window, climbed onto the roof, and threatened to jump! She bit a staff member and broke the skin. She was breaking mirrors. She put worms in our food. I don't know where she found worms. But now that she takes BEZEN regularly, the difference is like night and day! She's a whole new lovely person! She listens well in class, expresses interest in hygiene, and hits all the numbers—eight hours sleep, three meals a day, zero breakdowns! I would adopt her myself, if I could afford children!"

    We got out of Askewn zipping down a state highway to avoid the interstate-bound traffic, passing fences half-buried in dust, defunct wind farms with their impossibly large white blades still, listing in the dry and shifting ground. South and east for hours on roads used mostly by truckers, routed through Bailey and White Rock and smaller, emptier villages. I know there used to be fields there, farms with crops in rows, but now you pass abandoned silos, fields where floods arrived in the spring when corn was young, choked it with salt and silt, and then evaporated in a blaze, leaving endless rows of black ossified reeds that disintegrate over the slow course of a year. Hard yellow ground, sandy plains, those big brown squares that make you think *mud farm*. The light is always working on something off to your side and once it's finished working there are vast banks of clouds that never arrive. One of Linda's lessons: the Anadarko and Wichita and Caddo tribes, forced back and back and back, and meanwhile the land stays skeptical of our genocidal presence: *here?,* it says, rushing beneath the car but never really changing. *Here? Really? Are you sure?* The land asks, and just once you've convinced yourself, abruptly you're out of it, having swung wide around Paris to avoid the congestion of evacuees, trundling east towards Louisiana and its mind-warping view of sky, enormous enough that it is simply impossible not to be hopeful, hopeful in spite of everything, you see sky that big and the green beginning to rise again from the ground below it and you're convinced of hopefulness, might devote yourself to it.

We waited in line for another hour at the Texas-Louisiana border. I was sweating bullets, again.

"Don't worry," Arda said, touching my shoulder lightly so that I jumped. "They're giving the cards to everybody. It will work out fine." I nodded, mute.

"We're in international waters, baby," Maria sang from somewhere behind me. She pulled Zak up to wiggle in the aisle with her, trying to cheer her up. "Everything's legal!"

"Not true," Linda muttered, though no one was listening. "That's not how that works."

"I'm going to gamble," Amy announced, sitting primly with her pale hands folded in her lap.

"Let's all get married," suggested Lucia.

"This is not international waters," I reminded them. "We are in McLeod, Texas." I glanced at dreaming Teresa in the mirror and had some nauseous thoughts about fingerprints that I quickly crushed into a little ball and threw away. But as we waited, I counted fears. This van could easily be traced back to the rental spot. Could I come up with a convincing excuse to remove the license plate? But CASK MOVING LINES would still be stenciled on the side.

When the border agent finally came along, he gave a cursory glance around the van, took down our information, and then handed us 12 temporary Pink Cards, unlaminated and fragile. Arda held onto the girls', but Linda took hers in her hands for a long time, turning it over and over again, even reading the fine print on the back.

"My first Pink Card," she said, smiling shyly. She held it up. "God bless."

We got onto I-20 East towards Atlanta. The glare of the road and the burbling of the girls grew soothing, hypnotic. The smell in the bus was the smell of Twin Bridge, bottled and concentrated: old milk and mouth, a condensed human smell. Carmen and Linda chatted behind me, mostly Linda talking, Carmen acknowledging receipt of the speech with the occasional hum.

The radio played pop country, and in between songs an ecstatic jockey delivered bad news: the heat wave body count was topping 5000; the dust storm had grown after passing Askewn, destroying homes; rescue efforts were hampered by the blackout. It hit 130 degrees in Alice, Texas, where the pavement had buckled and stopped traffic, and at night, the riverbanks were swarmed with hundreds of families, sleeping outside to stay cool. Two young women had been arrested near Corpus Christi, charged with looting and gang activity in Fort Worth, Dallas, and Arlington; they'd beaten one man nearly to death with baseball bats. I changed the channel while the DJ played explosive sound effects but on the new channel a preacher, mid-sermon, kept repeating the phrase, *Grapes in the past, or grapes in the future? Grapes in the past? Or grapes in the future?* I turned the radio off.

The events in the garage had manifested as a kind of atmosphere in my head, a soundless noise, a pressure with no feature except its ubiquity. Rather than having thoughts, I was trapped in a room full of corporeal static. Driving was a decent antidote.

"We need gas," Arda interrupted, breaking me out of my spell.

He was right: the needle was almost to E. I hadn't been watching it. Cars shimmered in the heat before and behind us, traffic still thick. After a few minutes, Arda pointed: a sign swam up reading THE DOVETAIL, and underneath, in yellow outlined letters two feet high, *MEDICAL CLINIC / TRUCK STOP. WELCOME.*

Eighty years ago, in the early 1960s, Dr. Bartholomew "Bam" Cain took helm of a former fertilizer factory and converted it into a supply depot and walk-in clinic for the destitute. Dr. Cain ran the clinic, while the shops sold high-grade fencing wire and dual-action partial-stock rifles. From the start, the place was plagued by misfortune.

First, the clinic's pathologist tripped over a gurney and was impaled through the eye by his own best pen. Then the accountant was indicted for embezzlement and fled to Bucharest. The much-beloved clinic cat was found stone-dead with four kittens in the wheel well of the ambulance. Cain, increasingly anxious lest the Dovetail jinx reach him, bit his nails nervously until this habit led to a staphylococcal infection which spread, taking his right arm from the elbow down. Soon after, having turned to gin as he mourned his arm, Cain was found dead on the roadside in his smashed, upside-down 1990 Ford Pinto, wheels still spinning.

After his death, the Dovetail went bankrupt and remained empty, until it was auctioned off to an entrepreneur backed by venture capitalists who knocked the 'low-income' part off the hospital's mission and leased most of the square footage out for retail shops.

The New Dovetail was still mid-renovation.

All of this I read off a plaque in the waiting room.

We'd watched the truck stop / hospital loom up out of the desert: white, stone, the sun guttering in its windows. The large building had its own generator and backup generator; it blazed with light and pumped conditioned air.

Linda was first off the van. Carmen stayed behind to keep watch over those who were napping, while Arda and I guided the rest into the main lobby so they could use the bathroom.

"Slow down!" I cried to Linda, but she was off, actually jogging. She approached the doors but then made a hard left, and it became clear that her intention was to circle the building until she had sufficiently stretched her legs.

"This woman," Arda sighed, "With the spirit of a lizard."

I was mostly watching Teresa still. She was walking by herself, but no longer had that dreamy look on her face; now she just seemed sleepy, the BeZen wearing thin. I slowed down to walk next to her.

"Teresa," I said gently, "What are you thinking about?"

She looked up at me, as startled as someone can be when they're up to their eyeballs in pharmaceutical wattle. "Nickels," she said.

"Okay." I dug the heels of my hands into my eyes; when I took them away I saw stars.

"Why are they called nickels?" she went on.

"Are you—are you really asking me?"

"Is it because it rhymes with 'tickles'?"

"What?" I checked my brain. "No. No, it's because they used to be made out of nickel. Like the metal."

Teresa nodded seriously, absorbing this new input. "Metal," she said softly to herself. I checked the time. She was due for another dose of BeZen at the top of the hour.

We herded the girls to the bathroom, everyone gasping with pleasure as we entered the rarefied palace of fluorescent light and coolness. I wandered around the white, scuffed hallway to the toilets, looking at the wire racks of souvenirs. I found the plaque about Dovetail and Bam Cain near the door and read it while I waited. PLEASE EXCUSE OUR MESS, begged an embarrassed cartoon syringe at the bottom of the plaque, his gloved hands spread. DON'T MISS THE DISCOUNTS!

There is one other skill I learned which still comes in handy, picked up the night our father announced we would fire bomb the Elk's Lodge.

"This is the perfect day to do it," he'd been repeating endlessly, pacing the rooms of our home when we got back from school. I sat at the table and watched him, swinging my legs. My father was a fairly large man; he carried a bit of a gut back then. He had brown hair cut short over his square head. Once, he'd had a gang of friends, each attributed a nickname, like *The Bugman* or *Fat Dave,* which he still used when he spoke of them, smiling.

It was, by most metrics, a very poor day for fire bombing. The weather station had announced the approach of a big hurricane—that thing we'd made in class, with bottles and glitter. Hurricane Svetla. Svetla was coming, we agreed grimly on the playground, though we kids did not know from where, or why, or really what it meant. I'd taken out my bottle of glitter and swirled it.

"We need bottled water, Hal," our mother was saying. "We need to board the windows. We need sandbags." She said this in a gentle, reasonable voice. She was never angry, never upset.

"We will," he assured her, "This will only take a bit." My father hated the Elk's Lodge with a true hate. This was the kind of hate that sustained; a nurturing hate, the type that keeps people lingering for years on death-beds. He nurtured a baffling grudge against what he called "those Nazi deer fucks" in the same way that he nurtured the peonies by the front door. He fertilized the hate, guarded it jealously, shared it with loved ones. Mornings, if he were in the car with us as our mother dropped us late to school, he would tense up a block away from the Lodge. As we approached, he'd roll down the window. Two doors down, he'd stick an arm out. Finally, as we passed the lodge—a low ugly brick building surrounded by hedge— he'd holler, "Disband, you cretins! Disband!" Jemma and I would crow with delight, banging doors, echoing in our high-pitched girl voices, *disband, cretins, disband*! Our mother would suppress a smile and roll her eyes.

I think he hated them because, being a fraternal order, men went there and made friends. My father had no friends anymore. He'd watched them slip away in the midst of his wild flights and long, dark troughs. There was the summer when he'd spent three months in bed, dragging himself out only to hunch skeletally in his robe in the driveway, regarding every passing car with despair. It's hard, I guess, to be friends with that.

Let me spoil this quickly and say that we did not ultimately firebomb the Edenton chapter of the Elk's Lodge fraternal order. There are several reasons. First: I was eight. Second: we didn't really know what firebombing was. We were a generally pro-peace family. And lastly, I think that if we had bombed the Elk's Lodge, my father would have been arrested and/or the Lodge destroyed, and that would have been the end of his joyful loathing. He would have had to find a new hobby to replace it. So my father used the word 'firebomb' only to make the event exciting for us. But we were our father's daughters. We were excited when he was excited. He could have chosen any word at all.

The television played endless loops of rain. I sat on the couch, chewing on my finger, occasionally batting Jemma's feet out of my face as she scrawled around in baroque acrobatics on the cushions. On the screen, a reporter somewhere near Wilmington, nearly 200 miles south, shouted at the camera through the torrents, holding a yellow rain hat on his head with one hand.

Our father plopped onto the couch and we immediately snuggled up on either side of him. "Now's the time to strike," he repeated, as our mother left the room to nap. The smell of smoldering sage drifted out from the bedroom. "While everyone is distracted, hunkering down for the storm. Glued to their televisions like philistines and voyeurs. Strike while the iron's hot, girls!"

We agreed. The hot iron! Strike it! We followed him to the garage, where, a few years later, he'd show us the basics: how to change the oil, how to change the spark plug wires, where the radiator and air filter and fuel injectors were. The Cat 4 eye was spinning northeast towards us, but wouldn't reach us for hours; while a busload of tourists drowned in storm surge outside Charleston, in Edenton there were only banks of fast-moving gray clouds, pushed by a cool fresh wind. He handed me the packet of water balloons and handed the funnel to Jemma. Carefully, one by one, our father poured the paint from the cans through the funnel and into the balloons. Then I'd hand the balloon back to our father so that he could tie off the mouth. We made about a dozen. The paint marks from what we spilled—purple and blue and red splotches—stayed on the garage floor for the rest of its life.

While our mother napped, he closed the garage door softly and drove us (that rare treat!), slowly, hazards on, to the Elk's Lodge, parking several blocks away. And though it was still light out, he boldly climbed out and stretched his back and slammed the driver's door shut, and the three of us snuck up towards the building and hid behind a hedge.

"Are you ready?" he hissed.

"Oops," whispered Jemma. She had pinched one of the balloons too tightly and now green paint ran all down her front. I snickered.

"Good job," he said solemnly. "Camouflage."

"It's too far," I whined. "I can't throw."

"I can," Jemma announced. "I can do ten pushups."

"I can do thirty," offered our father.

"I can—" I racked my brain to think of something impressive. "I can—I can—I'm a vegetarian."

"No, you aren't," said Jemma.

"Are you?" murmured our father, looking around for witnesses. He held a finger to his lips. We cocked our arms back.

He gave the signal. We let loose.

The balloons soared across the yard in glorious arcs—or, his soared; ours mostly plopped—and one hit the side of the building, exploding in a thrilling punch of color that oozed down the side in bright fingers. We squealed with delight. He shushed us, though his own face was electrified with joy. We threw another and another; me and Jemma's pretty much landed in the grass and rolled harmlessly, but one exploded in an ecstatic purple burst on the sidewalk; another split against a rock and went rolling, flicking thin lines of paint up and around the grass. By this point we were suppressing shrieks, breathless with laughter; finally he grabbed both our hands and hauled us like a troupe of grinning witches the few blocks back to the car, flinging our joyful bodies into the back seat, and then driving—carefully; obeying the speed limit—to the home improvement store, where we got flashlights and battery-powered fans, him saving the receipt so we could get the money back later, and then home to hunker down for the hurricane. We got away with it—he'd been right; everyone had been busy preparing for the storm. When it did come, we huddled together, eating saltines with ketchup and store-brand cereal from the bag until the lights went out and Jemma and me were ushered to our shared bedroom. The rain slammed the windows, wracked the pines outside. The storm drains backed up. Outside, water spread across the black road, then crept across our yard, deepening, up the sidewalk, and stopped just before our front door, flooding the garage, ruining what we'd left on the ground, but not the paint marks. Down by the harbor, wrecked boats would sit for weeks. Three dozen houses would need gutting. Svetla erased towns down south; Dulac, in Louisiana, written off the map. But I didn't know any of this then. I just saw water, dripping from a gray bulge in the ceiling, wetting the living room carpet while I stood slack-jawed. For months, we'd have a blue tarp on our roof as our parents tried to navigate the bureaucracy of FEMA. The tarp was still there when the house went down.

"Dad," Jemma had said on our way home, "Aren't we going to be in trouble?"

"You only get in trouble if you get caught," he'd said, winking.

And this was the lesson which served me at Twin Bridge.

When Linda came back from her jog, it was my turn to stretch my legs. I went outside to the van, empty now as everyone else had woken up and gone in search of water and toilets. I popped the hood, climbed up towards the distributor, removed the air filter, did what I had to do with two quick twists, put the air filter back in place, twisted the nut tight and dropped the hood with a satisfying bang. Then I strolled back in and browsed schlock in the souvenir rack while I waited for my heart to stop pounding. I passed rooms labeled PATHOLOGY and LAUNDRY, past carts of soiled blue linen, people wearing dust-stained masks, exhausted, in hospital cots barely concealed behind papery curtains; two voices singing *happy birthday, dear*

Daniel; an aggravated man saying *I can't let you go, now, you've threatened to harm yourself;* rhythmic beeps. I turned a corner and ran into Frank.

"Good prices," he observed neutrally. He looked around at everywhere in the hallway but my face.

"You thinking of getting a procedure while we're here?"

"Actually," he said shyly, "I think I need a crown." He tapped his jaw. "The molar."

"Really?" We walked further along the hall, reached a curtain of plastic sheeting which I pushed aside. He followed me into dimmer halls: here they had not yet put up the drywall, and the bones of the building showed through. Old timber, insulation crumbled to dust. The tile had been pried up so we walked on baseboards, carefully, heat pricking at our necks again, keeping an eye out for holes in the flooring. "I've never had a cavity."

"Stay humble."

"Let me see," I asked, and turned around, craning to look into his mouth. He hesitated, then obliged, opening wide.

"Huh," he grunted, pointing at where. But I was looking at everything else: the ridged pink-white roof of his mouth, the stone-still muscle of his tongue, the dents and caps and chips and dark flecks on his teeth that told me his body was broken-in, that, like me, he hadn't been brought to dentists young, the evidence that he'd spent years and years moving through the machinery of life without me, terrible joys and letdowns and accidents, fights and candy bars, and the dense history of a life that didn't need me all written there made me so, so, unaccountably sad. I blinked. He pointed again and I spotted the cavity.

"Oh. Yeah." It was a tiny black dot on the left molar. "You'll probably need to remove the whole jaw."

"It only hurts sometimes," he said, pulling the finger out of his mouth. "How's my breath?"

"It smells—" I searched for the right word. "It smells familiar."

We walked further for a minute, along the un-built hall, dust motes floating around us.

"I think that was weird of me to say," I said.

He shook his head. "No. Yes. I'm not a good judge, I think." He looked at me somehow abruptly. We'd stopped at the end of the hall, where they'd installed new windows with shims, but hadn't yet packed in the insulation or done the molding, so bright paws of southern wind reached us. The smell of green was in it, hints we were out of the driest country. Way off across the land, the sun was sending its blades into the scrubby pines, and as it dimmed I saw the glow of natural gas flares, rising from somewhere I could not see. I inhaled deeply. "How are you?" he asked.

"I'm not doing very well," I answered, surprising myself.

He nodded.

"To be honest," I added, "I can't really think about it right now. We're going to start running out of the girls' medication tomorrow. And—other things are going on." I put my hands against my forehead and scrubbed them slowly back and forth. "Jesus. Jesus." All at once weird, hard tears started trying to force their way out of my face; my face was trying to cry, like an allergy. Frank briefly put a hand on my arm and my face almost won but then he took it away again.

"Hey, everybody seems okay. And we're out of Askewn. You're doing all right," he said kindly.

"Sure. Yes. We aren't in the morgue. We're cruising." I shook myself. "What about you?"

"Well. I kind of hitched a ride with all y'all from the teen prison at the last second out of a semi-collapsed town, and you haven't kicked me out of the van, yet. So. Yeah, same. Great."

I put my hand out toward the window and let the clean-ish air blow against my palm from the outside. "Yeah. This part's not bad."

"I'd only kill for some ice cream." He put his hand out too.

The sun dipped further and the world burnished itself. "It's a little beautiful," I admitted. Then we were in uncluttered evening time: thin clouds up against a dry and pinkening sky like strips of fruit pith, and through the unsealed window, night, breezing in sweet and slow. I hadn't felt evening like that for a long time: evenings with trees that hold shadows, where for a moment the underground river within you shifts and wakes. The terrible knowledge was at bay. We still both had our hands toward the window, parallel.

Frank said, "I had a lot of fun with you, that night. I get why you wouldn't call me back. But I'm kind of glad I ended up getting an excuse to see you again."

It had the tone of something he'd been practicing aloud. I was about to ask him what he meant by *I get why you wouldn't call me back*, but there was a noise behind us.

"Excuse me," said a young man in scrubs. ASK ABOUT OUR DISCOUNTS was printed across his chest. He was picking his way over the construction, rolling a cigarette. "I won't tell if you won't," he winked, and lit up as we turned back to join the group.

By the time we got back to the van, Linda, panting, was waiting for us.

"We've got a problem," she said.

"Don't say that to me," I flinched.

"The van won't start."

I nodded neutrally and climbed into the driver's seat as she continued speaking. "It cranks, but won't start. I was about to pull up to the pumps and refuel. Were we that low on gas?"

"No," I said.

"No," Arda confirmed.

I turned the key. The engine cranked, but the *ruh ruh ruh ruh* went nowhere. "Hmm."

"Combustion engines," Frank sighed from the ground. "Could be the battery?"

"Could be."

I popped the hood. Frank looked at the battery and jiggled the wires at the posts a bit. "Connection seems fine. No corrosion. But god knows how we're going to get a jump for an engine this size."

"Assuming it's the battery," I added.

"Right," Linda agreed, "But what else could it be? Jesus, so much for that rental company. Why don't you call?"

My heart flipped in my chest, but Frank saved the day—"No way they'll be able to help. The place was a zoo, and everyone's phones are dead out there by now."

Linda sighed and looked longingly across the lot, to the bank of electric chargers next to which were parked a row of the highly-reliable sedans of strangers.

I tried the key again. It cranked and cranked and didn't start. Linda, ignoring Frank's words, put the phone to her ear and tapped her foot while it rang. No answer. I tried the key again as the girls crowded around Frank around the engine compartment, until he detached himself from the mob and stuck his head in the door again.

"I don't think it's the battery. If it were dead, you shouldn't be able to crank it endlessly like this. It should be getting lower and lower on juice."

"Hm."

"I don't smell fuel, either. So I think it may be a fuel delivery problem."

"Weird."

"Maybe from the dust storm. Dust and grit could've gotten into the tank, could've gummed up the lines and fuel filter."

"Could be."

"Damn."

"Dang," I corrected him uselessly. The girls admired this exchange from a medium distance.

There was silence as everyone absorbed this information. Stuck at Dovetail with no wheels. Then I broke the news I'd been preparing in my heart for the last hour:

"I have an idea, and nobody is going to like it except Hanan."

When we told her, at first Hanan looked worried. Like she was going to be in trouble. But once she believed us she lit up like Christmas, like Santa mainlining speed.

"Not a trick?" she repeated, following us to the new van I'd picked out. "You're for real? Really for real?"

Our new van—rust-spotted, navy blue, with three rows of bench seats on both sides and a faded 1990s-looking decal of a skier on the back—was one of several in the parking lot that had clearly been sitting for a while. The tires were low, a back window was covered by a garbage bag, and on the windshield were two month-old orange notices from the highway patrol noting that it was considered abandoned and was due to be towed—much like a dozen other vehicles we'd passed, waiting around for the Department of Highway Safety, which, to say the very very least, had its hands full as its budget was slashed even as bridges further south warped and collapsed in successive heat waves.

"This a trick?" she asked again, but she was moving towards the driver's side door. It was locked, naturally; we requisitioned a coat hanger from a rack of t-shirts that read KEEP LOUISIANA SPICY and fished around until the latch popped. Hanan climbed inside, grinning, and with the help of Frank's screwdriver, popped off the panel underneath the steering wheel.

"I can't believe we're doing this," Arda muttered, chewing his thumb.

"No way this gets screwed up," I said under my breath. "Where's that lucky charm Maria had?"

We watched in silence while Hanan stripped two wires with her teeth. This was most definitely against the Twin Bridge code of conduct. I paced in circles as we waited. When I looked back, she was kissing wires together, and suddenly the van rattled to life. I let out the breath I'd been holding and uncrossed my fingers.

Hanan laughed with delight while I leaned in and checked the fuel gauge. "Quarter tank."

"One more thing," Hanan said. Without warning, she rammed the screwdriver into the ignition, hard. She fiddled with the screwdriver, twisting it back and forth, as she yanked on the frozen steering wheel. After a minute or so, she yelped in satisfaction as the steering wheel was suddenly loosened, and she made big cartoonish turns of the wheel, all the way left and all the way right, making low zoom-zoom noises before hopping out.

"Careful," she warned me, pointing at the wheel well. "I haven't duct taped the wires. They're live and exposed. Don't knee 'em if you wanna live." She put a hand around her own throat, stuck her tongue out to the side, and mimed a seizure.

"Don't tell anybody," Linda said.

"I am going to tell everybody," Hanan apologized.

"I'm going to gas up and fill the tires."

"Don't forget the duct tape!" Hanan reminded me as she skipped back to the rest of the group. I was touched by her concern. Though she didn't know that I'd twisted off the electrical harnesses of the fuel injectors on the Cask moving van, we were, for a moment, co-conspirators. I thought: Jemma would be proud. She would've pretended that she wasn't. But later that day, she would've found a reason to hug me. I gassed up the van, wiping the dust from the windshield with a filthy cloth I found in the back.

Chapter Eight

Linda drove some practice loops in the parking lot, and it seemed to drive okay—probably, we thought, the van was stolen, or else the driver had been on a delivery assignment and abandoned the gig. It would, at least, get us to a hotel for the night. Dark was setting in.

I checked on the girls with fresh piercings to make sure they were healing up right. Sabine's eyebrow hole was looking redder and angrier than I'd have liked. Hanan plucked at her shirt collar and diligently checked her own nipple while I averted my eyes, then gave me the thumbs up, beaming. I'd rung up antibiotics, saline and gauze at the truck stop / hospital before leaving, wincing at the cost, and with Carmen looking on, I cleaned Sabine's piercing site gently, as best I could as the van rocked, Sabine wincing while I dabbed it with cotton.

"Let's keep an eye on it," I said. She nodded and stopped herself from touching it.

I took the empty seat next to Frank and turned my phone on—I was nearly out of battery, but I wanted to check the news and see if there was anything I should worry about. Before I could do so Frank glanced at me, or rather, at my hands, and asked: "How could you do it?"

My stomach seized. "What?"

"Leave Askewn," he went on. "It doesn't seem to bother any of you."

I shrugged. "Maybe it'll bother me later." I gestured broadly around the van. "Anyway, we'd been planning on it. For months. What about you? You just up and left, no warning. Aren't you leaving behind your family? Friends?"

He shook his head a bit with his eyes closed, laughed a little self-deprecating snort. "Not in Texas." It wasn't bitter. He drew a speaking breath, but my phone rang, surprising me. I recognized the number as the office of TENDER KARE and picked up.

"Ms. Campbell?" came the voice of Bing Hooper's secretary.

"Yes."

"I've a message from Mr. Hooper."

"Okay. That's good. I've been trying to reach him; we had a delay and the medication is running—"

"He wanted me to relay the message that there's a problem with the clinical trial CRO report."

I went very still.

"There was a series of inconsistencies that require further examination."

"Could you please explain that more, please?"

I listened, keeping my mouth, my face, all very still. The secretary explained that the report had been flagged; further review was pending; be aware that the transfer to Atlanta may be suspended; more information incoming. I hung up while she was still talking.

"Everything okay?" Frank frowned.

"Okay." I closed my eyes and pretended to be tired. The next day we'd already be in Atlanta; good luck prying us out the doors, then, gremlins of the bureaucratic state. I refused to be intimidated. Linda, an aggressively defensive driver, slammed on the horn, derailing my thoughts, and Frank and I fell into loose, distracted conversation about the things we passed on the side of the road: Dog. Naked feet of man on porch. FROG LEGS 7.99/DOZ. White Chevy on blocks. He seemed a little bit nervous and kept making bad jokes, one after the other in rapid succession without waiting for me to laugh, which only made me laugh harder, despite myself: *What do you call a frog whose lost its legs? Unhoppy. What comes with frog legs? French flies.*

Somewhere past Monroe, we pulled over for the night at a place called the Sleep Tite Motel. It had a large, floodlit sign out front, with red block letters reading GENERATOR RUNNING! Linda parked the van carefully on one side of the lot. The girls were buzzing with the uneven energy that long-anticipated change will give. That, and we'd begun to titrate the BeZen out of necessity as the supply dwindled, and some of them had to have been feeling the effects of their first missed dose by then.

I went in and got rooms for everyone but Frank, who paid for his own, separately. I put the charges on the company card, which, hallelujah, was not yet frozen. The young guy behind the counter, a chicken-necked kid with a buzzcut and the kind of circles under his eyes earned by chugging energy drinks for days, snapped the key cards on the counter one by one. The lobby smell of stale coffee and the loudly buzzing fluorescent lights acted badly on my road hypnosis. I met back with the others in the parking lot, where they stood quasi-guarding the van door.

"Right," I sighed, looking around. "How are we going to do this?"

"We'll hand out the cards," Arda said, "Then patrol. And we keep checking on them until they are all settled down."

"It'll be chaos," Linda murmured, staring at the key cards in my hand with a somewhat haunted look. "They're all going to sneak out and visit one another. And who knows what else."

"Thanks God there isn't a pool," Arda said, drawing a hand slowly over his face.

"It's like summer camp," Carmen smiled. "It's so sweet!" Carmen bounced her eyebrows and tried to make eye contact, mouthing, *so sweeet.*

"I'm going to be honest for a second," Linda said. "I'm concerned about just what the fuck is going on."

"Let's concentrate on getting to Atlanta."

"Oh yeah? Are we going to have another girl commit a *criminal act?*" she shout-whispered, nostrils flaring.

"Your concerns are reasonable," Arda said quickly, "This is an emergency, however. We would not be safer, all of us sleeping outside at the gas station there."

"The van had obviously been there a while," I added, "And—"

"This is not okay with me," Linda said flatly. "I want that on record."

"Once," Carmen contributed, smiling, "When I was about 14, my friends and I took a car joyriding, but we accidentally drove it into a canal. We got out but it sank to the bottom. We left it there and nobody ever found out."

"*Thank* you, *Carmen*," I said, flinging my arms wide in exasperation and turning to Linda.

"We're tired," Arda interrupted. "We'll regroup in the morning and make a plan. A better plan."

"We're doing the best we can with the resources at our disposal," Carmen added, surprising us all. I agreed, Linda capitulated for the moment, and we opened the van's door to let the girls tumble out.

We distributed rooms and let the jackals roam. They squealed, they skipped. This was an adventure! Since there were an odd number of girls, I said I'd stay with Teresa, and Arda would have his room to himself. I brushed off visions of waking in a cold sweat to Teresa standing over me in the dark with the ice scooper, flexing her knuckles before she plunged it into my neck. Most likely there would be no more murder, but as the BeZen wore off, I wondered what, if anything, Teresa would start to remember.

The girls spread out into their various rooms. We walked from door to door, knocking and dipping our heads in. All the rooms were on the ground floor, in the same L-shaped corner of the motel that faced the van. Carmen walked beside me.

"They're just so *cute*," she was saying, "Excited to have a sleepover."

I felt she was misunderstanding the root situation. She ducked toward me and touched my arm.

"Oh my God," she said, in a conspiratorial voice, "Wouldn't it be great if they made a pillow fort?" She leaned back and pursed her lips, tilted her head, slapped my arm lightly with joy. I felt her fingers brush over my wrist, dry and soft. "That would be the best."

"Mmhm."

"I miss that, you know? Like, girl bonding. You know?"

I nodded vaguely. I was trying to pretend like I didn't know what she was talking about but I did know what she was talking about. I simply didn't have room inside to muster up enthusiasm. I told her good luck without meeting her eyes and went to check on the rooms in the opposite direction.

All the girls were watching television. Sabine and Amy, who kept poking her finger into the gap where her tooth once was, sat on the foot of the bed, faces slack, watching a program about hot surgeons. Maria and Zak were jumping from bed to bed, squealing, until I asked them to stop, settle down, go to sleep. Hanan and Lucia, whom I'd always liked because she laughed at my jokes, were cuddled in one bed together while Hanan rattled off a high-octane story about her first two boyfriends fighting at a Dairy Queen and Lucia let out the occasional low, appreciative chuckle. And then there was Teresa.

I stood outside the room for a moment. When I rubbed my hand along my bicep, a layer of grime curled and beaded under my fingertips. All at once I realized how physically exhausted I was.

I stepped into the room and the door swung shut heavily behind me. Teresa didn't look up. The overhead light was off, only the lamp and the bathroom light shining, so the TV did things with the shadows around her nose and eyes. Through the walls I could hear the thumping of girls wrestling and jumping. Voices on television hooted and moaned.

"How are you doing?" I asked cautiously, still standing by the door as she flipped through channels.

"You keep asking me that," she said, shooting me an annoyed sideways glance. The BeZen was fizzling out.

I walked forward quickly and snapped off the TV. "Teresa." I stood in front of her, arms at my sides, while she wailed *hey!* Then she leaned around me, pointing the remote, and turned it on again. I yanked the plug out of the wall so hard the TV shifted on the dresser, one corner poking into thin air.

"What the fuck," Teresa said, letting her jaw drop indignantly. A curtain of hair swung free of her shoulder.

"Talk to me," I said, my heart starting to work hard again. "What happened in the garage? Talk to me. Tell me what you were thinking."

"What?" she said, her brows furrowing even further. She drew her lips up to reveal her teeth. "What?" Then her face changed; she leaned back, wrapped her arms around herself and kicked her legs in the air a bit, still sitting on the scratchy carpet. "Oh my God, wait. You don't remember?" She barked a laugh. "You were wasted, weren't you? God, I knew it."

"Wait—"

"Wow. I mean, sometimes you come in stinking like liquor sweat or whatever, but fuck, I never thought you were getting lit at Twin Bridge." She laughed again and sprawled out against the end of one bed. "That's kinda badass."

"No!" I cried, frustrated. "That's obviously not what I mean."

"Oh my God," she said, speaking over me in a high, forced laugh, "This is hilarious."

"I don't drink," I lied wildly. Things were not going the way I'd foreseen.

"Ooo-kay," she said, rolling her eyes hard enough to move her head.

"Of course I remember what happened," I said in a rush, "Samuel, the garage, all of it." My voice had changed without my consent, becoming hoarse. "Teresa, you hurt Samuel."

Teresa looked skeptically into my face, but she must have seen that I was serious. Maybe she even saw that I was scared. She shook her head a few times in silence, looked at me, and found things the same, me still watching her, stern and frightened, and she shook her head again as though to clear the vision. She dropped the remote on the carpet and stood up.

"What, is this some weird therapy trick?" She took two steps back, toward the bathroom. She was wearing an old t-shirt screen-printed with a bank logo, blurred with dust and so overlarge that it reached down to her knees. Between that, and her round bloated face, and the gray circles under her eyes, she looked as though she was recovering from a long illness. "What are you even talking about? I didn't do anything. I didn't do anything!"

"Stop shouting," I whispered.

"I didn't do anything," she repeated, looking around wildly at the floor.

I'd been unconsciously moving towards her. Now I stopped. She looked truly mystified, shaken, not faking. "We were at the rental place," I started. I put my left hand out, fingers spread, patting the air with each sentence in a slow rhythm. "Are you being serious with me? You don't remember? A dust storm came. We went inside. It was crowded."

"Okay," Teresa nodded vaguely. She was wary, watching my face as I spoke.

"You're with me so far?"

Her hands were balled into fists by her hips, a pre-fighting posture. "Yeah. Okay. It's a little fuzzy. I was tired." Something slammed the other side of the wall and we both jumped. Laughter exploded from the next room.

"We were in the lobby," I continued. "You got the keys for the van."

"I got the keys?"

"You were helping—"

"Okay," she said, nodding rapidly, "Yeah, okay, I got the keys. They were on a hook behind the desk."

"We had to run through the dust to get to the garage."

"Yeah."

"Samuel was there."

She nodded.

"He and I had a kind of—an argument." She held herself still, breathing with her mouth open, watching me. "Teresa? Then?"

She blinked hard and just barely shook her head. "Then I went to the van and waited for you." She looked around the room, at the sick-mint walls, the nylon quilts, the black television screen. "I was really thirsty. You brought me water."

I looked at her carefully. But there was nothing struggling to hide behind her face. No secrets. Or if she was lying, she was remarkable. "Is that it?" She yanked on the hem of her shirt.

"We were in the office. Samuel grabbed my arm . . ."

Teresa shrugged and shook her head. "No. No, I don't know."

"I hit him first. On the head. Hard." I swallowed. "You were leaving the office, but then you came back. You picked up a bottle—"

"What!" she wailed. "What are you doing?"

"Look, just—"

She shut her eyes and shook her head hard. "You're scaring me," she said.

I dropped onto a corner of the bed. "Sorry," I said.

"Then what happened?"

I opened my mouth. Here it was. I cleared my throat and tried again. "You hit him on the head with the bottle."

She coughed a sort of disbelieving laugh. "I what?" she cried. Then she seemed to relax; she almost laughed for real. "No I didn't. That's not true. I'd remember that."

I opened my hands in my lap and looked into them. A guilty stone was sinking down within me, black and dense. We had done this—the adults in charge. Of course the warnings were there. The power of BeZen. The paper insert in Nurse Bell's office, with its laundry list of side effects. And now brutal music sunk in through my glittering carapace, a dreadful thrumming bass that whispered *find the locus of control*. There the dreaded locus was, in my lap. We'd medicated their needs away, and this was the result. It would be a while, I knew, before the stone in my gut hit bottom.

Yet when I spoke, the words came out smoothly. "You did. You did, but it's okay, I can see you don't remember. It's the BeZen. You hit him on the head with a bottle. It didn't break. He fell down. We got in the van and left. We left a note behind, apologizing. It's fine." I waved vaguely in the air. "I talked to him. On the phone, later. He understands. He won't press charges."

The motel had gone quiet.

"That can't be true," Teresa said. She sat down on the floor, looking at me with that unblinking habit she had.

I let her work on it for a minute in silence.

"Oh man," she said, mostly to herself. She touched her face with her hands, patting gently at her lips and nose. Then she glanced sharply at me, as though the thought had occurred to her that I was lying. But the look on my face must have convinced her because then she started to cry, to take big, heaving, shaky breaths, something I'd never seen Teresa do before. I put my arm around her and felt her relax into me after a minute, because she was just a kid.

"Sorry. It was just an accident. It's our fault," I was saying. We were having a normal moment, I guess. She cried while I said things like, "There, there. It's going to be okay." And, "It isn't your fault."

Eventually Teresa went still. I told her she should get some sleep. After she crawled under the covers, I brought her a cup of water and then sat on the edge of the bed for a few minutes, encouraging her to take box breaths, combing her hair back until her eyes drifted closed. This was the sort of kindness, the maternal intimacy you were not allowed at Twin Bridge. I stood up carefully when her breathing grew deep. When I was sure she was asleep I went into the bathroom and got into the shower, turned the water on cool and scrubbed my arms and neck and armpits until all the dust was gone, and the smell of me replaced by cloying motel soap. Then I stood under the water for a while, listening to the drone of the water against the tub's plastic. My shoulder was stinging. I examined it and found a long, thin scratch I hadn't noticed before. I thought about my sister. I pictured Jemma, remembered Jemma holding my face between her hands while our house burned down behind her, black shadows licking her shoulder while she said, fiercely, shaking, not yet crying, *We are in this together, do you hear me? I'm with you, Beat, it's you and me, forever*, and how desperately I'd loved her at that moment. Jemma, if I ever have a daughter, you will be an aunt. I shut off the water and dried myself with the rough motel towel. Back in the room Teresa was fast asleep, the covers pulled up to her eyes, snoring lightly.

I sat on the other bed, on top of the covers, with my back to the headboard, watching the television with the sound off but really watching her, taking the kind of animal comfort you take in seeing another living creature fed and safe and sleeping the sleep of the deeply exhausted. My own eyes were squinting with fatigue. I turned off the TV and left the room, shutting the door as softly as possible behind me and pocketing the keycard.

When I came out of the room, raw and subdued, I saw Linda, Carmen, and Frank, sitting on the curb a few doors down, each of them smoking a cigarette. I shuffled towards them, taking big gulps of the humid Louisiana air.

Carmen turned around and waved at me. Linda glanced and went back to smoking, which she did with a sort of grim purpose, switching the cigarette from one hand to another awkwardly. Frank kept his head turned and watched me come up. His hair was wet from showering and he didn't say anything.

"Friends share," I said, squatting on the curb next to Carmen. I made a punching motion with my fingers and Frank reached across her lap, shaking a smoke from the pack.

"This is my first cigarette in two years," he noted.

"I have one every once in a long while," I said. "For special occasions."

"This week," Linda said, keeping her eyes on the pavement, "Has been one long special occasion, that's for sure." What's awful is that the cigarette was delicious. The best I'd had in years.

We all sat for a while and looked out at the big night. Past the motel parking lot there was the one road, and then some marshy fields and the sky. The sighing of the occasional car, the size of the night, the ticking motel lights; they all added up to a giant loneliness, one so enormous and cool I could almost see it, just past the horizon, forty-feet tall and wading slowly through the scabgrass, all gunmetal and blue. But that was off in the distance. For the moment we sat in a row.

"I've never been to Georgia before," Carmen offered. We nodded silently.

Linda tapped ash into a Styrofoam cup between her feet. "We're in Louisiana, right?"

"Yes," I confirmed. "We're maybe halfway to Atlanta. Six or seven hours tomorrow."

"Where you from?" Frank asked, turning his whole torso towards Carmen.

"Galveston," she said, "Before it flooded." She stubbed out the cigarette on the sidewalk, half-smoked, twisting it thoughtfully into the concrete. As she did, she pulled up her right pant leg, pointing to the tattoo on her ankle. I recognized the scrawled X, dotted with numbers, that the National Guard left on evacuated houses after floods.

Frank nodded as we all waited to see if we should ask more about the Galveston flood. Frank's neck where it went beneath his shirt was damp. Carmen asked Frank where he was from.

"From Nebraska," he said, clearing his throat. "Nebraska City. Straight north of Askewn, basically." He flicked his own stub into the parking lot, where it landed at the edge of a circle cast by parking lot lights. He leaned back on his hands. "So no one is from Askewn."

"I am," said Linda. She kept her same still posture, rolling the butt between her thumb and fingers. Then she blinked hard, as though released from hypnosis. "I've lived in Askewn all my life. My parents are from there, too."

I watched Frank's hands as he gripped his knees. I thought he'd ask her about her parents, but instead he stood up and said, "Look, could anyone else use a beer?"

"God, yes," said Carmen.

"Because I got some while you all were doing the bed-time routine."

Carmen turned to me. "I like him," she said, which made me blush.

"Arda is sleeping—"

"I got a separate room," Frank reminded me.

"We should stay up for a while, anyhow," Linda reasoned, "We ought to keep checking for the next hour or two to make sure everyone sleeps." We were already walking in a line to the end of the L-shaped motel wing where our rooms were.

Frank was in 102, where he'd already opened his suitcase and spread things around. He'd stripped the red-patterned quilt from one bed and bunched it up in a heap against the wall. The other was still made up. On the table between them, an ancient digital clock blinked the wrong time.

Linda and Carmen sat on the beds, facing one another. I sat down next to Carmen. Frank opened the tiny fridge and pulled out a twelve pack and a mostly-empty bottle of corn liquor. I laughed out loud.

"It was in my trunk," he said bashfully.

He dragged a chair from the corner and sat by the foot of the opposite bed.

"I'll try some of that," I said, pointing to the bottle, which had a green label that said Heaven Hill.

"Me, too," said Carmen.

We found a couple dusty Styrofoam cups by the sink. I added tap water to my Heaven Hill and Carmen poured in cola that she'd gotten earlier from a vending machine. Frank and Linda opened the corn beers. I took a deep breath. Frank was looking at the art over the beds, first one painting, then the other. Linda stared mutely at the carpet, which looked plastic and flammable. She still seemed angry about the stolen van. We commented on the art and our various levels of exhaustion, everyone zonked, irradiated by sunshine and highway. The whiskey was also the best whiskey I'd ever had. I tried not to gulp it.

"I saw this in a dream," Carmen began. She cleared her throat and rolled her shoulders. "Six days ago." I tried to make eye contact with someone, panicked that we were about to be subjected to hearing someone's dream. "I dreamt that the four of us were on an airplane. Out the windows the sky was all red-pink, and the land was pink. The airplane was big and empty. And silent. The chairs were big and empty. We were the only people on the plane. I walked to the back of the aisle and the light was weird. And then in the closet back there was a man, or—a deflated man, like his skin, naked, his eyes empty kind of." Carmen coughed into her hand. We were all spellbound by her weird, droning non-story.

"Then I turned around. I couldn't hear my footsteps anymore. I went up towards the cockpit. I was walking up the aisle and the empty guy was behind me. I opened the door to the cockpit and there was no one there. There weren't even—what's it called—the controls, the instrument panel. Just an armchair, a big empty armchair facing the window, framed by curtains, and down there out the windows all this land, red-colored, going on and on and on. But I felt good on the airplane. The empty skin guy was behind me, but I sat down in the armchair. It was so quiet. It was peaceful." She had gradually pointed her speech towards me. She smiled and shook her head. I thought there was going to be more to the story, but she stopped and looked up where Frank was still looking, at the paintings on the wall. "Pretty crazy."

"I'm sorry," Linda said, chuckling nervously, "But what the fuck?"

I was unable to stop myself from bursting into laughter. I don't think I'd ever heard Linda cuss before. Frank laughed at both of us, and then all four of us were laughing, laughing the way a dog shakes itself out after a fight, clutching our bellies laughing like we'd been poisoned, laughing until we couldn't speak, flight-or-fight-or-laughter.

When we stopped, I felt better; I was watching Frank; it's such a pleasure to simply look at another person. The cords in his neck above his black t-shirt with the holes in the collar.

"I never thought I'd leave Askewn," Linda said, still catching her breath.

"What, didn't you ever want to?" I asked, taking a gulp of Heaven Hill.

She shook her head. She was holding the beer in both hands but hadn't taken a sip yet.

"It's good to travel," I offered uselessly.

"Not everybody wants that," said Carmen.

"I moved around a lot when I was a kid," said Frank. "I lived at my dad's house, then my mom's, then my dad's again, then my grandparents. So when I got older, I didn't want to travel at all. I wanted to stay in one place," he said, poking his knee to punctuate the words, "one place, with a family, friends, the works."

"I wanted kids," smiled Carmen, "I thought I'd be married by now."

"I was married, once," Linda said.

"What?" I shook my head. "I never knew that."

"Fresh out of high school. Marriage only lasted a year. After we divorced, I moved in with my mother." She took a sip of beer at last. "She was a wonderful girl. But we were just kids. Too young. We didn't know how to argue. We only knew how to fight."

I looked at Linda and tried to imagine her, 19, in love, fighting.

"I knew it," said Carmen.

We laughed. "You know everything," Linda said, softening.

"What about me," said Frank playfully. "What do you know about me?" Against my will, I felt, what—a little flare of jealousy?

Carmen squinted at him, deepening the sun-sharp wrinkles around her eyes. "You're straight," she began.

"Nobody's perfect."

". . . and you fall in love with every girl you date," she continued. I took a big gulp and finished my cup of Heaven Hill. "You don't talk to your mom, but you still call your father sometimes. You've got a sibling who's in trouble. Prison, maybe. You like dogs. Used to think you wanted to be a teacher. No," she corrected herself, "A drummer."

Frank's face, meanwhile, had gone very still. Now he was looking hard at the plastic phone on the stand between the beds.

"All you really want is to move somewhere where you can go swimming," she concluded, "and you've been learning to play Parcheesi, and you've got an awful sweet tooth, and you like only the worst, dustiest museums."

We all looked at Frank.

"Everybody likes dogs," he said neutrally.

"Was she right?" Linda asked. "About the rest?"

"That was good," he admitted. "Jesus. Okay. Not bad."

"Every girl you date?" repeated Linda. She rolled her eyes. "Ugh."

"Carmen!" I cried. "You're a goddamned psychic!"

"It's true," she said humbly.

"I'm a shitty swimmer," Frank added.

"Do Linda next!"

"Do not, witch," Linda said sharply. But she was smiling.

"C'mon," I begged.

"Don't y'all know each other well already?" asked Frank, stretching out his legs between us.

"Guess new things," I said, nudging Carmen with my shoulder.

"You've eaten a scorpion . . ."

"Wrong!" Linda barked.

". . . and you liked it."

"I would never eat an endangered animal," Linda said, shaking her head.

"Only ticks." I got up to refill my cup.

"Let me try," Frank said. He pointed at me, where I stood by the cupboard with the cup in my hand. He held one claw-shaped hand to his temple like he was receiving a message from the spiritual realm. "I will now share ten facts about you. Right, okay, you're a vegetarian—"

I grimaced.

"—who makes exceptions for human flesh."

"Yes."

He continued to tick off facts, counting them out on his hands without pausing: "You don't clean your ears because you're afraid you'll puncture your eardrum; you do not know what the Iditarod was; you're addicted to manifestos of every kind, Marxist, ISIS, whatever; your best friend is your sister; your favorite smell is the smell of gasoline; you haven't touched a piece of fruit in four years—"

"I just touched a fruit," I lied, shaking my head. "I just ate an entire grapefruit."

"That's only seven," Linda said.

"That isn't really about her, though, is it?" Carmen said, picking at her lip thoughtfully. "That's just a list of facts."

"Like the kids make," Linda said. The kids love to describe themselves with lists. Likes and dislikes. Colors. Favorite seasons. Things which were never interests but *obsessions*. We talked for a bit about this habit of the kids, how they liked to be categorized and particular.

Frank said that, really, if you wanted to know someone, you had to ask them about choices, about right and wrong. Carmen said you could find it out by asking when someone was last truly happy. We all were quiet for a second, trying to remember our own last moments of perfect happiness, but it was hard since happiness tends to go away when you pay too much attention to it. Then for a while we took turns relaying Twin Bridge stories with the thinly-hidden intention of shocking Frank, each in turn recalling something stranger, remembering girls long-gone, who'd moved out of Twin Bridge and on to foster homes or independent living, we didn't know, weren't allowed to know; what they left behind was stories of deliberate food poisoning, stick-and-poke bathroom tats, bogus funerals and the one time Lila had registered as a mail-order bride on the sly using a burner phone she kept under her mattress: just one more doomed attempt at getting out.

"Incredible," Frank said, somewhere on the border of disturbed and amused.

There was a knock on the door that made us all jump, then scramble to hide the cups and bottles. Linda looked around the room and opened the door. But it wasn't a girl, it was the motel clerk.

"Somebody left this at the front desk," he said, and held up a Pink Card—Frank's. Frank jumped up and snagged it, though not before I learned his last name, which I'd never seen before: Caston.

"Not used to having it," he said, stuffing it into his wallet.

The clerk left. Linda suggested it was time to check on the girls, holding herself straight, speaking carefully enough that she must have been tipsy already.

We split into two and two. Carmen and Linda took one arm of the L, and Frank and I walked the other. We walked slowly, listening at the doors and also checking the corners where ice machines and vending machines glowed, looking for signs of rabble-rousing. I slid my hands in my pockets as his dangled loose at his sides. The sidewalk was narrow and we kept our voices low as we spoke.

"I can't believe this is your job," he said.

"What, drunken cross-country babysitter?"

"Bus driver," he said, glancing into my face. "Motel travel agent. Nurse of fledgling vehicle thieves."

"I think we're well past fledgling."

"Sweet-talker of cops."

"Nothing sweet about any of that," I scowled.

"Yeah. Right." We took a moment for disgusted reflection.

"What about your job," I asked. "Your jobs. Your million different jobs."

He waved his hand in the air dismissively. Frank had a kind of loose jointedness that, for whatever reason, made me trust him, like he never thought about how he might appear to others. "My job's no job," he said, "I was only at Cask for, like, six months. And now I guess I'm not. I've got enough trade skills. I'm not worried. I'll be something else in Georgia." He caught himself. "Still going to get the rest of that furniture, though."

"Sure. Right."

We paused in front of a room where low voices emerged. It was the sound of TV, and the curtained windows were dark, flashing blue as a commercial came on. "Fell asleep with the TV on, probably," I said. We moved on. "You're going to stay in Atlanta?"

He shrugged. Then added, "My brother's there."

"The one in prison?" I joked.

But he nodded, slowly. "He was, before."

"Oh, shit. Sorry—"

He waved the apology off. He kept turning to look at me as he spoke, and my eyes fell again on the C-shaped line in his cheek formed by his smile. "It's fine, it's fine. He got out years ago now. It was short. Relatively. Married now. Got a kid."

"That's good." We stopped at another door and leaned our ears towards it, listening. I pressed my shoulder against the door and looked up at him, inches away. For a moment I felt his breath. No noise in the room. We moved away and kept walking.

"What about you," he went on. "You've got a sister, right? I think you told me that."

"Yes. One."

"She in Askewn? I guess not."

"No."

He didn't press the subject and I appreciated that.

"We used to live in North Carolina," I offered, since he'd let it alone.

"I remember that. How'd you get out here?" I shrugged, too tired to explain. "You keep it kind of mysterious, don't you?" he said, which surprised me, and then made me sad. He wanted to flatter me maybe, or he felt resentful a bit, saying I was unreachable. But I wasn't unreachable. Or didn't want to be.

"No," I said firmly, "I'm transparent."

He laughed in an embarrassed way. We stopped at the end of the walkway. All during our stroll we'd seen the soft glow on the sidewalk falling from the lit window, and now we heard the voices of girls behind the door.

"Here's the party," I said. I knocked hard, three times.

Giggles rose to a high sharp point, followed by shushing, then cut off. *Sh, shut up, shut up. Shut up!,* they hissed.

I tightened up my face.

Maria slowly opened the door. "Hi," she said bashfully. Behind her, in pajamas, half a dozen girls.

"Bedtime," I said, in a nearly bored-sounding monotone. "Everyone back to their own rooms. Let's go, let's go, same rules here as back in Twin Bridge. Bed time."

Very slowly, grumbling, the girls gathered up sweatshirts and pillows and sandals and trundled out of the room one by one. Frank waited off the end of the sidewalk as I escorted them. "Sleep," I pressed them, "sleep." In a flash, I had a jarring out-of-body moment—wasn't this normal, wasn't this all impossibly normal when just a few hours ago the seizing white face of—

Quickly, trying to drown all that out, I paced in circles round the departing girls, brushing past Frank, catching the smell of smoke in his clothes. Once they'd all filed out, Frank and I headed back to his corner room. Linda and Carmen must have finished already because no one else was around. I wanted to linger out there, and when he offered another cigarette I took it. We smoked standing, leaning against the motel's cinderblock wall, not talking. This was it, I thought, the desire right before the object of desire. The parking lot smelled like gasoline and something else, the smell of soft, rotting matter, the slow organic turning of whatever was wet in the wet warm air. A weather for deliciousness, stolen luxury. Hotwire weather for sure. He finished smoking first and waited for me, not touching, though he could have. I followed him back into the room for a last drink.

"Some fun coworkers," Frank said. I was sitting on the foot of the bed again, and he was back in the chair.

"I like them," I said, and meant it. "There's a lot of turnover at Twin Bridge, a lot of duds. I'm glad they ended up forced to come with."

"Unlike me?" he grinned lopsidedly. "Maybe less happy I invited myself?"

"No, it's nice."

"Because I brought beer."

"No," I shook my head, "Because you brought whiskey." I turned so I was facing him, our knees a few inches apart.

"I'll be honest. I don't think anyone in that building gets paid enough."

I shrugged. "Yes, but they were willing to hire me." His statement irked me—underneath it was the myth of the soft-minded do-gooder, the belief that any work of nurturing means the worker is uninterested in self-preservation or profit. Little did he know. I yearned for money, slobbered at the concept. For now I leaned my elbows onto my knees. "I think it's good for me," I blabbered, "To see how emotionally overwrought and hyped-up the kids get. Like, I used to feel bad that I didn't express myself strongly and clearly. I thought I was doing something wrong. But then I see the kids, and it's like, 'Oh, having more emotions definitely isn't *better*.' But I guess that's obvious." I rubbed my forehead. Maybe I was drunk? "I mean, I have feelings."

"Sure."

"But there's some other version of me, I mean the world, I mean this world, where I spit out everything I feel instantly. Terrible."

"Messy."

"A mess!"

"Better to shove it all down deep and then, thirty years later, get cancer."

I laughed and he leaned forward, pleased. "What about you. You get in trouble as a kid?" I asked him.

He scanned the ceiling for a moment. "My brother was always in trouble, so I was the straight man." He briefly sketched out his brother's misadventures, which ended with methamphetamines snorted in a car which he then immediately drove into the Missouri River. "Anyone else would have died," he said, "But Andy had the luck of an idiot. Climbed out the back windshield. Sprained his wrist is all."

"The luck of an idiot," I repeated softly.

Frank reached out and took my wrist then, lightly, circling his thumb and pointer finger around the joint of my free hand. I watched and let him lift my arm lightly; the pads of his fingers were soft but the rest, the pillow between each knuckle, was rough, just enough that I could feel the slight and thrilling friction against the tender skin at the base of my palm as a thin electric charge shot through me, from stomach to thigh. I kept the rest of my body very still; he lifted my wrist a few inches, like he was idly curious; then in a slow, fluid movement he gently turned my hand over so that it was resting, palm-up, on top of his own. No goblins, I noticed; no shaking.

"So Carmen reads palms?" he asked.

"Yes," I murmured, still watching our own hands.

"What did she say about yours?"

I tried to cast back in my memory—on a recent morning after we'd both been up all night on basement duty, she'd held my hands in much the same way, drawing her fingertips lightly across the lines. Delirious with sleeplessness it had given me a kind of shivering, animal pleasure, awoken a craving that was less about sex and much more about contact, just as Frank was doing now. I couldn't remember what she'd said.

"She said I'd live a long and healthy life," I lied, "With lots of travel."

He nodded. The coarse denim of his pants, the brass button of his fly, the sparse black hair on his arm, the occasional white nicks and scars there, the tendon moving in his forearm as he slowly ran his thumb over the knuckle of my pointer finger; then his shoulder beneath the t-shirt, his collarbone and the shadow beneath, his jaw, his lips, which looked somehow crushed, not quite symmetrical, though I kept myself from looking too closely there.

"What about you," I asked, making myself look into his eyes now. "What do you know about your future?"

I was smiling a little but he wasn't; his lips were parted and his face was open and even surprised, as though already something had happened which was surprising. His hand tightened slightly on mine because he was nervous, which made me like him so I kissed him. Once, long, still, his mouth soft, and behind that the hard pressure of tooth; then he slid his hand around the back of my neck and up my scalp into my hair and I gasped, just a little, and he caught my act of breathlessness as he kissed me, with more urgency, more hunger. I was the less patient one. I twisted his shirt collar, pulled myself onto his lap and sat astride him in the chair, clothes too in the way to feel much of each other's bodies until he reached both his hands all the way up the back of my shirt and drew them down so his nails scratched lightly from shoulder down to the base of my back, sending a hot spring up the length of my spine, so that without meaning to I very quietly moaned into his mouth.

The drinks had made me brave enough to act and to touch him. But they had also put a kind of coat between myself and sensation, so that I couldn't be enveloped by it and couldn't turn off my awareness, yet, couldn't stop performing at least a little. He pressed my shoulder down so I sank deeper against him, pressed more firmly against his lap until he stood up, and with my legs around him walked the few feet to lay me down on the bed.

On my back, on the quilt, I felt too aware of myself. While I unbuttoned my fly, he tugged at my cuffs. And things could have gone anywhere then, they could have moved blindly ahead, my movements dumb and rote and automatic, following the same blank usual tracks, but instead, suddenly, he flipped me over and kissed the back of my neck. He slowed down, he slowed way down. He slid my arms up over my head and breathed on the back of my neck, the delicate hairs at the base there. Nibbled slightly at the curve that turned to shoulder. He pushed my shirt up and then pulled my shirt off, and I wasn't wearing a bra, so I was beneath him in only my underwear, which I was vaguely aware was dingy and ill-fitting, but he drew his hands lightly over my back, my ribs, the sides of my breasts, my neck, my ears, reading all my lines, the future in his palm all over me, sliding his arm under my belly and pulling my hips back towards him until my nerves burned and my head turned off and I wanted, I wanted, I wanted.

Later we talked again. Do you believe in conspiracy theories? The moon: that isn't real. The common cold was engineered by the CIA. Fluoride in the water doesn't allow for mind control, but it does make us emotionally brittle. None of it was serious, and the more he said, the stranger he became, and I liked him more. He ran one hand idly over my side, my chest, my hips, as we talked. It felt nice to the point of being bizarre; I tried not to squirm beneath it. He asked me if this was my first disaster, this blackout; I said yes, up close I'd seen no floods, no tornadoes; other than a housefire and one minor hurricane my life had been sheltered and cotton-soft. Almost everyone had lived through one or two of the big ones at this point, and we all politely declined to ask one another about it, since the stories were exhausting to tell.

"You're lucky, huh?" He closed one eye, still pressed into the pillow, and looked at me with the other through an L he made with his hand. "Yeah, you look lucky."

"From day one. Lucky baby. Lucky woman. Someday I hope to be a lucky corpse."

"What happens to lucky corpses?"

I gestured sleepily. "Shot into space. Out of a big cannon."

"Living the dream," he sighed. "Escaping from Earth."

"Right. My parents had strange views on luck. And Earth. They were kind of—religious? You know—" I yawned. "When I started working at Twin Bridge, I used to do this thing," I mused, using the phrase *used to* in its loosest sense, "Where I'd, like, send cockroaches in an envelope to state legislators. Or, once, I looked up who the richest man in Texas is and tried to put down spike strips all around his driveway. But you can't buy those online. And there were cameras everywhere."

"You never got into trouble?"

"The postal system's such a mess, nothing probably reached anybody."

"Right. So how come?"

"I don't know. I felt mad. Don't you get mad?"

"Sure," he said. But I could hear it in his voice that he wasn't angry in the same way—not the anger I had, Carmen had, Teresa had; the anger that I suspected was inescapable, inherited, that slept in our bodies. Amy's goddess, Lamia, devoured children. Frank looked at me and ran his eyes all over my face, so that I blinked and turned into the pillow.

"I like you," he said.

"Ah," I said nervously.

"I'd like you most if you mailed cockroaches to the governor."

"The man's a fan of vermin," I smiled into the pillow, drifting off.

"What housefire?" he asked me dreamily. I floated back up. "Didn't you say there was a housefire?"

"My house burned down," I said, "when I was about seventeen."

"Oh. I'm so sorry," he said, making a move to get back up on his elbow. I pushed him back down.

"It wasn't so bad," I whispered. "Not really a disaster."

"No disasters," he repeated softly.

"No disasters," I agreed, and I guess we must have fallen asleep like that, in the midst of saying we had always been okay.

Chapter Nine

The next morning, in the van, the good-natured squabbling of the girls had taken on an audibly darker character. Headaches abounded; it was as though the whole vehicle shared one dark migraine. I sat at the wheel.

We moved deeper into Louisiana. Petrochemical plants spat fumes by the highway; fat, shiny lakes sprawled out on either side, chemical runoff ponds full of material with names more suited to stars: cadmium, selenium, dry ash. Pumps nodded against a hot white sky. We drove for hours, traffic thickening, trapped at a crawl on tarmac over ghost cypress swamps, where saltwater had rushed into marshes and left white, skeletal trunks sticking crazily out of the flats, crisped. Sitting in a stand-still jam, heat shivering in every direction, no one spoke; the girls leaned separately against windows or folded over with their heads on their knees, letting slip the occasional groan. Van crawling, no wind, sun irradiating the metal roof, it grew smotheringly warm. The AC wasn't as good as the other van's and couldn't keep pace; it threatened to send me sleeping. Cars honked uselessly. A hand-lettered cardboard sign attached to a mile marker announced gas was for sale at the next exit, in 1-liter and 5-liter jugs. After just an hour, witnessing me droop, Linda volunteered to drive.

"I thought you didn't want anyone unlicensed driving," I teased, though I was glad she'd offered.

She shrugged her shoulders, bare and freckled and knotted with muscle. "What's the point? There's no point. I'm as qualified or unqualified as anyone." The effects of the night before—drinking, sharing—shone on everyone's faces but Arda's, with different symptoms. Linda's hangover seemed to take the form of flattened affect. She had spoken relatively little all day, herding the girls into the van in silence, gingerly pinching a neon-green can of energy drink. Carmen was visibly anxious; she kept making eye contact with me and smiling, briefly, and once I'd settled into a seat next to her, she nervously asked, *was I . . . embarrassing last night?* I assured her she hadn't been, or else we were all embarrassing, to which she gave a curt nod.

Frank and I didn't get a chance to talk. Arda had sat down next to him and was peppering him with questions about the Midwest, whether it had cowboys, a series of questions that not-so-thinly disguised his feelings on the history of American genocidal tendencies. But I was keenly aware of his presence all the time. I glanced his way trying not to be conspicuous. Sometimes I felt him look at me. Just before we'd left, I'd been in the van alone, scanning the seats and picking up trash, when he stepped on.

"How'd you sleep?" he asked. He walked down the aisle towards me slow and easy, pushing himself off the tops of the vinyl bench seats.

"Wonderfully," I answered, honest. Once I'd left him, after a quick and dizzying doze thin enough to let in the soft distant rumble of heat lightning, I'd slipped silently back into my room without waking Teresa, collapsed into my own untouched motel bed, and slept a ravenous sleep. "You?"

Frank shook his head. "I woke up before dawn, by accident." As I'd walked forward, he moved slowly backwards, letting me get closer. We looked into one another's faces, pleased, and didn't touch as the van door opened and the girls began to file on.

Now I stretched out in the seat next to Carmen with my eyes closed, lulled by the warmth and the drone of traffic. In bursts I allowed myself the dreamy pleasure of remembering the night, then had to fling the thought away because I was at work in a van during an actual emergency.

The radio gave us updates: people had leapt at the opportunity for Pink Cards. Border patrols were overwhelmed. Traffic frozen. Heat wave intensifying, thousands dead in New Mexico. Evacuees swarming the border; they really used the word *swarming*. It took me a minute to realize that they meant us—*we* were the evacuees, we were going to swarm the border, we were on our way to swarm it right now.

The commercials still sounded jubilant: lung purification treatments so you can breathe easy! Investments. Lottery tickets. Has your home become uninhabitable due to floods, dust, mold? We'll buy anything, the worst homes, fair prices. Mattresses. Cheeseburgers and window AC units. Homeowner's insurance at low, low, low rates. Shoring services will lift your house for free, there's a government program, call today to apply! Two more girls had been arrested in Corpus Christi for strangling a man with an extension cord: *can you imagine*, said the DJ, and shot off a whackadoodle laugh. Just as I started to nod off, Arda, wide awake across the aisle, tapped me on the shoulder.

I sat up blinking to see him hunched toward me, his sun-wrinkled face lowered between his shoulder blades in a posture of conspiracy.

"What?" I rubbed the sting of sweat from my eye.

He jerked his thumb towards the back of the bus. "The girls," he said in a low voice, "They're going into withdrawal."

"I know," I said, but straightened up and looked behind me, at the rows of nodding heads. Some were awake—those faces were dour and stared out the windows, panting slightly, or had their faces in their hands like they were trying to concentrate on not feeling sick. "What can we do?"

He shook his head, put his chin in his hand. The threat of disorder hung thin in the air around me, like dust after a structural collapse. I proposed a bad idea, hoping it would jog his own imagination. "We'll stop at a pharmacy and load up on painkillers and anti-nausea meds. That'll help with the headaches and such. Just until we get to Atlanta and can get more BeZen."

He nodded slowly, knotting his wooly eyebrows. "If we get to Atlanta by tonight, there will be no problem."

"We should be able to do that," I said, and my stomach dropped into a queasy pit as I remembered the TENDER KARE phone call from yesterday. We would simply have to get there before they could stop us.

Easier said than done. The motel where we'd spent the night was no more than 70 miles from the Louisiana-Mississippi border. But the traffic grew thicker and thicker. Soon there was the near-constant staccato of honking, sometimes near, sometimes far, irritating since it seemed pointless; nobody was getting anywhere. The air conditioning chugged against the heat but it was still growing warmer. I fanned my shirt against my damp chest. Outside, SUVs and early-era hybrid sedans were loaded with bicycles and pet cages. I began to notice some cars cross the median, heading back the way we'd come—more and more, in fact.

"What's that about," Carmen said quietly, leaning across me to tap the glass.

We watched the traffic in the opposing lane as we rolled. Then Carmen cursed. She pointed: up ahead, a roadside sign in big orange letters warned us that the interstate, where it crossed the Mississippi River, was temporarily closed.

"Are you shitting me?" growled Linda, articulating the growl inside us all.

We scanned the radio. We tried AM. Everyone on the AM frequency laughed louder and somehow more obnoxiously. We found news: there was a pause on crossings, they said, due to the border control being overwhelmed. Even those with legitimate Pink Cards would have to fill out an application to cross.

Leaning across the aisles, we staff attempted a hasty discussion of strategy, but with ¾ of our language centers obliterated by hangover the choosing largely fell to Arda, who, with confidence, decided we had to turn around and take a detour. Immediately, already, the chances of Atlanta-bynightfall were dropping. We turned south, headed for the next-nearest crossing, almost two hours out of our way down in Natchez and not handy to any interstate. And we hoped that it'd be emptier, or at least less packed, due to its closeness to the Louisiana coast.

After Jemma left that day, stricken at the sight of our parents' extreme devotion to Double Truthism, I got into a habit of standing at the doorside window, chewing (in an icky habit) absently on the corner of the red sheer curtain, until our parents took that away, too.

I was 15, 16, and tired all the time, as though all my energy had lately been spent on the enormous concentration it required to ignore my parents' deteriorating stability. Since the argument that night, when Jemma had come to dinner, she had barely ever come back to the house. She and I hardly talked. When we did, she talked in a kind of code that felt designed to shut me out, making jokes I didn't understand and at which she laughed alone, meanly; she referred only to people I didn't know, her co-workers, her friends, her boyfriend Ugly Dan, her other boyfriend Other Steven. I sensed vaguely that my continued presence in the house amounted, to Jemma, to a form of treachery, which made me feel both guilty and furious for reasons I couldn't untangle yet.

Life, meanwhile, in our house on Moseley had gotten murkier. Dad was increasingly strange. Mom was increasingly frantic. It wasn't helped by the cession of the Louisiana coast, an event that made the older generation behave weird to the extreme, that seemed to prompt an epidemic of unhinged-ness among US adults, as they could no longer deny that things were changing, drastically and irrevocably. Yet everyone seemed surprised.

"It's not a surprise," my civics teacher was saying. "It's predictable." It was September, it was hot, it was still hurricane season and Lake Charles had, recently, gotten shredded to ribbons by a Cat 5—a storm that had eventually reached us in coastal Carolina, where even after that distance it took our power out for four days, collapsed an abandoned bar on the own's outskirts, and killed eight Filipino itinerant workers who'd tried to ride it out on a 40' trawler. "They've been talking about it for years."

It was a special day, a television news day, which happened once or twice a semester when major world events happened: an election, a new war, an old war we'd revived. On this day we settled on hard plastic seats and watched a series of maps of the Gulf Coast flit across the screen.

". . . in what could herald a major policy shift for this administration," the newscaster was saying. Quick succession, then: submerged buildings; shrimping boat; bitter fisherman; weeping woman on a bridge; roofs two feet above the waterline; white-gray haze of hurricane rain on street.

Mr. Sinclair, with his square glasses and perpetually damp pink forehead, began to explain. The United States of America would no longer include the sections of Louisiana outside the federal levee protection system. The sacrificed area only about 400 square miles of actual land, at this point; the rest had dissolved into the sea like wet cake, eroded by thousands of miles of oil pipeline canals, and hurricanes, and rising water. This ex-Louisiana coastland had been purchased jointly by a real estate / tourism development company and an oil and gas conglomerate, who would allow the residents of the now-sovereign area to continue living there tax-free (Mr. Sinclair snorted) as long as they signed a liability clause, while the companies built liquid natural gas terminals the size of space stations and sold luxury hunting trip packages to Montana tycoons; a tempting offer, if you ask me, Mr. Sinclair went on; land and no taxes? This president, etcetera, and so on. It meant little to me at the time. I'd never heard of the towns down there, at America's ragged hem, towns named after extinct pirates and the French: Jean Lafitte, Grand Caillou, Dulac.

And though I didn't pay attention to all that, it was the signs of my own parents' strangeness I could no longer ignore. It was the constant, non-stop disaster fixation, the tally of hurricane dead they kept near the fridge; it was entering the living room one afternoon to find the couch and armchairs gone, removed without explanation. The accumulation of odds and ends piled on one side of the hallway, forcing me to pick my way carefully through old rakes and discarded plastic tupperware and snapped dog leashes, and then their disappearance as well; it was the bland empty rooms of the house. And their singing, sometimes, at night, both their voices united in an eerie charmless tune which woke me up with a hammering heart, electrified the hairs on the back of my neck, always in the small dark hours. I pressed the pillow over my face and willed my way back into sleep.

I moved through the house then like a deep sea diver in a bell jar. I imagined myself a giant, wading slowly through the detritus of meager human lives, to get to my cave, my room, where things were clean and neat and safe. I ate most meals away from home, or tucked away in my room: cold cheese and tomato sandwiches, dry cereal, whatever I could make without going to the kitchen. I straightened my books. I made my bed. I worked part-time at the gas station so I could buy my own groceries. By effort of will I managed not to think much about my parents' behavior. Out the window, I saw them dragging cardboard boxes full of their own clothes to the curb, my father chattering non-stop for minutes. I drew the blinds. I only left my room to head out the front door. Sometimes the phone rang, the line carrying the nasally, bored voices of creditors. Sometimes I heard my name, my parents' voices coming muffled through the wall in grave tones, but I ignored it; they were busy all the time, it seemed, and rarely tried to talk to me. And I couldn't bring myself to call Jemma, to meet her head on with the loneliest question of all, which is, of course, *are you mad at me?*

Instead, I made myself even smaller, trying to say and think and do as little as possible so that I wouldn't do another thing to make Jemma or my parents upset. This exhausting smallness meant I didn't play sports, didn't make friends or do drugs (yet), meant I ate spaghetti sandwiches alone in deep concentration at a corner table during lunch, meant that in class I doodled meaningless shapes on paper or rested by looking out the window at blank sky, and so did badly at school.

The teachers were checked out anyhow. At this stage, the press to leave Edenton was powerful; our class shrunk as fast as people could get their hands on Pink Cards, heading north and inland, which, from what I understand, had its own problems. In January, windows were left open for warm breezes to come through, torturing us all with the smell of sun on mulch.

"Mitochondria," we repeated in biology.

"Revolution," we said, sleepily, in history.

"Managed retreat," we said in civics, repeating after Mr. Sinclair, and sometime that month I must have thrown away the photocopied map that showed us the new shape of the coast.

All to say: driving south was not a broadly popular choice.

Lucia was straddling the back of a seat when I turned around, her head out the window. "In my next life," she announced, her voice warped by the wind, "I will be a squid!"

"Get in the van," I barked, lunging for her sleeve.

"A bobtail squid!"

I scrabbled over Carmen's lap and reached Jamie as she was saying, *they glow in the dark*, hooking my fingers in her collar and giving it a light tug.

"Arms and legs and heads inside the van at all times," I said.

"Get off," Lucia snarled. I left off and moved swaying back up the aisle, head like a zinc bucket, empty and sour, watching as Carmen tried to have a serious conversation with Sabine, sitting behind her, about the camo baseball cap she'd shoplifted from Dovetail.

The girls were slowly, gradually, going off the rails.

"I'm too hot," cried Maria.

Jamie climbed onto the back of a van seat to touch the vehicle's roof. Behind her, other girls moaned *shut up* and clutched sore heads. Don't worry, I said to Carmen, just as a projectile flew through the air and hit the windshield behind my head: someone had gotten hold of Linda's empty energy drink can and chucked it forward, spinning, so it flung its contents at all of us. Some landed on my cheek and I wiped it off as I stood: not energy drink green but clear and viscous; I chose to believe a girl had *not* spent the last twenty to thirty minutes slowly and deliberately filling the can to the brim with human spit.

We handed out 500mg bars of ibuprofen from Nurse Bell's office like Tic-Tacs, but it didn't make much of a dent. When Maria started kicking the seat in front of her, Zak spun around and smacked Maria across the face; then it was a scuffle, which Linda separated bodily.

After an hour's worth of hazy, bumping heat, something odd had begun to happen out the window.

We were still hours from the coast, but the movement of so many people from the water-ruined towns had done strange things to the geography. Or anyhow, the towns looked abandoned. Storefronts were shuttered. Trash bags sat in piles six feet high, uncollected for months.

"Look," whispered Carmen, making me jump. She pressed her fingertip against the glass, pointing: a series of faint gray lines, like a collapsing musical staff, ran along the buildings at varying heights, below which they were all browner, as though once steeped in tea. "Water lines," she said. Which reminded us we were still close to the Mississippi. Somebody had set out a sign, right before the bridge turn, that said, *Real Pecans, Buy Hear.* Someone must still be living there, in between the moldering slats. I must have nodded off, because when I blinked we were pulling into a rest stop.

Frank had been recruited into our operation by then; he listened to Arda divvy out tasks. Carmen and I distributed lunch from a cooler: dry sandwiches we'd assembled at Twin Bridge the day before. They were made with fried pork skin and a mysterious cheese produced from corn syrup.

Simply intolerable heat: heat that throttled, heat that jammed its fingers down your throat, heat that wrapped your head in wool, snickering, heat that made burning weapons of any outdoor metal. We spread out at the rest area: a bare patch of earth off the highway studded with picnic benches. We stuck to the dirt where the shade was, but still, soon we were sticky at our legs and necks, towards which tiny invisible gnats, one of the still-abundant bugs, kamikazed themselves. A hundred yards down the road an old metal bridge crossed the river, made faintly unreal by heat shimmer. I sat back, panting, too hot to eat, watching my assigned delinquents chew miserably.

"I'm gonna die," Amy said flatly.

"No you aren't" I said, then added, "Why?"

"Hot. Hot, hot, puking hot," she groaned, then put her sandwich down and began scraping at the ground with a stick; once she'd cleared the dry grass away, she lay her belly on the relatively-cool dark earth with a sigh. It was a decent idea. A couple other girls copied her.

"What's it so green for?" Hanan asked through a mouthful of food, squinting around with distaste. It wasn't *that* green. The grass was spiky and coarse.

Sabine, near Carmen, began to emit a piercing howl, then abruptly quit. All over, the girls kept throwing tantrums the length of a blink, flinging sandwich wrap to the ground, shoving a girl who leaned into them, prompting fights brutal but so short that we had no time to intervene before they'd both surrendered, gasping and nauseous, gripping fistfuls of torn-out hair.

"I fucking hate dirt," Hanan added, brushing at her pants legs. "And my head is killing me. Where are we?"

"I like dirt," muttered Amy. She was wearing the same black t-shirt and black sweatpants she'd been wearing for days, now smudged with white sweat stains. She ignored her food and pressed her fingertips into her eyes.

"Eat your sandwich," I encouraged.

"I'm not hungry, my head hurts, you're not eating," she replied without opening her eyes, tossing the protests off without conviction.

"You'll feel better if you eat something."

"Why aren't *you* eating, then?" Hanan frowned.

"Because I already feel fine," I lied.

"Well, I feel like flayed dick."

"Hanan!" Linda must have taught them *flayed*. In an effort to connect, I said, "Well, you don't look flayed."

"What do I look like?" she asked, her voice slurred with exhaustion, lowering her pecked-at sandwich. A weird, rotten smell floating up from the nearby river wasn't helping.

"A ghost," Teresa said before I could answer.

"You do look pale," I frowned.

"Ghosts are *invisible*, you *fucking idiot*. How could I look like one?" Hanan snapped at us all, suddenly flicking into hostility. Then she lowered her head into her hands. "I'm gonna puke. My head, my head . . ."

Amy pounded both her fists on the ground. "Holy Lamia," she began, "Let me invoke you—"

"You're so embarrassing," Teresa interrupted. Amy rolled her eyes back into her head and started swaying back and forth, groaning.

"Amy," I said, sensing that she was building up to an act of retaliation, "Let's all just take a deep breath."

Hanan promptly pretended to faint, going limp facedown before us on the dirt.

"You *killed* her," Teresa cried, affecting a wail, but she must have seen how that sentence made me jerk like a pin to the brain stem, and she froze. So it was suddenly very quiet while I fixed my eyes nervously in Hanan's direction.

"Hanan," I said, touching her lightly on the shoulder. "Hanan."

She didn't move.

I shook her a bit more urgently. She rocked, boneless.

Using both hands, I turned her over.

She was unconscious. Her face was bloodless, her breathing shallow, her skin strangely cool. *The piercings,* I thought at first, and quickly glanced beneath her shirt; no redness or sign of infection there.

"Arda," I barked, once, trying not to spark panic. But everyone in the field heard the fear in my voice and snapped their heads my way. Frank stood up. Arda leapt.

When Arda reached us—Amy and Teresa stepped back, Amy's face furrowed with guilt—he moved his hand swiftly over Hanan's face, as though wiping it clear. He pressed the back of his hand to her temples. He said, calmly, "heat stroke," as though he'd been expecting it.

"Ice," I said, dashing to the cooler, which we'd re-stocked with ice that the motel made us pay $30 for. Teresa met me there, her eyes soft, holding a white hand towel she must have taken from the motel.

"For the ice," she said. Quickly, we bundled up a cold compress. Arda took it and began applying it to Hanan's forehead, neck, and palms in succession.

"Take her shoes off," he instructed me.

"She needs a hospital," said Frank; Frank was suddenly next to me, giving off more heat. Without thinking I lightly took his arm, then realized what I was doing and released it. I caught sight of Zak: she'd come to check on Hanan but then stopped abruptly, gripping her head, and sunk to her knees.

"Hey." Reaching her, I gingerly pushed the black hair back from her face. "Where's that lucky tooth." I was going for a tone of comfort but it came out sounding bleak. Zak bent to the ground and began to dry heave. Sweat had abruptly broken out in great, rolling beads across her forehead and neck. She gagged and spit into the dirt. Teresa dutifully handed me another ice compress from another motel handcloth. I passed it to Zak, who took it, panting, along with a bottle of water, another crucial item we'd grown too low on. Zak chugged.

"Look," someone shouted behind us: Hanan was coming back to bleary consciousness. Arda and I leaned her up against one of the van's tires in the shade, and began covering her skinny arms and legs with the wet rags, like bandages.

"The armpit," Linda said, crouching in between us, "Stick some ice in there."

"Ugh," groaned Hanan, whose eyelids fluttered. "Gross, gross . . ."

"It's too humid," Arda murmured, holding up one of the wet rags. "This is hardly cooling her." The girls were standing around us in a silent ring, chewing on their fingers, eyes wide.

I put the back of my hand against Hanan's forehead. What else was I going to find except clammy heat? Heat stroke protocol usually involved calling 911, but we were outside the easy reach of emergency services. "We can't put her back in that hot van," I whispered to Arda, using my best sensible tone. The AC was only making a dent in the heat at that point.

"What else is there?" he muttered, "The van is all there is . . ."

"Look," Hanana croaked, lifting one weak wrist, "I'm a mummy."

Linda crouched between us and gently pressed Hanan's arm down. "We could flag down another driver."

"She needs medical attention," Arda said. "The real stuff."

"There's a clinic in Natchez," Linda said. She was pointing down the road towards the Mississippi. Natchez was right across the bridge. Yes: what she needed was air conditioning, the good stuff, freezing blasts of motor-compressed air. The heat was melting our own heads. The heat was standing just behind us, shrieking nonstop, making it impossible to think right.

Hanan was still slumped against a tire, soaked from sweat and the damp towels we'd pressed on her. She breathed the tiny gasping breaths of a chipmunk, her eyelids fluttering. Her dark hair was plastered flat to her forehead. Easy to see now how skinny she really was: her ribs, her bony knees, all too visible. Once we got to a hospital I inwardly pledged to serve her infinite corn/cheese sandwiches on infinite pewter trays, if only she'd promise to survive.

"Well," I said. "Let's go for it? Now, right now?"

"Yes–" Arda started, when Linda, in one deft movement, lifted Hanan and slung her over her shoulder, fireman style, to carry her into the van.

The others filed quick and quiet back into the van, leaving behind the sad abandoned crusts of our unloved lunch. We'd laid Hanan's limp form across one of the vinyl bench seats, and as the girls filed past, they paused and stared briefly, rubberneckers at a car crash of the human body. *Go, go*, I hurried them, and in the back Lucia quietly began to tack some of her t-shirts over the windows, to block out the sun. Amy followed suit.

"Can we help?" Sabine and Maria asked. As attentive as I'd ever seen them.

"Wait," I said, and leaned around Linda, who was settling back in the driver's seat, polishing sweat from her eyes. I picked up the old cardboard someone had stuck in the wheel well to cover the ratty carpeting, ripped it in half, and handed it to Sabine and Maria, making a fanning gesture. They understood: plonked themselves on the benches behind and before Hanan and began fanning her as though their lives, too, depended on it. I handed another piece to Carmen so she could wave it at Zak, who was seated behind her with the little bundle of ice pressed just below her neck.

"Okay?" I asked, looking around, running the head count. A dozen faces, drawn and shiny; a dozen heads of hair gone limp and filthy with sweat. Okay. Linda took off the emergency brake and we lurched towards the bridge.

That morning, in the hotel room, when I'd awoken for the second time, I'd found Teresa already awake, sitting up against the pillows and flipping through a pamphlet from the Church of Latter Day Saints. I'd stared at the lump of my feet under the covers as the night came back to me: bottles, walking, each of us trying to relay the story we'd made of our lives, then the kiss, his hands, my body. All profane and secret and maniacal in the light of day. Then Teresa spoke and broke me out of self-hypnosis.

"Didn't I protect us from Samuel yesterday?"

"What?" Snapping my head back towards that part of reality gave me vertigo.

"All I'm saying is, I don't need you to protect me."

I sat all the way up, scrubbing at my face. "Listen, Teresa–"

"I got 17 years practice protecting me."

"You're not—"

Tap-tap: Arda knocked on our door, making the rounds at dawn-o-clock: time to get loaded into the van before the heat walloped us. I told Teresa she wasn't responsible for protecting anybody. That was supposed to be the adults' job.

"I've heard that." She went quiet and I thought maybe she'd drifted off again. I stood up, stretched, and her voice floated over: "Only, sometimes I think: what if the government really *was* sending my dad secret messages? Through the weather patterns, just like he said. Maybe he really was a genius, really built a spaceship that really would've worked."

"Maybe, Teresa," I said softly. Maybe it was easier to say no one had let you down, because you never needed anything from them anyway. Maybe she and I could be collaborators in the project of pretending everything was, and always had been, absolutely fine.

She'd looked at me then and her face hardened, back to the one I was accustomed to. "What do you know," she spat, and flung the pamphlet into the far wall.

The bridge wasn't far, and it seemed odd that we weren't surrounded by stalled traffic aimed at the state border checkpoint; rather, a thin stream of vehicles were cruising in both directions. Hanan was sprawled out on the bench as Maria and Sabine continued fanning her at speed; she looked dazed and unhappy but at least she was maintaining consciousness. Small victories.

"Have we got a destination?" Arda asked softly.

"God, I can't *wait* to sit in an air conditioned clinic," Carmen sighed. Despite the medically vulnerable addicted teenager panting nauseously on the bench seat, things seemed good, suddenly; soon we'd be across the border, and if we pushed we could even reach Alabama before having to pull over for another night at a hotel, but in the meantime, there'd be gas stations and convenience stores with chilled interiors galore. Yet now it was still too hot in the van, it couldn't be good for Hanan.

"I'll find the address," I said, and fished out my phone, using its dwindling battery to search for the nearest clinic. We crested a small hill.

From the top, looking up the road which sloped gently to meet the bridge ahead, we could see the river and opposite bank stretched before us. It was an old iron bridge, which crossed the muddy Tensas, sank to kiss ground, then arced across the Mississippi River at a relatively narrow point. Beyond that lay Mississippi the state. The bridge rested on pylons and arced steeply; we couldn't see the road's surface there. But we could see the road that rose towards it. And we could see how every car up ahead was slowing, stopping, and then making a U-turn to go back the way it had come. And we could see, on the left, in bright orange letters, the sign: BORDER CLOSED TO ALL THRU-TRAFFIC.

Frank took the wheel so we staff could hold a quick conference as we approached the backed-up U-turn, the four of us leaning our heads into the aisle, gripping our respective seatbacks, sweaty fingers slipping on the vinyl and leaving dark hand shapes behind.

"We haven't got time to find a new route," I said.

"If there were someplace we could stop and cool down, I wouldn't worry," Linda said, rubbing her scarred chin, "But there's nothing open nearby. Not on this side."

Motels would be filling up already, we agreed; campgrounds, probably, too. Of course, I was nervous for reasons beyond Hanan: every day we were delayed meant more time for TENDER KARE to figure out the falsified elements of the BeZen report and retract the transfer offer; i.e., another night in Louisiana could possibly doom us all.

"We've got to let them rest," Carmen was saying, "To cool down. They're going to get sicker."

"There's nowhere to rest," I pointed out. "There's nowhere to go."

"Getting across is our best bet. Hanan's not the only one facing heat stroke," Linda added; I could have kissed her.

"We'll find a way" I said, and with my phone made a series of brisk, unsatisfying searches. I searched for "evacuation news Louisiana" and read highlights aloud: borders closed except for two bottleneck points at the northernmost point, hours back the opposite direction we'd gone. No power still in much of Oklahoma and Texas and Louisiana; National Guard deployed; heat-related death count ticking past 6000 (*records shattered*, read the headline). Then I searched "Louisiana Mississippi border." I searched "ferry crossing Mississippi River," then "narrowest point Mississippi River Louisiana," "how smuggle over river," then "how smuggle children border river," "how best smuggle children," "how smuggle best child drug withdrawal," "how make teen sleep," "how make teenager sleep long time," "how many sleeping pills fatal," "mississippi river dangerous?," "mississippi river how many drowned dead die year," "mississippi how easy swim dead drowned missing die" and then Arda asked me what I was doing just as my phone finally died.

"Looking for answers" I said, pocketing the phone as we continued to crawl forward. "No luck."

"I'll try," he said, and retreated to frown into his phone, which he handled surprisingly well, I thought, for a relatively old guy.

"I still say we head straight to the nearest hotel," Carmen said. I looked ahead out the windshield. We were approaching the turnaround point, where orange barriers with flashing lights blocked the lanes.

"Withdrawal is going to get worse before it gets better," contributed Frank from the driver's seat. I met his eyes in the van's rearview mirror.

"I say drive through the barriers," said Linda. Arda raised his eyes in surprise as Linda burst into a tight, anxious bark of a laugh.

"All right," said Frank, and pulled over onto the baked-brown grass of the median, the van canted slightly to the left. He leaned on the emergency brake and twisted around to look at us as the engine idled. "What's the plan?"

The plan we reached was to split the difference between retreat and storming the barriers.

Carmen moved the van into the shade across the road, where they'd idle with the AC on to, hopefully, cool down.

Frank and myself would walk across the bridge to the border checkpoint, in order to alert whoever was there that we had minors who needed medical attention, that we needed to cross in order to get to the clinic. For a minute, we argued in subdued voices about whether to bring Hanan. She was sitting up now, looking sallow but calm. If she came with us, she might get ice and AC faster. She'd also give credence to our story. It would be easy to wave off adults; it would (perhaps) be harder for them to turn away an actual, flesh-and-blood, sickly-looking kid.

"She'll faint again," Arda said, shaking his head. "In the heat, walking? Twenty, thirty minutes? Impossible."

We all nodded.

"What if we bring someone else," I offered. "Another girl, someone who isn't ill, but it shows that we're telling the truth, that we're transporting minors. Maybe make them cave."

"I'll do it," Teresa said. She'd been sitting on the bench seat behind me, her hands between her knees, wilted, jaw stuck forward in a dour expression. One seat further back, Hanan was listening in. Her eyes were closed and she was taking big, nausea-proof breaths through her nose.

"Okay," I agreed quickly. Arda gave his uneasy assent.

Frank, Teresa and I borrowed baseball caps from Sabine's stash for the sun. We grabbed waters from the cooler. The few bottles that remained inside were lukewarm.

"Ready?" The three of us stood at the door of the van, bracing for the blast of tarmac-charged heat outside. I looked down the van aisle. Most of the girls were dozing fitfully. Arda, pale with fatigue, gave us a two-fingered wave. Frank slapped the ceiling for luck and opened the door.

It would be a decent walk to get across the bridge. We weren't sure where, exactly, the border check would be—the bridge's height hid the opposite side from view—but the cantilever bridge looked about a mile long. It felt weird to be on foot, walking a structure not designed for human feet. Below us slid brown grass, then a few yards of yellowy scrub, and then the river, brown and swift, its muscles flush to the surface.

But it was hard to notice anything for long, really. The heat ground us down. Beams overhead created stripes of shade, and we paced our walking to linger there. Off behind us came the occasional honking and squeal of air brakes as a truck inched forward, only to turn around. My mouth tasted faintly of gasoline. If you'd taken a snapshot of that moment—two adults and a child miserably trudging a huge empty bridge in the heat wearing, by now, let's be honest, totally filthy clothes, the country powerless and sun-stripped behind them—it would look like the snippet of a nightmare; but it wasn't a nightmare, it was only a walk. The glare had created a dull buzzing in my head. When I glanced up, the crest of the bridge doubled and winked out, shimmering in the heat-wavy air.

"I don't know why they didn't put wheels on the human body," Frank muttered as we walked, Teresa slightly ahead of us.

"Hm."

"That's what rollerblades are for, obviously," Teresa volunteered. Frank and I glanced at each other.

"Good point," he said, and then caught up his step for a moment. He touched my shoulder and pointed to either side of the road ahead, where signs on reflective construction barrels told us, again, that the border was closed; entry beyond this point was forbidden by the Department of Homeland Security. Below, indecipherable statute numbers.

The minutes passed slowly, but the open air, the nearness to resources, the smoking industry in the distance that indicated the presence of electricity, they inspired in us a kind of giddy lightness. As we reached the center of the bridge, more signs started cropping up, the usual border stuff. First there were the stands of the Louisiana side, looking like tollbooths. Normally they'd each house one or two agents; bored-looking, unmovable federal employees who checked Pink Cards and rifled through trunks, just regular normal people who traded funny asides and sleepy workplace jokes with their colleagues while casually exploding the dreams of strangers. Who could blame them, in the end. We all need jobs. But now the tollbooths were empty, which only added an uneasy layer to the scene. The red-striped barrier arms were down, barring each lane. We ducked beneath them. When I touched one to steady myself, my hand came away black with soot. By then we could see, maybe half a mile ahead, the Mississippi border control booths, but we were still too far to tell if they were manned. No man's land yawned between the booths.

"Race?" I offered. I looked at Frank, his lank body, his face baked a darker brown than yesterday and shadowed by the ugly cap; he rolled his head on his shoulders and nodded.

"This'll be embarrassing for you," said Frank. We both feinted beginning to run, stifling little psycho laughs. Teresa eyed us skeptically.

Our humor flagged as we walked on under the brutal light. The sun poured straight onto our shoulders without a drop of shade anywhere, now; something weird was happening in my own body, as another round of sweat pricked up, a painful and unfamiliar chill shivered through me. It was starting to seem like exposing Teresa, or ourselves, anybody, to this heat was a mistake.

As we trudge toward the Mississippi booths, we saw that there were more barriers, some chainlink and pylon, climbable but secure enough that scaling them would require time and effort. In all-caps black, the barriers warned: THIS AREA WATCHED BY CAMERAS. They warned: IT IS UNLAWFUL FOR ANY PERSON TO CROSS, etcetera, whatever, it was too hot to read. Two yellow emergency lights flashed and flashed at a few points along the fence. All in all, these features added an element of deliberateness to our trespass. The booths ahead were dark. No vehicles parked nearby. It didn't seem like anyone was there. God, get us off this black asphalt. The buzzing had grown louder in my head.

We stopped and stood in a line, Teresa between us, looking at the empty booths ahead. Frank seemed to reconsider, too, chewing his lips, damp hair stuck to his forehead. I breathed through my mouth in case that might cool me off, like a dog or a vulture. I was trying to think about what we should do but thinking was blotted out by an animal need to get out of the heat. It was making me nauseous.

"Maybe you two should wait here," said Frank, frowning as he eyed the Louisiana booths behind us.

"Maybe fuck yourself," Teresa said. I failed to suppress a laugh.

"Well, good point," Frank said, scratching the stubble on his chin.

"We should stick together," I said. "You going on ahead kind of defeats the point of bringing Teresa."

He tilted his head in acknowledgment. As he did so, a wail went up: ahead of us, some proximity alarm was going off, screeching. The orange lights above the DO NOT CROSS signs started blinking. *Go back*, was the message; *you're danger and we're danger too*. The orange lights meant, *Anyone who passes this light is a criminal.* But we'd expected something like this, and maybe it was good, anyway; maybe this would get the attention of an actual living person, who could come talk to us, understand our situation, and let us through. Teresa stuck her fingers in her ears, but then the alarm stopped, though the lights kept flashing. Frank and I glanced at one another and kept moving, as sweat slipped down and stung my eyes.

Walking again, slowly. I was eyeing the shaded patch of tarmac next to the Mississippi guard booths. We could sit down there and drink water. I put a little bit on my fingertips and dabbed it on my temples and neck, but they were already damp with sweat, and I was scared of running out. Buzz buzz, went the heat inside my skull.

"Mississippi sucks," Teresa volunteered. She was lagging behind a bit.

"We aren't in Mississippi yet," I said; the speaking took real effort; I was trying to concentrate on moving ahead, step by step, towards the shade that was in front of me somewhere.

But as I spoke, I began to realize that the buzzing wasn't only in my head.

We slowed, then stopped. We could all hear it—Teresa, who was fanning her face with both hands, froze. In the reflection of the tollbooth windows twenty feet ahead, I could just make out our reflections, washed-out and small on the tarmac, Teresa now craning her neck to look straight up.

"Oh," she said.

We all looked at the sky.

At first, I couldn't see anything but hot, white, empty space, even as the buzzing grew louder, more distinct. In the corner of my eye, Teresa stepped back and lowered her gaze. I followed her stare, which seemed to be tracking something ahead of us. There was a shadow, flicking over the pavement ahead, moving steadily towards us.

"Wait," Frank said, touching my arm.

Teresa looked hard at us and frowned. I waved her over with my right hand and found myself gripping the back of Frank's shirt with the other, my knees slightly bent. As I stepped carefully backwards toward Teresa, staring upwards again, I spotted it: a small white shape, sliding across heaven. An angel, I thought; a zeppelin loaded with relief, water, gasoline, non-perishables, batteries. I glanced around; there wasn't anyone else in sight, it must be meant for us. I let them go and raised both my arms toward rescue. The buzzing was almost directly overhead now, and loud. Frank had his eyes glued to the sky.

"Should we wave?" Teresa said, her voice tight with anxiety. It must be very small, or very far off, I realized. Even though it was nearly overhead, it still seemed miniature–like a model plane, moving slowly.

Abruptly, Frank shoved me back. He pointed to the Louisiana guard booths back the way we'd come.

"Hey–" I coughed.

"The booths," he burst, "Go, go, behind the booths–"

Without explanation, he took off the other direction, sprinting for the border, running across the five empty paved lanes toward the fencing; I trusted him, I guess, because I grabbed Teresa by the hand started yanking her towards the Louisiana booths.

The tone of the buzzing changed. I glanced up: our angel was directly overhead, hovering. The shadow draped itself near our feet on the hot black pavement, and then all at once, my understanding snapped together.

"Drone," I breathed. Breathed it upwards, at the machine.

We needed to run; we ran; Teresa stumbled, I yanked her forward, I looked back towards Frank, shouting his name, caught a glimpse of him clumsily vaulting the furthest border gate, looking back up at the sky and crazily waving both arms. We were 40 yards away, 50 yards. I slowed, looking back, Teresa protesting and trying to pull us back toward Frank and Mississippi. I should have dragged her. We were 60 yards away. Then 70 yards. Then we heard two clicks.

A clean, crisp noise.

Like this: *click. click.*

I pulled Teresa to the ground, but felt her snatch her hand from mine. I reached out after her, clutching air. There were a few seconds of absolute quiet. One second. Two seconds. Three.

Then it arrived.

A wave of white heat on my left swallowed me, then dust, then the noise of the explosion, distinctly in that order. The noise was hardly a noise. It was much more like a knife that cut through my head and erased whatever came after its blade, and at some point I was thrown down hard onto the pavement and slid, scraping my arm badly and ripping out a chunk of my hair. Objects fell down through the air, arcing and landing on the asphalt around me, both nearby and distant, bits of wood and plastic and chunks of road. I waited as they hit the ground around me, covering my head with my forearms. *Get up,* the snake god whispered to me in my dizziness. *Get up right now.*

I was okay, I stood up, I touched my ears: the world had been clamped down upon. I paced in a circle, coated in dust, coughing as it filled my mouth, my throat full of glass, gray dust stuck to my eyelids, watching my feet, talking out loud to anybody.

"Teresa," I said, "Frank. Teresa! Hello! I can't hear," I said. My voice was nested deep in cotton, emerging from someplace very distant, very faint. "I can't hear. I can't hear." I tapped my hands over my ears. My right hand was bleeding and I'd smeared blood into the hair at my temples. The air was thick with gray; I reached out with one foot, tapping along the ground in the direction where I hoped the others were; reaching out to grab air. I moved with the paralysis of nightmares, afraid to go closer to whatever was in front of me, the echo chamber of my body the only thing I could really hear, then bent over double; something landed on my back, and I straightened in a panic, nearly cracking Teresa's jaw with my head. She was standing there, arms out and hands working, her mouth open in a mask of screaming, though there was no sound, and she was all gray except for her eyes which were wet and clear and enormous, much too soft to be out here. She stumbled toward me, skin furry with grit, and I put out my hand. She grabbed it with one, then both of her own, pulling herself limply toward me. Sound began to come back: I heard the knock and crack of shrapnel still falling around us. Teresa's mouth was still frozen open, still soundless. I pulled her toward me and without thinking, up into my arms; she was too grown to be lifted but I lifted her anyway, wrapped my arms around her and squeezed while she dropped her muddy face to my neck, made fists into my back in a painful way, choked, shuddered, and finally began to wail.

The night before our house burned down, I had a funny little dream about coyotes. In the dream, I'm in a hallway, and coyotes trot past, one by one, with their bouncing steps, panting but silent. I wait for them. Through the hallway window, I see squares of sky, the deep navy blue of chilled light and silent dawn. The coyotes' tongues are nested snugly between their rows of teeth, like a key in lock. The house is white and blown open. Wind moves through. The cabinets have no doors. The chairs have no seats. Rooms open into other rooms stripped of meaning: the kitchen bare and sandy; in the beds where we used to sleep is a steel frame piled high with trash. Up above the roof is full of toothy holes, and beyond it the darkness receding, as though night were a fluid material that the earth was thirsty for and which slowly soaked down. In the dream I lie down. Sand sticks to my cheek. Jemma is there. Violins come on the radio. On the hob boils a kettle of blood, and the whistle is rising, rising, louder, louder–

I woke to a scratching sound. I was in the van. It was dark. Something moved. Crouched on the floor, a gray shadow. An enormous bird huffed, its claws clacked against the dirty seats, its black eyes rolled in its wet sockets, it cocked its head and looked at me, opened its terrible mouth–

I started awake, again, boiling hot, on the bridge. The sun directly overhead.

The bridge. I was on the bridge, in the sun. Yes.

I tried to get up. Pain shouted through my head. I winced and touched my scalp: yes, I'd gotten dragged across the asphalt a bit. Then had found Teresa. And come to the side of the bridge, and sat down. I rubbed my eyes and blinked around, wiping my forehead with the hem of my shirt, which made the shirt muddy. Steps came toward me and I squinted in their direction.

"Are you awake?" Teresa kneeled next to me, her face flushed scarlet with heat and worry. "I found Frank. He's coming."

I shook my head; I wanted to ask if she was okay, but my throat was so dry it seemed I couldn't speak.

Frank arrived, shaken and scraped to bits but alive. We all began checking one another to make sure we were whole: Frank went down on his knees and grabbed my shoulders; I clamped down on Teresa's hand, afraid she'd take off again, and spun her slowly to look for wounds; my other hand hooked the collar of Frank's shirt, my arm hanging as dead weight. *Are you okay*, we kept saying, again and again. Quit plucking at me, Teresa said.

Frank's face was gray with dust, his eyes so bright by contrast that they practically glowed. Two dark, thin trails of blood ran from his ears to his chin, already dry.

"Blood," I said, touching the blood.

He frowned and shook his head, gesturing to his ears. "Something happened to my ears," he said in a weird half-shout. Teresa leaned over and tried to look inside his ears. Frank didn't notice. I stood up and braced myself as a wave of light-headedness came and then passed.

We began to move back towards the van, past the unharmed border booths. Because what had just happened was impossible, I felt it wasn't happening, and I wasn't myself, and so glided almost pleasantly above the unfolding present moment, the way one can bound weightlessly in a dream. Teresa and I kept up a silent pact of listening for buzz and clicks, jaws clenched, eyes down. None of us talked, save to check if there was water. There wasn't. There were no shadows, and my throat filled with glass when I swallowed.

"Wait," said Frank once more, stumbling a little. He bent over in a stripe of shadow and put his hands on his knees. I stopped; Teresa slowed down but kept going, looking over her shoulder a little; I understood she couldn't stop. Frank held up one tanned hand, blinking continually as though trying to clear a hair from his eye, taking huge breaths through his mouth. I moved closer to him in case he needed balance. His clothes were stuck to him by dust and sweat that had together turned to mud. "Okay," he said, and started walking again, unsteadily, inhaling deep breaths through his nose.

After one thousand years we finally saw the van, shimmering in the distance. Then the road, then the heat-pale figures on the road. Carmen resolved out of the flaming hot blue, saw us first, and came running, though she was still small and far away, and then Maria. And then Sabine. Teresa took off running towards them, and as she did so she burst out with one strangled furious noise like someone leaping from a burning window, and then was gone, sprinting, while Frank, limping behind me, caught my hand. I turned into him, very slowly, discovering only as I moved my scraped palms to his shoulders that I had scraped my palms, so we very carefully leaned against one another, barely touching, only breathing into one another's necks for a moment, because you can't hold up anybody who's that scraped raw.

Back in the van we got cleaned up very cautiously, using some of the dirty melted ice water from the cooler and a rag that Arda dug out of the glovebox, while repeating nervous questions like *what happened*, and *did you see people*, and *did they see you* and *are they coming after us*. I sat blankly on a van bench seat, touching the new bald spot on my scalp where a chunk of hair had gotten ripped out.

"Border security," Frank said finally. "One of those non-lethal automatic drones," he added, his voice still weird and loud. Arda's face changed. He touched his forehead once and nodded. Carmen and Linda were nearby, too, making shapes and concerned-sounding noises; it was hard to keep track of anyone just yet; I poured a tiny bit of water on my face from one of the last water bottles, spinning my finger in the air in the universal gesture of *let's get rolling*. I wanted to be away from there. Immediately. We didn't start driving, but the other staff went into a huddle without me.

On the bench in front of me sat Frank. The blood on his arms turned out to be from four thin identical slices, shrapnel scars the width of a razor blade, so thin they clotted immediately and which all pointed like a compass needle in the same direction. I tuned into the world around me about the same time we started moving again, headed the way we'd come, along with all the other traffic, in a great hot noisy mass of fumes and nobody saying much, everyone with big dumb dinner plate eyes in a way that was almost funny, maybe. "Automated border security" and "non-lethal drone" had just been formless word-shapes ripping by in the dark, on the news, before now; now they arrived in real life and these rhetorical gestures turned out to have weight and smells, to cast shadows, to abrade skin and burn and terrorize. I stared ahead into Frank's dust-pale hair. Teresa on the bench seat next to me. He hadn't washed off the two thin trails of blood below his earlobes, which I wanted, very badly, to touch.

    The others were talking. They were trying to make a new plan. Okay. Atlanta. Okay. I was picturing it again: Atlanta, clean floors, a room for each girl. Therapy that works. Green tea in clean cups (imagine: real tea). And me, living on gin and good intentions, and I would exercise and grow muscles, and do art. The world's hostile youth would cook elaborate recipes, oxtail and marrow, squash blossoms and pozole. And there would be rain. Not too much. I followed the noise of talk back to the surface and re-entered the chatter.

    ". . . we can't go back," Carmen was saying. "The national guard, no food, no electricity, no nothing."

    "Someplace we trust," muttered Arda.

    "No group homes, no police," Carmen went on. She talked animatedly, throwing her arms around, but kept her voice at a low register, feet glued to the floor.

    "Everywhere's full," Linda added, "I heard it, the radio said it, while you were talking before. All the hotels around the border are booked.

FEMA said they'll set up reception centers. Or send trailers. But that could be weeks."

"Months," Carmen corrected.

Arda made a humming noise and dropped his head, scrubbing his hands through his thin hair. His scalp was red and tender from the sun.

"I've a friend," Frank chimed in. He sounded normal again. I slid to the edge of the bench seat to see better. He seemed to have forgotten, already, that he had been hurt; if anything he looked, now, feverish with energy. The slice over his right eyebrow had opened back up but he pulled himself forward to the edge of his seat and leaned into the semi-circle of adults. "My sister-in-law, really. My brother's wife. She's from Houma. Louisiana."

I heard Linda suck her teeth. "That's the coast."

"We could maybe cross down there. At least we could maybe get put up."

"It's dangerous."

Frank scowled. "That's just rumors."

"There's nothing down there."

"*People* are down there," Frank said, but not angrily, not trying to convince anybody, just deadly serious, running the side of his fist back and forth along the edge of the seat compulsively.

"And then?" Carmen said. "Camp out forever?"

"People run across the border down there all the time," Frank said. "Or around Pearl River, further East. It's all marshy maze. There's boats–"

Arda coughed up a miserable-sounding laugh. I was dimly aware that something had shifted for him—sometime between when we'd left to cross the bridge, and when we got back, he'd begun to look very, very tired. The laugh made us silent for a second. I think it was dawning on each of us, with a shockingly stupid delay, that this was an actual crisis. It had emerged around us, slowly, enveloped us shade by deepening shade like the approach of badlands dusk, a gradual accumulation in the atmosphere, until all at once we recognized: we were in an emergency.

"How far?" I asked.

Frank hesitated. "We must be about two hours from the coast."

Two hours didn't seem that bad to me. But Linda was shaking her head vigorously. "We should drive north. Getting across the north border won't be as hard as the river."

"It's swamped," Arda said quietly. I had to stay still to hear him better. "Everyone's going that direction. I got a voicemail. A neighbor. She said she'd been in traffic ten hours trying to get to Arkansas."

"We're getting low on gas," Carmen added.

We were quiet for a minute.

"What are you guys talking about?" said a smaller voice.

Sabine, at my elbow, looking grave. We adults all straightened up, like we were in trouble.

"We're figuring out where to go next," I told her. She blinked at us. We had parked again on the shoulder, and it was quiet except for the traffic whooshing by, and the metal of the van creaking as it heated in the sun.

She asked what our choices were. We looked at one another—honesty, honesty? Was now at last the time?—and then we told her: the menu options included south towards uncertainty, north towards standstill, or—well, drive around blindly, try to find shelter until it turned dark or we ran out of gas, probably park in the lot of a BigSave, sleep in the van. She nodded solemnly.

"One sec," she said, and turned around.

"Should we ask what they want?" Linda hissed anxiously.

"They're the ones who are sick," said Carmen.

Sabine was huddled with the others. Us adults waited quietly.

"At least," Carmen added cautiously, "The town—Houma?—could be a temporary place to stay. Until things settle down."

I had boulder-sized doubts about any of this really ever settling down, but I nodded and kept my mouth shut. Really, was it the worst thing? Ideas clambered; it was hard to slow down my thoughts: no, not Atlanta: constant movement, our lives stitched together from smaller and smaller blocks of lives. That might not be so bad, I thought, staring at the side of Linda's face as she said something worried. We could achieve some nomad routine. A new tribe, yes, and we'd learn violin by the levees and train ourselves out of rage. As we sat there, a rock thrown up by a truck tire thumped hard against the roadside window, making me and Frank flinch.

"Okay," came Sabine's voice, suddenly swelled with confidence; she'd been elected speaker for this particular moment, it seemed. She put her hands on her hips and set her sharp freckled jaw. "We say south."

"Guys," Linda said, alarmed.

"Down to the coast," Sabine nodded.

"The traffic fumes are making me sick," Hanan said from behind her. She still sounded weak, but at least wasn't worse.

"And I've never seen the ocean," Zak called.

We adults all looked at one another. Linda threw up her hands. Carmen stood up and took her turn at the wheel.

For the next two hours we raced straight south, more or less along the river's route. I stared blindly out the window, trying to keep the ragged hem of blind panic at bay by having zero thoughts. Under the sound of the others' voices pulsed anxiety, chittering around the van from seat to seat, gnawing on our hearts. Outside wasn't safe, and inside was ticking into danger too, now, degree by literal degree.

Maria hopped onto the seat next to me.

"Where are we going?" she asked.

Houma, I told her. A town on the coast, on what is now the coast. As soon as we'd started moving, Frank had used precious phone battery to call his brother, who put Frank on with his wife, who called back twenty minutes later with an address for someone who, she said, would help us out. Frank listened with enormous concentration, plugging his free ear with one thumb so he could hear them with his damaged eardrums. Then he hung up and turned around to tell me, "She says we should stop at a grocery store before we get there, if we can." His face was smudged, and he'd been silent and serious since the bridge, and the solemn look on his face got all mixed up with my own tenderness so that I had the unshakeable impression that what he was feeling was heartbreak for the world, heartbroken by the drone and what it all meant, and I could see him push this feeling out of his mind in deliberate moments when, for example, Arda leaned across the aisle to point out an overturned boat, at which Frank shaped his face into an expression of interest and gratitude, praising the view, so that this intense grief for the world was hidden from anyone who wasn't looking constantly and closely and which all spurred in me a wave of desire and love so acute that I had to look away.

From under her eternal pink sweatshirt, Maria pulled out a flimsy, spiral-bound *Guide to Louisiana* that I assumed she'd shoplifted from the last gas station.

"You've got to stop doing that," I mumbled pointlessly.

"Doing what?" She flipped through the pages, then stopped with a cry of delight. "Houma. There! Does it have a beach?"

"I don't know. I don't think so."

One thing we'd been right about—the traffic in this direction was much thinner. No one else wanted to go south.

"It looks pretty."

I leaned over and saw a tiny, black-and-white photo in the guidebook of a house on stilts.

"I hope so," I said. "It might look different from that guidebook."

The sun sank lower, sending pink knives of light across the highway.

We passed an abandoned Dairy Queen, a church, a tractor center, all dark. We entered the outskirts of a town, houses crawling with bushkiller vines that burst through their windows, blinding them. In the yards, the skeletons of lawn chairs, canvas long since rotted away. We passed some cars. People still lived there, but whoever could leave had clearly left already.

Carmen stopped in front of a Food Lion. She threw the van in park and we all sat there, staring out across the parking lot, idling. No other cars in the lot. The interior was dark.

"Betcha they got potato chips," said Maria.

"It's an emergency, and we need food," Linda declared, from her chest, as though it were a magic spell.

And ice. And water.

We all got out and walked slowly towards the grocery. The doors' electric eye was dead, but Carmen pried the doors apart easily enough with a tire iron, then winked at us. "Still got it," she said.

The inside: absolutely still. It was dizzying to be so still after hours on the highway. The checkout registers stood dark and unmanned. I touched a rack of candy. A cart with tortillas, powerade, and jerky was parked in the nearest aisle. The air in there was warm and close, having been closed up for who-knows-how-long in the heat; a faint smell of spoil wafted from the fruit aisle.

"I hear this shit is full of cancer," said Maria, breaking the spell. She'd ripped open a bag of cheesy snack and began going to town. "You want?" She offered to Zak.

"No, no," Arda frowned. "We are not taking cheese snacks. Let's please stay on the van."

"Let's go," Carmen said, and we walked them back to the van. Frank paused with me at the van's door as the girls filed back on. I felt him looking over my face. Then he carefully took my hand, looking at the fresh white scar on my hand where Teresa had bit, a lifetime ago.

"How sharp are that kid's teeth?" He wondered aloud. He probed his own teeth with his tongue. I let him trace my hand for a minute, run his fingertips along the blue in my forearm. His attention shy, his cheeks hollow, his hair oily and dark; he reminded me somehow of a Belgian monk from a brutal era, someone using their meager resources and declining health to concentrate on brewing golden Trappist beers and scrawl baroque illuminated letters, while all around him, plagues raged. I mean he often seemed to miss the point. And that it made me want to crawl into him. He was so calm that I was afraid.

"Would you do me a favor?" I asked him.

"Sure."

I led him onto the van and waved my arms like a conductor to get the kids' attention. "Wait here," I begged them at large. "Torture Frank."

"Wait. Wait," he said, but I skipped out and swung the van door shut behind me.

I walked back into the dark of the Food Lion. "Hello?" I called. Arda and Linda made noise from other aisles.

I followed the sound of Linda's voice and found her crouching behind the seafood counter, eyes wide, poking the spread gills of a display plastic lionfish with the handle of a can opener.

"I've never touched a fish before," she was saying. "I've never touched the ocean."

I thought of her strange lessons. The deep sea eels. "That is plastic," I said gently. Along the back wall hung hyper-saturated, aging photos: swordfish, tuna, sardines, sharks. Stuff I hadn't seen for real-real since Edenton.

"I know," she said. I came around to the back of the case and stood beside her.

Below the case were stacks of cans with actual fish inside. I caught sight of my reflection in the Pyrex, streaks of something—dirt or Frank's blood—on my neck. I stepped around Linda through a door marked STAFF (that's me!) and ran the gloriously cold tap in the employee bathroom, splashing my face, soaking my hair and wringing it out in a wet mouse-colored rope.

Stepping out I bumped into Carmen, who had blown up one of the deli's white latex gloves like a balloon and was bouncing it happily on her palm as she strolled about, plucking up packages of dehydrated egg, electrolyte pouches, sweet corn crackers.

"Okay?" she said.

"Okay," we said.

And so we did the shopping.

The aisles were dark and gleaming. Despite myself, I began to hum something cheerful as we plundered the shelves of abundance, dumping them into a trolley: wet wipes, bread, imitation cheese, corn flakes, canned peas, lots more water. The aisles lush with bright and delicious packaging; Arda was in the cookie section, ripping open a package of caramel snacks; I moved to the meat counter; stood above the vacuum-packed and unexpirable imitation-beef cuts, real tendon, and compact chicken gristle and trailed my fingers over the plastic. I felt 100% indisputably high.

We tried to focus on protein and carbs and whatever might pass for vegetables, and after a half hour or so, satisfied, we headed for the van, balancing cases of water on top of yucca snacks, then went back for more water, then some more. I found Linda taking a break just inside the door, scraping the side of a pudding cup with a cookie. She looked up and smiled shyly.

"I haven't had a pudding cup since I was just a kid," she said, maybe embarrassed.

"Where is everybody?" I said. "I mean the town." I dipped the tip of my pinky finger in the remains of the pudding and licked it clean.

"They must have evacuated, too," she shrugged. At that point I was facing the creeping sense that we'd been driving not for two days but for years, decades; that time had been compressed for us like astronauts at the rim of the event horizon, and everyone we'd known, and everyone they'd known, had grown up and led productive lives without us, that everyone else was already long gone. I looked around the shop as Arda returned the trolley.

I turned to Linda. We, the refugee swarms, eating pudding. "Well," I said. "Guess we're looters after all."

Linda turned the cup upside down in her hand. "This fucker comes with about three spoonfulls of pudding," she frowned, and crushed it in her fist.

The last time I saw my parents, they made me a big dinner. It was delicious. Exquisite, even. Mom hadn't cooked with enthusiasm in months, or years, it was a sign; it meant something. They wanted to have a sit-down dinner! With me! Maybe this was it, the sign they were done with the whole Double Truthism thing, that they were finally oaring back to shore.

But "I'm not hungry," I'd scowled, already well used to procuring and eating my own meals in my room. They wouldn't win me over that easy.

"It's that stew you like," my mom said, smiling anxiously in the doorway. She'd lost weight, and she hadn't had extra in the first place, so her muscular arms, the bones of her chest, they stuck out more than ever, though it was, I thought, a pleasant angularity. It suited her, or else she was just my mom: made exactly as she should be. Her hair had grown longer than I'd seen it in years, and she'd stopped dying it, so gray streaked down from the roots, but it was softer, less frazzled than it had been before. "Come on," she said, opening her arms, and that was all it took, really. How could I say no? I followed her to the kitchen, walking within the soft smell of soap that trailed behind her.

"Hey, chickadee." My dad was setting the table, and he squeezed my shoulder when I came in. He'd lost weight, too, and I think he'd stopped going to his ophthalmologist, so he was squinting even more than usual.

I started to pick up my spoon, but my parents were making prayer hands and closing their eyes. So I steepled my hands, too, and mimicked their concerned expressions without really meaning to; a spy in the house of crazy. We hadn't had dinner together in a long time. The praying thing was new.

"Speak it and make it be: I will find a better version of the world," said my dad.

"I will find a better version of the world," said my mom.

They looked at me.

"Same," I said weakly.

My father cleared his throat and squeezed his eyes shut tight. "I make $85,000 a year before tax. We live in Ann Arbor, and have barbecues. We own a boat."

My mother: "I am a celebrated artist. Our roof isn't damaged. We are not in debt."

"Ann Arbor?" I said.

"Nothing fancy, just a pleasure yacht, 16, 18 foot," my dad added.

"We are friends with our neighbors. We don't plan for evacuations."

"We take vacation once a year, on a warm island. We swim in the ocean. No one gets cancer."

"Our girls are content. They bring friends over to the house. Their grades are decent."

I started to get it. It wasn't really like praying; it was more like affirmations, like reading a self-help book out loud. They were describing the other, better versions of the world that they believed in, the ones they thought they were so close. They kept skipping me because I kept shrugging. I was hungry and let my gaze wander around the kitchen: without the curtain, without the kitten-shaped soap dispenser, without the fake orchid or pewter pitcher or hideous paisley-patterned dishes stacked above the fridge, having been emptied of nearly everything identifying, the kitchen now looked sterile and cruel, someplace meant for cooking batch hospital meals or for a divorcee to hang himself. Then I noticed my mom was crying. Her eyes were squeezed shut tight and her lips were pressed in a white line, her hands clamped together tight till they shook. I don't think I should have been allowed to see that: my mom weeping with her eyes shut. Nobody should be allowed to see that sort of thing.

"Self-abnegation will allow us to travel from this world to another," said my dad, his voice down in his chest the way it went when he was trying to keep the emotions out.

"Self-" said my mom, but her voice got too shaky to finish.

"Ugly world? Begone!"

"Yeah," I agreed.

"Beautiful reality? Come here!"

"Git on over here!" I crowed, getting into it, because hell, why not.

"We're heading back to clean air, cold winters, and housing stability."

"Yeah," I said, "We're going to go back to the Middle Ages. To joust. And have *mead*."

Instead of laughing they opened their eyes.

My mom blinked and sniffed, delicately wiped under her left eye with one finger. "Well okay!" she said, in the cheery tone of a pilates guru.

"Bit of a freakshow, that prayer," I said.

They tutted me and then we ate.

The food was hominy and mushrooms and beans with tons of salt, the kind of cheap, almost-meat-tasting stuff more and more people had switched over to. I was a junior in high school. Ms. Trindad had gone back to Illinois after the latest summer, when there were heat advisories every day and ten died at Chowan County nursing homes, simmering in their wheelchair-accessible apartments. I chewed and they heaped more food into my bowl. My mom wasn't eating. She leaned on her elbows and asked me questions she hadn't asked in ages.

"How's school?"

"Full of villains and dumbshits," I said around a mouthful of corn.

"And are you doing any sports?"

"Only intravenous drugs and recreational screaming," I imagine saying, to shock them, but I don't. Anyhow I didn't do drugs, yet.

"And do you have a boyfriend?" She went on, getting sing-song.

I rolled my eyes. As though I would ever tell her. I had given one miserably dry handjob and kissed a warm-mouthed girl at a house party; that was it, so far. They'd ignored the silo of my life all year and now the door was barred, unless they begged. But at least the food was good. She must have used the last of good ingredients: it had tomato paste, and cumin, too, both grown hard to find and pricey.

"And Jemma?" Dad said carefully. "You see her a lot? You two are still good friends, right?"

I shrugged. I'd tried extremely hard not to become a mediator among them, but the rift that remained there pawed at me often.

"Oh, I'm just so proud of you," my mom said abruptly, looking into her bowl. She looked at me and her eyes were shiny. With a start I realized she was talking to me. "You're a remarkable young woman, BB. I'm just so glad you were brought into the world—into this world, I mean."

I coughed.

"We love you," my dad added, his voice thick with feeling, squinting his good eye at the wall somewhere over my head.

I was annoyed, I was embarrassed, I shook them off. They wouldn't let me wash the dishes. They gave me big, lingering hugs; it was clear, I thought, that they were on some tear, had probably done big-time rehearsing of their humiliating affirmations and group crybaby time over at the Church of Dumbfuck. Bitter but not quite giggling, I slipped out of their grasp, back to my room.

The next day, normal life went on. School with the usual pointless data points. "Nucleus, ribosome, cytoskeleton," we said, in chorus, in biology. But towards the end, before my last class, Jemma found me in the hallway, snagged me by the elbow. I was surprised; she hadn't stepped foot in the school since about a month before her own graduation.

"Mom and Dad called," she said coolly. "They want to talk."

"Again? I asked. "About what?"

Jemma shrugged. Without another word she turned and headed for the exit, her black dress billowing; I followed, happy to play hooky.

I was surprised to hear they'd called, and that she'd answered. But I was happy; I got in her beat-up car, I loved to sit there, inside the cool pink bubble of my big sister's life. The car was warm. Dust motes and flecks of pollen floated around in the lemony sun. The car smelled sour and bright. We passed the broad, musical sounds of spring: radio from open window, child shouting. I felt normal: with family, and on the way to family, on a warm afternoon, near the end of my junior year.

We parked on the street. Our mom's car wasn't in the driveway. Jemma trudged in front of me across the muddy lawn and knocked.

When there wasn't an answer, she tried the knob. The door swung open.

I followed her inside. The smell inside the house was different. And it sounded different, too; I could hear Jemma's footsteps reverberate.

"Hello?" she called. "Anyone here?"

I stood at the threshold of the living room and looked around. At the bare floor. The bare walls.

The house was empty. Not empty like it had been, but completely empty: the kitchen table we'd just sat at was gone. So were the chairs. So too the couch, the television, the newspapers once plastered on the wall, the pink glass lamp that stood at the end of the couch that our mom had loved, the green wall clock Jemma and I once used to time ourselves holding our breath. Each room was stripped, as though made clean for strange tenants.

Jemma charged into their bedroom. Empty. Nothing in it but dingy gray carpet and the broken venetian blinds.

I opened my room, worried about my things, the way a dumb kid worries, as though I had anything precious in there. Everything remained the same: my bed, my desk, my tatty clothes lumped on the floor.

I met Jemma in the kitchen, where she stood with a piece of paper in her hand that she'd plucked off the bare counter, her face slack. She handed it to me.

Dearest baby girls, BB, Jems, It began. *I wish wish WISH you could come with us. If you had BELEVED Double Truthism, you could have Okay so maybe some day you will. But now we need to leave. We are headed to the other world. Pls dont be mad. Your dad has seen a path. Please look up "self negation DOUBLE TRUTHISM" and you will see!!! Don't believe the darkness of this world bcuz we know IT ISNT REAL!!!!!!!!!!!*

That was how the note ended, along with Xs and Os and drawing of hearts. And: *mom and dad.*

They'd left. I blinked at Jemma, then the note, waiting for one to explain. She was looking around at the bones of the empty house. I kept drifting towards singular reasons they could not have left, like, "They can't have left; his peonies are still here," and then my thoughts would gently rebound back to blankness, away from the thought of the doomed petunias, a thought like a glacier, cold and silent and intractable and which represented only a tiny, tiny part of the terrible whole.

Chapter Ten

We used the wet wipes to clean ourselves off. We wiped grit off our faces and arms and legs, from the creases inside our elbows and knees, and tossed the dust-streaked trash onto the van's floor. I glanced over Carmen's shoulder where the needle hovered ever closer to the E.

Less than an hour to Houma. The van was filled with the warm, content sound of snacking as myself and Arda wrapped a bag of frozen peas in one of Amy's black t-shirts and gave them to Hanan, who was still conscious but limp and damp and yellowy, like a newborn. Amy watched, sticking her pinky finger into the gap where her lucky tooth had been kicked out.

"I'm gonna scratch my skin off," I heard from the back of the van; Lucia had gotten eaten by mosquitos while she'd napped with the van window open, red welts coming up on her forearms. I gave her a bag of frozen peas, too.

The van rocked, the roads buckling more and more, shifted and cracked by the uneven water table. We passed a Keppler outer belt of garbage, heaps of discarded tires, burnt auto husks, upside-down boats shedding fiberglass. Then electric poles at skewed angles, some seeming to dangle by their own wires. Gutted house mounds lined up neatly and pink as tic tacs: tongues of insulation, shingles, shattered futons, the matted pulp of old clothing scattered across the crabgrass. It seemed almost embarrassing how it all looked the same, all our collective possessions just wads of damp paper towels in the end, Styrofoam and ash trays.

Thin strips of lifted trailers ran along either side of the bayous. We crossed a bridge over a narrow canal choked with green hyacinth. Half-rotted docks pointed at where the pink hull of a shrimping boat stuck up among a carpet of invasive aquatic ferns, twists of storm-blown aluminum siding. Spiky palmettos sticking their fronds into the road. Then green lots spotted with concrete slabs and columns holding nothing, or houses totally done for, face ripped off, roof across the road, mouth open screaming. Flights of cement stairs climbing to nowhere. Carmen steered slowly around craters in the overgrown road. Frank pointed her into a huge slab of parking lot on the water and she parked.

He wiped his face, thoughts very far away. "From here we get the ferry."

The outside smelled warm, like moss and gasoline. The bayou widened here into a lake so bright it blinded me. I stumbled into Frank's back, one foot landing in wet, sucking roadside mud.

"Careful," he said, putting a steadying hand under my elbow. I start to make a joke about how his elaborate plot to kidnap us all, but the possibility feels actually just realistic enough for it not to be funny.

A hush had taken hold of all of us, like heathens in a cathedral. Ten yards ahead, past an orange barricade stamped HAZARD, lapped the waterline. Across it to the south, you could see Houma, sprawled atop, a brackish, shallow marsh. Seagulls (seagulls!) wheeled overhead; as we watched, one dipped crying to the surface, canted back, and emerged with something blue and wet. It landed on the signal box of a half-submerged stoplight and gulped in a fluid motion.

"I'm gonna gag," said Sabine softly.

I frowned at her. "Careful not to touch that eyebrow piercing if you touch the water."

"This way," Frank called. We gathered what we had—coolers, bags of groceries, the girls' tatty luggage. The office materials we left behind.

Down a gangway bobbed a pair of water taxis, one with a few passengers already aboard. It looked like a recommissioned fishing vessel. Below the outriggers, bench seating had been installed, while the buffalo-sized cap drum, patchy with old paint, dripped orange life jackets. The words FOR HIRE and DAY RATES were painted in white strokes on pieces of canvas hung from the booms, like the skeletal wings of an enormous marine bat, a monster from folktales that sucks the blood of children and goats.

Carmen and I handed out life jackets as the girls boarded, tightening the straps and saying *do not take this off under any circumstances*. The taxi's motor churned up eddies of brackish water dotted with algae. Somewhere below our feet swam shrimp, maybe turtles. The thought exhilarated me. If Frank didn't murder us all perhaps I would slip off, change my name, spend my last dollars and days at a gas station slot machine and assume the personality of an exhausted gambler or just become full bitch. It was good to keep in mind these possible offroads, and/or I was probably majorly concussed.

"I'm excited," said a voice; Amy was tapping me on the shoulder, shy, then skipped past me and onto the boat. Everyone stood in a clump near the stern.

"What if it falls over?" Hanan said warily.

"The word is *capsized*," corrected Zak, pleased. Something with a long white neck took off from the opposite bank and everyone under 21 applauded.

"My sister-in-law's mother, Rosa, she's going to meet us," Frank was shouting at Arda over the engine. "She'll give us a place to stay." We took our seats on the damp bench as the water under the stern came to a boil. Arda chattered anxiously with the captain about the ferry schedule while we began to slide away from shore and the van, our little doomed heat capsule, dotted on the inside with our blood, spit, and almost certainly piss. I sat down next to Frank, who was in the midst of a whispered conversation with Linda.

"They must patrol the waterway, too, right? The state borders here must be closed?" she was saying.

"They do patrol," Frank said, "But Rosa has a commercial license. She's allowed to cross the border. If we want to take that route." He rubbed at his nose and by the way he stared hard into the middle distance it was clear our tenderness was no longer in his thoughts at all. "It's 100 miles to Mississippi."

"And they're not going to see seven teenage girls on her boat and say, 'Hey, that looks like human trafficking? And arrest us?"

"I'm thirsty," said Amy at my elbow, "and bored," and then clutched the railing, grinning ecstatically as the boat steered into some wake and sent her sideways, prompting technicolor visions of Amy catapulting backwards off the side of the ferry and disappearing beneath the surface of Lake Houma, or whatever this body of water was.

"Down, sit down," barked Linda, upon whom the last two days had been also hard: a scratch on her left cheek from a girl's nails, eyes red-rimmed from sweat and dust. She cracked the knuckles on one hand thoughtlessly while she looked at me, turning with her powerful shoulders, her taut and sun-gouged cheeks. "Youths!" she said.

After a moment I realized she was being funny. I was so surprised I laughed like a maniac. Then I put my face against my knees and rested my eyes. I felt okay for a full minute's time. The swells were gentle and the sun was going to go down, eventually. For now it shone through the region's dissipating industrial fumes and created a psycho easter palette, irradiated pinks and tangerine so bright I almost tasted it. Beneath my face, the laces of my shoes were brown with caked Askewn dust. My pants had smudges of dirt and sweet ketchup and maybe old brown blood. There was grime under my nails, chewed short like a child's. I touched my hair. It was dry like a horse's. Someday it would fall out, or turn gray like my mother's. The sour air, the russett-tinged light, it was all achingly familiar, but I didn't want to connect anything to the past because it might suggest repeating, might suggest that I had come back and would come back, again and again, to everything unthinkable that's happened before; or worse, that nothing comes back, only comes back as a thin, diluted shadow of whatever you had before, and no one gets to return.

"Hell yes," said one of the girls, and I looked up to find we had reached the edge of the half-submerged town.

"Hands inside the boat," barked the captain, who sported a silver mustache and the folded mouth of a man who has removed his dentures. The taxi was chugging down what had once, by the looks of it, been a main thoroughfare, following a course marked by pink buoys. Dying trees, hickory and black locust, roots long swamped and crowns gone brown, branches cracked and sagging; some cypress dragging long, gray beards of Spanish moss, made skeletons by saltwater encroachment. Through a flooded intersection where blank traffic lights swung. Frank rolled his head back to watch the rusty traffic boxes pass above us.

The avenue narrowed. In the buildings' shadows, without the glare, it was easier to see and I guessed that the water was as deep as I was tall, deepening as we pushed further into town; wavelets suggested a lazy current. We slid eye-level with the tops of sunken front doors, or looking up at the brine-chewed bellies of houses on stilts. On a brick wall the painted letters MIKE'S QUICK STOP were bisected by a ruler-straight high water mark in mossy brown, and by looking around we learned that also CASINO and FAMILY DOLLAR were beneath the water, caked in silty mud, whiskery catfish swimming the pharmaceutical aisle. Up here the dented roofs of pickups all rippled sweetly with reflected light. The water was spackled with red gas cans, shiny foil snack bags and the rinsed detritus of every curb and storm drain from half the country, come here to rise again.

We slowed to a crawl as we passed a hand-lettered NO WAKE ZONE sign, nailed to a rotten telephone pole. Briefly the captain revved the engine and turned the rudder sharply to correct the drift.

Surprise: downtown Houma was fiercely alive.

Half the buildings did look abandoned, but those in use had been refurbished so that gangways floated at the fronts, like an aquatic sidewalk. In a window a hand-lettered sign advertised duck eggs. Finely woven blue and red nets and rope thick as my waist on platforms under houses, next to planters on pulleys and floating garden boxes that rose and fell with the wake. We pulled up next to a food float, strung with candy-colored lanterns which swayed and knocked in the breeze, sizzling grills and the rich smells of grilled fish and hot oil, onions in butter, shrimped slathered with pepper, charbroiled oysters.

"Thanks, all right," said a passenger stepping off, while Maria threw her remaining Flamin' Hot Cruds into the air off the stern, prompting seagulls to swoop and fight. The other girls cheered, then moaned when it ended.

Next we pulled up to a dock that extended from the top half of a submerged church. The steeple still towered above our heads. A crowd at the dock was already plucking up their bags, ready to board, and when the captain unlatched the handrail we all filed off, me nervously counting and re-counting the girls' heads (seven, all seven), and then huddled together on a floating platform inside the nave.

Jemma quickly took me away from the empty house. Away from the parent-shaped, burning black shape where our mom and dad were supposed to be standing. Obviously, I didn't think they'd stay gone. Later, I'd become angry, and then angrier still, but that afternoon I was just washed-out, empty. Limply I let her load me into her awful car. Then, outside, the world slid by, the world which had not changed at all for anybody else, a fact that just plain made no sense.

"We're going to get some rest," Jemma was muttering, shaking her head continuously, like there was water in her ear, "and then we'll make a plan. But good riddance. To them. First we just need some rest."

We slowly climbed the stairs to her small apartment and she pushed me towards the shower. When I came out, she'd made her best attempt at making up the couch. I climbed into a Minnie Mouse sleeping bag and drifted into a thin, anxious sleep, roused sometimes by the soft clatter of care: Jemma washing a pan, Jemma boiling water for tea, Jemma in the hallway talking on the phone in a low voice. The strangeness of our parents leaving loomed over me like a dark yard of fabric, snapping in a violent wind such that it could at any moment loop around my throat. I had to slip it. I slept. I woke again with my throat full of the achey taste of crying. There was the black shade above me, waiting for me to wake up fully before it lowered upon me, those few empty seconds before you remember what's happening. I remembered. Oh, oh. Jemma was there, sitting on the couch.

"You're squishing my feet," I whispered.

She waggled her hips as though to crush me more.

"Stop."

"Are you hungry?"

I shook my head and sat up. The kitchen smelled good. I scrubbed my face and looked at the window; I must have slept a long time, because outside the light was fading. Our parents had left; it ran over me again like a shiver. Her phone rang and she stepped out for what I would later realize were the first of many calls with the Division of Social Services, the Department of Family and Child Services, and so on. She must have been exhausted but she burned with the white-hot energy of panic; she knew if she slowed down she wouldn't get back up, another thing I'd learned as a kid in our house that served me, years later, at Twin Bridge *(lesson seven)*.

She moved, then and ever after, constantly, stirring tomato sauce with one hand, pulling out a toothbrush from a bag of odds and ends that someone must have dropped off. She had direction, she knew what to do. She would take care of me. She had changed so suddenly, become an adult all at once.

"I have to run down to the basement laundry," she was saying, then froze and came over to me. She sat next to me and put one arm around me, hushing while I wept hard, bitter tears that came up painfully, until the last of the light drained out of the room.

For months, I slept in Jemma's bed while she took the couch.

"I don't mind the couch," she'd insisted, while violently sorting through old car parts she kept in a jumble in the closet. I watched while twisting the point of my shoe into the linoleum. Since our parents had left I'd grown painfully shy. When teachers called on me, they did so so gently that I burned with shame.

Jemma became always busy—cleaning, cooking, going to work at the call center where she'd asked for more shifts. She was always texting me, letting me know where she was. *I'm at the grocery store. I'm getting my oil changed. I'm talking to the landlord, I'll be back in ten.* When she was home, she spent long, frustrating hours arguing on the phone for food stamps and subsidized internet, a heartbreaking process that usually went nowhere. What made her happy was finding a deli that let us put hot food on EBT. School didn't interest me and I excelled at no subjects. Jemma bought secondhand practice books for the ACT that she spotted at a thrift shop and told me to study up, which I agreed to, numb, happy to have my head filled with something besides the bone-cracking longing for my parents, for who my parents used to be a decade before. Jemma fielded calls about second mortgages and property taxes. She didn't know what to do with the empty house, which was underwater financially; storms and floods had bankrupted insurance companies all along the Carolina coast, and as they folded, rates skyrocketed; Jemma began to realize that our parents had been facing crushing, insurmountable debt. In the margins of my ACT book I wrote down vocabulary words: *imminent, relevant, multilateral, devastate.*

"We'll get you into community college," Jemma would say as she packed her things for work. "You work hard, Bee, and we'll save money, take out loans, move someplace. It's good we're just two now, hm? Travel quicker."

At night I heard her moving all the time. If she slept, she slept with the lights on.

The church was probably very beautiful, as all the broken colored panes had been replaced with blue tarp, and up above us the sun was angling through regular windows, so the buttery light turned navy as it sank towards us, like we were the ones underwater. Way up above our heads a half dozen fans spun lazily, which, I'd later learn, were crucial to keep mold at bay. But at the time I didn't notice; at the time it was just one more waiting room in hell, one more institutional cube-space gumming up the works while we tried to get someplace calm.

"I feel fucking weird," Hanan announced, standing stiffly next to me with her arms out at her sides like a gymnast on a balance beam. I put the back of my hand to her forehead but she felt normal, it wasn't heatstroke. It only meant that in the blood-brain barriers of the girls around us, the BeZen was beating its final retreat, dragging its nails as it got dragged out. I'd not noticed during the half hour on the boat but now it showed: each girl jittery and uneven, scratching themselves, panting; as I watched, Amy reached up and started trying to pluck out one of her eyebrow hairs, then another.

"We can walk from here," Frank was saying, but jumped when Maria threw herself down at the edge of the platform and stuck her arm elbow-deep in the murky water.

"Oh no no no," Carmen said immediately and dropped to her knees, then hauled her backwards by the waistband. Passengers picked around us. Out of the corner of my eye I saw Lucia swiftly hook her arm through the crook of an elderly stranger's elbow and spin with him, away from us, chattering happily to the man who frowned and clumsily tried to disentangle. Linda caught her as she was already lighting a filched cigarette and knocked it from her mouth, prompting an indignant cry.

". . . And not good weird," Hanan was saying, "Like, comedown weird. Like, day after taking molly weird," while I waved them in the direction of Arda, who was leading us toward the exit.

"I know," I agreed, distracted, "Just try to keep it together, would you? Set an example?" The others coagulated in a loose twitchy bunch and we all headed outside to a sunny corner of the dock. I looked around.

"Linda, Carmen," I said, flagging them, "Teresa? Have you seen Teresa? Anybody got her?"

"Check the roof," someone joked.

"Not funny."

"Is this normal?" Frank asked, at my elbow.

I turned to him and held his beautiful, crooked, idiot face in my hands. "Please hear me when I say none of this is normal," I said slowly. But he was roaming his funny, fox-colored eyes around my face, really looking, so closely I got spooked and let go.

I looked around, calling Teresa's name, which went bouncing all over the houses' peeling bargewood walls, over the jerry-rigged pontoon boats made of empty plastic tubs, through the green woody stalks of banana trees and elephant ear plants growing valiantly out of narrow strips of alluvial mud that had accrued along the church walls, finally tangling down somewhere far off, with a cornet playing a scale, low but clear. There was no documentation. There were no policies. Teresa could simply disappear. Teresa, who, at that moment, wandered calmly out the door of the church, and waved. Look at that. Nobody had to disappear, nor be a thief of joy.

"Okay," I said instead, and leaned down briefly to look into Teresa's face. "Keep your shit together. Yeah?" Then I looked into Maria's face. "Maria, how you doing? You gonna be able to keep your shit together?"

"Yes," said Teresa, giving me a little three-fingered salute.

"No," confessed Maria.

I looked at Hanan. She made the so-so gesture with one flattened hand.

"That's okay," I said, putting both my hands on Maria's scalp. "I'm blessing you with Lamia's protection spell, okay?"

"Who?"

"She's the goddess of snakes or some shit," Hanan told her.

"I don't like snakes," she frowned.

"She's the god of muscles and gold bars," I lied. "I know you don't feel good right now but just stick with Arda and soon we can rest."

"Follow me," said Frank, and led us down the floating sidewalk to a warehouse, pausing occasionally to consult directions from his sister-in-law that he'd written on a scrap of paper, then up a ramp to the second floor, where we arrived in an almost entirely bare former office. A large Pyrex section of wall opened onto not the concrete factory floor but a small enclosed dock, a few jon boats tied up.

In the center of the former office was a woman about Arda's age. She and Frank hugged. He introduced the woman as Rosa: short, tan, clear-framed glasses, hoarse voice. She moved with the kind of brisk efficiency typical to EMTs or child gymnasts. Her glasses seemed to be too strong or too weak, because she had the habit or craning her neck back when she looked hard at you, down the length of her wide nose and blinking hard, frowning deeply. When we filed in she closed the door behind us, smoking continuously, so the space was filled with the sound of the water knocking the boats. She patted Frank on the back and he visibly relaxed. They chatted about Frank's brother and her daughter. She brushed some dust from his clothes. Her laugh boomed around the room more than his. Then professionalism came over her like a colored lens.

"How many of you are there?" she rapped out. She addressed Carmen, holding her elbow with one hand and tapping out ash with the other.

"This is all of us."

"Are there any people with mobility needs in your group? Diabetes? Anybody pregnant? Anybody have seizure disorders?" We shook our heads. Then, "If I say it is extremely important to be quiet, can you be quiet? Do you get seasick? Do you believe in God?"

"Yes, no, yes," said Carmen.

"No, I don't know, I don't know," Linda corrected.

"All we need is a place to stay for a few days," Arda interrupted.

"Aren't we going to Atlanta?" Linda frowned.

He apologized and asked Rosa to excuse us. Arda said there was news to share.

Of course, there were wonderful parts to living with my sister. She took me to the dumpster behind the Food Lion and we fished out precious bags of softening fruit, bruised and rejected, worth a fortune. We ate sour tangerines and mashed pears on our backs on the sofa, luxurious as cats, cutting out the rotten parts with a pen knife she shared. It was March and already very hot. I let the juice burble out of my mouth.

"You have to grow up," said Jemma, frowning, and for her this meant something specific.

One Friday I came home to find the couch turned backwards, and a board laid across our two half-broken stools.

"Time to learn to drink," she said, producing a six-pack from behind the couch. She gestured for me to sit on the boards.

For an hour, she handed me the beers and recounted her own bad drinking stories, ones I'd never suspected: windows punched out, chins gashed, violent finishes to several relationships. She was only 20, she had a fake, she'd been busy. I listened in silence; after two beers I was drunk; after four, flooded with courage, I demanded she arm wrestle me. She won twice and I lunged at her across the couch, missing.

We fought, too: my brooding was so intent I could hardly think of hygiene, and she scolded me for not showering, for not talking, grew frustrated because I couldn't finish things or sit still. And I raged against her; any demand at all on my time or my energy seemed ludicrous, borderline obscene. I was already working as hard as possible to get up, to go to school, eat meals. I wanted space, space, more than she could possibly give me without catapulting one of us into the sun.

When we stepped away from Rosa, Arda turned on his phone and showed us the headlines. He said he wasn't sure how to explain it by himself.

The words on the screen were bold and in various fonts, a range of major news outlets from Florida to California. This collection of headlines said things like, "Death toll at hands of possible organized violence climbs." Some of the details were familiar; we'd heard them mentioned on the radio during the drive: that strangulation, that beating in Corpus Christi. But the story had taken a new shape since yesterday.

Across the blackout region, it said, in four or five cities, from Dallas to Beaumont to El Paso, a spate of murders and maimings had occurred at the hands of unsupervised girls, some as young as 13. They'd all been residents of other public-pharma group homes. I scanned an article. *The victim says he made sexual advances on the perpetrator in jest, when the girl, whom authorities have not identified, gouged out the man's eye with her thumb*, it went, with no photographs. *He is expected to recover.* Media reports strongly hinted it was a form of domestic feminist terrorism. Or maybe a brain parasite from Mexico, suggested another. They'd arrested some girls. But maybe not the right ones. Motivations unclear. No names released at this time.

"It's all of the company's group homes," murmured Carmen, reading over my shoulder. "It's everywhere." She looked at us with wide eyes. "Should we be scared?" Arda handed her the phone. He was giving me a strange look. Then he pulled me aside while Carmen and Linda shared the phone, reading with their hands over their mouths.

"I received a voicemail," he said, speaking very slowly and quietly, like his voice was a garrott and I was a pheasant and soon he might need to behead me but only to eat, only to survive the harsh winter. "It was from an employee of Tender Kare. This employee said he had been trying to reach us for two days. He said there was a problem."

"Oh."

"A serious problem."

I kept very still and Arda kept very still, watching me. I cleared my throat. "Very serious?"

"Beatrice," he hissed, "They're withdrawing funding. They're ending the study. Closing everything. The reports? What did you put in them?"

"Not lies," I said too quickly.

"He read me excerpts—made up names. And crazy things to say. 'Patient has inhuman focus'? BeZen curing food allergies? 'Patient able to survive falls from great height'?"

"It *could* be true."

"You said Sabine learned piano and Hanan was an engineering genius."

"She engineered the van!" I protested, making a gesture that was meant to be a screwdriver. Arda wiped his hand over his face. "I'm sorry. I don't know—look. I'm sorry. Just tell them I'm crazy, I wrote a crazy report, I'm fired."

"None of that fixes the problem."

"I just wanted to get us someplace better -"

"*Stop* trying to get us someplace better," Arda snapped, and sucked his teeth for a moment before adding, "It does not matter; they stopped the whole trial, it is over. No BeZen anymore for anybody. All of it, everywhere. There's no going to Atlanta." With that he turned back to Carmen and Linda, who looked up, worried. I sensed he wanted to be far more furious with me, but that I had the advantage of having been recently drone-striked. When I joined them again, Linda was saying: Okay. Let's do it.

Just before my high school graduation, my pink card showed up in the mail. The timing was dumb luck. I'd applied almost three years earlier, after Jemma moved out, never expecting I'd get it. I wasn't a doctor or an engineer. I had no merit. I just found good fortune in the general pink card lottery system.

"What'd you get?" Jemma asked when it arrived, glancing over. I had it in my lap under the kitchen table while she made toast.

Nothing, I said; just the school asking for money.

"What, fees?" she said, putting down a butter knife and turning around, her face instantly tightening with concern and money math flashing behind her eyelids.

"No, no," I said, "Asking for donations."

She relaxed and barked a laugh. "Good luck with that."

For days, the letter burned in my pocket. I looked up Texas, the geographically closest state my Pink Card permitted, online, and scrolled around imagining where I'd live. I experimented with a going-away frame of mind. What if I were to say goodbye to the Food Lion? What if goodbye street? What if goodbye curtains? What if goodbye Jemma's apartment, goodbye sagging couch, goodbye mailbox where our parents used to leave pamphlets and tracts that said, *This World Is Not Right!*

I imagined what that would feel like, leaving, and pedaled my bike around Edenton slowly in the heat, trying to stick to shade islands and streets without standing water. More houses sat vacant. More roofs had blue tarps. They would never reopen the library or the Baptist Church. Families had moved into RVs temporarily and then never moved home; they parked by the dozen in gravel lots off the state road. And all this though there had been no One Big Storm, yet; no One Big Storm was necessary when we kept getting hammered with lots of medium ones. Around that time, when bridges washed out in Chowan County, they stopped getting rebuilt. That's how our retreat got managed.

But once, it had a post office. Once it had trash pick-up days. Once I biked around for hours, unable to go home to Jemma's apartment and tell her the news, which was news, now, because I had accidentally made my decision; I would leave Edenton and never, never come back.

"You seem quiet," she said that evening as I picked at dinner. We didn't have a kitchen table, so we ate our meals in our laps on the couch.

"I'm okay," I said. She didn't push, preoccupied as she was with her own worries, the tax liens and mortgage payments and house bills scattered around the counter. She'd listed it, *FOR SALE BY OWNER,* but nobody wanted to buy a house in an increasingly doomed flood zone in a shrinking town. "Just thinking about the future," I'd added.

Rosa and Arda drove us in two jon boats, motoring slowly down the canals under a violent-colored sky, to the safehouse where we'd stay a few days. It was medium-decrepit, a double on nine cinder block pillars that stuck up out of the still marsh.

One by one we climbed a short ladder onto the wraparound porch and stood there, looking over the darkening water and catching our breaths. The whole house canted a little to one side, and its daisy-yellow paint bubbled and peeled. We had neighbors. Their boats now alight with electric lamps. Two brown pelicans bobbed on the water underneath the house next door. Three young boys in shorts and bare feet passed underneath us, paddling a canoe and squabbling. Beneath us, too, reflected the impossible cloud palaces over the polluted marsh, towering pink-blue fortresses that smeared at the edges into rain. *Rain,* I thought, skin tingling. Something living in the water leapt.

"Mullet," Rosa noted.

"Who lives here?" Carmen asked.

The girls had already rushed through and around us into the house, and we could hear the somewhat alarming sounds of them settling in: furniture banging around, windows slammed, a shriek of *I claim this bed!*

"This house," Rosa explained, "is for people passing through." It was for us as long as we wanted it. "There are plenty of empty houses here. Most of them are too storm-damaged to be habitable, but we're slowly fixing up a few. The families who got bought out moved inland and left empty houses behind that get eaten up by mold and wind. The people who can't afford to live inland anymore—some of them come down here." She ran her hand along the doorjamb and looked at her palm. "You got people whose great-great-grand dad is buried in an Indian mound that's underwater now. So the people who are still here, they're real stuck on staying." She brushed her hand on her jeans. "New arrivals are mostly undocumented people, people with records and bad credit, elderly couples whose life savings were their house—you know. The usual." I didn't know what was usual. She bent down to examine a bit of termite-chewed board, tapped it with her fingers, then went inside without looking back.

She showed us around: three bedrooms on each side of the double. She told us how to switch to solar panel energy during the day, back to the battery at night, what to do with the trash. Arda began telling her about the groceries we'd brought; she said we could trade some of it for fresh stuff, crab and shrimp, if we wanted. Frank and I went back out to the porch. He was watching the water move, faintly lit by the windows, light which bounced off the wavelets and gave no heat. They left a cool, hollow ring in the eyes, like the taste left after drinking water from a cold metal can. I leaned over and rested my forehead on his shoulder for a minute. I wanted to lie down on the floor for days.

"Rosa used to work in seafood processing," Frank was saying softly. "Moved here from Honduras when she was like, twelve." He glanced behind him. "She kind of scares the shit out of me, to be honest."

"She's great," I said sleepily.

We sat down on the edge of the little porch. Leaning into him made me aware of my body again, the deepening bruises from the bridge, the sore ripped place on my scalp, my sunburned neck radiating heat. He had tender places too. Against the darkening mountains of clouds to the east, sheet lightning unfurled in silence. A chorus of frog sounds paused, then resumed and multiplied. Waterbugs sent rings outwards below us. Here was this town, existing like a miracle. Maybe there really was another, stranger world fit snug up against our own, like two jigsaw pieces the identical color of sky.

"I like it here," Frank announced. "And I like–" he turned and kissed the top of my scalp—"the boats."

"Funny, funny," I said, and when we kissed he was warm and alive around me, and I had that sense of being surrounded by silent music, of a great rush of physical invisible noise, a pressure almost like the fear pressure that had filled my head the day before but was its identical inverse. I pressed my face into his human shoulder, gasping.

After everyone took turns washing up, they slowly turned in, still squabbling over who got which of the two twin beds in each of the bedrooms, some of them saggy but all with clean sheets.

"Go to sleep," we repeated, walking from room to room, speaking to the shadows piled in beds as they tossed and huffed.

"We can't sleep," cried out Hanan, sitting up, kicking fiercely. "It's hot, and mosquitos are biting my leg. I am fuckin' uncomfortable." She beat her thighs with her fists.

Linda flipped a switch and the ceiling fans began to slowly turn. "That should help with both."

"You know what this night is like?" said Amy from the other bed.

"Please just sleep."

"This is like a sleepover in a morgue."

"It's too warm for a morgue," I said.

"What's a morgue?" asked Hanan.

"Please, sleep," I begged, and kept walking through the rooms, their high ceilings, the curtains drifting in air currents sent down by the lazy fans. Far away a barge sounded its horn. I walked until the noises from the rooms smoothed into one sheet of breathing, then joined Frank in the sixth room. The thunder had turned to rain, which drew some of the stickiness from the air. I closed the door and found him, ran my hands over his face, his arms, then retreated wordlessly to my separate tiny bed. We were too hot to touch, too exhausted to talk; in the dark, under thin sheets, with the heat at our throats, we curled into a sleep so delicious and black I swear we shared it.

Chapter 11

When I left Edenton for good, it was very early in the morning. I'd planned not to tell her. I'd planned to leave a note, explaining everything, commanding she join me once she get her own Pink Card, forswearing goodbyes. But I couldn't do it.

My heart was pounding while Jemma and I ate our last dinner. It was microwaved soy nuggets cut into the shape of stars, with some kind of corn-based sauce. There was no taste, I couldn't eat it, my heart was fluttering. I had a bus ticket and a packed bag. She still made up her bed on the couch each night. Early the next morning, while she was still asleep, I'd decided I'd slip out the door. After all, she'd left me once. And it had all worked out. Now it was my turn to make a choice, any choice; in fact the need to commit some singular definitive act that was mine alone had grown almost painfully urgent.

Jemma's small apartment looked different than it had nine months earlier, when our parents had left—cleaner, neater, sparer, but also stripped of some exuberance she'd once brought to it. The overstuffed couch was now draped with a baby blue sheet she tucked in as a cover to hide the wine stains and cigarette burns. The windowsill that had once been lined with oyster shells and dried beetle husks was clear. Behind me, the counter was spotless; the cabinets were full of neatly stacked plastic promotional cups we'd accumulated and handfuls of wooden chopsticks.

"Everything's so sweet," said Jemma, miming a gag as she forked her food. She blinked at the bottle of sauce on the table and frowned. "The first ingredient in this is 'imitation corn.' What does that mean?"

Behind her, out the windows, sun hit the brick building opposite and bounced a warm light into the room, red clay light, the kind of light that makes you speak more softly because it's tender, and sudden movement risks puncturing through the curtain into night. Goodbye to the brick light, too.

She was so tired from working a double she was drifting off to sleep at the table. Ever since she was little she'd had one eye that went a little lazy when she was tired or drunk. How many people will I ever know a thing like that about, ever in my whole life? I watched her lean on her elbow, chin on her fist, eyes closing for a second, until she slipped and started to attention.

She scrubbed her face in confusion and looked at me. "Are you all right?" Even exhausted, her first instinct when half-conscious was to make sure I was okay, and I felt it all with a bolt of clarity so sharp it nearly sent me to my knees.

"I love you too," I said, without thinking, and then burst into tears. Jemma was already there, my sister already with her arms wrapped around me, not asking anything. She pulled me over to the couch and kept us there. Soon I wasn't crying about leaving. I was trying to catch my breath, while I thought about all the things I imagined she imagined I was crying about, and her thinking made it so: our parents, their madness, their absence and before that their withering of care; our house, the holidays, pictures of anything more than ten months back; our neighborhood, my classmates and their families taking RVs inland; all of it spoiled, now, because the world was spoiling and our parents had gone mad over it, over leaving a worse world for their children. The world slipping away, undeniably, growing more sterile and violent, the land itself dissolving under our feet. This was too much; I couldn't get it out of me with crying.

I gulped a breath and wiped my face and said "Jemma, I'm moving," and then started speaking quickly so she would comprehend everything at once. I knew how important it was that there be a single blow, not a series of small ones. "I got a Pink Card, I'm going to Texas, I'll start over there and get a job and you can apply, too, and join me as soon as you can, okay? I'm sorry, just can't stay here, you know that, I'll go crazy." It came out all shivery.

"That's okay, that's okay," she said, barely flinching. She asked when I was leaving. I told her tomorrow. She shook her head. "No, no," she said easily, confidently.

"You'll get to join me soon. There's a family reunification application-"

"No, look, we'll get you a new ticket," she was saying. Her face was drawn and pale. The little scoop under her doll nose was damp, her crisp blonde hair stuck up at weird angles. She rubbed my back in a circle. "You've got time."

"The Pink Card will expire," I told her, which was true. "I have to go now. If I delay, I'll never leave."

"Where will you stay? What will you do? Don't be crazy. Finish school, then we can talk and make a plan."

"I'm going."

"No," she said again, with such confidence I began to fear I'd made a mistake; she seemed prepared to physically bar the door.

"You can't stop me," I said wildly, jumping up. I began to back away; she leapt to her feet, too, and for a moment it seemed she really would wrench me back and lock the door. But suddenly she changed, she went still, she held her hands down by her sides in fists and stood very straight.

"All right," she said. "You're leaving? Really? You're decided?"

"Yes."

We were quiet for a minute. Jemma seemed to be engaged in some complicated internal conversation. She kept swallowing, shaking her head, narrowing her eyes. A semi truck went by outside and the windowpanes rattled.

"Okay," she said, nodding. "Okay," she moved slowly back toward the couch, keeping her eyes on me, "Then I need to tell you about what's going to happen to the house."

I glanced at the clock on the stove. My bus was in 12 hours.

Jemma sat back down and began to explain things. She spoke mostly in the direction of the floor.

The house was done for, she said. Financially. The mortgage was months behind, it was in default, we had about 18 days until foreclosure, mostly because of repeated repair costs and because the homeowner's insurance had skyrocketed, the policy had more than quintupled in the last few years. Yes, she'd listed it, but no one wanted to buy here; the insurance was too high for anyone to get a loan even if they wanted; no one even wanted to rent it. And it was worth less every year. And if we let insurance lapse instead it could get damaged by a storm, and we'd have no way to fix it, and Jemma would be saddled with the debt because our fool parents had, in a fit of idiot good intentions, transferred ownership to her. FEMA had never given us, or anyone we knew, enough to get out of the hole. And then—she painted a picture, growing alarmingly energetic, interrupting herself; it became clear she'd run over this image in her head many times—then the bank would foreclose and just let it sit and the shingles would be torn off by storm winds, and so rain would come in through the roof, the ceiling would collapse, and then mold would flourish inside the walls, into the drywall, and as the water encroached the foundation would sink unevenly and crack, the whole house with its sad empty eyes growing bleaker year by year, until it collapsed, leaving only debt, and us with nothing we could do, not legally.

"What's that mean?" I asked. She was cracking her knuckles over and over, a habit she had when she was nervous.

She explained her plan to me. Immediately I rejected it. It was ridiculous and offensive. It was brutal. All risk. I wouldn't hear about it. Sure, she was my big sister, but she could be dumb, too, I tried to point out gently.

Her mouth got small, which meant she was angry, and she left the room. She came back a minute later with a cereal box. Before I could ask what it was she dumped it upside down, and a flurry of papers fell out: bills past due, warnings, notice, envelopes ripped or unopened, bank statements in pink. "Tell me how to do this better," she snapped. "Go on, go through it, you look, tell me."

Of course I had no clue where to start.

Of course at the end of the day, I didn't believe she'd do it.

There's that feeling, sometimes, when you wake up at some nowhere hour, still dark, and all your lonely thoughts are there in front of you on bare, spindly branches. I got it that night, repeatedly, when I woke up, again, my heart thudding with anxiety because my bus was in ten hours, eight hours, five. Jemma was upset with me, and had proposed crazy things, of course, but it didn't matter; it was only something she'd said because she was mad at me and wanted to bully me into staying. We'd argued and then she'd stormed out, and I, bitter and correct, had thrown myself sulkily onto her bed and anticipated her apology when she took me to the bus station in the morning.

After kicking around the sheets for a minute, I got up to get a glass of water. In the living room, the blue-covered couch was empty. I walked over and touched it. No sheets, no pillows; she'd never come back, never made it up. I got a bad feeling. I put on a sweatshirt and went down and got my bicycle.

I was still two blocks away when I knew things were wrong. The smell in the air turned acrid. The thin night-time traffic grew congested. A firetruck, horn blaring, turned a corner up ahead, speeding from the opposite direction. I followed. Getting closer, gray smoke, its belly orange from the glow on the ground, stood in the sky.

"Oh no, no," I said quietly. Everything had been all right as long as Jemma was all right, and now, abruptly, it was not. Here was our street. Here was our block. There were our neighbors, our former neighbors, the ones still left. And our house.

I threw the bike down onto the ground and flew towards the edge of the road, pushing my way violently through the small crowd that ringed the scene. But the house was already in flames.

It's hard for me to say whether it had gone up quickly, or if it had been burning already for a long time. But the fire had already done its work. It was obvious the house was lost. Black smoke billowed thick from my parents' room, lit red-blue by emergency lights, and poured in great muscular bursts from my room's window that faced the street. Sprays of red-orange embers showered the driveway and skittered towards us. I unconsciously took two steps forward before Jemma's hands shot out, barring my movements. I saw her but it didn't move through me; I couldn't take my eyes off the house.

The front door had scorched black at the top, and the long windows on either side had shattered, a specific which made something small twist and crack in my chest, as though this were, so far, the only truly irretrievable damage, the broken windows. The fire moved happily; it pounced on the kitchen and began to devour, surging and retreating in its liquid way, and all I could think was that this was a joke, a joke; Jemma had done something reckless to prove she would, and now it was done, so she could take it back.

The heat was sharp even from where we stood in the middle of the street. I was vaguely aware that people were watching us—the two dozen or so who'd come from around the neighborhood to witness the fire, hands over their mouths, shaking their heads. In my nose, seeping into my clothes and my hair was the smell of plastic melting, and wood and drywall and screen and the fake veneer counter top, and the grout between the bathroom tiles, and burning mirror, and my burning old bed, which I'd stripped, stuffing the little I owned in boxes that sat in Jemma's basement nook, but with pieces and flakes of mattress writhing and surging up in windy vortices in imitation of pleasure or seizure. I kept stepping forward and Jemma kept pulling me back, though we didn't speak or take our eyes, both of us, off the burning house. Every so often some key beam or stud would give in a big wrenching crash, and a shower of sparks would arise to mark the place.

I looked at Jemma, her face orange from the fire, and I didn't blame her, didn't know what to think, thought again of my boneless tail, the no moral compass—it was so unclear what was fair sometimes, the rules changed it seems, for everybody, for reasons arbitrary, so maybe this was the right thing to do after all. I wasn't angry, I just needed her to explain things to me in a way I could understand. The heat lapped at our faces in waves. I had a terrible, shuddering vision, one that sometimes, even now, in the dark of motionless sleep, rises slowly from some black depth to lend nightmares, a dark bubble in a fetid lake: our dad, coming to his feet in the kitchen window, where the table would have been. The flames behind him, and around him, and within him; only his bones and denser organs remaining, lit through like an X-ray but driven by the same force of will that had propelled him always, staring with his hollow skull at my sister and me where we stood, frozen, at the edge of the crowd.

I blinked and the vision dissipated. Of course he wasn't there. Their car wasn't in the drive. Their phones had been disconnected for months. The fire would have looked like an orange smear to him, every object in flames casting its own strange halo. But Jemma was there, standing next to me, her round face switching red and blue now in the emergency lights. I leaned against her shoulder and clapped my free hand over my ear, trying to hear the blood in my own head, or in her head, over the clatter and shouts. Behind us our shadows ticked back and forth on the pavement as the lights blinked and the fire moved. Then I stood up straight again.

"There it goes," Jemma was saying, in a voice that had changed from the last time I'd heard it, grown tight with something. After a little time had passed, she said, "When's your bus?"

We left. We were mostly quiet on the drive. We reached the bus station in just a few minutes, then sat in the car in the parking lot, watching the line form for the folding doors. The sun was coming up and the air tasted cold and hard. I looked at the people in the station, holding styrofoam cups of coffee and thought, *coffee*. We must have smelled like smoke but I couldn't smell it. The streets here were almost empty. A bus went by. A man with terrible, crumpled shoes put his chin on his chest and slept against the wall.

"It was squatters," said Jemma out loud, then looked at me hard, making sure I understood. We knew—I knew, she knew—that she'd set the fire in hopes of an insurance payout. To be rid of the house and everything that was no longer inside. But she wouldn't ever say it aloud. And neither should I. "Do you have any money?"

"Enough for a couple months."

She nodded. "It'll take longer than that," she said, an oblique reference to how long the battle with adjusters and investigators would be, though I didn't understand it then. She was looking hard at the bus line, biting her upper lip, a line deepening between her eyes. She must not have slept.

"I'll job hunt when I get there," I said, repeating the lines I'd meant to say. Part of me must have been excited, but most of me was play-acting. Later on I'd sit down and sort out what all this meant. Right now there was something I was meant to do; I had a ticket; I had a seat; I would take my bus ride. She took my hand and gripped it painfully. She walked me to the bus line and stood with me. She waited until I got onto the bus. She stood outside, like our mom did when we went to elementary school, watching until the last possible second she could see me, until we pulled from the space, pulled out of the station, paused at the end of June Street, turned a corner and were gone.

In Houma, we entered a dreaming season.

CURRICULUM FOR MARCH 12TH

Rescue swimming

Basic self defense

Goal: DEESCALATE. DEESCALATE.

Biology: intracoastal fauna. Note: PLEASE DO NOT BRING SNAKES INTO THE HOUSE. They escape and are very hard to find!

Mechanics and logistics: knots

Why the hitch? Why the bow? Don't let your rescue craft get away from you.

Reading comprehension (Maria's pick (no gore!!))

Life took on a nodding, easy beat. We handed our looted groceries to Rosa, and then nightly we staff made big pans of whatever she brought back, drum, shrimp, crab, mirlitons. The girls found new roles, new rhythms. We tried, at first, to caution them: "You're exhausted, don't push yourselves," I'd say to Lucia and Sabine as they set off in a pirogue for the old coast guard post. "Keep your life jackets on. Don't get lost."

"We're not stupid," they'd say. "We won't get lost,"

"I just mean take care of yourselves," I said, following them down the wooden hallway, the brackish water outside sending chimes of light all over the walls, boards creaking.

"We are," they swore. We struggled to believe them. Linda, emperor of structure, made a schedule, Carmen and I peering over her shoulder: she broke it down into shifts, a suggestion about time use that the girls took as a loose suggestion, skipping the homework Linda invented to instead squat on the porch with a fish hook of rancid bacon for caching crabs, or to paddle up to Houma's only operating restaurant, Guidry's Pizza Express, to flirt clumsily with the pimpled teenage cashier. They'd come back hours later, zonked by sun and squinting glare-strained eyes, smelling faintly of the stale weed they'd found in some long-abandoned drawer, sighing contentedly with the exhausted satisfaction of run-out desert horses.

Most of Houma was people with limited options. A retired surgeon from Metairie ran a free clinic out of his motor boat. In certain parts of town, orange hazard buoys warned of drowned land posing danger to propellors—a sunken barge, the tops of old gas pumps—which turned out to be favorite spots for the girls to congregate, since such sunken debris now bristled with oyster reefs.

"Don't eat 'em if they're already open," said Rosa, motoring Amy, Hanan and me to visit a dentist. Amy had gotten a false tooth to replace the kicked-out one. Rosa translated the dentist's Spanish, a stout and handsome man who joked continuously. He'd been a certified DDS in Tegucigalpa, then a roofer in Houma, and now he was a dentist again. If not in the strictly board-certified sense. There were a few trailers on a high ridge of dry land that FEMA had left behind after Hurricane Svetla, which had been turned into a community center, with couches and a microwave, where the girls once more practiced their dances.

Class lessons touched on what was useful, like the water cycle, as outside great shadows massed, cumulonimbus clouds drifting across the warm surface of the marsh, dropping blurry sheets of rain in the distance (rain!), which turned to sticky humidity, traveling back up. One morning

Frank gave a guest lecture on electricity, volts and ampules and basic generator maintenance. He knew how to keep their attention:

"How many ampules of electricity," he asked the girls, gathered on rescued stools or lying on the ground or lounging in window sills, "do you think it takes to stop the human heart?"

"One hundred!"

"Less."

"Thirteen."

"Less."

"One?"

"Even *less*."

I sat in while Linda, in her element now, devised math problems centered on the rate of land loss, subsidence, erosion of the coast. Everybody in Houma knew Houma wouldn't last. A storm would take out the last of it soon, maybe a few years. But it wasn't gone yet. Rainbows of oil bloomed and drifted in the water below our feet. We took a field trip to the Terrebonne Parish public library where the second floor was still dry and secure, not even a window smashed. All the desks had warped from humidity, but the metal shelves and plastic-jacketed books had held up fine. A possum nesting in the printer nook among shreds of paper got spooked and bared its needle teeth. Something flapped by wetly on the first floor, through the dark. The girls browsed and came back with crates—some pulp, some thrillers, some how-to manuals and comic books. Some equilibrium was emerging that I wouldn't question.

After about a week, I began to believe no one would come looking for us. The blackout was still going, and Tender Kare was embroiled ever-deeper in what was now unfortunately referred to as "The Girl Gang Murders." When

I turned my phone on I tried to search up what had happened to the girls who'd killed people, but nobody seemed to be saying. I put my phone away.

Then one evening, over dirty rice, Rosa explained her other work. She asked permission to enlist the girls. Did the girls want to help? They did.

The work looked like this: Hanan and Teresa scanning the intracoastal waterway with high-end binoculars and low-end night vision scopes scavenged from the abandoned coast guard post. They monitored the channel in both directions, a blank strip that demarcated the permanently flooded road. Way on past the horizon was the open Gulf, spotted with tiny distant oil rigs.

They worked in pairs and took shifts. If they heard a motor or spotted the orange of a dinghy, they called Rosa on the Walkie, who'd speed a Zodiac to intercept them before they were spotted instead by the CBP: usually they were cheap dinghies, overloaded with plastic-wrapped luggage, chilly-fingered young parents wearing fake plastic life jackets that wouldn't have kept them afloat. Rosa would guide them to the nearest boat ramp, where the other girls would meet them with silvery foil emergency blankets, water bottles and snack bars. Back at one of the other free houses the travelers got to take a nap, brush their teeth, put on dry socks, hug their children in liquid-boned relief. Sometimes they continued on to Mississippi. Sometimes they turned inland. They all got a room in a clean but forgotten house, and boat repairs and bottled water. Every once in a while, someone stayed. The girls flourished, eyes alight, like they'd been spoken to in their native dialect for the first time in their lives.

"Where are the clean sheets?" Amy would say, striding from a recently vacated room.

"I left some big sticks at the last landing spot," Hanan told us over dinner, passing the spaghetti, "So that we can beat the brush for snakes."

"Tampons, Greg," Maria scolded, following one of Rosa's colleagues down the ramp, "You've got the hygiene closet stocked with condoms and floss and, like, three pads. Have you ever had a period in wet jeans?" Greg looked at me, hoping for mercy, but by then I had largely quit intervening at all.

What else? Carmen and Frank both liked to go by the free house and make chat with the people who boated through. Sometimes I tagged along, lying on my back in the jon boat and watching the tops of buildings slide by, then the underbelly of a house, and the occasional black branch or the long, slender golden grasses that grew thick along the edge of the town's thin high ridge. Frank and I tied up the boat in the shade under the house and bobbed among the traveling families, trading gossip about canals and routes, sometimes sharing icy beer. The people who came through in boats weren't grizzled smugglers: they were cousins from Franklin, which flooded now with every storm surge, where the shops were all closed and the roads impassable. Or it was a dad and his epileptic toddler, or an exhausted-looking hunter with a folded-up wheelchair, or a doe-eyed teenage boy who said he had a little sister in Dulac.

"We're from Pointe-aux-Chene," they told us. "We're from Cocodrie, we're from Grand Cherniere, we're from Theriot. We're from Bayou Sale, from where Burns Point Lane goes all the way to the Gulf and stops."

People who couldn't afford to stay put or rebuild, who had waited two years for FEMA or insurance payouts, whose town now had no grocery store, no gas station, no church. People who'd waited months or years for Pink Cards and couldn't wait any longer. Who'd heard there were people in flooded-out Houma who could help you forge a Pink Card, or put you on a rigged-out shrimping boat and get you across the line. We didn't find everybody. Sometimes we heard about a dinghy getting picked up, people pushed back, boats whose motors broke, people stranded on mud islands for days. But some got through.

LESSONS FOR MARCH 29:

- *What does the future look like? What's the future ground made of? How often does it future rain? What's the electricity of the future? Is it bright? Is the future dreadful? Can we trust it? Are you part of it? On which planet will the future be hosted? What animals will be permitted in the future? Please provide examples. Where do you envision living in the future? Under what kind of roof material? How do we make that? The future? Here? For us? In our lifetime? This lifetime, here? How are we going to keep one another alive in this world, this one, this one right now? Please, show your work.*

What, anyway, could I have ever said to Jemma on the phone to fix it?

I called her from the bus, at every long stop. She answered immediately, on the first ring, always asking, "Are you okay?" Yes, I said, things are okay.

I got to Askewn, I lived in a concrete room with no window and no yard, I unloaded packages from a truck at a big box store. I got laid off, I moved, I was robbed. Called Jemma, left a message. Bussed tables. Slept during the day. Mail found me, about the fire, the insurance company's investigation. Police found me, called, asked a lot of questions about Jemma, who'd left the state and maybe the country. I pled ignorance. I called and left a message. I ate like garbage. Dated somebody angry, then stopped. Biked off a curb and broke a tooth. Developed a pain in the jaw. I searched my parents' names online, got nothing. Got on drugs, got off drugs, got on drugs, got off drugs, developed fellow-feeling with crows and worms. Fished a cigarette butt out of the ashtray, woke up in somebody else's truck, drank tequila out of a plastic bag. Got evicted. Ruined my credit. I got a check in the mail, many months later, when the insurance investigation wrapped up; a staggering loss in light of the house's original value, but also more money than I'd ever had at once, enough to live on for a couple years if I was careful. Put the insurance payout into an emergency account that slowly shrank. Started working in a call center. Called Jemma, said *Call me back* aloud over the message that said, *This number has been disconnected or is no longer in service.*

A couple years later, I saw Edenton on the news: the big storm everyone had been waiting for had finally swept through. Edenton was evacuated, residents scattered. Clips of men and women sitting on cots, lined in rows in a sports stadium. Clips of water two feet deep on roads, seeping up through lawns, thigh-high in drainage ditches, rotting the bottoms of doors. There was no going back ever again. I ordered a fake diploma off a sketchy website based in Armenia and applied for a job at Twin Bridge. The first time I went in for an interview, and met Arda, I was sweating bullets, so nervous. *How do you do*, he asked.

Over stuffed shrimp one night, Carmen started talking about returning to Askewn.

"I think it's over," I said, later that evening, in a whisper to Frank, squished together on the skinny mattress.

"What," he said, "the blackout?" He was sitting up, shirtless and leaning against the wall, half-scanning a diagram for a jet engine. He and Rosa had pulled an old airboat out of where it had tilted into a bank and they'd been idly considering what it would take to get it working.

"Not that," I said, "I mean the child prison." I kicked off the sheets and stretched myself out as long as I could, while his eyes scanned the diagram. As disaster ebbed, his attentions diffused elsewhere, like steam in a larger room, steam which I, as an adult and theoretically independent woman should be able to easily live without, but it did take a concentrated effort for me to imagine doing so, to remind myself that I had a life before this and will have a life afterwards, replete with secret plans and mornings alone and personal armpit odors that only I would smell. Of course nestled inside me was the long-held, unspoken assumption that we'd go back—everyone, all of it; that this entire life, from age 13 onwards, was temporary, a brave experiment in leaving the house, and any moment now we'd wrap it up, button our jackets, collect the lost mittens, and return to our childhood homes and childhood friends next door to catch each other up on our ill-advised adventures, and finally get some rest. But there is no back.

"Do you think we could find some diesel?" Frank frowned, and behind him on the water a green channel marker seems to softly blink *go, go, go*, though really any captain knows it's saying, *keep me to your left*.

We decided things that weekend, when we were all stuck inside by a brief but tremendous thunderstorm. Carmen would leave on Wednesday. She'd bring Sabine, Zak, and Lucia, who'd all gotten in touch with family members they wanted to go back to. In the morning Greg and Arda set off to check on the van, stock it up with water and road food and extra gasoline, the day still cool with dew and not sticky yet. Zak and Sabine were already awake. They joined me on the porch as the boat motored off. I brought them each a cup of instant coffee while they whispered about how they'd come back to Houma, trying not to cry. "I'll visit," Sabine said, though this was another place that you couldn't really plan on returning to.

Linda and Arda and the other four girls would stay, at least until the heat of summer grew too oppressive. Then, maybe back to Askewn. I'd stay for as long as I could. Hurricane season began May 1.

Frank would go to Atlanta, where he'd meet his brother and look for work. We traced the outline of his plans from the back-breaking twin bed. First a month in Gulf Shores, where they were hiring, a big federal work program sealing up chemical plants shuttered by storm damage. As he was saying, *ethylene oxide, gas masks*, I grabbed his hand impulsively.

"I'll think about you too much," I blurted.

And so we didn't talk about the going away. There were still days and days left to enjoy. The knocking of water, the sigh of the house, the coffee on the porch on dark salted mornings.

On Monday, before the others left, Teresa knocked on my door. She came in and sat in the wicker chair I'd shoved against the wall, facing the window, where Frank sometimes sat to chatter sleepily and mess with the emergency broadband radio.

"How are things," I asked her. She was hunched up, facing the floor. I worried if she thought of Samuel. For me, my sleep was strange and I never dreamed. I kept losing track of things. Every once in a while, when Frank and I slept together, a cold creeping feeling would come over me from the back of my head and I'd have to say *let's stop*. He knew only a curtailed version of things. I remembered the loopy dust-storm blur, the slice of black time, and then emerging as though from behind a veil, sitting in the driver's seat while I shook and muttered bizarrely.

Now the ceiling fan ticked; far off, a barge sounded a low, moaning horn, and a pushboat responded.

Teresa pointed at the window.

"That screen doesn't fit."

She meant the bug screen. She was right, it was too big, not snug in the frame.

"It's fine," I shrugged, throwing up my hands like, *these things happen.*

"But you live here," she protested, standing up and stretching her arms above her head. "We can fix it." A breeze came through and lifted everything soft, the corner of the sheet, the gauzy curtain, my damp hair.

"All right," I said. "One of these days, sure."

"No," she said, "Now." She was already picking up a flathead screwdriver. The house was already full of mosquitoes. But I let her show me how.